An Outsider Inside

R J SAMUEL

Cover Design
by
Treehouse Studio

DEDICATION

To Jesse, Hamish, Clio, Rags, Piglet,
and the rest of the menagerie, past and present.
Love is not a strong enough word.

BOOKS BY R J SAMUEL

A PLACE SOMEWHERE
(Extract available at the end of this book)

THE VISION PAINTER SERIES:
FALLING COLOURS – The Misadventures of a Vision Painter
CASTING SHADOWS – The Further Misadventures of a Vision Painter
HEART STOPPER

COPYRIGHT

AUTHOR'S NOTE

This novel is entirely a work of fiction. The names, characters, and incidents portrayed in it are fictional and the work of the author's imagination. Any resemblance to actual persons, living or dead, events, or companies is purely coincidental.

While all the characters and situations are fictional, I would like to acknowledge the people who shared their stories with me over the years as their experiences educated me. There are some parts of the book that will be upsetting and I hope anyone experiencing such a reaction has support from the various organizations that are available. My thanks to Raksha for the support they provided me, and I hope to pay it forward.

Raksha - meaning "protection" in several South Asian languages - is a Georgia-based non-profit organization for the South Asian Community. Raksha's mission is to promote a stronger and healthier South Asian community through confidential support services, education, and advocacy. Guided by values of consensus in decision-making, diversity in leadership, and the dignity and worth of every individual, Raksha strives to empower and serve the South Asian community.

ACKNOWLEDGMENTS

Thank you to my 'alpha editor', Rachel Gold - because of you, this book is a whole lot better and closer to what I really meant. Thank you, Elaine, constant beta reader through my struggle to find the best version, I'm sorry to have caused so much confusion, but you will be one up on everyone else when the 'lost stories' make it into another book.

To my second readers, Ingrid Sherman (if any typos escaped into the book, it is my fault, as you could not have put in any more effort), Elizabeth Anderson, Orla Turley, Lex Kent, thank you for your helpful feedback and support.

To Ann McMan, Famous Author, thank you for the beautiful cover design that captures exactly my vision for the story. And for teaching me the concept of 'honey badger' even though it didn't apply to either of us.

The idea for the book came over ten years ago and there have been many ideas since so it is hard to name those who helped along the way, but thank you Alé for the spark that led to Lana and thank you Melissa Brayden for taking the time (and emotional energy) to write out as many of the stereotypes you could that many bisexual people face on a daily basis.

To Guneeta at Raksha and Heather Hale, you kept me going, changed me, and continue to teach me to see who I am. Thank you for guiding me on a path to knowing better love.

Thank you to all my readers for your continued support and interest. As always, the most precious gift I get from writing is hearing from readers who have connected with my words and enjoyed my work.

For my writing companions, Clio and Rags, both lost too soon during the end stages of writing this book, I love you and miss you, and your pawprints are all over the place.

~ 1 ~

Dublin, Ireland. 2012

The shove on my spine was rougher than expected in the jostling, but cheerful, crowd.

I spun round.

He was a typical fecking lesbian-hater. Even had a handwritten 'No Women Screwing Unless I'm Watching' sticker on his metal-covered leather jacket. At a Pride march.

I moved towards him, anger outweighing fear. My head came up to his pierced nipples, inches from the swastika tattoo hidden in the jumble of skulls, crossbones, and chest hair. The smell of armpits and the stale sweat of beer on his beard invaded my nostrils.

I took comfort in the *gardai* I'd noticed about 20 feet away, standing in a group, bantering with the crowd. A female guard who'd eyed me up earlier, now turned, her interest piqued by the altercation.

I glared up at him. "Did you *push* me?" Raised my voice. "Did you fecking *push* me?"

He grinned, and I flinched at the stench of his breath. I glanced to the side again, almost wet my pants. *Where were the cops?* I couldn't see them on the crowded sidewalk. Too late to back down now. Fecker couldn't shove me, and get away with it, not here, not now, not with thousands of us marching to be seen and heard.

He said, aiming the comment at the guy beside him, "A fucking loudmouth lesbian." An English accent. Didn't think my blood could boil.

"Yes, a lesbian." Looking him straight in his red-stained eyes, I said. "Do you have a problem with that?"

"Yeah, bitch." He towered over me. My gut crawled into my chest. Fear and anger had clumped into an adrenaline-soaked ball in my stomach. *Where were the women?* The fading chants of my group dissolving into the crowd of marchers answered that.

Where was the guard? I risked a glance to where the cop in her now welcome navy uniform had been. *There!* Two uniforms, pushing through the bodies.

My eyes flicked to his.

His mouth twisted into a snarl. "Not just lesbian, a bastard mulatto."

The matching, but bigger, companion snorted from his right. "Which one of your parents was the black bugger?"

The first thug leaned in, inflamed eyeballs receding under heavy lids. "Bet a pound twas a dirty black fucker fucked your cheap white mother."

The fear got swallowed up in the old dark cloud that rose from my heart, fogged my brain. I screamed above the noise. "He was an Indian motherfucker and she is a gorgeous Irish woman who'd eat you English Nazi bastards for breakfast."

The cops barked warnings, getting louder as they neared, but I yelled into the angry face above me. "Hope you get what's coming to you in our Irish jail tonight."

He swung. I ducked and his fist and arm ploughed through the male cop. I leaped to my left as the female cop's baton crashed down on the thug's skull, felt a pinch on my jacket as I fell past the other Nazi.

A few colleagues surrounded her, their batons ready, but the thug was out cold and his buddies backed away.

"Are you okay?" Her voice held more concern than required, seeing as I'd escaped and her partner had taken the blow.

Time crawled by on its knees.

I nodded.

Grinned up at the cute cop.

She knelt. "Don't worry, there's an ambulance coming."

"Why?" The word trudged off my tongue. My mind wandered, not sure where.

Gentle hands on my clothes, my lapel badges clicking through the buzz in my ears.

I looked along my body.

Darkness crept out in a circle on the pocket of my pink jacket. Chloe had given it to me a long time ago, but she'd only gone last month.

My hand fretted at the stain, fighting a strange, uncaring, gravity. I squinted at my fingertips. Crimson blurred from six of them.

The breeze touched my brow, chilly on wet skin. I shivered.

The cute cop's hair shone above me, a dark halo against the sun.

My throat protested, muscles tired, but the words needed out. "My name is Jaya Dillon. I am a lesbian. I am Irish-Indian. I have the right to walk the streets of my country."

Her eyes were kind. "Yes, you do." She smiled, held my blood-splattered hand, the only part of me that felt warm. "How bout doin that without pissin off the nut jobs who'd beat up anyone who's different?"

I wasn't sure if my lips arrived at a smirk though my cheek muscles started the journey. "Wouldn't be as much *craic* now, would it?"

The bursts of a siren picking its sluggish path through the throngs pierced her surprised laugh as the light faded from my day.

~ 2 ~

Kerala, India. 2005

Red paint. Red painted hands. From the tips of her fingers to the intricate bands circling her delicate wrists. Lines of betrothal, lines of bondage, of freedom. She imagined a single tear dropping from her eye dragging mascara with it on a downward journey, streaking its blackened trail through her powdered cheek, and landing in a sprawling dark stain on her hands. Hands so lovingly and patiently decorated by her mother. She stopped the giggle that threatened to escape from her reddened lips, but the urge welled up again, to release it and the multitude of its relatives shoving impatient on her tongue. To shatter the potent kin-filled gravity pressure-cooking her into a well-bred well-seasoned Indian bride.

The white and gold sari she was wearing for the first half of the two-hour-long service appeared old and staid, bowing before all present, awaiting the promotion of its wearer to a new and blessed station.

The *mandragoti* lay in waiting over her aunt's arms. Gold flecks on the red silk glinted and winked at her. The sari to be laid over her head to signify her new state. She was to wear it for the next part, its soft folds enclosing her in marital servitude.

A moment of panic.

The 'white half', as she referred to it as opposed to the second "red half", had almost ended. She had seen little, could not have described it. The stranger beside her had said the right words at the correct times. She presumed she must have too, otherwise she would have been prodded by heavy aunt fingers.

She needed to focus, at least try to remember these moments flying past her. After the sudden changes, the instants she should treasure, filing away for future perusal, perhaps describing to attentive offspring.

She relaxed slightly as she remembered the videotaping taking place. She would have to re-live every moment in dreadful multi-coloured, dancing-titled glory, the faces of the newly joined strangers plastered onto floating cubes bouncing off the sides of the screen. She lost focus, willingly this time, her mind not needed here, her body was enough, to be passed on in the eyes of the law, the family, the church.

§

The reception was winding down. They had broken the tradition and stayed. For that, she was glad.

At the far end of the banquet hall, her new husband said something to the DJ and, after a pause, his request soared from the massive speakers. She recognised with pleasant surprise the notes of a song from *Sholay*, one of her favourite Bollywood movies from childhood. The dramatic cymbals clashed into the space, the drumming echoed in the clapping and laughing from the guests who remained.

The heroine's wail resounded through the hall before her voice formed any words. It was not strictly a dance number though it spoke of dancing to her death. The ultimate sacrifice she offered to make for her hero, helpless, arms tied above his head, body wrestling and straining against the shame.

It struck her how inappropriate that song was at a wedding as the drunk stragglers shuffled to the heavy breaths of torture pounding from the speakers. The heroine had danced over broken bottles shattered into her path by the villain. Her feet bled, blood marked her way, the sun blazed into her thirsty face, but she danced, leaping between glass shards, hands reaching for pity, for mercy from the merciless, and to her love, singing of the endless dance for love, the sacrifice as life drained from her in the splotches of movie blood that followed her every step on the hard soil of the villain's lair.

Her sisters and cousins were mocking the movie sequence, the men standing in a swaying circle around her older sister, Kavita, as she waved her arms in the air. The small number of guests from the groom's side sat at the tables bordering the floor, faces stern.

She grimaced and shook her head at her cousins as they waved, urging her to join them. She was smiling as she turned to her husband who had crossed the room and was standing across the main table from her, to explain to him they were teasing her about her teenage fascination with that song and the movie and she thought it sweet he had found out.

Her words halted, swallowed, as she saw his expression, altered into a smile that did not reach his eyes. An emotion she would not recognise until later introduced itself and settled in for the long haul it knew lay ahead.

The music was reaching a crescendo. He inclined his head towards the exit. Her body rushed out of the chair, skirted the dishevelled banquet table to reach him. They did not say goodbye to anyone as they departed their wedding reception, she followed, a few hurried steps behind the stranger.

CHAPTER ONE

Dublin, Ireland. 2015

"I dropped out of the womb of an Irish-American who'd been banished to Ireland by her white family, onto an Irish hospital bed so that gave me the Irish part, the shocking sight of my darker than expected skin and hair lessened slightly (and a little later) by eyes,"

"Ooh, interesting start."

I glance up from my printed pages at Fiona and she covers her mouth with an exaggerated gesture. She stretches and I admire the fluid grace of her muscles before returning to my piece.

"all of me darkened by the genes of an Indian student visiting New York then gone, lightened by my mother's pale blonde blue gave the nurses and my mother's extended family pause before condemnation, gave me a chance in the depths of seventies rural Ireland, a tanned baby rather than the black babies they were instructed to be charitable to, but who'd never drop into their midst, who'd never be one of them."

Fiona runs her finger down my arm, brushing my breast. "Nice. Bit harsh though, isn't it?"

I sigh.

She says, "Go on, go on."

"My mother's fierce protectiveness, fierce as a lioness who knows her cub is unique, damaged, different, special, beautiful, would inspire unwelcome feelings in the village, even the good feelings uncomfortable, who wants change, but the lioness banned from the wild for being too wild was not to be tamed by the laws of rural life. She flowed through, her cub in tow, demanding the glory for having produced such an exotic seed."

"Sounds like your mother, alright. Zara Dillon, the lioness." She grins. "Sorry, shutting up now." She reaches across me and peeks out of the gun-metal blinds at the grey-water slice of Dublin rooftops. "Do you hear that rain? Damn, it's going to be a wet shift." Her smile gets wider as she wriggles into our quilt cave. "Talking of wet shifts…"

My voice drops a few notches into huskiness.

"And the family and village, dazzled by her leonine charm, opened their hearts to the bedraggled cub who didn't officially know she was not full lion, more half-lion, half-tiger.

I was occasionally reminded of my difference, not by accuracy, but by the chants that followed the Travellers when they stopped by the village, I look more like them, the easy-tan skin, the dirty-blonde hair, and amber eyes glowing with the same wildness though I kept it hidden under the necessary tameness of me."

"Hadn't thought of that. You do kind of look like a Traveller. Just sometimes, mind you."

"Fiona, are you going to let me fecking finish? This has to get written if I'm ever doing this blog thing."

"Well, sorry then. Was only trying to help."

"Feel free to help all you want at the end."

"Fine, fine. Keep going." She hums as she opens the lower buttons of my blue shirt, rather, *her* cop shirt, that I'm wearing over nothing. It smells of starch and traces of deodorant. She's naked apart from panties, and she wraps her long bare legs under her and sits beside my knees.

"I'm ashamed I didn't stand up for the Travellers, not that they needed my help and I didn't add to the chants, but inside I found myself counting the ways I was Indian-Irish or Irish-Indian and the ways I was special rather than different, oh, that hair is so thick and lush, your eyes, holy jesus, they are like something else that colour, you lucky thing, you get such a nice tan, not a fecking freckle in sight."

She has worked the sheet past my hips and it tangles around my thighs. Her gaze on my skin is followed by her breath on my belly. She lays her head on me, her cheek cool against my scar. Her eyes are a darkened blue in the soft light coming from the lamp clipped on the wrought-iron bars of the headboard. I linger on the sight for a moment, then return to the pages with a sigh.

"See, that's my Indian side. Though the impression most of the village had of Indians was the roaming Sikh salesmen so I guess I was an itinerant to them anyway. I hadn't yet seen, and neither had they, the explosion of medical and scientific staff from India and Pakistan, the gentrification of the Indian image in Ireland took place in towns and

cities beyond my child eyes and happened only in my twenties when I was away from the rural, when I was in the new urban of Galway, when I creaked and groaned with the growing pains of modern Ireland, growing, but yet unable to graft new shades of skin, unable to see beyond into the Irishness of birth, of soul, of thought, of presence. There were scales everywhere. I felt sorry for the blackest of the Irish born here, but never Irish to the Irish; the half-skinned, born here, but considered a curiosity, a half image of Irish; and the light-skinned right-blooded, not born here, but Irish by heritage, a full image of Irish, but still not full Irish to the Irish.

There are years and years of Irishness I don't get to claim as there are years and years of Indianness I don't get to claim either, except in my genes, but they only produce the features that give me access, the legal right to be present. They don't give me the key to the Irish and certainly not to the Indian. They give me a door to the displaced, the window on the itinerant passing by, who at least belongs in his own world of motion."

I peer down my open shirt at her. "The words came in a burst in that hospital bed. Those guys attacked me not just because we were marching in the Pride march, proudly lesbian and out, but because of my colour as well."

She focuses on my face, and then her gaze drifts lower, between my breasts.

She says she loves the contrast of her fair hands on me. I like the way she reacts to my body, though I sometimes ponder whether she compliments the agelessness of my brown skin to make me more comfortable about being 42, 12 years older than her.

Her hair tickles against my belly button. "Not saying nothing until the end. Is that the end?"

I must concentrate, need to get ready for work soon as well. "The media didn't get it. They went on about me being stabbed for being lesbian, but nothing much about me being brown. That's why the need to write it."

"I hate that you were stabbed, but we wouldn't have met otherwise." She smiles. "And that would've been awful."

The media liked that part. Me being 'saved' by the dashing female guard.

We made the news again when we got together months later.

The national news. *Raidió Teilifís Éireann*, no less.

Possibly too much in there on being brown. The blog post is meant to describe how I ended up being stabbed in Dublin during a Pride march coming up to three years ago. And I can't mention Chloe. She's the reason, for that, and for so much wrong with my life now.

"That's my excuse for being changeable and flaky, for not finding and fixing on any life that makes sense. For being a white guy's 'exotic' girlfriend in college, to being an Arts degree graduate who couldn't find a niche in the world of careers, to chasing every interest and fancy, to playing with hearts until mine was felled, by a woman of all things. To never looking back, to becoming a lesbian activist, to fiercely worshipping the female, to fighting for lesbians with a passion, to stopping the straight white male system from winning, to paying lip service to the other minority rights fights, but the cause was us, the love of women."

Fiona says, "I love that." She has moved and her words whisper into the space between my thighs.

"Which was why it shocked me and my lesbian activist world when I fell in love with a bisexual woman. A bisexual woman. And English to boot. But love and lust ruled, and I spent two years hiding out from my society and she spent the same time and effort hiding us from her society of English Methodists. I'm not sure if the bisexuality was the chief reason I hid with her, it was bad enough though she'd decided to be strictly lesbian with me, but she couldn't decide not to be English and many in my group couldn't handle the being English part."

Hmm… This might not fly. Not sure they need to hear this. And really it was the bisexual part.

Fiona straightens herself up and considers the papers I'm holding, rustling in the air above us, out of her eyeline. "You sure you want to add that?"

I read on, silently.

I know why she hid me. Not as much because of the Indian part though it probably didn't help that her father had been a colonel in the time of the British Raj and carried a view of Indians he formed in those days, but the fact I was a woman made me untouchable in his eyes, not to him obviously, but to his daughter. So I didn't meet him and my girlfriend never met my friends and my colleagues. Not a recipe for longevity or much more than a two-year relationship, but she gained something from us, and I lost everything when she was there and when she left, my identity, my self-respect, my vigour, and fight. I spent the three years after she walked out on our ceremony being the best lesbian activist in Ireland, getting myself stabbed for the cause, taking on two big fecking English Nazi bastards during a march in Dublin, growing the scar after months on disability, and my old group appear to have forgiven me.

Have they? Didn't notice them helping with the medical bills.

Fiona says, "Did the group not talk to you when you were with your wan?"

"We didn't go out on the scene. I couldn't tell them much about her."

I read the next line in my mind as well, keeping the printed words at the bottom of the page out of Fiona's line of sight. *The motherless Chloe gained a relationship with my mother. And I won't begrudge her that. Zara Dillon is a woman I'd want as a mother no matter how difficult she can make my life.*

I fold up the papers. "Well?"

"You might be better to take out the parts about growing up dark in Ireland. People don't like to hear you went through that sort of stuff."

I unfold the papers and stare at the text. There won't be much left if that's taken out.

"And maybe don't mention that woman. After her leaving you for a guy and all?"

I shake my head and wince at the twinge in the tightened muscles of my neck. "No. I left her." I rub my neck. "Mostly."

"Ah well." She sits up, facing me, and massages my shoulders. She touches my lips with her tongue and murmurs, "Mmm, nice."

I taste what she does, and nod, rubbing my mouth against hers.

She whispers, "You don't have anything in there on us. Did you decide on what the reporter asked? It's the Irish Times supplement. They want a photo too."

I'm finding it hard to concentrate. "Did they ask you because you're a cop?" Part of me had hoped she'd forgotten the reporter, I don't want to deal with writing that piece. Or a photo of us being used as part of any campaign.

"Don't think so. The piece needs women, and men, from different jobs and places, a bit of diversity. She's working with the new gay and lesbian group that got together to campaign for same-sex marriage." Fiona turns so her cheek is against mine and we're posing for a pretend photo, her smile nudging up my cheek. She enjoys the way we look together and the story of how we met. "And the co-chair of the group wants more lesbians on it, otherwise the gay guys will take over as usual."

I sigh. "You know what Theresa is like. Don't want to lose my job."

Fiona moves back, squeezes my muscles. She climbs off the bed and stretches. "I've to get ready for shift soon." She frowns. "How come you keep working for your wan? You go out and get stabbed in a gay Pride march and then return to work for a group that doesn't want gay marriage. Kind of fucked up."

"Everyone has a right to their opinion. I prefer to keep my job this time."

"You could always get another job, or start the journalism course at uni." She's pacing in place beside the dresser, picking up and putting down my awards and my miniature ceramic animals. There isn't much other house stuff left, I hadn't replaced all the stuff I threw out.

I say, "They took me on again, even after I left them."

She swivels towards me. "Of course they did. Why wouldn't they? Not that they'd have kept you on then because of your bi girlfriend, anyway. It's not your fault they couldn't handle you being with a bisexual."

"They'd have been fine, just given me a hard time for a little while."

I put the papers on the bedside locker and slide down in the bed. It was me who couldn't handle them knowing, not after the acrid views we shared on bi women. And then I mess up and fall in love with one. And we'd been right, hadn't we? Chloe had left me before our commitment ceremony. Probably for a man. Like every other bloody closeted lesbian who pretends to be lesbian or bisexual to experiment. Thought I'd left the last of those feckers in college. My bad for falling for another.

Fiona is rifling through the drawers. "Don't go sleeping in my shirt. I need it."

I groan. "Come back to bed. Don't you have any other shirts here?"

"Forgot them in my dryer. Thought you had work to go to?"

I nod and slide further under the quilt. This cave is warm with the scent of our bodies, our sweat.

She mutters, "Why do you have to go to Galway today? Is *she* going to be there?"

"My mum asked me. And I'm only getting to visit her again after ages." I peek at her over the edge of the quilt. "Chloe's away. Seemingly she isn't there much anymore."

"Will you get a chance to sort out the mortgage stuff?"

My voice muffles into the featherdown. "I'll do it soon."

"I need to inform the bank if it's going ahead or not. Difficult as fuck to get a mortgage, wouldn't do to mess around with them."

"I know, I know. I'll ask mum to ask her." Chloe's name still on the deeds of this apartment, a shared mortgage. Remnants of our life that can't be erased by throwing away every single item we bought together. Even the mirror. That was hard. I kept having visions of seven years of bad luck as the gilt-edged mirror, framed by taped-on pictures of Chloe and me, bounced away in Padraic's van, peeping through the rear window, reflecting me standing on the middle of the street, deserted save for the mist in the lamplit dawn.

Fiona's voice is slow, as if she's pondering. "Who knows what the parents will say if we are on the front page of the Irish Times, even if it's only a supplement. They read mostly the Sligo Tribune, but the neighbours are sure to show them."

A frown pinches at my eyebrows. I stick my head out of the covers. "But they know you are lesbian."

The central heating is on, and pink dusts her pert breasts. The blush racing up Fiona's neck is obvious on her pale skin even as her silhouette blends into the shadowed cream walls. "We don't discuss any of that."

"I thought they were okay with it?"

Fiona grabs her navy trousers off the floor. "They are. As long as it's not pushed in their faces."

"So, it's what? That I'm *brown*?"

She throws the trousers on the floor and they slide across the shiny wood. She sits on the bed. "They're not racist or anything. They just haven't met any black people, you know?"

No point correcting her. I'm not technically 'black people,' not here in Ireland, anyway. I'm 'brown,' 'Indian,' sometimes even 'coloured.'

Her cheeks are dusky, she stares at her fingers playing with the pale blue sheet, silk because I have silk sheets now, no more cotton, threw those out too. Her voice is low. "Don't want to upset my parents. They're too old to change. And especially not now when they might be ok with me being gay. They want me to be safe and secure, that's what's important." She releases the sheet, combs her fingers through her short black hair. "Sure, isn't that why you should write the article? And put you and me on the cover as a reason people should vote Yes for gay marriage?" She smiles, strokes my fingers. "Write it for me? Something showing we're normal decent people who deserve the chance to marry. You write stuff for your weird group all the time. That Theresa one is just nuts, why try and get people to vote No? If no one fecking wants to marry her, then let her stay single, why fuck it up for the rest of us."

She leans over me and it brings back the memory of her face above me as I lay bleeding into the cobbles.

The cute cop and the lesbian activist she saved.

She's right. I should write the article for the Yes side. But I'd managed to finagle my job back and Theresa is my boss and she will go completely mad if she finds out. And an easy job is handy while I figure out how to work in the online journalism field.

Fiona's kissing me. Which is always a welcome distraction from ending up in the middle of these bloody wars, despite wanting a peaceful fecking life.

CHAPTER TWO

"Did you read Catriona's article in the bloody *Holy Catholic Review*?" Theresa's voice from the doorway breaks the silence.

I sigh. What now? The office had been quiet, Orla and me dawdling through a Friday. The others are attending some training course on equality at the far side of the Edwardian house that serves as the Dublin headquarters for the organisation. Orla, too late to hop out of the armchair, buries her face in her book, moving her head in time to whatever music is flowing into her ears.

Theresa grunts as she pushes the carpet-tight door fully open. "Sorry, I should have said *Sister* Mary Catherine." She aims for my desk brandishing a sheaf of green papers, staples glinting, multiple fonts vying for prominence.

At this rate, I could be out in time. The tapping of raindrops against the tall bay windows has been a peaceful murmur all morning and a reminder to take a taxi to the train station. Walking those tree-lined avenues, I'd be soaked before I get there and end up a pile of steam for the three-hour journey to Galway.

"What does it say?" I clear my throat. "I need to leave early today if that's okay? Have to catch the 3 pm train."

Theresa waves the papers, wafting a welcome breeze over my face. "Fine, fine. Is it the mother again?"

I nod. It hasn't been the mother for almost three years, just didn't want to let my boss know my need to escape on a Friday when I couldn't bear a moment longer in the overheated fluorescent-light office, stuffy despite its large windows and raised ceiling, smelling of old coffee, old papers, and old smokers.

Theresa reads from the newsletter in a faux holy voice. "We must all learn to live our truth, to show our true love for God without fear, no matter what our secular politically correct society says, because that is

.e only way to avoid a living death." She flings the papers on the antique coffee table, raising dust from its pocked surface. "Fecking cheek of her."

Margeta strolls in from the lobby. "Fucking cheek of who?" Her Polish accent makes the words sound clipped.

Theresa says, "Whom, Margeta, whom. You're okay, even us English speakers get that wrong sometimes."

I say, "She was reading from Catriona's piece in the church newsletter." I turn to Theresa, hiding my grin. "How's Catriona getting on in the nunnery? Someone so cute, what a waste. Though I bet she's charmed a few of the nuns into bed already."

Margeta says, "You mean the Catriona who was your girlfriend?"

We both turn to her.

Theresa says, "Yes, that one."

I say nothing.

The kiss had been enough to make me join the group, but it hadn't meant anything to Catriona except a flirtation. Her repentance seemed a bit extreme, though. The return to the order of nuns was unlikely to be due to our kiss. The other kisses, with the other women, might have played a part.

Margeta says, "You're better without her, boss. You would not have met Ginger." She takes a folder out of one of the three beige filing cabinets huddled by the magnolia wall and slumps into her chair with a loud exhalation. "I wish we would include refugees and asylum seekers in the cases." She glances up, sunny blue eyes wide in her broad face. "It might help the group to obtain diversity funding, and not leave it to the Yes side?"

Theresa shakes her head. "It doesn't fit into the remit of our funding. I'm sorry for the people of colour who are now trapped in our institutions of racism, but we have to work with what we have. The others go searching for diversity to prove their openness, sure don't we have diversity here?"

I frown. I'm the only one in the group who's got as much as a tint of dark. Hope she's not going to ask me to be the poster black baby for the No campaign.

I remember the train, and tap my monitor. "Are you certain you want this logo?"

Theresa strides around my desk. She moves with the energy of a thirty-something. Her tattoos, however, are sagging on almost seventy year old skin, the head of the labyris drooping in prayer and the green and purple yellowing.

Her voice pierces my eardrum. "What's wrong with the logo?"

"Well, it goes with the name of the organisation."

"So? Isn't it supposed to?"

I nod and ask. "Are you still happy with the name?" Brace myself.

She barks, "What do you mean?"

"Well, would you not reconsider going against the marriage referendum now?"

The wall clock ticks and I wonder how long it has been there.

Margeta clears her throat. Orla nods faster, headphone cables dancing on her chest.

Theresa's voice is firm. "We got government funding. And I still believe marriage is a prison of the patriarchy. Because the stupid laws in this country refuse Ginger the right to stay though we've been together two years does not mean I will change our fight. Do I have to remind you how many years we have been fighting for the 'I', the individual?"

I sigh. "Just checking." The logo stares at me from its perch on the typed name '*The I's Should Have It*' as if it would rather be anywhere else.

My boss is now on a march zigzagging between the motley collection of office furniture. "The tax codes, how our society is built around this notion of family over the individual, around ownership of women, how can any woman, lesbian or straight, consider marriage? All this talk of family and children, who speaks up for the individual? Why should I have to pay more taxes because they want to have bloody children out the wazoo, to breed into this already overpopulated cesspool of a world? Why is everything geared to favour men and procreation? Surely the individual has to be treated right first and only then can any couple or group or institution come into the equation."

I adjust the shading on the 'I' shaped symbol, tone down the red, scale it down in size too. It's the best I can do with what Ginger gave me. Not sure what they do in America, but she said Texans do everything bigger. Then she laughed. With all her bright white teeth and blonde hair. We were all as surprised as she was that she couldn't stay and work in her own right. What with her Irish roots, distant as they were, and white skin. But it turned out Immigration was now obliged to come down hard on all non-Irish, all non-EU citizens.

Theresa's voice continues to drill through the air. "We have to stand in our truth alright. Sister bloody Catriona can write from her institution in the clouds. The rest of us have to live in the real world, we have to protect ourselves, protect true lesbians is more like it. If we go begging for the right to be imprisoned, if we grovel at the feet of the institutions, then we deserve nothing better. All those closeted lesbians don't help. And the bisexual women who are really closeted lesbians without the guts to tell themselves the truth. Or worse, the women who try it with a lesbian and it's too hard to be ostracised by their straight world and so they feck off to men."

I catch Margeta's glance at me. She looks for a second like a deer in the headlights then she grasps a sheet of paper and stares intently at it.

Before Chloe, Theresa and I used to gripe on this topic at length over pints in the pub down the street. Well, she used to complain, while I nodded sagely with the occasional rant about Jojo fecking O'Hara who had been the first woman, the woman who when I fell for her, everything fell into place. She was four years my senior, in college terms, had also never slept with a woman, was convinced she'd burn in hell, and took the time with me in bed, after, sure enough, to patiently explain the wickedness of my ways. Last I saw her, she was showing off her engagement ring to her friends. She didn't notice me in the corridor, staring at the results on the bulletin board, tears streaming down my hoodie-covered face though I had aced the exams. No doubt she noticed when I wasn't there for her tryst with her pet lesbian. I guess I owe her a toaster oven.

Theresa turns to me, her arms open, her palms facing the ceiling. "Sorry to bring up such a painful topic, what you lost in those years away from us, but you confirmed all too well why we must keep this fight going."

For Chloe's sake, in our two years together I worked at another non-profit, where nobody needed to know I was lesbian. For my sake, I didn't talk to or meet anyone from the lesbian scene I'd been such a part of since moving to Dublin, not wanting to deal with anyone knowing I was with a bisexual woman.

After Chloe left, I returned to my job here, and we resumed our pub tirades but I rarely refer to Chloe, not by name, though I'm more vocal against bi women in general.

Theresa is still talking. "You poor thing. That woman should have been the one stabbed, not you." I recoil at the image of Chloe facing the bastard, the wound in my gut stings with the memory three years later. And I haven't mentioned to anyone at the office, especially Theresa, that Chloe now rents my mother's garden flat in Galway, the only way we could manage the joint mortgage and my refusal to lose my home here in Dublin because of her.

Theresa steps toward me. "She should suffer the consequences of hiding love for women, not you, the brave soul who faced down two huge English thugs and took a knife."

I blurt out, "I'd never want for Chloe to have been stabbed instead of me."

Lying in that hospital bed, I'd wondered why my group had walked ahead of me, left me on my own. I guess it's the individual strength thing. And they weren't around for my hospital stay, probably because in the boss's opinion government funding should not allow for private health insurance.

"For sure you don't! You're too sweet for that. But you're right to be so angry at her. To hate her. If it was me, I would have outed the bitch."

I mutter, "I'm not into all that stuff. Nobody should be outed against their will. Not even bisexual women." I know what else won't happen. I absolutely will not date someone now who says they're bisexual.

Theresa snorts. Thwacks the pages against her palm. "I'm sick of all this shit, biphobia, transphobia, etcetera etcetera etcetera. I'm not fucking phobic of anything. But *no one* is going to determine who I should or should not be with. *That's* what we've been fighting for, isn't it? The right to love who we want, to prefer whoever the fuck we want to go to bed with. Everyone is getting so brainwashed, demanding we all think and feel the same way. I mean, what about the trans women, Goddess knows I'm all for them, but when they tell me I can't choose *not* to have feelings for a trans woman, *for feck's sake*, I fought for the fecking right long before they were born, male or female or whatever. We are fighting for the right to be I N D I V I D U A L," She pumps out each letter with a clenched fist, "I E if I don't want to marry a trans woman, I fecking well won't and no institution, not even the L G B T Q fecking I institution will tell *me* what to do."

Orla pipes up, annoyingly perky, louder than she probably intended from her music cocoon. "You forgot the A for Asexual." She aims at me, "You and Chloe were getting a civil union, no?"

Theresa swivels to me, frowns. "You were?"

I say, quickly. "Just a commitment ceremony. Nothing legal or institutional."

I log out of my PC and stand. "Do you mind if I leave a bit earlier? Might be able to get to the station without a cab." I point at the window.

The sun is peeking through the grey, water drops shine and dance on their journey down the glass.

Theresa nods. Her voice is ripe with understanding. "Of course. It must be so hard for you to even hear her name." She moves closer and gives me a hug. The patting of her palm against my back echoes in my chest, my nostrils fill with the linger of tobacco and hash on her T-shirt.

She leans back, her hands now gripping my upper arms. Her faded blue eyes in their wrinkled surroundings are bright with a new hope. "Can't wait to read what you write for our 'No' piece in the Irish Times. You fell from the same tree as your mother, such a true and eloquent voice. Give our love to Zara. Tell her Ginger was asking after her." She releases me and turns to Margeta. "Ginger's American connection and all, she's psyched to hear of another American woman settling here happily. Me, I knew Zara Dillon in the old days, such a strong brave woman, bringing up her brown child outside of the institution of marriage in those times, and in rural Ireland. And marching for abortion rights for women when she didn't want one herself." Theresa glances at me. "No offence." She raises her hands, a sure sign of an imminent speech. "We need more strong women, more Zara Dillons if we are ever to win this fight to be true to ourselves."

I grab my stuff and smile apologetically at Margeta on my rush to the door. The heavy click of it closing behind me shuts out the drone of Theresa describing Zara's feminist activist exploits to what's left of her captive, equally unwilling, audience.

I'm shoving my dripping bag into the overhead container and cursing my misplaced optimism about the weather when I remember. I never informed my boss of the Irish Times photo and article for the 'Yes' side."

CHAPTER THREE

There's too much stuff lying around my room, can't find my bag.

I wander down the stairs following the aroma of baking scones into the kitchen and stand for a few moments at the doorway struck with homesickness, and regret for the lost years.

Zara has a letter in her hand. I didn't think anyone used snail mail anymore. This is on an actual sheet of paper. There might be floral patterns on the pastel. The handwriting is undecipherable from this distance as it winds under her fingers.

"Someone wrote you a letter?"

My mother nods. Her smile is wide and so warm as her wrinkled fingers smooth the paper it makes me regret for a moment all the technological advances we've made.

Zara's voice is unusually timid. "Yes, isn't that lovely? I wish more young people used letters, understood the beauty of words on paper, and not just in computers."

"Who's it from?"

My mum puts the letter beside her cup. The morning sun catches the flecks of purple on pink, delicate against the burnished wood countertop.

She stirs her tea and sighs. "You know, there are so many places I never got to visit. I used to travel all over the US in my youth. And then there were the trips to Ireland. But I didn't get to go to Europe, despite living in Ireland."

I frown. These forays into memory usually came with baggage. Which reminds me, need to find my bag. "Why didn't you? It's right next door here, not like having to fly from America."

She smiles, sadly. "Yes, you'd think I'd have been all over. But only England. I haven't been to Spain or France or, Goddess forbid, somewhere further such as Greece."

"Mam, who's the letter from?"

She pats at her silver hair. "Don't you want to know why?"

"Why what?"

"Why I haven't been off this fecking island except to go to the next island?"

I peer into the utility room, but my backpack isn't in the pile of bags and boots. It's not all that appropriate for an interview, but I don't have a briefcase and anyway I'd look silly with a briefcase. Not for a library.

"Jaya?"

"Yes, mam. Have you seen my backpack?"

"No." She frowns. "Wait. That pink thing?"

I nod.

"No, haven't seen it."

I wander through the kitchen to the living room.

The living room is as bright as the kitchen. A small front garden, framed by large windows, differentiates itself from its neighbours with a lawn sign proclaiming 'Vote Yes'.

Zara's voice follows me. "I'm not saying it was anyone's fault. Life turns out different sometimes to what you expect."

I snort. "You can say that again. Never thought I'd be 42 and going for an interview because my mother set it up."

I move aside the records stacked against the old player I'd found for her in the second-hand store. A bunch of leaflets titled 'Yes to Same-Sex Marriage" and other 'Yes' paraphernalia is strewn around the room.

Zara stands in the doorway, a dishtowel clutched in her hand. "It would be so nice to have you home. What about Fiona? Are you two not getting serious?"

"I don't know." I sigh. I do. "Yeah, she'll probably be pissed off at me if I get the job here. She wants me to get another one in Dublin or go back to college. Guess it will be better for the magazine article."

"I never thought my wee cub would be the face of the lesbian marriage fight. I knew you could be on the front cover of a magazine, didn't I say so to Nona. She was going on and on, our Paula being in the Bugle, blah, blah, Goddess knows, Paula's my niece, but there's only so many times you can hear talk of her and her perfect husband."

I smile. "It *is* a national magazine. But I am not *the* face of the fight, I'd only be one of them, there's a whole group of us."

"The most beautiful and unusual one. My brown baby cub on the front cover of an Irish national magazine. Isn't life so twisted."

"And my words inside. I have to write something for the article. On why we should be given the same rights as straight people. To be honest, I want the right to marry, but I'm not even sure if I want to get married myself." I frown. "I should describe how we are invisible in Ireland as lesbians, how we are second-class citizens. And how closeted lesbian women pretending to be bisexual hurt the cause. That's what I should be writing."

Zara says, "Come on over and have a cup of tea with me, will you? I'll find your rucksack for you later. Or better, you can take one of my bags, will make a much better impression than that pink thing. Are you even going to take off all the lesbian badges?"

I turn to scowl at her. "Did you take off all the feminist symbols when you succumbed to the patriarchy?"

"Jaya, it's a library. Perhaps the fact you are lesbian might not affect the actual job?"

I state, "I'm not going to hide who I am," then mutter, "Not anymore." I pat the site of my scar on my stomach.

Zara lifts a hand as if to ward off the sight of the scar. "It's quite okay, you don't have to show me that awful thing again. Come on, sit down. Take a break. I promise you'll still be lesbian after a cup of tea and a chat." There's a giggle in her voice and my mouth opens to launch into an attack, but her grin makes me giggle too.

I sigh and surrender. We return to the kitchen and I sit in the breakfast nook by the window, a counter with two stools. She pours from the pot and places the cup and saucer in front of me. The letter is face down on the kitchen table.

The flat where my bisexual ex lives squats in the garden, visible out the back window. That's how I regard her now. My bisexual ex. The bitter anger surges into my stomach. I had walked away from my relationship with my mother, had not let either of them visit me at the hospital, I couldn't believe my own mother had not ripped Chloe apart for what she'd done. Instead, Chloe had moved down to Galway, into the flat in Zara's back garden. I had stayed in our sleek city apartment, now unable to spend time in the bustling house that was home to my gay cousin too. Chloe had managed to steal my extended family too.

Fiona had been the one to visit me in hospital and during my recovery. And my old friends from the lesbian scene in Dublin, the ones I'd lost when I was with Chloe, they'd been my haven, as was the group at work though I didn't agree with many of Theresa's views. But I haven't told Zara any of this. To her, to Chloe, to everyone, I'm in great shape, in a new relationship with a hot cop as my friends describe Fiona, part of the scene again. I'm glad at least to be a vocal, working lesbian activist once more, not man-hating, but woman-centred.

Zara takes the tray of scones out of the oven and puts one on a plate in front of me. "Will you go with Padraic and Nestor? I'm a little tired today."

I frown, anxiety needles whenever I remember my mum ageing. I noticed more lines on her face when I first saw her in Dublin two months ago after the almost three years I'd kept away, but her back is straight, her energy the same as when I walked away from this house, from her acceptance of Chloe. "Are you doing okay?"

She nods and sits, supporting herself with her palms on the table. She sips from the cup, smiles. "It's good to have you here, my little cub."

"Uh-huh." I finish off the scone, the butter warm on the sweet crumbly pastry, and almost forgive her. "What are Padraic and Nestor up to?"

"Don't talk with your mouth full." She's smiling as she puts another scone on my plate. "Nestor is moving old stuff from a friend of a friend's house and Padraic is going to help him with the van. I would help too, but I'm not as limber as I used to be." She moves forward in her chair. "So, as I was saying, or asking. Do you know why I never went anywhere?"

She's a dog with a bone. Which is normal for her. I'm not sure which bone this morning.

"Money?"

"No, we weren't that poor." She pats my hand gently. "We were lower middle class. But it was tough being a single mother."

"You had Nona and Uncle, and Bridget and Bernie, Padraic and Paula, and Nestor and Nuala, and Fionn and Freda. You were hardly a single mum?"

She gives The Smile. A bit sad, a bit brave, a lot martyr. "Yes, we did have the family. It was still hard as a single mother though. You were my special cub, couldn't be leaving you to the rest of them to bring up."

"Am I somehow getting the blame for you not going to Europe?"

"No. No, of course not. I loved having you and wouldn't do anything different." She sighs. "It was all my fault in reality. I got so scared of travelling after I had you. Couldn't leave you on your own, you know, if anything happened to me. So the most I did was go to England a few times, took you with me."

"Must be where I get my love of the English." I'm muttering again, glaring out the window, thoughts of Chloe bring up chest burn.

She frowns. "I like the English, especially the Queen. Though I didn't like her when Princess Diana died. No. No way."

I nod. "See. Remember what they did to Di. You can't trust any of them. Eight hundred bloody years of rule, and then they arrive and screw you and feck off back to England." I'm building up a head of steam.

Zara sighs again. "I'd love to be able to feck off somewhere. To do the travelling I couldn't do as a struggling single mother."

I stare at her with full suspicion brewing. "What's up, mam? We haven't had so many mentions of your struggles before a second cup of tea since Nona suggested you move back in with them."

"The bloody cheek of her. Like I'm an invalid. Is this not a fantastic house? Am I not able to pass for 50 years old? Just because she's in her fecking seventies and all her kids have moved out and she's bored with himself."

Now I'm patting her hand. "You're 67. And you do appear 50 sometimes. But she meant it for her sake, not yours. The house must be so empty for her now."

"At least she has all the kids. They take her places. I mean, outside of Ireland. Nestor lives here and I can't get him to take me anywhere."

"For feck's sake, mam! Where do you want to go?"

Her smile is radiant. "Saint-Sebastien-du-Lac."

"Where the feck is that?"

"France. It's somewhere in France, a village I think."

"Why on earth go there?"

"There's a holiday complex by the lake. I got a coupon for accommodation, huge discount, twenty-five percent of normal. I saw a picture. It's so lovely. That's where I want to go."

I sit back, forget it's a stool and over-correct forward, smacking the counter. The teaspoon jangles in the saucer.

She picks up the spoon and wipes up the drops of spill with her palm.

"And when do you have all this planned for?" I don't bother to ask any other questions. There is no point. I try avoid it with logistics rather than reason.

"I need to use it by next weekend? That gives us enough time to get ready and Nestor can keep an eye on this place when we're gone."

"We?"

"Of course, we. How am I supposed to get there on my own? It's way in the middle of rural France somewhere."

"Thought you were a limber 50-year-old?"

"Now what fun would that be? I want to travel to Europe with my little cub."

"Oh Lord. Seriously, what's going on?"

She gets up from the table, straightens herself gingerly and puts the letter in the pocket of her dress. She's weirdly smartly dressed, but that's usual for her, eclectic is the word most commonly used to describe my mother and it can be both complimentary and puzzled at the same time. Colourful, too.

She says, peering at the calendar on the wall, "Will you organise the trip? I know I can leave all the ticket and travel stuff to you." She puts on her purple-rimmed spectacles and examines the dates. "If we leave on the Friday, it's the first weekend in May, and return the next Monday or Tuesday, that would be perfect."

"What if I get the job? I can't take a holiday straight away."

"Who said?" She opens a closet and pulls out what can only be described as an eclectic bag. "Here, take this to your interview. And if they don't let you go on holiday with your poor mother who raised you singlehandedly as a young brown child in rural Ireland without nary a word of complaint, then they don't deserve you working for them."

I sigh. Glad I have a few years of savings set aside. Didn't want the job that much anyway.

No more thinking. My career, Fiona, the group, the magazine articles, my joint mortgage, Chloe, all of it.

Running off to France with my mother sounds like so much more fun.

CHAPTER FOUR

I climb into the bench seat of the van and Nestor nudges me along the seat as he clambers in. The leather is hot against my thighs.

Padraic gets in the driver's side and starts the engine. He says, "Where to?"

I frown at my cousins. "I've no idea."

Nestor pulls out a scrap of paper. "It's in Laurel Park. Here." He hands it to me. I recognise my mother's sprawled handwriting. I peel the sticky pink paper off my fingers and show Padraic.

Padraic puts the van into gear. "I stayed near there in college. Those were the days."

Nestor says, "Those weren't such great days."

Padraic drives away from mum's house. "Well if you hadn't been so gay, it would have been fun." He chuckles as we wait for his brother's reaction, but Nestor is in a thoughtful mood. He gazes out of the window and says, "Is mam going to vote Yes or No?"

Padraic pulls out into the line of traffic. "I don't know, man." He sighs, reaches across to turn on the radio and Aerosmith soars over our heads. "I think she's not voting."

Nestor winds down his window. The sun is shining, but the air coming in is chilly. "Why can't she be more like Aunt Zara? Mam might as well vote No by not voting. Auntie is actually going around town with a 'Vote Yes' badge and she has a banner across the window of her car. Feck, she even took on your wan, Mrs. Whatshername, you know, Jay, the old biddie who lives in number 54, Auntie Z wrote on her wall." He giggles.

I turn to him. "She did what?"

He's laughing too hard now to talk. Padraic's laugh rumbles on the other side of me.

I wait until Nestor catches his breath. "She did what?"

Nestor gasps. "She painted on your wan's front garden wall. 'Vote

Yes or I'll marry your husband'."

"She did not!" I twist in my seat. Padraic is nodding. I turn to Nestor. "That doesn't even make sense."

Nestor smiled. "But it freaked the hell out of Mrs. Whatshername."

Padraic says, "Mam doesn't have the same chance as Auntie Z. She has to go to church with lots who don't think it's natural." He smiles apologetically at me, the blush of red working its way up his stubble. He doesn't think it's natural for his brother to be gay, but he loves him. Me, he loves anyway. And I adore him and forgive his clunky homophobia. He's always been the one who ruffled my hair after chasing off any lads who made fun of me at school for being brown.

He turns up the music. I sit between the two silent brothers as the plaintive notes swirl across them.

§

We pull up at the address and Nestor opens his door and jumps out and walks up the driveway to the front door.

Padraic sighs. "I'm just saying it like it is."

I pat his hand on the steering wheel. "Maybe don't say anything until the referendum is over." I gather myself to climb out of the van. "But, do me a favour. Please vote Yes and please tell auntie Nona to vote Yes too. This affects your brother and me. Whether I fecking want to get married anymore ever, at least let us have the right to decide."

Padraic nods. "I was going to anyway. It's God's place to judge anyone, not mine. If I got to marry Bernadette, everyone should have the right to make themselves as miserable…"

I swivel. "What?"

He laughs. "You two are so easy to make fun of. I mean, look at what ye get up to."

I sigh. "I know."

He switches off the engine and the music dies away. He swivels to examine me. "How are you getting on? You haven't been back at Auntie Z's for what, two, three, years?"

"Almost three. Mam got in touch two months ago. Chloe hasn't been there as much, she thought I might come visit." I poke at the black plastic of the dashboard. "All I'll say is thank goodness Chloe isn't anywhere around right now. No idea what I'd do if I have to see her or talk to her."

"I can't keep up with all this stuff. Was she not gay?"

"No, bisexual."

"Isn't that half gay?"

I frown. "I guess so." I slide out of the seat and land on the pavement. "All I know is bisexuals have a choice and I fecking don't. And Chloe made her choice."

Nestor has disappeared inside.

I look back into the van. "What are we here for?"

Padraic says, "The Bible says to love our neighbour, to love everyone."

I smile. "I meant, what are we at this house for?"

His blush deepens. "Oh, Auntie Z said a friend of a friend needed us to move gear out of storage because the place is being rented out again and the friend is away."

I say, "Thanks for moving all our stuff that time. Did you get rid of it all?"

Padraic nods. "Sold most of it. Some good stuff there." He gets out and comes around to my side. He looks down at me. He's the tall one in the family. And the wide one. "Are you sure you don't want the money for it?"

I say, "No. Keep it. Take it as payment towards the moving you do for everyone."

He ruffles my hair. "Family. The moving I do for family." He turns to the house. "Now, where's that ponce?" He guffaws as I jab him in his stomach.

§

The estate is suburban. In a college-student, poorer-worker way. Compared to the houses in my mother's neighbourhood, which itself is an ordinary suburb in Galway, here the grass is not as green, the trim is loose around cracked kerbing, the tarmac driveways shine with more tints of grey than black, the fatigued brickwork extends only halfway up the façades.

Padraic and I stand by the van, eyeing the house. It's nothing special, like its neighbours.

37

Speaking of neighbours. There is a twitch of the net curtains next door.

It's a Sunday afternoon and the sun is determined to reacquaint us with its heat despite the efforts of a scatter of puffed-up clouds. There aren't many cars parked in the driveways and I guess the college kids are studying for exams. There's always one week of blazing sunshine in May right before the school and college exams in June. I'd solved the dilemma, along with most of my classmates, by lying on the college lawns with my textbooks. We were a sea of almost all white flesh interspersed with white pages, turning over occasionally, burning gradually. The red sunburnt skin by the next day never stopped the week of desperate sun worship. We did it religiously, without fail. Sunshine was as precious a commodity as a good exam result, only rarer.

I'm aware the neighbour must be getting impatient watching us stare.

Nestor frowns at us from the doorway. "Auntie Z said there would be stuff in the attic and in the shed out the back. Will ye two head round and clear in there. Key's under the pot or something. I'll do up here." He disappears again.

Padraic chuckles. "Doesn't want to get his dainty hands dirty in the shed. Does he not know the spiders in the attic will get him?"

I smile. "Are you not the one who runs screaming? Or did the therapy work?"

Padraic cuffs me gently over my ear. "Who needs therapy? Only you two disturbed yokes. Come, let's get this done, Bernadette will have kittens if I miss evening mass as well."

We follow a concrete pathway leading off the driveway, around scraggly shrubs, and through a narrow lane between the grey spackled walls and the green-stained wood fence that is taller than me by four or five slats.

It is cold here in the shade and I hurry through, Padraic strolling behind me.

The fence continues through a corner behind a simple garden shed, surrounding a patch of brownish-green shaved grass. Three earthenware pots stand watch, each bearing a mostly dried twig, their twist and colour blending into the wood of the structure. I tilt back the nearest pot and a key blinks in the forgotten light.

I pick up the key and wipe specks of rust off it, the stain seeping into my fingertips.

A pane of Perspex serves as a window and the inside is dark even without the shading of grime.

Nestor's voice comes from above us and we both jump. "Hey, Padraic, will you give me a hand with the boxes. Jay, you could start there, sorting out the stuff and we'll carry it after."

We look up at him, his head poking out of the upstairs window. The rear of the house is the same spackled grey, but it has waist-high splashes of mildew. Rented, not a lived-in home.

Padraic gives an exaggerated sigh. He mutters, "Orders. That's what I get for doing him a favour." He walks towards the side lane. "Don't hurt yourself in there. Leave the heavy lifting to the strong men."

I don't rise to the bait as I usually do, turning instead to the shed.

The key faces resistance in the turn. It's wet and my fingers slip. The door sticks as well, but I get it open, wincing at the screech it makes against the bare concrete floor.

The sunlight sneaks in before me, trips up on the cardboard boxes stacked on wooden pallets. They come up to my chest. The air smells stuffy, with a trace of mould. There's a layer of dust on the top boxes that sifts into the air as I lift a lid. Papers, textbooks, medical titles. The next box has more books. I test the heft of the boxes, it's going to be hard to lift the top row off the others.

I peer beyond the barricade of cardboard. and wait for a minute for my vision to adjust to the dark space beyond the reach of the invading oblong of sunlight. Objects take shape, more boxes, not as neatly stacked, something resembling an armchair draped in cloth, an exercise machine, its straight rubber arms pointing up to the ceiling. I wish I'd thought of bringing a torch. Then I remember my phone has a flashlight.

I finally remember where to find the flashlight feature on the phone and switch it on and wave it over the boxes. Most of the cardboard boxes in the space behind are open, stretched, containing loose household items. A hairdryer sticking out of one box, a green sneaker with yellow laces peeking out of another. I aim the circle of light further back and more objects emerge, suitcases.

I find a foothold on the base wooden pallet. I push each box back a few inches, each one further, creating a narrow space for my foot and I use this cardboard staircase to climb to the top. I balance on my knees, swaying, under the crossbars of the roof. The cobwebs stretch against my hair and face, the dust creeps into my nostrils. I'm glad I'm wearing jeans.

I drop to the other side, landing awkwardly, but not hurting myself.

There's no path in the pile, so I have to move objects aside to get to the stuff at the rear.

I check out the first box, the one with the hairdryer. There are other toiletries in it, a hairbrush, concealer, tweezers. Skin lightening cream. Interesting. I examine the orange-coloured tube labelled 'Fair and Lovely'. I didn't realise there was such a thing. The next box has the companion green sneaker along with a pair of dress boots, black high heels, one sandal, furry bear feet slippers. I remember when those were all the rage, bears, and all kinds of animal shapes ended up encasing our feet. I nudge the boxes aside and work my way to the suitcases. There's red gauzy fabric in one of the suitcases. I pull it out like a magician's silk trick, it keeps coming. Red fabric with heavy gold lining in an intricate pattern. It's a saree. I've read about these and seen pictures. It's an Indian wedding saree, I can't remember what they're called. I push the material into the suitcase.

The armchair is brooding beside me. It seems so out of place. The cloth draped over it is heavy, smells of must and dust. I pick at the hem, lift it up, shine the light into the tented space. The fabric of the armchair is a light-green almost mushroom colour, it's smooth and the cushioned seat is plump. The arm is rounded, smooth. I raise the cover higher. The other arm is stained. I stop. Hold the phone closer. It's not a stain of age or mould. It's rust-coloured, irregular, and covers most of the front section of the arm. There are dark streaks, with fainter areas fanning out.

The phone buzzes and I let out a tiny scream. A curse word is mangled in the sound.

It's a text from Padraic. "HI". I mumble a full curse.

I wave my phone around. see a closed box and open it. There are two CDs, a video camcorder, the old analogue type. One CD is a movie, a Bollywood movie, the title 'Sholay' is designed in a fire font from the seventies. The other CD has got a typed label on it. 'David and Lana Matthews Wedding" and a date, 'July 30th, 2005.

I pick through more open boxes. There's one with mementoes from trips abroad, a knickknack version of the Leaning Tower of Pisa, the Eiffel Tower. There are empty photo frames, one bordered with shamrocks. A loose photo, quite dark. A man and a woman, Indian-looking. I hold the photo towards the open door, throwing more light on it.

"Nice looking pair."

This time I drop the phone and the curse words are not silent. "For feck's sake, Padraic!"

"Sorry." But he's not. He lifts a top row box and weighs it in his arms. "What they have in here? Rocks?"

"Textbooks, I think." I've found my phone and I shine the flashlight at him. "An Indian couple lived here?"

He walks to the door carrying the box as if it's full of confetti. "That should be interesting for you. Nestor will probably let you keep some of the stuff." He stops. "There was mostly crap in the attic. But there was a box of notebooks hidden away. You might want them?"

I nod at his back. "Cool. Can you keep it separate? I wouldn't mind hanging on to stuff from here too. I think the saree is an Indian wedding one."

He turns and grins. "You lesbians. Can't think of nothing but marrying. Sure, haven't you just met the woman?"

I sigh. "You crack yourself up, don't you?"

He's laughing as he walks out. "And Bernadette too. Don't forget, I crack her up too."

§

I survey the boxes strewn across my room with a twinge of guilt. I'm glad Zara was out when we got back. No clue who these people are to my mother, but I doubt they're going to mind me hanging on to a few bits, as the rest of their items are on their way to the dump. And I couldn't pass up on real Indian stuff.

I don't bring up that part of me with my mother, I don't want to upset her into thinking it bothers me not to have known my father.

I pull red and gold silk fabric out of the suitcase, run it through my fingers. The raised edges of the gold embroidery slow the smooth flow. It is a *mandragoti* saree according to the internet. Placed on or carried by the bride.

The women in the online pictures are so graceful. I stand in front of the mirror and hold the material up against my chest and face. It is from another world, one without the jeans and t-shirt I'm wearing. I'd be laughed out of that world if I wore something like this, a foreigner trying to fit in. I stare at the stranger in the mirror, my thoughts taking a trip to another land, one that should feel at least partly like home.

I sigh and put the saree back into the suitcase and open the box Nestor had rescued.

Printed sheets lie loose, along with a stack of A4 legal pads. I pick up the topmost printed page.

Lana M.

Intermediate creative writing class

Week 2 assignment - prose

Rainfall

Rain pulls you down. You struggle up, but your feet slip and you fall and just for a moment, maybe more, you wish you could lie there forever, until the soggy mess that is you is just another bump in this land that has been sodden for so long it cannot ever wring itself out. Trees leak, eternally running into the ground, leaves drip from their branches weighed down with the drops that fall in continuous anonymous streams merging the dirty grass and leaden skies and slip into the earth to be forgotten in the crowd. You cry into the ground beneath the pounding of raindrops until your tears turn to anger and you laugh. You roll over and jeer at them that there is nothing unique about a raindrop, unlike its colder cousin, the snowflake. The snowflake, the celebrity of the world of falling water. Richer, whiter, admired and feted, with tongues held out in wonder to taste them, study them. But they all end up as slush on the earth, absorbed and forgotten, like you will be, because this rain will never stop, but you will.

Interesting that I can't imagine an Indian woman going to creative writing classes here in Galway. I didn't realise I had that view too.

I pick up the next sheet.

Lana M.

Intermediate creative writing class

Week 3 assignment - poetry

The Coffee Table

The coffee table remains topless, bare.

As the glass lay shattered by your fury

I saw razor-thin slivers of past beauty, reflected

refracted ruins of our now.

The tragedy is not that you were there

But that I was. Now, I refuse to fall.

I refuse to drown in the alcohol

teemed rivers of your madness, your sadness.

I write to say this is me. This is me.

Not that shrivelled grey victim of a crime

Played in black and white silent movie time

In front of a crowd blinded by colour.

I wrote you onto a million pages

I write because I have no other way

I will write till you are carried away

Sinking in the ink. Disappearing. Gone.

"Jaya?" Zara's voice floats up from downstairs.

I drop the sheet back into the box and close the cardboard flaps. I yell, "Yes, I'm in my room."

"Are you packed yet?"

I'm not.

I yell back as I re-open the box. "Almost done."

"Nestor says he won't take the blame if we miss the plane. He's gone to get petrol."

I sigh. Take the printed pages out and lift the cover of the first legal pad.

UNTITLED

By

L.M.

CHAPTER ONE

Sapna

Tuscany, Italy. 1999

The wind slammed the shutters closed startling her awake. It swept into the bedroom and over her, bringing relief from the stifling heat. The shutters creaked open to reveal the Tuscan countryside, Lucignano sitting proudly, curled around the distant hills, its circular maze of red brick buildings basking in the mid-morning sun. Though they had only been in the village three times since the start of their honeymoon in Tuscany, they had used its name on road signs as their homing beacon, its Italian syllables flowing off their Indian tongues as they played with the sound. Made it like they were always on the road to Lucignano while in fact they were on the road to Arezzo, so often that they joked about it as they traversed the hills and plains of Tuscany in their quest to see all, feel all, taste all of this new land. The strange and foreign sounding names that they shaped in the privacy of their air-conditioned rental car- Sinalunga, Montalcino, Montepulciano, some flowed, others didn't. They both stumbled over Castenuove Bernadenga and she resorted to mumbling it out as a mangled sound when navigating "turn right, follow road for Castel... Blah... Blah..." As she tried to follow the typewritten directions they had been provided with by the villa owner.

"Jaya!" My mother's anxious voice breaks through my reluctance to leave the newfound discoveries.

"Okay, okay." I gather up the printed pages and the legal pads and frown at my wheeled suitcase, small enough for the Ryanair carry-on. I remove two pairs of shoes and put in the papers and the first two notepads and manage to get the suitcase closed.

The van pulls up outside with a squeal and I rush to change my clothes and swan off to some strange village in rural France.

CHAPTER FIVE

There are vehicles zipping along on the single-lane carriageway as it winds its way through the wooded landscape towards Saint-Sebastien-du-Lac which, from my quick internet research, has a population of 50. I'm sure there are more people in the surrounding area, but from the pictures and the size of the village on the map, they could probably fit only 50, if they bunked up together.

We'll be staying at something called a gîte complex.

The snores are gentle from the passenger seat. Zara has been asleep, wrapped in a large blue shawl, for most of the 5 hour ride from the airport, even when I stopped for petrol.

I have to cross the middle line to avoid scraping a blue van parked at the side, with '*Gendarmerie*' sprawled in white letters along the door.

I open the window and breathe in the sunny freshness of the rural air.

Zara shifts in her seat. I glance across. She's awake and seems uneasy.

"What's up, mum?"

"Nothing, nothing." She swivels to gaze at the scenery. "Isn't this so lush. It is so like Ireland, isn't it?"

"Yup, green." I'm focused on driving a rental, in the left seat on the right lane, both wrong to me.

"It rains a lot here too. That's why it's so lush. It's a National Forest area, you know?"

I nod. She has forgotten I printed out the info for her.

She clears her throat. "We'll be there soon. The holiday place."

"GPS says we're fifteen minutes away." We turned off the dual-lane highway and I'm concentrating on not driving head-on into the crazy French drivers. They're capable of causing an accident, they don't need a wandering Irish woman contributing to the confusion.

The roads narrow and quieten until we finally turn left onto what must be the smallest possible. It's fully tarmac, but gives the impression there should be a strip of grass growing down the middle. The trees are dense on each side, separated from us by grass-filled ditches.

Zara shrieks as a dark shape hurtles across our view. I've reduced my speed, but for a few seconds of adrenaline flood I close my eyes and expect a shattered windscreen and two squashed Irish women.

I open my eyes. The deer is running ahead of us, his rear end zig-zagging in his haste to get across the road he so suicidally merged onto from the forest. I glance at Zara and she's clutching her chest, her mouth open, but I don't think it's a heart attack, more shock. I smile to calm her down and say, "He's fine. We're fine. It's okay, mam."

I press my foot down on the accelerator in relief, and shriek as another brown body dashes across from our right. My swearing drowns out my mother's voice which has descended into a pained muttering. This time, I slam my foot on the brake, get it wrong, the car jerks forward and tips the doe on its hind quarters, the animal leaps in the air, gives me an accusing glare, and dashes over to join its mate who is now staring back at us in a similar, but haughtier, tone.

I yell after their white backsides as I pass the spot where they're disappearing into the safety of the trees, "Pick a bloody English car the next time ye decide to carry out a suicide pact, fecking French deer."

The yelling is good for my blood pressure. I turn to my mother to help hers. She is laughing, a repeated hiccup of nerves and relief.

I stop the car, taking up most of the road, and we both laugh helplessly. I need this. A break from the emotions built up in me for three years, ever since I lost Chloe. Being back in Galway, the place where she lives, the mention of her, the old pain and anger resurfaced. If it ever went away. Right now, laughing on this deserted forest road feels and tastes like freedom.

I'm wiping the tears away when Zara is able to speak again. She reaches across and grasps my lower arm, pulls my hand over into her lap, and envelops it with both her palms. "I have to tell you something."

I grin. "What, mam?"

Our destination is close according to the GPS. "Shouldn't we get to the place? It's right there." I gesture to the windscreen, pointing out the cream structure visible two hundred yards away.

There's someone driving towards us and we need to move to let them pass. It's one of those Citroen Dianes, the stereotypical image of a French car. Funny enough, I hadn't observed any others yet.

Zara tightens her grip on my hand, which I need for the gears. I frown at her, puzzled.

There's no space to pass us on the narrow road and I'm surprised the driver hasn't thrown choice French curses our way. I wouldn't mind learning a couple.

Zara's mouth is working, but nothing is coming out.

"Mam? Is it shock?" I check the pulse in her wrist, with my other hand, the one she's not still gripping.

A loud rap on her window makes us both jump. First a red jacket blurs, then a face pops into view, a huge smile taking over most of it.

Now it's my mouth that works with no sound emerging.

Zara keeps one hand clutching mine and lets down the glass with the other.

Chloe leans in and kisses Zara's cheek. "Saw you had stopped and got worried. Come on out, let me give you a proper hug."

My chin drops even further. Zara gives my fingers a tiny squeeze, smiles sheepishly at me, and climbs out.

I watch numbly as they hug, trying to work out where I am. This is familiar, them hugging, but in the wrong time, the wrong place.

I catch the nervous whisper. "Is she okay with this? I still can't believe she agreed to come."

Zara's voice is full of bravado. "She'll be fine." She dips her head to peer through the window. "Chloe is staying at the holiday complex. Why don't you follow us, I'll go with her."

"What?" I'm able to retrieve one word from my brain.

Chloe's face joins Zara's in a framed rectangle that makes absolutely no sense to me. Her smile is as sweet as I remember it, as I've tried to forget it. "Hi Jay, thank you for coming, and for bringing Zara."

"What?" I try to dislodge another word with a shake.

Chloe frowns. She stares at my face. Her dark green eyes match the forest behind her, her skin a shade more tanned now, cheeks glowing and framed by blonde-streaked hair and a red shirt.

Zara coughs and her face exits the picture as she straightens out of sight.

The frame is filled solely by Chloe. She says, "You didn't know?"

I manage to shake my head, still no words coming out.

Chloe bites her full lower lip. It was something she did that drove me crazy. Turned me on, but also ran a knife straight through my heart.

That pain reappears, tinged with the shock at her beauty, a revelation each time I saw her, for the fiftieth time, or the hundredth time.

She is looking right into my eyes which must be betraying my mixed emotions. Her face softens and her brow creases in confusion. Then anger creeps into my face, my body, my voice, taking over, reminding us who's in control of me.

I say, "No. I didn't know. Otherwise I would never have come. Why would I fly across the sea and drive halfway across a fecking big country to visit my ex who jilted me at the altar?"

Chloe winces. "So, Zara didn't tell you why I invited her?"

"The crazy woman did not tell me we were going anywhere *near* you! I assumed you were in England. What are you doing in the backside of nowhere? In a gîte thing and all?"

Chloe says, "I'm staying there for a few weeks." She peeks over her shoulder, as if for help from Zara, but my mother is examining the grass ditch with undivided attention.

"So why on earth are we here?"

Chloe rubs her cheek. "We should get you both to your cottage to settle in?"

"No. Tell me what the hell is going on."

Chloe sighs. "Please don't drive off or take it out on Zara."

"What am I, a childish jerk?" I gesture towards my mother. "I should be used to her crazy, though this is beyond fair, really, this is too fecking much, even for her."

Chloe grimaces, and I realise there's more. She speaks, holding each word in before letting it land in my angry lap. "I asked Zara to help with my wedding plans."

I'm aware my mouth is doing that hanging open thing again.

She continues, words rushing out now. "I didn't mean for her to bring you, though you're welcome of course, but if it is a problem, and I thought it might be, then you shouldn't have to put yourself through it. I wanted Zara to be here, she's the closest thing to a mother I've ever had, and she'll be my maid of honour. My dad will be giving me away, but I couldn't imagine getting married without Zara, and I need her help to plan it."

The words won't digest, they're sitting uncomfortably in my belly wondering what they are too.

Chloe rushes on. "David doesn't know I'd like the wedding here."

I find my voice. "Who's David?"

Chloe closes her eyes. "He's my fiancé." She blinks open.

I hear Zara, timid through the fog in my mind. "Jaya, baby, are you okay?"

I'm lost in the rural depths of France finding out my worst fears have taken concrete shape and hit me on the head, and my mother and ex are wondering if I am *okay*?

Zara says, "Chloe, how about you drive on and we'll follow you to the house. I could do with a nice cup of tea and Jaya could probably do with a shot of something."

Chloe almost jumps out of the view in her haste. "Yes, yes, of course. Follow me. It's only around the corner." She mutters to Zara. "Can she drive in that state?"

I press the accelerator, make it roar, lightly, though I'd rather gun the engine and crash into her petite straight French Diana excuse of an automobile. Two years with her, three years getting over her, I've enough rage to do it, but enough practice at swallowing the anger. The struggle to get over Chloe, being stabbed, Fiona, talk of mortgages, marriage, everything. It's swirling up inside me with nowhere to go. They better move the hell out of my way right now.

Zara leans in and says, "I'll ride with Chloe, it's right up the street." She smiles, wafting her calming energy, as she calls it, towards me. She pats the door awkwardly. "It will all be fine, my sweet cub, really."

I sit and watch, shocked, helpless, and fuming, as Chloe helps my mother into the Citroen, walks to her side and gets in, makes a five-point turn, and races away.

CHAPTER SIX

The two-storeyed house is a smooth patchwork of cream and grey brick under a burgundy slate roof and it sprawls a few rooms wider than the driveway. Eggshell-blue shutters frame the windows and match the front door, pots on the windowsills and patio overflow with cerise, pink, purple, red. Driving up the tree-lined avenue to it, I notice the charm with the same loss and anger that had engulfed me as I watched Chloe pack her stuff. We'd spent our last minutes together arguing, always the same thing we argued about when we met, and in the two years of our relationship.

I guess I'd been right all along. She had been biding her time with me, with a woman, while she waited for Mr Right to arrive.

Rage rises in me again, the familiar slow burn lighting into open flames. Having known right vies with having loved wrong.

Chloe is helping Zara out of her car. I ache seeing her through the barrier our past has constructed.

I stretch getting out of the car. After a long drive, I now need to carry this mask as well. This armour against everyone is heavy, but it works, enough to hide what it truly did to me when she left.

Zara comes over to the rental car, an apology of sorts in her eyes. "Isn't this such a pretty place? Even nicer than the pictures. Come, let's get our stuff to the cottage. Chloe says to drive behind the main house and she'll meet us there. All the cottages are there, she is staying in the lodging rooms here."

"That's all you have to say?" Though I don't want them to know the degree of hurt and anger, I'm amazed my mother is being so casual.

Zara whispers, "She invited me, and I wanted to be here to help. She's asked me to be her maid of honour. What chance have I got of being anyone's maid of honour again?"

"You don't think I might marry some day? To someone who might

53

actually stick around for the wedding? Don't you see this is unbelievably cruel of you, to drag me here to watch that same ex plan her wedding, to a *guy*?"

She sighs. "You're my wee cub, but we obviously don't' see the same things."

"What's that supposed to mean?" She's often hinted at her feelings on our breakup, but has always fallen short of blaming anyone.

"Nothing, nothing. Come. A cup of tea will help. Perchance a glass of wine." Zara makes a sweeping Gallic gesture and purrs. "We are in the wonderful French countryside, we should behave French."

No use saying anything. Since Chloe and I broke up, my mother and I haven't been able to communicate and we argue every time. This is already hellish and an argument with Zara is the last thing I need.

I notice she has added a blue and white and red scarf to her ensemble. Taking a deep breath, I work on the armour, and say, "Did you forget your beret?"

She perks up. "No. It's in my bag. Will I put it on, or should I wait until I meet everyone?"

I sigh. "Why wait? Let the embarrassment begin."

She smiles.

I add, "And the torture."

She waves me towards the car. "Let the games begin."

The cottage is delightful. As Zara describes it.

I'm too shocked to inspect it.

Chloe had stayed long enough to open the door and leave the keys, promising a tour of the place after she checked us in with the staff. She asked us not to mention her fiancé to anyone here. She stressed that three times.

Zara is oohing over the Belgian chocolates arranged sweetly on the antique oak coffee table. I guess everything is French furniture here. The wardrobes and desks and beds were probably discovered in the many quaint 'restoration' stores I saw on the roadside.

I can't sit here.

I leave her admiring the gîte.

There are more cottages, surrounding a large sandy rectangle, a shared courtyard, complete with a water feature. On the furthest side of the courtyard, opposite our line of cottages, is a barn-shaped building in the same sandstone material, and the sign says 'La Ville du Lac' and it has a picture of wine glasses dancing over a plate and knife and fork.

The wine glasses are enough for me.

A lake comes into sight when I clear the building and, despite my mood, I gasp at the blue-green water sending white shards of sunlight, painful in their intensity. I climb the stairs to a raised stone-tiled patio full of tables and chairs, empty now, but which I imagine must often be packed with tourists eager for that view. The remnant smell of food hangs in the air along with pine-scented detergent.

The inside is dim after the bright glare. I head straight to the bar counter through double glass doors which snap shut startling me, but no one's there to witness my little jig. I resist rapping on the smooth dark oak. Instead, I wait, impatient and hot and tired. And full of an anger I cannot escape.

A young man comes hurrying out pushing aside the swinging doors beside the counter and the metal insides of an industrial kitchen are visible for a few seconds. A woman's voice follows him through the narrowing gap. "We're closed. Tell whoever it is we're closed, no serving."

I'm not sure what flavour the man's skin is, but it is only a shade darker than mine. His even, white teeth contrast as well with dark-coffee eyes. I'm pleasantly surprised to see brown skin here in rural France. I like not being the only person with colour I haven't had to bake into me. Chloe is blonde and green-eyed and her skin has acquired a shade of tan that is regarded as perfect rather than offensive. In the summer, we lay in bed and admired each other's tone and wondered how skin that looked so similar could bring out such different reactions in people.

He has said something and I missed it. I say, "Sorry? Pardon-moi?"

"I'm sorry we're closed. For the next hour. It's kind of a siesta time here." His voice is soft, almost husky.

I don't mean to snap, but I really want wine, or beer, or something stronger. "I thought they only did that in Spain? Good Lord Jaysus Christ, is there anywhere in this fecking place I can get a drink?"

His smile widens, but he snatches a glance over his shoulder before whispering, "If you ask nicely, I could sneak you a beer. But you'd have to sit out on the terrace and drink it."

His grin is infectious. I return it, lower my voice. "I'll beg if you need. Sorry, I'm not normally this way, but it's been a strange and screwed-up day."

He's gazing at me, his smile taking over his eyes. His black hair is straight with a wave that seems to resist any attempt to tame it. I get the impression he is also enjoying the sight of another brown person.

The same woman yells from the kitchen, startling us both, "Ishmael! What did I say? Are you coming to help?"

He calls back, "Coming. There's a bird in here."

I'm set to quarrel with his description, but he puts his finger to his lips. He steps up and grabs a glass from the shelves built into the wall.

He leans towards the kitchen door and continues in the same soft, though louder, voice, "I have to release it, it keeps flying against the glass."

He places the beer on the counter.

I reach for my wallet. He shakes his head.

The woman's voice is muffled. "Oh no! Poor thing. Let me clean my hands, I will help."

Ishmael grimaces. "No, no, everything's fine, Isabella. It's out now. I'll be right in."

His smile returns as he swivels to me. "Go on. She can't see you or I'll get in trouble." He sweeps his fingers through his hair and the rebellious strands rise further. "Again."

I whisper, "Thank you." I grab the beer and creep outside. I wave in at him from a table in the far corner where I will be hidden from this woman with the strict voice. He's already rushing through the swinging doors, unaware of how much he's brightened my day and my view of French people, and people in general.

I sit and allow the lake to capture my attention. I want to see beauty in a way that doesn't wound or infuriate me now.

§

The lake, adorned by a string of lamps, provides a shimmering backdrop for the covered dining area, almost full of people dressed a touch more formal than the afternoon array of shorts and T-shirts, bikinis and bathing suits. The chatter in the air is a mixture of French and English accents. Our server was a young woman who spoke good English with a strong French accent.

"So, do we get to meet this David anytime soon?" I whisper the name. Not that I want to meet him, but I detect a discomfort in Chloe whenever she mentions her fiancé.

She picks at the elaborate salad piled on her plate. She's changed into a light green summer dress that shows off her tanned skin.

We are sitting at the same table where I'd sat nursing a beer for the afternoon. They had joined me when I didn't return to the cottage.

Zara forks the last bite of steak into her mouth, slumps in her chair and sighs. "That was so good. They have a hell of a chef, the brandy sauce was divine. I understand why they have a crowd here."

Chloe nods. "Yes, Isabella's fantastic. I'll introduce you to her after the service. She's frazzled because the guy who normally manages front of house is away. I've been helping out too." She faces me. "David's in Saudi Arabia at the moment. He needed to tie up things there with his parents, his mother is ill and they may not be able to travel and he wanted to arrange it if possible."

"Now isn't that so nice?" Zara studies me as though imagining having a good child.

"Yes, how sweet of him." Though my tone is light, Chloe glances at me searching for the sarcasm. I push aside the braised pork dish, the sweetness of the delicate sauce suddenly cloying on my tongue. The white wine is dry, cleanses my palate. "Is he Saudi Arabian?"

I hate the tenderness in her voice. "David's Indian, a nice guy, very involved with his family." She glances around, at the restaurant windows. "I'll explain later, but don't say his real name here. I said his name was Matt. It's not exactly a lie or anything, his surname is Matthews."

My gut hurts as though I've been shoved and it has to do with her hooking up with an Indian guy. "Does he know about your… about your me, I mean about me. Does he know you were with a woman?"

Chloe shakes her head, a dart of fear flies across her eyes.

Zara lifts her glass of red. "Here's to nice family men. I wouldn't mind meeting one myself."

"Mam!" I swivel in my chair.

"What? Just because you think of me as an old woman?"

Chloe gives me an accusing frown. Did I imagine the fear?

I hold my palms up and say to Zara. "What? When did I ever say you were too old? I just didn't realise you were searching for a man?"

Zara snorts. "I'm not necessarily. But it wouldn't be awful if a handsome French man charmed the pants off me."

"Mam!"

Chloe laughs. "Hadn't thought of finding you a French guy, but who knows, there might be cool guys for you here." She takes my mother's hand. "We'll find you a date for the wedding."

Zara nods. "That I can go with. Speaking of cute guys, who are they?" She points with her chin towards two men who are walking towards the restaurant from the cottages. I recognise the younger as my friend who sneaked me beer. He has a black apron on over black trousers and a loose white shirt. The man with him is older and pale-skinned. His salt and pepper hair and beard both rest on his purple shirt.

Chloe turns. She smiles as she swings back. "Sorry, no luck there. They're a couple."

"Blast." Zara says, "They're both cute, though the brown one is a wee bit young for me."

"That's Ishmael, Isabella's brother. They're Algerian. His partner is Frank. He's English, a retired surgeon who moved over from England." She stands. "And part-owner of this place."

I say, "Real family affair around here, isn't it?"

Chloe shoots me a look.

I hold up my palms again. "Just saying."

Zara asks, "Are you going to introduce us?"

Chloe nods. The men have reached the terrace and are heading into the restaurant. She calls out, "Ishmael, Frank."

Ishmael stops and then grins when he sees Chloe. He makes his way through the tables, nodding at the customers. The other man follows, after a pause to kiss cheeks with someone.

Chloe gives Ishmael a hug. Turns with her arm around his waist and faces us. "Zara and Jaya, this is Ishmael, my new best friend here."

He has the trace of a blush on his cheeks, sounds huskier now. "I managed to sneak Jaya a beer earlier, without Isabella catching me." He addresses Zara. "Delighted to finally meet you both, I've heard so much about the two of you." He lets Frank into the circle and Chloe performs the introductions again.

I fancy being examined by a coroner as Frank sweeps measuring eyes over me. His eyebrow rises a tiny bit at the rainbow pin on my top. "Ireland? Where in Ireland? I used to visit friends there." He has a similar English accent to Chloe's, his tone pleasant, but both he and Ishmael have tensed.

Zara says, "Galway. Where were your friends?"

"Galway, in the suburbs. Lovely place. Have you been living there long?"

Zara crinkles her brow, "Since the nineties? Jaya went to college there, so I moved from Dublin to be near her."

Frank glances at Chloe, but doesn't say anything.

Chloe asks, "Would you care to join us? We're thinking of ordering dessert."

Ishmael shakes his head. "I'd better go and help Isabella out. She can be cranky when the service is busy and she has to work with new people."

Frank gives him a peck on the cheek and watches as he hurries into the restaurant.

Chloe pulls over a chair from the next table and we all sit again.

Zara says, "That's a lovely mix of an accent Ishmael has. Where is he from originally, he doesn't sound French?"

Frank smiles. "I love that, much nicer than 'he doesn't look French,' that's what he usually hears."

"I didn't mean any offence." Zara laughs. "I brought up a brown baby in rural Ireland in the seventies, I get it with the 'not looking Irish' thing. I wasn't thinking that. It's his accent, very unusual. Of course, it helps he has such a sexy voice."

I open my mouth to admonish her but shake my head instead. I'm not her minder, this isn't like my college days when she almost took pride in embarrassing me.

Frank chuckles. "Yes, isn't it dreamy. He's French-Algerian, but he has lived all over the world. We got together in London. I think his accent bears the trace of every place he's ever been." He says to me. "Must have been interesting growing up in rural Ireland with your skin colour. I lived in a fairly diverse part of London for a long time, but living with Ishmael here has been an eye-opener."

I nod. "I had the impression when I met him he was glad to see another brown-skinned person. It's almost as white as Ireland here."

"It was easier when we lived in Paris. There are so many more North Africans there, he didn't stand out as much. If it wasn't for Isabella, he'd be the only brown in the village." He shifts in his chair, towards Zara. "Do I detect a hint of an American accent there?"

Zara groans. "Only a hint? Have I lost it?"

Chloe laughs. "Are you still trying to convince everyone you only speak American?"

There is a weight in my chest as I watch Chloe and Zara interact. It had never mattered, not deeply, whether my girlfriends got on with my mother. I deemed it safer when they didn't, or when they didn't meet. But Chloe had captured both our hearts.

I listen to the three of them and it feels surreal sitting here in the glow of the lights, a home that could have been. I drink the wine, warmth buzzes down and across my body.

Chloe catches me looking and her eyes gleam. And for a moment, it's like she feels at home too.

CHAPTER SEVEN

Night is seeking to replace dusk, and the terrace has emptied, leaving only our table.

Frank and Zara have settled into a comfortable chat. Chloe has gone to the kitchen to help Isabella and to bring her out to meet us.

A French police car sidles by the building, the glow of white lettering on the black side dying as it fades past the lake

Zara says, "I've heard you never tangle with the *'gendarmerie'* here."

Frank follows her gaze. "They're not too bad. As long as you don't provoke them. And you at least attempt to speak French. English people bought cheap here to take advantage of the strong pound and quite a few are reputed to be tax evaders or ex-cons in England. Many don't bother to learn French and expect life here to be the same as back home, but with an accent."

Zara leans forward. "I could have been a soldier or a CIA agent."

I sigh. This story became urban legend in our village.

Frank lifts an eyebrow. "In Ireland?"

"In Brooklyn where I grew up. I applied for the CIA." She's told the story countless times, but that never stops her telling it again or giggling as she does. "Don't know why they didn't hire me." She preens. "Don't you think I'd have been great? They could have let me infiltrate the hippies and the artsy neighbourhood. I knew everyone and blended in well. No one would have suspected a thing."

I mutter, "Can't believe they didn't welcome you."

"Truth! I'd have been such an asset. They had ads in the newspaper. Big ads. For agents. So, I dressed up one morning and slipped out of the house. The interviews were being held in Manhattan. I never told my mother where I was going. I was in my twenties, sassy and bold and just knew I'd be excellent as a spy."

I've heard it all before, but never fail to shake my head. Frank is smiling, his eyebrow half-cocked.

Zara waves an arm and the sleeve of her pink blouse flaps in the air. "I had on a leopard-print top over my lace bra and under a full-length white coat with a fake leopard fur collar. Red leather mini-skirt and black fishnet tights. And the shoes, oh my Goddess, they were stunning."

I say, "I still can't believe you walked into the CIA dressed like that."

"I could turn heads in those days."

Frank laughs. "I'm certain you did."

"It was in a skyscraper in Manhattan. They were on the top of the building, they'd commandeered a whole floor. They ushered me into a boardroom and did the interview there. Two guys in black suits. There were a lot of people there, they kept passing in the corridor and looking in through the big windows. They kept me there for hours, couldn't grasp the idea I could have done the job."

I say, "But you left."

"They asked me to fill out this humungous application form. I got to the part where it asked if I took drugs. And I was to list the names of people in the neighbourhood to vouch for me. Can you imagine? Me having to go back to Brooklyn and the CIA coming to find the folks I'd named. Not one of us who didn't smoke weed?" She shrieked with laughter. "I pretended I needed the loo, and I ran out of there as fast as I could on my heels."

Frank tries to hide his grin. He says, "I think you might have been excellent at the espionage game."

Zara nods. "I've been known to be good at a variety of games."

I say, "Not sure we are spy material, considering we were screaming like babies when attacked by two deer."

Zara sighs. "I could blame it on my age, but you screamed too."

Frank laughs. "So, you had the deer experience?"

I say, "The one following the other in a suicide pact? Yup."

Frank says, "That's what they do. The first one lulls you into a false sense of security and you're crossing yourself and next thing, pow! the mate runs in front of you."

Chloe and a woman approach the table, and the change in Frank's expression is so slight and fleeting I would have missed it if he hadn't been speaking to me and smiling. I haven't time to process what it was before the women arrive at our table.

Frank stands and drags over two chairs from the adjacent table that's laden with scraped-clean dessert plates and cutlery.

Chloe says, "This is the wonderful chef, Isabella. Ishmael's sister. She's the temporary fill-in chef, but you wouldn't guess from the food."

The woman is brown-skinned with dark eyes that are familiar, but then I realise they're replicas of her brother's. She's beautiful in an intense exotic way that makes me skip a breath. She runs one hand through hair she has released from a white cap and the black waves fall past her shoulders.

Her brows pinch when she glances at Frank, but her lips widen into a smile as she greets Zara and me.

"Chloe tells me you enjoyed your meal. I wish I could take the praise, but our regular chef prepared everything, and I handled the service. I don't formally cook, but I wanted to help." Her voice is soft and accented, with a hint of French, but more of a texture, when she speaks, honey pours down my spine.

Zara says, "That was so good, I could have eaten it twice. You should accept the praise, it was wonderfully presented. Please sit with us, you must be worn out." She pats my shoulder. "This is my daughter, Jaya."

Isabella's eyes widen. She smiles and the resemblance to Ishmael is even more remarkable. She says, "I love your eyes!" Her cheeks redden. "And your face! How striking. You must get asked this all the time, but you remind me of that Afghani girl who was on the cover of National Geographic, so unusual. Where are you from?"

My tongue is tied. Isabella has this air of composure as if she's experienced too much to be beaten down by the world. I should have gone to the cottage and freshened up, rather than sitting here for the whole afternoon and evening, in jeans and a top which I selected more for comfort for the long journey.

Ishmael has joined us and he pulls over another chair.

I say, "Ireland. I'm half Indian." I hover, unsure whether to shake hands. After she has been so complimentary, why I am so gawky?

Isabella kisses Zara on both cheeks. She reaches across and touches her lips to each side of my face. The scent of sugar and warm skin tickles my senses. Behind her, Ishmael and Frank exchange a look, but again I can't read it.

Everyone settles into their chairs and Chloe says, "Jay, do you want to tour the village tomorrow? Zara's promised to come shopping with me in town and you hate shopping." She turns to Ishmael. "Are you free? Frank and Isabella are working."

My forehead crinkles. I smooth out my expression.

Ishmael smiles. "Of course. I'd be happy to show Jaya the square. The village hasn't tourist spots as such, but the area is so naturally beautiful as it is."

I return his smile. "Thank you, I'd appreciate that." My tone is friendly, but I'm confused about what just happened.

They settle into a conversation, general chit-chat, restaurant, staff, local attractions, but after a half hour, the voices are bees around my ears.

I am exhausted. Overwhelmed.

I get up. "I'm heading to bed, it's been a long day. See you in the morning."

Frank stands. He nudges Ishmael's chair, and Ishmael jumps up.

I smile at them as I pass.

So, I have an escort tomorrow.

Where does Chloe's fiancé, David, fit into all of this and why did Chloe introduce him by a different name to her new friends? Matt. What's that about?

Has Ishmael been tasked with keeping me from disclosing my relationship with Chloe?

Or simply keeping an eye on the jilted lesbian ex-lover of his new BFF. I grin to myself as walk away from the terrace. '*BFF*', what am I, down with the kids?

I stroll to the gîte, the heat of the day seeping into my soles, the sand gritty under my feet. There is an aura of loneliness around the cottage. I can hear laughter and chatter from the other *gîtes* and from the restaurant and bar in the distance.

I'm bone-tired, but restless. There's a bottle of red wine on the kitchen counter. I pour out a healthy glass A call to Fiona will open the door to awkward questions. I won't lie to her, but any mention of Chloe being here is bound to cause trouble. Which I don't need. My nerves are a tangle of anger and confusion as it is.

A handful of English novels lean against each other on a small bookshelf, but I'm not in the mood for cosy mysteries.

The wine accompanies me to bed. Sipping it, I sit in the comfortable warmth trying not to feel sorry for myself, but my thoughts are in turmoil and self-pity is waving its arms around to get attention.

I remember the writing I brought with me, by an Indian woman who intrigues me. I need the distraction.

The air is chilly on my bare skin as I crawl out of bed. The notebooks are in my suitcase and I pull out the untitled novel.

UNTITLED

By

L.M.

Sapna

Tuscany, Italy

The wind slammed the shutters closed startling her awake. It swept into the bedroom and over her, bringing relief from the stifling heat. The shutters creaked open to reveal the Tuscan countryside, Lucignano sitting proudly, curled around the distant hills, its circular maze of red brick buildings basking in the mid-morning sun. Though they had only been in the village three times since the start of their honeymoon in Tuscany, they had used its name on road signs as their homing beacon, its Italian syllables flowing off their Indian tongues as they played with the sound. Made it like they were always on the road to Lucignano while in fact they were on the road to Arezzo, so often that they joked about it as they traversed the hills and plains of Tuscany in their quest to see all, feel all, taste all of this new land. The strange and foreign sounding names that they shaped in the privacy of their air-conditioned rental car-Sinalunga, Montalcino, Montepulciano, some flowed, others didn't.

They both stumbled over Castenuove Bernadenga and she resorted to mumbling it out as a mangled sound when navigating "turn right, follow road for Castel... Blah... Blah..." As she tried to follow the typewritten directions they had been provided with by the villa owner.

They always mistimed the daily tours, starting out late after a lazy breakfast on the little terraced patio leading off their holiday apartment, and ending up walking the streets of the small towns or villages in the height of the afternoon sun, joined only by other tourists who hadn't figured it out yet either. The locals were safely tucked away in cool dark havens probably looking out in amused tolerance at the slow baking taking place. She had grown used to the humid heat of Kerala wringing sweat from her but Tuscany was different. The dry heat scorched the sweat off her as soon as the drops ventured forth, the only place they remained was on the nape of her neck under the curtain of her black hair.

She suffered from the Keralite preoccupation with not getting darker so she religiously applied sun cream every day. There was no protection, however, from the merciless sun and she watched daily in quiet dismay as her sandaled feet and ankles grew more darkly brown, and knees too as they peeked out from under three-quarter length shorts.

She stretched slowly in the bed examining her arms as she did so. She noticed again the new ring, the diamond glinting in the sun, the gold band tighter now as her fingers swelled gently in the heat. The sound of the shower coming from the tiny bathroom in the corner of the bedroom brought her fully awake and she scrambled off the bed and wrapping herself in a robe, she sat at the dressing table, her back to the bathroom door. She watched him in the mirror as he stepped gingerly down the step out of the bathroom, the thin white towel wrapped around his waist. She was suddenly anxious realising he would need the dressing table and she was in the way again. She jerked up guiltily and grabbed her hairbrush off the dresser then sat back onto her side of the bed. He did not notice her dance around him as he strode over to the dressing table. He sat down and started his morning ritual tutting at the occasional misplaced item that disrupted his smooth flow.

Sapna pulled the brush through her hair, wincing as the tangles resisted. Her hair was straight with the occasional twist when she woke. She was used to coaxing it into shape in the mornings, taking her time, planning her day.

Her body felt changed now. She had assumed it would, after marriage, after the first time. But the difference was unexpected.

Used.

She pushed back the word that intruded.

Searched for the sensation.

Sexy.

Womanly.

She noticed his frown in the mirror. She wondered if he realised he was frowning, his eyes had a faraway look she was already becoming used to seeing. She worried she might be noticing too much, trying to pick up his needs from his words was difficult and she was not tuned in to his wordless signs yet. She felt decidedly unwomanly, un-Indian, wasn't this supposed to be automatic?

"Would you like breakfast?" She put the hairbrush on the bed.

He was examining his right cheek in the mirror, stroking the stubble with his finger, his forehead furrowed. "I didn't think I could get sunburnt. I might be peeling."

Sapna laughed, in surprise. "I think anyone can get sunburnt." She saw his finger stop, his eyes change.

She said, "I have sun cream in my bag, very high protection factor.

One of my friends, Reena, you didn't meet her, she couldn't come to the wedding, but she lives in Saudi too, she said she uses sun cream all the time now since she heard about the effects of skin cancer." Sapna was aware of her voice running on and on, she couldn't stop the stream of words. He had returned to examining his face, the other cheek. More words came out of her. *"We didn't know if Indians get skin cancer though, but she wouldn't take the chance, she's fair, like me."*

He hadn't seemed to be aware of her chatter. But now there was something else in his eyes. She thought back quickly over what she'd said. "Not that your skin can't be at risk, but the extra melanin might be a further protection."

She wished she could sink into the bed, that there were manuals to go with arranged marriages. How could anyone be expected to work out what to say to a perfect stranger, what would annoy them, hurt them, please them? What did she really know about him? The arrangements had been made through compatibility testing and star charts and relatives, but not for her. He was not much darker than her, but there were enough shades to notice. Her hastily compiled 'resume' had included 'fair skin', his had not mentioned anything like that. And her height had been left out, she had understood why at the wedding. She wasn't tall at 5'6", but he was around 5'7" she thought, it was hard to judge as they hadn't stood together properly since the ceremony, and she definitely didn't want to ask. She didn't know how to assure him none of that mattered to her. And to tell him what did matter to her. She assumed that would come in time, after all, theirs was an arrangement created through families.

And this arrangement had not followed the usual course, it had been created through bedlam, unforeseen and unwanted.

He was looking at her through the mirror. He gave her the smile, the one that didn't reach his eyes. "I like a good cup of coffee in the morning, eggs. I had the woman bring eggs. Do you know how to do sunny side up?"

"I think so." She sprang up, hoping her relief was not obvious. She was surprising herself. Relief was not what she'd ever expected when ordered to cook. She'd managed to make eggs for herself, but she wasn't exactly a good cook.

"Clean whites, soft yolk, but not running." He turned back to his reflection, gently eased off the offending peel of skin.

She hurried towards the living room with its tiny kitchen and heard him mutter as she left the room, "At least we have lots of eggs."

CHAPTER EIGHT

Ishmael is sitting on the steps to the terrace, gazing out at the lake where the morning sun chases diamonds on the surface of the water.

"Is it possible to get tired of beauty?" I ask, standing beside him. "I can't imagine that happening, but I've never lived every day with such a view." The wine and exhaustion from a long journey coupled with the shock of seeing Chloe wraps around me, an invisible shroud.

He looks up at me, shadows clearing from his eyes. "Good morning, Jaya. No, I don't believe I'll ever tire of the sight of beauty in its many forms."

If he wasn't gay and in a couple, I could have taken that as a come-on, especially with the way he was smiling at me as he said the words. Are attractive gay French-Algerian men charming with everyone, including lesbian women, just because they can?

He gets up and dusts off his stone-blue jeans. He's wearing a loose long-sleeved white shirt that glows against his skin. Even in the simple act of standing up, his movements are sensual. I give an internal shake, wonder if he is reminding me of his sister. I have a textural memory of her lips on my cheeks. The sandstone walls, the shimmer of the water, the languor of the trees, all lean in with a scent which seeps into me and fills me with attraction. That's the only way my tired mind can describe the sensations, the confusion.

I glance at the restaurant. The terrace is empty, but the double doors are open and the bustle of activity wafts out through them.

Ishmael follows my look. "Isabella is getting ready for the lunch service. We don't serve breakfast here. Not yet. Besides, most visitors prefer to walk into San Sebastian and get croissants at the bakery."

"Ooh, yes. Sounds great." I clap my hands together and Ishmael grins.

"Come on then." He turns and makes the short jump off the deck look elegant. I aim for the steps conscious I'm more likely to trip and fall on my face if I try that.

He holds up his hand. I grasp it and he helps me. He's five six or seven, only an inch or so taller than me, which means I land level with his cheeks, close enough to notice the slight widening of his pupils and the flicker of lashes. There's an alarm bell going off in my head, but I don't have time to pay attention because the moment is over and he has pulled away with less of his former grace and is striding down the road that winds around the complex and recedes between two lines of trees.

My heart thuds as I follow him.

We arrive at the tree-lined avenue, forest thick on each side, and I say, "How far is it?"

He stops and turns. "It's only a mile. Are you happy to walk? There are nice spots along the way you might appreciate."

He examines my sandals, light but comfortable. I'm wearing knee-length shorts, and a blouse that matches my eyes. It's an unusual shade of grey and turquoise and I wore it for Chloe. The thought flashes across my mind, surprising me. Confusing me further.

"What?" He's noticed the expression in my eyes.

"Nothing. Sounds good."

I walk past him, onto the avenue of trees.

§

The countryside is lush in a way that reminds me of Ireland, but with a drier quality. The shades include more brown smudged in with the green. We pass the occasional house, set back from the road, farms with cows in the field and some with wood-cutting machinery, chips spilling out of their maws. The air is humid, woody, fertile.

We walk in a comfortable silence of words, the forest is alive with the chatter of birds and the scenery requires no commentary.

I assume we are approaching the village as more houses dot the landscape.

Ishmael says, "I want to show you something. We've had an unusual visitor in the last two weeks." He is bustling with the excitement of a child. "A young deer has been hanging out with the cows in a farmer's field. It's wonderful to see the children so thrilled to be close to it. Parents have been bringing their kids, but we adults are enjoying it too."

"That does sound unusual. Isn't the deer afraid of people?"

Ishmael's face is bright with wonder. "Normally they are. But we think this little one is staying near the cows so the hunters won't kill it." His eyes dim. "There are crazy hunters around here, fanatical when it comes to their killing. There's a petition up at the bar to protect this one, I'm not too familiar with the politics of it all, but there are hunting families and those who are opposed to it and the laws here can be brutal." He looks like he's far away. "It appears to be a quiet, idyllic place full of beauty, but sometimes that is a veneer and underneath, waiting to be exposed, is the cruelty of humans."

He shivers, puts a smile back on his lips. "It's the field close to the village. We're almost there."

The road widens, by a couple of inches, and now lines of houses and the spire of a church are visible in the distance. Groups of cows stand and lie around in the fields, a dozen people hang out at the barbed-wire lining of one field. A man is holding a child up to the cows that have gathered near the people.

Ishmael says, "Can you see it?"

I move closer. One of the animals is brown and thin and isn't a calf as I first thought. "Wow, amazing."

We stand and watch as the deer grazes beside the cows, occasionally nuzzling at the outstretched fingers of a squealing child. The laughter from the children is filled with delight. The adults are smiling.

"I don't think we'll get to pet it today." Ishmael waves at a couple with a baby. "We can try tomorrow, if you'd like"

I nod. Smile at the couple who are waving back. "How long have you lived here? Do you know many of the people in Saint Sebastian?"

Ishmael says, "A few years. Frank moved before to set things up and I moved here later with Isabella and her husband."

"Isabella is married?"

"Yes, her husband, Henri, is the insurance broker here. Sweet man." Ishmael smiles. "You sound surprised?"

I am. Isabella gave the impression of a free spirit. I don't know which part surprises me more, that she's married, or that it's to a man.

I say, "No, why should I be?"

Ishmael chuckles. "You're not a good liar. I think you find my sister...interesting?"

The heat steals up my cheeks. "She's an interesting woman."

"You thought she was gay."

We're walking by small commercial buildings with signs for real estate, insurance, property management companies. There's a bank, a post office, a garage with French cars on sale in the forecourt.

"It occurred to me."

"That's fascinating. What makes you think a woman is gay" I look at him and he adds, "Not Isabella specifically, but in general."

I have to think for a minute. We turn onto a street lined with narrow buildings, half with calligraphed signs and colourful walls, the others boarded up with dirty grey scraps of wood, walls cracked and weeping paint dust stains.

I say, "I'm not sure. I've been a lesbian for so long and our appearance has changed so much over the years. Probably hasn't changed inside us, or even indoors, but the way we present to the world has changed. More lesbian women now resemble our old stereotype of straight women." I laugh. "And when I see an attractive woman, it's probably also wishful thinking."

Ishmael smiles. "Yes, Isabella is very attractive." He appears wistful for a moment, then his expression returns to smiling and he stops outside a glass-fronted building sandwiched between a boarded-up structure and a shoe shop. "Here it is, the best bakery for miles and miles."

The window displays rows of plain croissants, chocolate croissant, caramel slices, lemon cake slices, and more I can't take in before we enter the sweet-scented interior.

Ishmael says, "Why don't we get a sample of pastries here and a coffee to go at the café. We can sit by town hall in the square and I'll point out the women who are probably not gay though they might look it."

I raise an eyebrow.

He smiles. "Rural France has many women who match the old stereotype of lesbian women. They are not."

§

The warm doughy croissant spills chocolate as I bite into it. Flakes of pastry stick to my lips.

We're sitting on the stone surround of the fountain in the centre of

Saint-Sebastian-du-Lac. Droplets sprinkle and sparkle in the air, surrounding us in a mist. The village square stretches in front, one whole side taken up by a tarmac rectangle with poles sticking up which Ishmael explained is the site of the weekly evening market.

"How are you feeling about Chloe getting married?"

The question comes as I take a sip of coffee and I cough as the hot liquid goes down the wrong way. The cup shakes in my hand and heavy drops splash on the stone. A bead lands on his white shirt.

Ishmael hands me a napkin.

I clear my throat, wipe the chocolate pastry coffee smudges off my lips. "Did Chloe ask you to keep an eye on me? Find out if I'm going to say anything, cause trouble for her?" I use a clean portion of the paper and touch it to the stain on his sleeve. "I'm sorry."

Ishmael looks down at my fingers, at my ineffectual dabbing, and I am conscious of his arm and my hand jerks like I've touched the flame of a candle.

He says, "Don't worry, it will come out." He smiles. "Actually, Chloe didn't tell us you were coming until yesterday. She said she was inviting Zara."

"Yes, my mother did not think to inform me of this. She's always been that way, has good intentions, but bulldozes through life."

"It must be hard for you." His eyes are kind and captivated, and I can picture him looking at a new-born kitten with the same expression.

My voice sounds as husky as his. "What has Chloe told you?" I get my muscles under control, they seem to be sliding into languor under his gaze. "Sounds like loads considering ye only met recently."

White teeth peek at me between curved lips. "We connected straight away when Chloe arrived. She's told me a little."

I move my gaze away from his smile, focus on the coffee stain I caused on his shirt. "How did she meet her fiancé?"

"I think they were introduced through colleagues at a hospital charity event. He's a doctor and a bigwig in the children's charity she helps out."

That stings. I watch as a woman opens the blue shutters at the pharmacy, pausing on her way to wipe the doorknob with her matching apron before ambling inside. "Chloe said Frank was a part owner of the restaurant?"

"Yes, Frank and another man own the whole complex, the *gîtes*, house, restaurant. The commune owns the lake." He gestures behind us to the town hall, a cream stone building with a sign proclaiming ''Maire' hanging over the closed wood double doors.

"Who's the guy?"

Ishmael tears a piece off his croissant. "A friend of Frank's from many years ago, doesn't have much to do with the place."

"What did Chloe tell you about her fiancé?"

"She said he's nice. Most of the time. He can be a bit insecure though."

There it is. The gentle warning coming.

I glance at him, "And he doesn't know Chloe was with me. That she used to go out with a woman."

Ishmael shakes his head.

"So, he definitely doesn't have a clue she left me at the altar. I wonder how he would react if he knew?"

"Are you planning to tell him?"

I stare at the man who is asking me such direct questions. We are close enough now I realise he isn't as young as he appears at a first, or even tenth, glance. Soft lines radiate to his temples, one more on each cheek, dimples that don't age him as much as the depth in his eyes. The musky scent of his cologne intertwines pleasantly in the dance of coffee and warm chocolate,

The shops are opening and people are starting their day, wandering down the pavement, one or two coming in our direction. I watch them with a surprising sense of annoyance, like they are encroaching on our space. "Surely Chloe should tell him? She shouldn't be entering a marriage on false pretences."

His voice is sad. "Some people cannot face the chance of rejection. They live lives that are hidden even from those they love, but it isn't deceit, it's fear. Fear of what will happen when they are thrown out of their society. Fear there will be nowhere they are safe if even their family cannot love or accept them."

"Chloe never told her father. He was her only family when we were together."

"From Chloe's description of Matt, my opinion was that he could handle it. But she is afraid he will be like her father."

I blink. I'm trying to figure out who Matt is. Then I remember Chloe has told them a different name. I wonder why she picked a name that doesn't sound Indian. Though David doesn't exactly sound all that Indian either. I can't work it out, so many things confuse me about Chloe now anyway.

I say, "I don't think she ever gave her father the choice." My voice is bitter. "I guess she was never really lesbian so she didn't have to risk losing him, much easier to lose me."

Ishmael frowns. "Why do you think she was not lesbian? She was with you and going to marry you."

"But she didn't, did she? From day one, she was confused, hid me from her father, her friends. Then ran away."

"Did you ever think it's possible you didn't give her a chance?"

"Me?"

Ishmael smiles. "Yes, you. Answer me without thinking of the politically correct answer. What do you feel about bisexuals?"

"Fecked up," I look around guiltily. We both giggle.

He says, "See?"

"I didn't treat her like she was fecked up."

"Are you sure?"

"Did she tell you I did?"

Ishmael takes my hand. His hands are strangely comforting despite the crackle at his touch. "Chloe loved you deeply. She still does, but she found someone who doesn't question her love. And she fell in love with him."

The words stab at me. Tears press at my eyelids. "Did she blame me for her walking out on me?"

Ishmael's voice remains soft. "No. She has never spoken badly of you. She described you in ways that made us all want to meet you." He puts a hand on my upper arm. "And her description was accurate. We're very happy to meet you."

I sigh. "So you know I wouldn't do anything to hurt her."

"Not intentionally."

I frown. "What does that mean?"

"It's going to be difficult for you when they get married. If you see them together, know they are happy."

I twist my lips. "If Chloe is happy with this guy…"

"You sound doubtful." He smiles. "You spent two years convincing Chloe she prefers men and now you doubt her love for Matt?"

"I did that?"

He chuckles. "I wasn't there, but that's the idea I get."

"She's the one who left me." My hand slides out of his.

"And sometimes people only leave when they can't take being pushed away any longer." Ishmael squeezes my arm gently then releases it. "I was only asking for Chloe's sake. Let her at least tell Matt in her own way and time. She's happy with him, much happier than she says she's been for a few years." He picks up his coffee container and crumples the empty brown bag that had held the croissant.

"Warning received and noted. I won't say anything to Matt if I ever meet him." I smile, but the usual anger at Chloe is mixed with something else.

Jealousy?

It rises in me, a serpent twisted and coiled, and I want to lash out at someone, but Ishmael is sweet, so instead I speak softly, "That doesn't mean I won't spend my time here establishing if she really does prefer men."

Ishmael gives a surprised smile. "This should be interesting."

CHAPTER NINE

"I need to know what's going on."

The sound of Chloe talking is coming from a shaded wooden arbour built into the gap between our line of cottages and the back of the main house.

I pause, blinking in the sunshine after the cool of the gîte where I'd collapsed across the couch, sleep catching up on me.

"You should know him more before you marry him, love." Zara's voice is troubled.

I creep up as close as possible, step over the paving stones, the swept sand, between the apple trees, and sit on a bench under the shelter of an empty gazebo next to theirs.

My mother is more visible as she's wearing a mix of bright yellow and orange. I could be sitting here by myself anyway. It's not my fault I can hear their conversation. Though they are practically whispering and there's no one else in earshot.

The occasional shouts of the drinks supplier and the bottles and kegs clanging together from the delivery truck outside the open door to the restaurant kitchen are louder than Chloe, but I can make out her words.

Chloe says, "I should ask him, but David chooses not to dwell on the past. I'm trying not to be all paranoid, and I never told them why I'm here, I didn't mention his name, only the first bit of his last name, called him Matt, but I did say I lived in Galway. Frank got flustered and he wouldn't say more than his business partner lived there too, but later I overheard him saying to Henri they were not to mention Lana again. I felt bad eavesdropping, but it was weird hearing them talk like that."

"Weird in what way? Lana is the ex-wife of David, *your* David?"

The name is too unusual to be a coincidence. Same Lana as on the notebooks and classes? What had she used? Lana M.? L.M.?

"Was or still is David's wife. It's in limbo. Frank was urging Henri to take over David's share. That being partners was not appealing anymore, not after what happened."

"What happened?" There's a flash of yellow as Zara leans forward. I notice I am mirroring her, the curiosity poking at both of us. *Lana is Chloe's fiancé's ex-wife?*

Chloe sighs. "That's the problem. I don't know. They were debating how to break up the partnership and Frank was wishing he'd had enough money at the beginning to avoid David having the controlling percentage. He couldn't do it on his own, but was wondering if Henri could afford to help buy David out, but they needed him to agree to sell."

"Is David involved with running the business? Does he come here?"

"Not that I know. David was complaining about tax papers in French and I tried to translate them for him, thought my school French might help. I couldn't understand most of it, but there was an address in Paris, and Frank's name was included. Frank was a friend of David's. And his wife. I'm finding that hard to grasp. Frank was friends with this Lana woman. And he and David are still business partners, there's no sign of Lana, and something happened and no one will talk about it. How can I marry someone who might be married? And I hate the uncertainty. David said he'll sort out all the paperwork when he returns from Saudi Arabia, but it is overwhelming for him. He called from Saudi to say his brother was selling their old rental house in Laurel Park. He was upset he had to ask me to help clear out the stuff left in the attic and shed."

Chloe waves around her, her gesture encompassing the courtyard, the cottages, the restaurant. "This was meant as a surprise for David, exploring holding the wedding here, and I was concerned what he would think, me coming here without telling him, so I haven't said where I am. Or told Frank or Ishmael or anyone here he's my fiancé. I've had this, this apprehension, and I'm really curious, but no one can know." Chloe's breath rushes out. "It's so good to talk to you, I already feel better. Thank you for coming here. And for getting the lads to clear out the house, even without knowing why.

Zara says, "It was no problem, love. Jaya went along too. I might not have mentioned it was you who asked. The notebooks she found and the clothes must have been Lana's then. She's been reading them, but that's our Jaya, all excited with anything to do with writing and doesn't tell me, her mother, anything."

I realise the names are familiar because they were on a CD in the boxes. I hadn't paid close attention, but now remember 'David and Lana' written on the wedding CD cover, and a date.

Chloe says, "Lana had notebooks? What kind? David gets upset when Lana's name comes up at all. I'm sensing she was very disturbed." The strain cracks her voice. "David is so kind to everyone, he never demeans Lana, but it's obvious what it did to him. She thought she was gay and she couldn't deal with it and messed around and got depressed. He's a typical Indian guy that way, he can't even contemplate the whole gay thing, it's totally taboo. He was practically choking when he mentioned the word gay, couldn't even say 'lesbian'."

Zara says, "Ah. So that's why…"

"Yes, I can't." Chloe's voice rises. "It would affect him, not sure how. Or what to do. It never came up when we were dating. He was such a gentleman, so cultured, and I felt inadequate and I hadn't meant to date again for a while, and with how guys can regard lesbians, I didn't bring it up, didn't want to go into all that. I mean, I would say it to women that I was also dating men and some reacted badly. It was such a minefield anyway, this dating thing, I was going to give it up. Then I met David, and it was a whirlwind, he completely swept me off my feet. And I had the same effect on him. I was surprised I could fall so fast and so hard after everything that happened, but I did."

"But how are you going to hide a piece of yourself from him? Is that wise?"

"Jay would never understand, and even you probably can't. I've always wanted the dream, the picket fence thing. Partner, kids, being part of a unit that was stable and accepted. I've told you how my childhood was. All the moving around, India, England, Ireland. Pop and his anger at Mom leaving. I hate that insecurity, really, really hate it. All the while Jay didn't trust me, I was ready to settle down with her, but we couldn't legally marry, we couldn't have kids, at least not when she wasn't ready, and she could never bring herself to trust me because I was bisexual. And David's so into family, into being a unit too, and everything I pictured is within reach, with someone I love. With the magic as well as the steadiness. It's so perfect. How can I risk all that? Not when he's had such a hard time in his past, when he's desperate for peace and security too. After the hell with his wife."

"What happened to her?"

"She ran away, or she killed herself."

Shock pricks between my ribs.

Zara is silent. The sounds of the complex around us creep back, the clatter of kitchen service, the chatter from the terrace in the distance, the horseplay of kids at the lake even further. Zara says, "He doesn't know which?"

"No. He said she was disturbed, depressed. She might have had an affair with a woman and that pushed her over the edge because it went against all their taboos, the Indian culture. It's such a huge deal, like it's the worst thing ever to be gay. She tried to kill herself and then ran away, but because they never heard from her or found her body, she was declared missing, presumed dead. Her car was found at the Salmon Weir bridge. They think she jumped off there and the rough water carried her out to the ocean."

"My Goddess, how awful for him. Not knowing. Is that what he's trying to sort out now that he wants to marry you?"

Chloe sounds tired. "Yes. He's in Saudi Arabia because his mother is ill, but he's going from there to India, and then he'll have to deal with the legal paperwork in Ireland and France. Because they owned property, this place, in France. Enough years have passed, he thinks, for the timeframe he has to wait." She sighs. "I can't wait. I need to find out, help him put it behind him, behind us, and move on with our lives."

Zara say, "Did you hope I would investigate? You know, with my CIA background."

I choke back the cough that grabs my throat.

Chloe says, "In a way. But then, out of the blue, you said Jay was coming and I got this hope that she could help. The last thing I want is to ask her, but I also don't want to end up losing my chance at happiness. Not saying you couldn't help, but you're good at finding out things in person, she's good at searching online and she has connections on the scene in Galway."

"She does." Zara sounds thoughtful. "There's more, isn't there? You want Jaya for something else. Anyone can help you get information on Galway, on Lana."

Chloe is silent. I'm torn between being touched she trusts me and peeved she'd ask this of me.

Zara says, "You can tell me. Jaya may not be in a space to simply do you a favour. Especially when it's to check if your male fiancé is trustworthy enough for you to marry him or if he is still married."

Chloe expels a breath. "When you put it that way." She pauses. "David asked me to sort his tax paperwork and the property papers, everything is so bureaucratic and he was drowning and could I take care of the French paperwork. There were contracts from Paris and Saint-Sebastien-du-Lac. I saw pictures of this place and thought it was a beautiful location. When I got here, I talked to Frank about holding a wedding and he was getting material together for me and showing me brochures for the surrounding areas as well. Once when I went to ask him about the wedding, I caught him at a bad time when he was on the phone to the employment office and clearing out their storage space, and he pointed me to that small room off the bar they use as an office. There were boxes behind the desk and I sneaked a peek in them and found a box of letters and stuff." Her serious tone momentarily lightens. "I could hear him in the restaurant. Everyone could. He thought he was speaking French, but it was really just loud English with a French accent."

Zara laughs. "I'd say he wasn't polite."

Chloe sounds like she's smiling. "No, he wasn't. Anyway, when he was occupied, I rushed through the letters."

"Lana's?"

"Yes. They were good friends. And Lana had become close with Frank's gay friends in Galway. There were a dozen or so letters."

"Do you have the letters?"

"No, didn't want Frank knowing I'd seen them. And then he moved all the boxes, possibly to their gîte."

"Damn." Zara says, "Do you remember what was in them?"

"I only skimmed through them. Lana talked about her work, she was working two jobs at one stage, and the funny thing was her second job was in a lesbian bar. The rest in the box was clothes, women's clothes. It felt odd, it just did. And then when I heard Frank talk to Henri, and I started imagining Lana, well, all these things started mushing up in my brain." She is holding her head, fragments of her visible, her arm, her blonde hair, filtered through the leaves crawling up the arbour trellis. "I'm possibly being crazy, but I began to worry."

"About Lana?"

"Yes. I keep remembering how Frank sounded when he told Henri not to discuss Lana. I mean, even David can't be sure if she's alive or dead." Her voice trails off again, then picks up speed. "I know David now, but not anyone here. I mean, I've become friendly with Ishmael, but they're all close and have these confusing connections. David and Lana and Frank were friends. Frank moves to this village from Paris, and then next thing, Isabella moves here too. Ishmael is Frank's partner, but Frank is always so protective of Ishmael's sister, Isabella, though she's married to Henri. And Isabella is beautiful, as David once described Lana, I remember because he took a breath in, that way you do when something hits you in the heart with its beauty. Like what I felt when I was with Jay."

I frown in surprise.

Zara says, "You're happy now with David, except of course from this trust thing, but there's always been a part of me that hoped, really hoped, you two would find each other again."

Chloe's voice is sad. "I did too. But I could never convince Jay I wouldn't leave her for a man. She never understood the bisexual thing, she seems to have a gut reaction to it. It's as if she was born lesbian and doesn't understand how I could love a person for who they are, how they make me feel, and not what gender they are. I can't change, that's the way I am."

"Jaya wasn't born lesbian. She went out with a few guys but yes, she's pretty adamant now. She isn't normally intolerant you know, but she was torn up in college and then with you, and her pride won't let her see beyond that. I think she got the stubborn streak from me."

"You think?" Chloe giggles and my mother joins in.

My frown deepens. I'm not intolerant, normally or not.

Chloe says, "And you're the only one who can get her to do something whether she wants to or not."

"What do you need me to ask her to do? I'm not saying I will, but let me think on it. She may act tough, but I might have been a little thoughtless bringing her here." My eyebrows rise at her unaccustomed insight.

"I was thinking she'd be able to root out info about Lana." Chloe puts her hand on Zara's arm. "Hear me out. You are great with people, but you would ask them straight out. I sense they're hiding something and the last thing they'll do is answer direct questions. Ishmael and I had an immediate connection and talked a lot, but he didn't discuss the others with me. I have this impression the marriage between Henri and Isabella was a sham. He's not her type, don't get me wrong, he's a nice guy, so sweet and polite, and he's attractive in a pleasant way, but they're just not a match. And Isabella doesn't come across like she's in love with him. She does have this fire in her eyes, as if she's passionate, but hiding. And she and Frank spend a great deal of time together."

Chloe takes in a long breath, exhales. "Obviously I needed to talk this all out. Why am I letting this upset me so much? I'm anxious and that's the last way to start my married life, with this craziness going around my head. I've been there, when someone's misguided doubt ruins a relationship."

"So, you're thinking Jaya might get close to them? Maybe Isabella? Ask questions?"

"You know what Jay is like with women. She's a charmer. And she has this effect." She laughs. "Well, you don't, you're her mother. But take it from me, she does."

I'm speechless. If I was in the conversation, I would have been at a loss for words as well. I have no idea what Chloe is describing. She's talking of someone else, not the gawky-so-not-cool woman who's hiding in a gazebo to eavesdrop on her ex and her mother.

Zara laughs. "I'll take your word for it. I still think of Jaya as my sweet wee cub, though she's been more of a bear with a sore head lately. So you want her to charm the truth out of Isabella?"

Chloe nods. "I think so. Maybe. I need her to dig up anything she can on Lana. With the Indian thing. From her connections, she always knows someone on the lesbian scene, maybe getting close to Isabella or Ishmael."

Yellow and orange blink through the arbour lattice as Zara stands. I crouch down, press further into the sandy space under the wooden trellis. The sounds are more indistinct now. She says something, I hear my name, in her own way, the rest lost as their voices dwindle under the crunch of sand and stones.

I unwrap myself and sit on the bench. It is rough and hot under my thighs, the heat pushing into the shade of the arbour.

I'm trying *not* to imagine what I might unearth on Lana that would be damaging for David. I'm not *that* person, but with how Chloe spoke of me, I'm wondering whether I got her all wrong.

Maybe she's not bi.

And she still loves me.

And *I'm* the one who screwed up so badly by pushing her away.

I shake the thoughts away. *I can't go back there.* Can't go through all that uncertainty again. It took so long to stop the pain. And I'm with Fiona now. A definite lesbian. I belong somewhere now, finally. What's more fitting than being one of the public faces of same-sex marriage.

Who am I kidding? It hurts to think of Chloe, to see her, to be around her. And even if we are never together again, I couldn't live with myself if I knowingly let her enter into a marriage with a dangerous man. She hurt me so bad, but I don't want her being hurt.

A thought sparks and catches. *I need to find this Lana.* Or uncover anything about Lana or David I can use to show Chloe she's making a mistake.

Sapna

Galway, Ireland

The drive from the train station had been a blur, the events of the past few weeks catching up to her, the changes so extreme, so disorienting, leaving her unsure where she was on any day.

The house was like all the others in the estate. A little bit tired, a little bit proud, making an effort despite the effort involved. Grey speckled concrete walls, faded brick skirts.

Thomas insisted on carrying the suitcases into the house first, on his own.

Sapna stood beside the car. She tried to wrap her thick jacket around more of her. From the heat in Tuscany to the cold in Galway, another change that battered her body. The parts of her face and hands the jacket didn't reach were bewildered, too defeated to summon goose bumps. She noticed a woman's face peering through the lace curtains of the house next door. It was pale through the light, pockmarked with shadows. Sapna smiled though the movement hurt her lips. The face moved back sharply.

Thomas came out of the house. He glared at the neighbour. "That's Mrs Flynn. Nosey old woman." He turned to Sapna. "I wonder how she will like the old tradition."

"What tradition?"

He moved quickly towards her and she tried to stop the flinching of her body. He didn't notice as he swung her around, pulling her back against him before bending to scoop her into his arms. She experienced a mild sense of surprise at how light she felt, 120 pounds to his 185. He stumbled, for an instant, but righted himself, one arm supporting her shoulders, the other her knees.

Her hair fell black towards the ground, her face red with embarrassment despite the cold. Thomas swivelled to face the house and she saw Mrs Flynn rapt in attention. Their eyes met and though it was dark through the curtain, Sapna sensed the change in expression in the woman's eyes. Sapna could not place what it was straight away, but as he carried her towards the house, she realised it looked like pity.

The inside sagged, tired as well. Brown wallpaper, beige furniture, terracotta carpets.

"You'll be able to bring a woman's touch." Thomas put her down suddenly and the back of her head bumped against the wall in the hallway. He reached out and rubbed her forehead gently. "Sorry."

She nodded. Her hand moved towards the spot that was sore from the bump, but she diverted it to her upper arm, hugged herself through the down jacket.

He said. "Yes, it's freezing in here. Let me get the radiators going." He strode towards the kitchen at the end of the hallway.

The hallway was narrow, carpeted with an off-yellow floral print. The kitchen counters were visible ahead. She went through the open door beside her. The living room was small with one window that matched the neighbour's window, down to the grimy lace curtains through which she caught a patterned glimpse of the housing estate.

Thomas came into the room behind her.

She said, "I've never seen one of these, except in English movies." She pointed at the marble fireplace. "Is it possible to have a fire?"

"Everything is possible for my new wife." His voice boomed in the small room, then sank into the fabric of the wallpaper. "Chandy did not do much with this house, he rented it out to some Irish people. We can make it look better."

She said, "It's a good house. I like the -," she paused, scanned the room, "I like the marble." She ran a finger along the mantelpiece. "We can put decorations here." She wasn't sure what she had that would cover the brown vibe, but any of her prints and the red and gold and bronze of her various finds would surely help.

"Yes, yes, of course. Do whatever you want. Mrs Bennett's house was the same. I am used to it."

She looked at him.

"Mrs Bennett, my landlady in London. I told you I worked there for years?"

"Sorry, yes. With Chandy." She had a rough sketch, didn't want to say he had not fleshed out any details. Or said much about his upbringing in Saudi Arabia. Or his family there. She knew what her mother had passed on from his 'file', that Chandy was his brother. Chandy had been the one responsible for getting the two families together.

"Chandy was only there a few months. He married that Irish woman and moved out."

"Oh, I thought he left to come here?"

Thomas walked over to the window. "He moved out first with Karen. Then he moved here after the girls were born."

"I only spoke to him briefly at the reception. It was all so busy, I didn't

even remember the names of the kids." She smiled. "I think I was too scared of your parents."

Thomas frowned. "They were not nice to you?"

"No, that's not... Sorry, yes, they were very nice. Both of them. I was so nervous, and I met them all together. And Chandy was only at the reception for the first part."

Thomas nodded. "Good. It would not have been correct for them to be impolite to you."

She tried to picture the faces, through the strangeness of the wedding and the chaos of the days leading up to it. All she remembered of Chandy was that Thomas was a shorter, thinner, darker version of his older brother. She had been so relieved her unexpected husband was handsome she hadn't really noticed the others around him. She hadn't realized how shallow she was, if that was the term for it, that it mattered so much, that she had such a reaction on seeing him in the flesh for only the second time, that her body had gone from the cramped nervous waiting to relaxing, just momentarily, before all the craziness hit again.

Thomas tugged at the beige curtains that lay heavy against the wall, framing the outside into a view of grey sameness. The dust wandered into the air. He frowned.

She said, "Will it be okay for me to make changes, or should I wait until we get our own place? Do you think Chandy will want the house back if he comes back from Saudi?"

Thomas was staring out of the window. "Have they not ever seen an Indian man?" He pulled aside the lace and folded his arms as he glared across the road.

Sapna saw no one on the street. She moved towards Thomas. There was a twitch of lace in the window of the house directly across from them.

She smiled up at him. *"I could cook something Indian and take it to them."*

He chuckled. *"Yes. I'd like that."* He walked to the living room door. *"The house should be warm soon, I'll go and get some things from the shop."*

She nodded. *"I'll clean the rooms and unpack."*

"Good, very good. I need to rest for work. I have to be my best." He stood in the hallway, his keys in his hand. *"There's one Indian restaurant I know. I'll get something from there for you to take to the neighbours."* He chuckled again. *"That's a good idea. Shove the Indian in their faces."*

He was gone before she could say she knew how to cook two Indian dishes.

Sapna sat on the bed and watched Thomas adjust his tie.

He said, *"It's a Turnbull and Asser."*

She nodded.

"You have no idea why that's a big deal, do you?"

She smiled, shook her head.

"It's so much better than the one I purchased with my first paycheck in England. That one was plain, when I wasn't as style savvy." He turned to examine his reflection in the mirror on the dressing table. *"This one, in honour of my first day at work at a private clinic instead of the public hospital, is a Spiral Circles Purple silk tie."* He smoothed his hands down his blue cotton shirt, the one she'd ironed for him last night. *"See how well it goes with this shirt, simple, but expensive, and the Michael*

Kors suit. Navy. Bright colours contrast well with my skin, and I use accents rather than the embarrassing stuff the Indians wore at the hospital. Even Chandy."

He did look very stylish. Much classier than the guys she'd seen in suits in India.

"Did Chandy not follow your style?"

He sighed. "I tried to help Chandy when we worked in the same hospital in London. I was glad when he moved to Dublin." There was a hint of a smirk on his lips. "My efforts to style him failed."

He turned to her. "Where's my white coat? It's a pity to hide good taste under a white coat, but I found it calmed the nerves of the elderly patients, especially the women when I checked in on them before their surgery. The women want their surgeon in a lab coat for some reason. Or scrubs."

She went to the closet, swept her hand along the line of shirts and trousers. She had ironed his white coat as well, hung it up for him. They'd gone to scope out the clinic, walked up the paved driveway, bordered by manicured grass, to the sliding glass doors and stared up at the sign. The hospital shouted private money. They'd watched the doors slid open with a respectful swoosh, ushering patients and staff into a glass and pine lobby with elevators and escalators covering three levels.

He picked a tiny piece of lint off the lapel of his jacket. "Years and years and a ton of hard work, but this is the start of payback time, a consultant role in a year or two."

Thomas checked his hair in the mirrored closet doors as he passed. He eased a few loose strands back into place. He used black hair dye sparingly, left streaks of grey in appropriate places. He saw her watching him. "It's good to emphasise the difference here in Ireland. Might as well do it in a stylish way. There aren't as many Indians here as there were in

London." He smiled. "Not at my level. And they're all white here at the top."

Sapna gathered up the items he'd left lying on the top of the dressing table. Thomas spoke with a slight English accent normally. It was more pronounced this morning. He'd said the Saudi-born Indian accent had almost disappeared in England.

She heard him chuckle. "I'm glad there's no long Indian name to deal with, this one fits easier on those small hospital badges and white staff always prefer it."

He walked into the hallway and down the stairs.

"Where are my keys?" His voice floated up and she heard the irritation in it.

She hurried out of the bedroom. Leant over the bannister. "I put them in the box by the vase. There." She pointed at the ornate wood box she'd bought in Cochin.

He flicked back the lid and she winced as it hit the glass table top.

He took out the keys, left the box open. Inspected his hair in the mirror hanging on the wall.

She said, "Good luck," but he didn't seem to hear in the opening and closing of the front door.

The house settled into a quiet hum around her.

Sapna ladled more curry over his rice. She put the saucepan back on the stove and sat down at the table.

He paused, his fingers dripping, dark shadows on his cheeks and chin. "I interviewed by video with Mr Brady, the Deputy Chief of Surgery. I *just assumed Professor Casey Ryan was a man."*

Sapna said, "Is she nice?"

"Who cares?" He snorted. "I can't believe I have to work for a woman. She joined them last year from Minnesota. In America. She's married to an Irish man. She has Irish heritage." His voice became a parody of politeness. "All the best people do." He dipped his fingers and grabbed another handful of rice and curry. "Must be how she got the top job. I was in a hurry, should have checked all of this, but I wanted to get you settled here. So much disruption with the betrothal mess and the wedding and honeymoon."

"I'm sorry." She was apologising for Lalitha again. For a moment, she wondered how long she would be doing that, and then her mother's voice nagged into her that he could have destroyed them all by not accepting their alternative.

He nodded. Sighed as he pushed away the almost empty bowl. "I can't eat. I'll adjust. I always do, but just once it would be nice if something worked out right away. More exams, more slogging away. And now a woman will be telling me what to do and can decide whether I get promoted."

Sapna got up and took the bowl to the sink. She emptied the few soggy grains of rice into the garbage and washed the bowl.

"I'm going to be so busy. I need to focus on getting on Casey's good side. She's not as encouraging as I'd expected." He sighed. "Why isn't Brady the Chief of Surgery instead of the deputy? It's so frustrating. So many years, all to end up working for a woman. Now I have to charm Professor Casey Ryan. Which means having to study all her achievements, when I could be concentrating on mine. Bloody boring too."

Sapna got a wine glass from the cabinet and the bottle of red wine he had opened last night. She placed the glass in front of him and filled it. "Are the others on your team nice?"

He said, "I only met one of the other senior residents. He's Irish, not as experienced as me." He took a gulp of wine. Leant back. "The nurses love me." He smiled. "I think they were disappointed when they saw my wedding ring. And my patients love me." He stretched. "I appreciate people who don't make arbitrary judgements based on skin colour or any other such superficial means of determining ability. Or at least, those who get past the difference in skin tone quickly. That's why I said this morning, make it a stylish difference. Some didn't even notice my skin colour. But not in a 'I'm going to avoid the fact you are Indian' way. I don't appreciate that reaction, but I get a whole heap of it. I decide on a person-by-person basis whether I'll put in the effort to educate them. I'm not just the colour of my skin. The Indian culture is more than the depth of a few melanin skin cells."

He smiled. "They are usually surprised by my 'Western' ways. What do they expect, a barbarian, or I'll need an outside toilet?"

"It will be nice to meet them all."

He twirled the wine glass slowly. "Later. When I'm more settled." He drained the last of the wine from the glass. "I'm exhausted." He frowned. "The work is fine, it's all the smiling and chatting that is tiring. As if I care what county a nurse is from or how many sprogs Brady has fathered."

He got up from the table and stretched again. "A few more years. And the stupid exams." He patted his abdomen. "I'm going to read up on Professor Casey. I should be going to the gym." He looked at her. "It rains quite a bit here." He smiled and reached out to stroke her belly. "We can both get pleasant exercise later."

All the words she'd been bottling up during the silent day crawled back down her throat.

Thomas walked his fingers up her arm, slid them under her hair. "I should skip the study tonight." His breathing had quickened. "Why read another woman when I have a good-looking wife to examine right here."

His palm cradling the back of her neck was warm. He was staring at her mouth, the light from the bare bulb brightening his eyes.

The thought swept into her mind again, how much his smile changed his face. When he focused on her, she felt beautiful, like she was the only woman in the world."

Sapna

Galway, Ireland

Sapna poked her head into the living room. "Could you get the dinner set from the shed?"

She heard a grunt from the armchair.

She said, "Victoria is your friend. The least you could do is get the plates out for her visit. We might as well make use of Ammama's good china."

She heard him sigh.

"I have to study. Vic doesn't have to worry about all that anymore."

"Then why did you agree to her coming now. Why not wait until the exams are over?"

She heard his textbook slamming shut. He got up and ran his hand through his hair. "She was good to me in London. What was I to say, 'Don't come to the house on your trip to Ireland?' I think she is coming to visit us specially."

"She is?"

Thomas put the book down on top of the pile of textbooks on the coffee table. "She wants to meet you. And she wants to propose something in Paris."

"What something in Paris?"

Thomas looked tired. "I think she wants me to go in on a property in Paris." He brushed past her. "Where is this china?"

"In the shed, with all the other wedding gift stuff. What property in Paris?"

He frowned. "It's all going to get damaged. Even months in this rain is bad."

"I have them well protected." She said. "No need to unpack all of that if we are only going to pack it all up again when we get our own place."

A hint of guilt trickled across his face. "Soon." He moved towards the back door. "Which set? Where is it?"

"After a year, I take 'soon' to mean maybe another few years." She smiled to soften the words.

"I'm working on it." His tone was angry, but then he saw she was smiling. "Okay, 'soon' might be one more year." He grasped the handle of the door. "If I pass the exams this time, it will all change."

"I'm not complaining. This is a nice house now. I was just teasing." She walked to the stove and lifted the lid. The rice was almost ready. "I could work, use my degree?"

She hated when his shoulders tensed. She said, quickly, "It would get me out of the house, not because I'm not grateful. But wouldn't things be a bit easier if I could contribute? It won't be as much as when you have the exams done, but it might help until then?" She turned the heat off, the gas flame puffed as it went out. "Or we could use my dowry money?"

He opened the door. The early darkness falling did not help either of them. Nor did the constant rain. She reached across the stove and switched on the porch light.

He said, his voice quiet, "You don't need to work. I will pass this exam and I'll get the raise."

He stepped into the wet evening. "Which set? Didn't your mother send a hundred dinner sets?"

She smiled. "She sent four. Pick any, they're mostly floral patterns anyway and I don't think your English surgeon friend is going to care what type of flowers are on her plate."

She heard him laugh. And then curse as he sploshed through the rain.

Sapna watched Victoria clean her plate with the chapatti. She grabbed her napkin and wiped away the stray drop of curry on her chin.

"Sapna, that was so good. Where did you learn to cook?"

She smiled. She opened her mouth to reply.

Thomas cut in, "I had to teach her." He laughed. "You would not have almost cleaned off the flowers on your plate with the chapatti if you had to eat what she used to cook."

There was a crinkle of the skin on Victoria's forehead. She smiled at Sapna. "Well, this was delicious. Thank you for cooking and being so welcoming."

The smile that had fallen slightly flew back onto her lips. "But of course. You are welcome. Thomas told me how you took care of him when he was in London."

Victoria shook her head. "Oh, I didn't do much. The occasional good meal when I sensed he was fed up of Mrs Bennett's meals." She turned to Thomas. "I'd say you don't miss suet much."

Thomas grimaced. "Definitely not. Or kippers. The sausages were great though." He drank half his glass of wine. "I can even manage the black pudding here. I never imagined when I lived in Saudi I would one day be eating the clotted blood of a pig." He took another gulp. "I never imagined a whole heap of the ways my life would turn out."

Sapna got up and collected her plate and Thomas's. She gestured at Victoria's. "Would you like more?"

Victoria shook her head. Then said, "Actually, that would be nice. I could eat another few plates of your cooking."

Sapna put the empty plates down and took Victoria's plate with a smile. Picked up the half-empty bottle of wine and turned towards the counter.

"Hey, bring it back." Thomas's voice had a hint of a laugh. "It's not empty yet. Here Vic, have a glass. Enough of that soda shmoda stuff."

Sapna held the bottle towards Victoria. She shook her head. "No, thank you."

Thomas reached across and picked up the empty wine glass in front of Victoria. He gestured at Sapna. "Bring the bottle. Come, give it to me."

Victoria said, "No, really, thank you. I don't drink anymore."

The serious note in Victoria's voice finally pierced Thomas's joviality. He frowned. "Okay, then I will drink it." He flapped his fingers at Sapna. She put the bottle down and he filled up his glass. Put his hand over hers when she went to pick the bottle up again.

She picked up their plates and dropped the empty ones in the sink. Ladled out another chapatti and a generous helping of the chicken curry onto Victoria's plate and placed it before her.

Victoria smiled. "You're probably under the illusion I won't be able to eat all that." She patted her belly. "I can fit lots in here, especially *when it's so good."*

Sapna smiled. "Thomas can keep the weight off without doing anything. Me, I have to work at it. And it is so cold here, I walk up and down the stairs for exercise."

Thomas said, "I'm glad we have a staircase." He poked Victoria in the shoulder. "You should have a staircase too."

Sapna said, "Victoria, I have dessert. It's an Indian one, but I can't boast I made it. I got these from the local restaurant." She took the white cardboard lids off the tinfoil container and showed her the brown dough balls, glistening in clear syrup, specks of almond clinging on to the almond-honey cakes.

Victoria groaned. "Gulab jamun? Mmm, I love them. I am going to have to run up and down the stairs more than you. May I borrow your staircase while I'm here? If you insist on forcing me to eat all this irresistible food." She laughed and shoved another curry-soaked piece of chapatti in her mouth. "I'm not complaining. At least my cranky old doc says my cholesterol is fine. Must be all the diet food I have to eat at home." She turned to Thomas. "See? I need to get away from London. Otherwise I will drown in package food instead of the wonderful croissants and pastries I could enjoy instead."

Thomas drained his glass. "You think that house is a good investment?"

Victoria snorted. "It's a fantastic investment. I tell you, there's no way to lose money on this. Everyone goes to Paris, especially honeymooners, but also families, from everywhere in Europe. And America. We could give it to a company to manage as a rental until we're ready to move there."

"Move?" Both Sapna and Thomas spoke at the same time.

Victoria smiled. "Okay. Until I'm ready to move there. I can't imagine myself staying in London for more than another year or two. We could all make a little money until then, and I would buy you out if I move or we could keep it together and I rent from us. I don't mind having you two as joint landlords."

Thomas gestured at the house around them. "As you might have noticed, we don't live like kings. I pay rent to Chandy and he is good not to charge the full market rent." He tapped his fingers on the table. It made a hollow sound. "This estate is mostly for students to rent so they are close to the college. I was planning to buy a bigger house in Barna, some of the consultants live there." He sat back. "I never thought of France."

Sapna emptied the curry into a container. She hadn't realised he had picked a place for their house.

Victoria said, "The London market is insane. Way too expensive. You get a matchbox there for the same money you would get a chateau in France." She laughed. "Not that we need a chateau. We don't need much to get a decent-sized house in Paris. The pound is so strong against their francs." Her face reddened and her voice rose slightly. "I have a friend who is a real estate agent in London and the agency he works for has a partner in Paris. He said they've been watching the trends and they're predicting a huge rise in prices soon. We need to get in before that. I trust this guy, he made a killing in London."

Thomas frowned. "How can you know it isn't some scheme? To get you to buy a house no one wants."

"I promise, I wouldn't have come all the way here and shown you if I didn't think it's the opportunity of a lifetime. I can buy a smaller house on my own with what I have saved." She took a piece of paper out of her shirt pocket. Carefully unfolded it and handed it to Thomas.

Sapna walked over to the table, stood behind Thomas and peeked over his shoulder.

She gasped. "It is beautiful."

Thomas smoothed out the paper. "It is selling for that? Not too bad, is it? For such a big house."

Victoria nodded. "See? And it is in such a nice area. The tourists love to stay there. There are lots of bakeries and cafes." She smiled. "Boulangeries and patisseries." She pronounced the French words with a flourish.

Thomas twirled the glass around in his fingers. "I love French wine. No experience with French food, I don't have to eat frog's legs, do I?"

Victoria laughed. "No, the wine is cheap and there's lots of it. There are many immigrants and it's such a diverse neighbourhood, lots of ethnic foods." She said to Sapna. "What do you think? We might get to use the house for holidays for the weeks it is not booked out. Because it's going to be booked almost constantly."

Sapna said. "I like it. It looks very nice. and the sun is shining."

Victoria smiled. "The sun shines much more there."

Thomas leant against his chair. His head bumped into Sapna's solar plexus and she stepped back. He said, "Let me think about it. We have some money available, but I had planned to use it as a deposit here." He shook the paper. "This is interesting."

Sapna frowned. The money was her dowry, but now she had no say in where it was going to be spent. She felt suddenly disloyal when she saw Victoria's raised eyebrow.

Victoria said, "I believe it is a no-loss situation. I can't guarantee we will make a fortune, no one can guarantee that, but I wouldn't put all my savings into it if it wasn't safe."

Thomas rose, pushing back the chair. It came to rest against Sapna's stomach. He patted Victoria's shoulder. "I know, my friend, I know. Let me consider this over the weekend. While I am studying. Sapna is happy to show you around Galway tomorrow if you want?" He laughed. "Or maybe you would prefer to relax at home. I won't be responsible to your doctor if your heart suffers with her driving."

Sapna sighed. She said to Victoria. "I passed my driving test three weeks ago. On the first attempt. But my driving lessons did not go too well." She didn't want to say probably no one's first lessons on the wrong side of the road would have gone well with Thomas as a teacher, but instead she said, "There are lovely places in Galway if you'd like to go on a tour tomorrow?"

Victoria nodded. "That would be great. My friends live in Galway, in Oranmore. They always said it is a place you visit for a weekend and end up moving to. Music, arts, college, tourists. Eclectic?"

Sapna said, "I haven't seen much of Galway itself. Thomas has had to work a lot and the studying takes up most of the rest of his time." She noticed a curiosity in Victoria's eyes. Sapna glanced at Thomas, then asked Victoria. "Can you manage dessert now?" Whatever was piquing her interest would be better asked when they were alone in the car.

Victoria closed her mouth. Then smiled. "I would love the Gulab jamun. I may surprise you at how much delicious food I can eat."

Thomas swayed slightly. He gripped the back of Victoria's chair. "No surprise, my friend." He yawned. "I think it might be my bedtime, I will skip dessert tonight."

He turned to Sapna. "I'm going to sleep longer tomorrow morning and then study all day while you and Vic are sightseeing." He held out his hand and Victoria shook it.

Thomas walked to the hall. "I'll talk to you tomorrow evening, Vic. Sorry for being a damp squid, I need to get as much rest as possible in between the studying."

Victoria muttered, "Even a damp squib," when he'd left the room. She turned to Sapna after they listened to Thomas's heavy tread on the stairs. "I guess he doesn't need to come down and go up again like we do."

Sapna laughed in surprise.

Victoria gestured at the chair Thomas had vacated. "Sit, sit. I want to learn all about you."

Sapna pointed at the dessert on the counter.

Victoria shook her head and got up from the chair. "Sit. Please. Let me get that. It's the least I can do after your spectacular cooking." She smiled. "I must be missing a touch of home, as only a lovely person can make a house a home."

Sapna smiled as she sat down. "I see you are a charmer."

Victoria shared out the dessert, two of the almond-honey cakes each, a pouring of syrup over all. Her back was to Sapna, but the smile was obvious in her voice. "It is easy to be honestly complimentary to you, my dear, very easy. Thomas is a lucky man. If I was aware of what this arranged marriage system could do, I'd have had my parents don a saree and mundu and pretend to be Indian."

Sapna laughed out loud. Victoria turned and smiled. "You need to do that more. Sounds wonderful, but rusty."

Victoria brought the two dishes over and sat beside her. "Have a glass of wine, relax. I can't drink wine, but I don't need it when I have your sparkling company." She smiled. "Don't worry, I'm not chatting you up, not that way inclined. You need a friend, someone to talk to." Victoria poured a glass, handed it to her, and raised her glass of orange soda.

Victoria clinked her glass off Sapna's. "Mrs Sapna Ninan. I think we're going to be good friends."

Sapna drank a mouthful. "Ms Victoria Adams. Somehow I too think we are." The loneliness slipped away. Even if it was for just a weekend, she would enjoy the friendly attention of this Englishwoman."

CHAPTER TEN

There are customers on the terrace and in the dining room. The restaurant offers the '*menu du jour*,' a three-course meal and wine for 8 euro and it attracts locals and tourists. Ishmael had explained how Napoleon made it a law for restaurants to offer these meals at a low price for the working class, and lunchtimes in rural France are busy and noisy.

An image of a box of Lana's letters sitting in Frank's gîte niggles at me.

And the novel.

The gay friends in Galway.

The property in France. Though there's no Lana and David. Just Sapna and Thomas. Is it really a novel, fiction? Or the writings of a 'disturbed' woman.

I wander into the dining room. "Jaya!" Zara waves at me. She's on her own at a table by the window, wearing an odd mix of yellows and oranges and a blue sun hat that flops over her back. I haven't seen Chloe since their chat in the arbour earlier.

I make my way over, aware Isabella, Ishmael, and Frank are in the kitchen, the noises of a busy service clattering out with every swing of the doors.

"The lunches here are amazing! We need this '*menu du jour*' thing in Ireland." She motions me into the seat facing her. The lake sparkles through the large windows though my view is punctuated by the people eating on the terrace.

I turn and examine the handwritten menu on the chalkboard. "Did you and Chloe have a productive morning of shopping?"

She says, "We cut it short. I was tired after the long drive and Chloe was sweet enough to sit and talk instead."

I sigh and straighten in my chair. Somehow, she makes me feel guilty about something.

"Nice chat?"

She nods. "We mentioned you."

"All good, I hope." I swivel towards the menu board again. "What are you having?"

She sounds disappointed. "I was planning on trying the *charcuterie*. Ah, here's Ishmael, let me ask him."

I watch Ishmael with different eyes, wondering what he's hiding about his sister, and Frank.

He smiles at me as he reaches into his apron for a notepad. He takes my order and talks Zara through each item and they finally select three courses for her. And the wine. She wants the whole Napoleonic experience.

Zara waits until Ishmael has disappeared behind the swinging doors. "Jaya, I need you to do something for me."

"For *you*?"

"I don't ask much of my wee cub, but it would help you too."

I sigh but stay silent.

She says, "I want you to keep away from Chloe while we're here."

I frown. That is not what I expected. "Why? Did she say something? Did I do something out of line?"

"No, not at all." Zara reaches across and takes my hand. "I know this is tough and I probably should have warned you what was going on before we left Ireland. But I wanted you to see her again, to know she's happy, to get some, what do the kids call it these days, closure."

"And now I've seen her and closed whatever and shouldn't hang around her anymore?"

"Not exactly. I think you are both dealing with emotions that haven't been resolved and you both need space to sort out those emotions individually." She squeezes my fingers. "I had hoped there was a chance for you two. But she does seem to love David and unless you're better to her than you were, I do not want her to lose that relationship."

"*Me*? Better to *her*?"

Ishmael arrives with our starters and she hushes me with a look.

Zara tucks into the plate of cured meats, tearing chunks off bread from the basket.

I stare at my French onion soup. The aromatic steam reaches my nostrils and my stomach growls.

"Go on, eat." She pokes her fork at me. "The food is great."

I taste a spoonful of soup and have to agree.

"So, will you keep away from Chloe?"

"After we leave here." I can't leave things as they are.

Zara smiles. "Ah. One last try?"

Not sure if that's what I mean. After all, Fiona, and I are practically engaged.

She says, "Fine. Do you want some advice? Help from your old mother who was able to charm anyone into bed?"

"Ugh, *mum!*"

She laughs. "Believe me, men or women, it didn't matter. If I decided I wanted them, they were putty in my hands."

My hand swats her words away. "Advice is fine, but can we not mention your exploits?"

"Okay." She clears her plate to the side. "You should pay attention to another beautiful woman." She gestures with her head towards the kitchen. I wonder why she's attempting to be discreet when none of the three is in sight.

"Another beautiful woman?"

"Uhuh." She sounds slightly frustrated. "Did you not learn anything in college?"

I smile. "Obviously not as much as you did."

"You should pay attention to…" Her voice hushes. "Isabella."

"Ah, I see. In front of Chloe?"

"Of course!" Her hand sweeps the air. "And wherever. Not just in front of Chloe, that would be too obvious." She frowns. "But remember, Isabella is married."

"So. Let me get this right. Flirt with a married woman to influence one who is engaged to be married, while being the girlfriend of yet another woman."

"Yes, yes. Discreetly though." She waves at me to be quiet as Ishmael emerges with our main course.

§

Zara and I have moved to sit outside. The rest of the tables have mostly been cleared, apart from a man in a tight shirt nursing his post-lunch espresso, staring at the lake and ignoring his brochures for ice-cream machines.

My mother has filled me in on her morning conversation with Chloe.

Everything except how it might affect Chloe and David.

And Chloe's reactions to me.

Zara asked about the notebooks, but I said they were still in Galway and I hadn't read through them.

I'm reluctant to share them with anyone yet.

Chloe is helping Frank and Isabella and Ishmael clean up in the restaurant and kitchen.

My nerves are rippling, but twenty minutes pass before the four of them join us.

Isabella's face is drawn and her brown eyes are edged with red. She gives me a warm smile. I stand for the two kisses. Conscious of Zara and Chloe watching, I stumble over my greeting. Are they wondering the same, where is this charmer they've been lauding?

"Lunch was delicious." Zara holds up her glass of wine. "*Salut.*"

Isabella kisses her cheeks.

Frank stretches with a loud sigh. He tugs a dishcloth out of the waistband of his trousers and tosses it onto the next table before pulling a chair over to ours for Isabella.

He asks me, "Did you enjoy San Sebastian?"

I grin. "We were at the bakery, ate lovely croissants by the fountain, so the essentials have been taken care of." I settle back in my seat. "It must be a big change for you, from London to Paris, then to a tiny village in France with one bakery?"

Frank sits and smiles. "I'm a country boy at heart."

"So you must have enjoyed visiting Galway. Love that city, it's like living in a town and also in the country. Where did your friends live?"

Ishmael has pulled up a chair too and I catch the quick glance between them. "In Oranmore."

"So they're still there? Do you visit them often?"

Frank shook his head. "I haven't been there since…for quite a long time."

"That's so interesting. I was there for Pride around six years ago. Things have changed so much. When were you there last? Did they have a march there at the time?"

"I think I was there in 2007 or 2008. I merely dropped in on my friends. Not sure vis-à-vis the marches at that time."

"Oh, okay. I thought your gay friends might have been at them. I love to study the history of our movement, how the women, and the men, got the Pride marches started."

Chloe asks, "Doesn't your business partner live there?"

Frank shifts in his chair. "Yes, I was staying with him."

She turns to me, her eyes glinting with interest. "David is a partner in this place. He and his wife, Lana, also lived in Galway. Isn't the world such a small place? They're Indian, too. Not that you would know every Indian in Ireland, but it's funny, you could have bumped into them."

I smile. "Yes. And Ireland is smaller. Even fewer Indians around." I ask Frank. "How did they end up in Galway? Are they still there?"

Frank is rubbing at his beard. "David is. He's a doctor."

"Of course he is." I laugh. "Aren't most of the Indians there doctors or nurses or at least in the Science field. Is his wife a doctor too?"

Frank shakes his head. Ishmael and Isabella are watching him. "No. She was a counsellor when she started work there. She's not there anymore."

Chloe says, "Oh, did they split up? I was wondering whether they would visit here?"

The noise of a glass falling over and liquid rushing out makes us all jump. Ishmael leaps up and grabs the cloth out of the apron he's wearing. He mops up the drink and waves away Isabella's apologies.

Isabella pushes herself out of the chair, wiping at the red wine on her whites. "*Merde*, I was to wear this for dinner service if I didn't get it dirty during lunch and now I have to change it. I have to find a clean one." She smiles. "In my size. They don't keep chef jackets for women here."

Frank stands as Isabella is leaving. "I might have one in the gîte. I'll go check." He turns and smiles an apology at us. "See you all later. Work here never ends."

Zara raises an eyebrow as she watches them leave.

I frown. More than before, I want to find that box in Frank's gîte. And I need to read more of the untitled novel which may or may not be fiction.

Ishmael gestures with the wet cloth. "Enjoy the afternoon. Isabella has left tasks for me to do before the evening service."

Ishmael might be a way in. He is protective of his sister, but he's also fond of Chloe and he's worried I'll wreck things for her with David, or Matt, or whatever the hell his name is, Chloe's fiancé.

I realise with a start I've been staring at him. He's still standing, smiling, half-turned to go.

I can use that.

Sapna

Galway, Ireland

She'd never met a gay person. She wasn't sure what to say.

Victoria said, "And this is Sapna. Remember Thomas, the doctor who worked with me in London? Sapna is his wife."

The man she'd introduced as Garry stepped forward and smiled. He looked so normal, slim, tall, pale. Sapna smiled back. Garry's partner, John, was more what she associated with gay men. Or more accurately, he resembled the men dressed in sarees she'd seen on the streets in Trivandrum. He was a touch more effeminate, slimmer than Garry, with slender wrists and what she thought was a hint of eye makeup.

John's voice was higher than Garry's, higher than hers. "Sapna, how nice to meet you. What a beautiful name. It suits you so well."

Sapna said, "Thank you." She couldn't return the compliment, in her mind, his name didn't suit him. "I wish I could say the same. Not that John isn't a nice name, but you should have a name like Raphael, you resemble an Italian painting."

John's smile widened. "Beautiful, and perceptive as well."

They laughed.

Garry grinned. "I resemble an ordinary Irish farmer, right? Garry suits me perfectly, doesn't it?"

"Not ordinary at all, but yes, Garry does suit you."

Garry said, "You're welcome to our home. Come in, come in." He stepped back and waved them into the house.

Victoria placed her hand on Sapna's elbow and escorted her into the house. Victoria had told her a little about the couple on the way over, and Sapna knew Victoria sensed she was uncertain and shy. They'd talked like old friends for hours the night before and continued almost without pause as she took her on a tour of Galway. Until Victoria suggested visiting her gay friends. After that, Sapna had been quieter. She'd seen Victoria glancing at her as they drove to Oranmore. She refused to consider whether Victoria was gay too.

The house was larger than hers. And lighter, helped by the cream walls and large windows. They went straight into a living room separated from the kitchen by a waist-high partition. The view of fields and stone walls and sheep was visible through sliding patio doors.

"Oh, that's so nice," Sapna said. "I wish we had a view."

Garry nodded, "One of the main reasons we bought here. They can't build on the field, it's agricultural land."

Victoria said, "I miss having a view of the countryside. London is great when you're young, but I can't wait to move to France. Even if it's to the city."

John smiled. "You'll eventually get back to the country if it's in your blood. Me, I'm a city boy, but I'm okay with this as a compromise. Garry is country at heart, like you."

As she wandered around the suburban home, Sapna realised she was surprised at the normality around her. This wasn't what her mother had warned her about. Not in real words, but in hints and nudges away from any association with people 'like that', especially when she reported to Sapna that Mr Patel had been fired from the school, for being 'mentally depraved'. Sapna had never questioned what 'like that' meant. She had wondered, though, why her mother's comments had become snider after she got back from college, after they discussed Sapna's friends, especially Anjali.

Garry brought over tea and they sat in the living room on couches with a real log fire burning and Sapna had the sensation of being warm for the first time since she'd moved to Ireland. She found it strange it was happening in the company of gay men. She'd never been so comfortable with men as friends in India. All her close friends had been women, college friends mostly. The thought played in between the coils of her mind. A vague body memory of times with Anjali, laughing as they lay on the dorm bed.

"Sapna, why Ireland?" John had asked the question and was waiting for an answer.

Sapna returned to the present. "I'd never heard of Ireland. I think I referred to everything in this direction as England." She smiled, "That isn't something I should admit, not in Ireland, is it?"

They laughed. Garry said, "No, probably not."

"Thomas was working in London and then his brother, Chandy, moved to Dublin and bought an investment house in Galway. The one we're renting now. We had an arranged marriage, and he had recently moved to Galway. I didn't know what to expect."

"An arranged marriage?" John's eyebrow was raised. "Fascinating. I always meant to ask, and please don't answer if it's not appropriate, but how does that work?"

Sapna said, "It's fine. I don't mind answering." She realised she hadn't discussed her marriage with anyone, not since they'd left India, left her friends, her family. "It wasn't exactly the normal arranged marriage though, so I'm not sure if it will answer your questions."

John smiled. "Ooh, sounds even more interesting."

"I didn't get to meet Thomas before our wedding, not really, only one meeting where I was in the background as he was there to meet my younger sister."

Garry said, "You're kidding!" He blushed. "Sorry, I didn't mean that."

Sapna smiled. "It was a bit unusual. The marriage had been arranged between Thomas and my sister. I was already on the shelf." Her smile grew wider at the expression on their faces.

Victoria said, "What age were you?" She said to the guys. "All those Indian men must have been gay if they passed up on Sapna." She chuckled as she turned back to Sapna. "It always comes across as if I'm chatting you up, but I'm not. I'm not lesbian. I think you have even more than this exotic beauty, I can't imagine any straight guy not being enthralled."

Sapna felt her cheeks get warm. "I was 29. That's old for getting married. When I was the right age, there was an unexpected situation with my dowry and then it never happened and when my sister was the right age, my parents had the money again. I was not bothered so they went and arranged her marriage."

"To Thomas?"

"Yes, but there was a problem with him because he was 41 at the time. Some problem with his brother marrying an Irish woman and that had delayed his proposals. To be honest, I didn't pay attention to all the fuss. I was happy for my sister and his family were respectable, they were in Saudi Arabia. Thomas's brother, Chandy, who was working in London knew my cousin, Ishmael, who was living in London as well, and their

parents made the proposal for my sister and our families then started the arrangements. I stayed out of it, except for that one visit. My sister was so nervous, now I know why."

The tea trembled in the china, as she put it to her lips. The others were leaning forward.

Sapna rested the cup in her hands on her lap. "She wanted me to be at the meeting, she wanted all the family to be there. I think she was hoping we would recognise they weren't suited or something. Most of us were there, and I stayed in the background. I didn't want my opinion of a stranger to be important in such a decision." She realised as she spoke that she'd been engrossed in her chat with Thomas's cousin for most of the visit, she'd barely noticed Thomas. The cousin, she couldn't remember her name, only her face. She had come from Saudi to represent the family along with a couple of aunts who lived in Kerala. "The marriage was arranged between Thomas and Lalitha, my sister."

Victoria said, "So your husband was supposed to marry your sister?"

Sapna nodded. "But Lalitha hadn't told us she was in love with another man. She couldn't tell anyone, so she ran away with him." The shame for her sister flashed through her body. It brought her back to the heat of the room, the fan blowing the hot air around as her parents shouted, blamed each other.

"Why couldn't she tell anyone? Surely if she loved this man and he loved her, they would not have forced her to marry someone else?" It sounded like a plea for an understanding he had not experienced. Garry took his hand. Sapna's initial discomfort around two gay men had disappeared. She watched their hands clasped on the couch with something surprisingly approaching envy.

She said, "There were so many issues, the agreed dowry, the loss of face, the pressure from extended family, but the worst part..." She paused, found it difficult to say the words.

Victoria said, "The worst part...?"

"It was our first cousin. Ishmael's brother, Reza, who she loved. That is almost as taboo there as gay people." Sapna stopped. "I mean, not you." She looked at Garry and John, her face heating up.

John leant forward. "It's okay. I have an Indian friend, a guy, and he can't say Garry's name as my partner, but we get on like a house on fire. I have to make the effort to understand where he's coming from."

Sapna said, "It may be much harder for Indian guys. I didn't have any contact with gay people, but when I went to college, my friends were all women and we would be very close. Women are allowed to be so much closer. But it is totally taboo, no one mentions it except as a mental illness."

John said, "Yes! That's what I was thinking. But, it's not as if society here is all that accepting either, I mean, they only decriminalised homosexuality in Ireland in 1993. It's scary. Such a Catholic country. I have to be careful what I say at work, I could be fired if they found out. My friend's a nice guy and he likes us, but he can't allow the fact we are gay. Does that make sense?"

Sapna nodded. "He can think of you as nice people and as long as he doesn't see the other part, he can be friends. I don't know what my husband would do or think if he knew I had met the two of you. I don't think he could be in your company."

Victoria said, "So how did you end up with Thomas?"

"Things were horrific after Lalitha ran away. My parents were so ashamed, they couldn't hold their heads up in their society. They were fighting and so unhappy and my father's health was already bad, he had high blood pressure, they thought he might have a stroke. I was the only girl left in the household, they'd successfully arranged marriages for my

two older sisters. My aunt suggested it to my mother and they came to me." Sapna wondered how simple words could be used to describe that time. The crying, the unspoken words, the sacrifices expected.

Victoria seemed to sense her disquiet. "I worked with Thomas in London. I remember him moving to Ireland, and he informed me of his marriage, but he never elaborated on any of this."

Sapna said, "It was re-arranged quickly. Once the decision was made, they substituted my name where Lalitha's had appeared. But I did not do the other things that normally happen, like spend time with him, find out if we were compatible. And he was obviously furious about what had happened." She had been making up for her sister's behaviour, ever since then.

Garry sighed. "Wow. And I thought we had interesting lives."

Sapna joined in the ensuing laughter. Discussing it had helped, but it had opened her mind, and she wasn't sure she welcomed the prospect of more thoughts. Not when there was nothing to be done anyway.

John said, "Have you made any friends here in Galway?"

Sapna shook her head, "Victoria is the first." She smiled. "And she doesn't live here." She turned to Victoria. "You should look up my cousin, Ishmael, in London, though he might not be open to meeting a friend of his disgraced cousin's sister. I'm sure he's been affected by the scandal too." She sighed. "Just don't mention it to Thomas. We've all been affected. Thomas works a lot and he's having to do exams to get a better job, but he doesn't want me to work, so I spend most of my time at home."

John got off the couch and took her hands. "Don't know if you're allowed, but I'm gay and no threat so can I give you a hug?"

Tears sprang to her eyes and she blinked them away. "Of course." She stood up and he put his arms around her and squeezed.

John said, "We have mostly gay and lesbian friends so they will have to do. You're coming out with us, we'll introduce you to the scene. There's a straight pub where we hang out, but I hear one of the women is considering opening a lesbian bar. You shouldn't be on your own so much." He laughed. "And I don't mean coming out as in coming out, but you know what I mean."

Sapna said, "I'm not sure what you mean, but the idea of making friends makes me very happy."

John leant back to examine her face. "Girl, we're going to have to teach you all the gay and lesbian terms. Don't worry, the lesbians won't bite you." His grin was wicked. "Unless you want them to."

Sapna felt a prickle in her chest. She was happy to have made friends and keen now to make more, but she knew this was something not to mention to Thomas, however innocent it was.

CHAPTER ELEVEN

I wait until the door closes behind Ishmael before I walk across the courtyard towards the cottage he shares with Frank. The staff used two of the cottages in the rectangle of *gîtes*. I've noticed the servers going in and out of the one next to Frank and Ishmael's.

Ishmael is in the novel. Lana's *cousin*. But no Frank.

I need more, from other sources. More about Ishmael, to see if he and Frank match up to the characters. Through my own experience, not through the words of a writer's creations. I imagine Frank as the character of Victoria. It makes sense. Maybe Lana used some of the real names and changed others. And she might have been afraid if David found the notebooks, he'd find out Frank was gay and none of them could afford that.

I knock.

Ishmael raise his eyebrows when he sees me, but his smile takes over. "Jaya, how can I help you?"

My voice comes out hoarse. "I was wondering if you had time to show me more of the sights. I want to get out of the way of Chloe and my mother and you did say you didn't want me hanging around her."

He laughs. "I don't think I put it quite like that."

I hope my smile isn't too wide, it feels like my mouth is stretched, out of my control. "Of course, if you're busy, I'll be happy to spend the afternoon figuring out if she's still a proper lesbian."

"No, no, not busy. I'd be delighted to be your escort." He gestures at his stained black apron and work trousers. "I have to change out of these."

"No problem. Should I wait here?" I gesture at the sun-soaked patio bordering the length of the rectangular courtyard. My hat is folded into my bag.

He hesitates and then moves to the side. "It's too hot. Come in, if you don't mind waiting a minute or so?"

I temper my smile. "Not at all. I'm a very patient person." Shock thrills through me as I realise I'm flirting with him.

The front room of the cottage is identical in structure to ours, but has a touch of home, not hotel. The kitchen is on the left immediately inside and, down three steps, a living room with sliding glass doors leading to a fenced yard, and a hundred feet beyond, the rear windows of the main sandstone house, where Chloe stays in a room on the guest side. Isabella and her husband live in an annex.

Ishmael waves me to the couch, face tinged with pink. "I'll just go and change. Help yourself to anything to drink in the fridge. I think there's beer. Or wine? Everyone drinks *rosé* here in the afternoon, would you like a glass?"

I clear my throat. "Maybe when we get back?"

His blush deepens. "Sure." He points upwards. There are stairs leading up from the far corner of the room. "I'd better change out of these smelly clothes."

My legs feel shaky as I follow him into the living room. He brushes by me and hurries up the stairs.

I can hear his footsteps on the wooden floor upstairs. I examine the room. Photos on the wall feature Frank and Ishmael posing at tourist sites in Paris. Frank looks the same, but Ishmael appears thinner in them, almost gaunt.

I scan the titles on a standing bookshelf with interest, but they're mostly tourist guides for the different regions. There are novels, including a humorous take on British expatriates living in France. Wooden sculptures of a boar and a cat act as bookends.

Two photos lean on the top shelf, one of Frank, Ishmael, and Isabella. The other, Ishmael and Isabella, stunning with their brown skin, wavy hair, and intense eyes. I pick up the second framed photo and notice my heart thumping as I stare at the pair.

They are so alike, and I want a closer look.

Without gawking at Isabella in person.

I'm already finding that hard to do without flushing into brown-tinted shades of red.

"If I didn't know you were into Chloe, I'd suspect you have a crush on my sister."

I drop the photo with a squeak that is so unsophisticated I want to sink through the floor. I'm grateful the frame hasn't got far to fall and it lands more gracefully on the shelf than I feel.

"Sorry, didn't mean to startle you." Ishmael's voice is husky with laughter. I turn and catch my breath at the sight of his smile, white teeth even, eyes bright. Eyes that mirror the confusion I fear is betrayed in mine. And then a veil lowers though his lips remain curved.

He has changed into dark jeans and a cerise shirt. The sleeves are buttoned up, emphasising delicate wrists.

I say, keeping my voice steady, "That's a great colour on your skin, I must remember it when I go shopping again."

He smooths the front of his shirt. "I got it in Paris. It's lovely, isn't it?" His voice is a study in casualness as well.

Why am I noticing everything about this man? Maybe because I'm so accustomed to being around lesbians, my reading of body language and my reactions are conditioned by that. Who knows in what way. What is happening to me, why are this brother and sister so confusing, so beguiling? I have no answer that makes sense. All I know right now is Ishmael holds the answers to questions that are becoming crucial to me, and I won't let anything distract me from my search for Lana and whatever secrets she might be hiding.

Ishmael grabs his keys off the kitchen counter. "This time I'll take the car. You might appreciate it."

I walk past him. "Me? Why? Do you think I can't do the hiking thing?"

He grins and closes the door behind us. I notice he doesn't lock it. "Hiking? It wasn't that far to the village, was it?"

"It was surely more than the mile you promised."

The sun beats on us as we walk through the courtyard. I wonder at the chill running through my veins.

Ishmael points with his keys at a low-slung red convertible, shiny beside other cars in the staff lot adjoining the restaurant parking lines. "It's Frank's gift to his wild youth, that he never got, he says."

Ishmael opens the door for me and waits until I've settled in before going around the car.

He drives slowly, but it's like we're skimming an imaginary grass strip on the narrow road.

He reaches across me for his sunglasses in the glove compartment, his shoulder warm against my bare arm, and I notice the wave of his hair that refuses to sit tamely.

I say, my breath tight in my chest, confused by his closeness and my body's reaction to it. "We'll take the deer out at their knees if they do their thing."

His chuckle follows him back into his seat.

"I'll drive between them instead." He puts on the glasses. "We can go and meet the friendly deer early in the morning if you want. Should be fewer people there then."

"That would be really nice, I'd love to." We arrive at the crossroads, a road veers into the village, the other is the way I drove in. "Where are we going today?"

He idles the engine. Glances at me. "Hmm... A drive through the countryside? There are many pretty villages. We could stop and have a glass of *rosé* at a restaurant café I know. Then I've to return to help with evening service."

I'm not accomplishing my mission, finding out about Lana, Isabella. But his proposal is tempting. And he might loosen up and tell me more after a drink.

I nod. "Sounds lovely."

He smiles, takes the turn away from the village.

I watch his lips, wonder again if it is his resemblance to Isabella making me notice these things. I sink into the seat and the breeze strokes through my hair, leaving the scent of summer in its wake.

§

"We were both born in Paris. To Algerian parents." Ishmael leans back, out of the shade of the beer-branded patio umbrella, and the sun teases his face. I watch his eyelashes flutter in delicate black tendrils.

The patio of the Café Le Pont borders the river's edge, its crazy paving separated from the restaurant building by a road that continues onto the eponymous bridge. Stone arches throw shadows over the green-tea water.

Ishmael had driven through picture-perfect French villages, flower boxes spilling a profusion of colour onto cream stone walls and I'd basked in the beauty. And we talked like we'd known each other forever, but thirsty for more, general things, spirituality, politics, pets. Not sexuality or family or background. Until now.

If he's Lana's cousin, then he is Indian, not Algerian. The novel does not match his story and I don't know what to believe. I ask, "Was it only the two of you? Any other brothers or sisters? Cousins?"

"Just us."

"Was that tough? Growing up brown in a white city?"

Ishmael nodded. "Probably not as bad as in rural Ireland. We had each other and other families. Not as many as now, but enough to have a community, to take over some *arrondissements*." He lifts an eyebrow. "I can't imagine what the experience was for you. I would say Ireland in, what, the seventies, was not a very multicultural place?"

"It wasn't. I was the only one with any brown, heck, any colour. My activism around lesbian issues is affected by my experience growing up in a place that saw me as an outsider. We are treated as outsiders, even when on the inside we're as much insiders." I lean forward. "I try and make lesbians aware they sometimes use the same judgements on women of colour as straight people do about them, we're so busy building communities for our safety, but we build walls at the same time, separating us further into outsiders and insiders."

Ishmael sips at his *rosé*. "And lesbians build walls against bisexuals too. Chloe experienced that."

The grey plastic chair wobbles on the uneven paving when I sit back. "Not the same."

His mouth quirks in a sad smile. "Isn't it?"

"Chloe chose to hide away."

"And what would the reaction to her have been if she'd been openly bisexual? From what I gathered from her, the lesbian community you enjoyed would not have been as welcoming. Of her, or you."

I watch the water flowing by. "We didn't risk it." I turn, catch him staring at me. He averts his gaze, his attention now aimed at the river too.

I say, "How come you discussed this so much? Are you bisexual?"

His skin is like mine, it betrays only partial proof of embarrassment. "My sexuality is a topic that fascinates Chloe."

My eyebrow rises. "It does? It's different in another way?" I smile. "Apart from the gay or bisexual thing?"

Ishmael is absorbed in my smile. My body tenses with the sense of power when you become aware of the effect you have on someone. It spreads, rippling through me, more an undercurrent than a wave.

Ishmael's gaze drops to his drink. "Yes." He shifts in his chair. "Chloe said you were not able to deal with bisexuality? I always find it - " He pauses, "*Interesting* when a gay or lesbian person cannot accept the concept of being bisexual."

"Why?" My hobby horse gets saddled. "Does it mean when someone loves women they must automatically understand a woman being attracted to men as well as women. In the same way that a lesbian is attracted to a woman and cannot viscerally understand the attraction or themselves experience it for a man, it's hard to fathom how anyone could be attracted to both." I jump on. "You know, many on the scene believe bi women who hide their lesbian side are actually closeted lesbians. And women who love women don't fall in love with men." I slide off, sidle away from the horse. "Besides, I don't have anything against bisexual people."

"So it is just this one bisexual person?"

My turn to shift in my chair. "I guess so. Maybe two. And I do have strong opinions. It's not like I hate men or anything. I was with guys before I discovered I was lesbian. I had awful experiences with bisexual women in college, after that."

"Straight women or bisexual women?"

"There's a difference?"

He laughs.

I smile. "I believe they were straight women who were experimenting. All of them ended up with men."

"So, you are into straight-looking women?"

A cross between a snort and a laugh escapes my mouth. "I love how you phrase that. Not straight women, but straight-looking women."

He grins. "I was trying to be gentle."

"Okay, maybe I do. Have a thing for more traditionally feminine women. Not femme femme necessarily. More of a soft butch I suppose."

"Have you ever had a thing for a man? Since you realised you were lesbian."

"No." I wonder why the liquid is trembling as I bring the glass to my lips. The *rosé* swirls into my mouth, scented and sweet. I rest the glass on the fidgety table, careful to keep it steady. It feels like I'm drifting into my college days, an alien and forgotten time. "You said you have an unusual sexuality. Not solely gay or bisexual. What is it then?"

He smiles. "Wouldn't you rather focus on Chloe?"

I push for a reaction, peeved he's avoided my question again. "How about Isabella?"

His smile stays fixed, but expressive eyes show hurt, whether he realises it or not and I regret causing the change.

He says, "What about her?" He watches the people walking over the bridge, his lips distorted through the glass he's holding in front of his mouth. "She should be lesbian, yet she's married to a man?"

I say, "Exactly."

"Are you sure that's not just wishful thinking?"

I purse my lips. Pause, then say, "Well, okay, at first, but there's something intriguing. She has great passion, a fire in her. And that doesn't match my impression of her husband. Was she ever with women?"

Ishmael's brow crinkles. "Funny enough, I don't know." He turns and his eyes drill into mine. "Would that be a factor? In whether you attempt to charm her?"

I may be unable to show a blush fully, but the rush of blood to my cheeks might as well be a red flag waving from my head. The words come out in a tumble "I'm not trying to charm her, simply curious."

I can see myself through his perspective and it is a strange experience and definitely not my normal self. I'm a lesbian activist. Sort of engaged to Fiona. I appear to be pushing to reunite with my lesbian-turned-straight ex and infatuated with his straight married sister. And obviously giving off some kind of pheromones whenever I'm around him.

Yes. That about summarises the look in his eyes.

He finishes his wine, puts the glass down with a clink. "Yes. We decided my sister is an interesting woman." He shoves himself out of the chair. "Speaking of her, she'll be mad at me if I'm late for evening service."

I hurry to my feet. "Sorry, I've taken up your whole afternoon. It was so nice to see the gorgeous villages. I suspect many tourists don't get to experience them. Thank you." I check my watch and my guilt worsens. The day has flown by and he has to work again now.

He bows. "It was my pleasure." He gestures towards the exit. "After you."

I examine his face, but it is a portrait of sweet innocence.

Sapna

Paris, France

"There are a lot of brown people around here, considering this is Paris." Thomas stretched back in the lawn chair on the balcony and took a gulp of red wine.

Victoria nodded. "That's why I love this area. There are Indian restaurants and Vietnamese and Chinese people and North Africans." She looked at Sapna. "You'll get to explore when Thomas and I go to the notaire's office. Will you be okay on your own? Most areas around here are safe and you can stick to the main avenues."

Sapna smiled. "I'll be fine."

She was excited to be meeting Ishmael though her nerves were raw from keeping that part of Victoria from Thomas, as well as the part of her with gay friends now. And she was going to meet Ishmael, the brother of the man who'd run away with Thomas's fiancé. Though Ishmael was her cousin and Lalitha was her sister, Sapna still thought of it through the shame Thomas experienced. Maybe because the only mention of the episode was through that lens.

She was glad something positive had come out of the whole mess. Victoria was so happy now and her letters after meeting Ishmael were full of a new passion for life. Something she needed after the years of self-loathing. Sapna could see the change in Victoria's bearing. She'd been friendly when she'd visited them in Ireland, but she now had a vibrancy in her step, in her eyes.

Thomas frowned. "I'm not sure I understand all this notary stuff. Or the SCI thing."

Victoria said. "It's a notaire. They handle all the real estate transactions in France. They're not notaries, more real estate attorneys, I guess. This guy is supposed to be excellent. He doesn't speak great English, according to Henri, my insurance guy so Henri is going to come along and translate, he speaks good English. We have to know what questions to ask, notaires don't instruct you, but they answer questions well."

Thomas put the glass on the terracotta-tiled floor. "Should we write down the questions then?"

Victoria arose. "I'll get a notebook. The SCI stuff can get complicated. But I think it's the optimal way to go ahead. It's a way to buy and manage property through a real estate type of company, but without all the company management. It's best for the situation when people who aren't married or related buy property together."

Thomas said, "We decided to do it through my name because of Sapna's immigration status in Ireland. She doesn't get Irish citizenship for a few more years and we don't want the hassle of the tax and paperwork. It makes more sense to do it in my name."

Sapna didn't say anything. Thomas had decided on his own. As her parents had always done. They'd arranged the dowry that was paying for this investment. He was dealing with all the paperwork and legalities for her Irish citizenship. She'd never realised it would take so long.

Victoria looked at Sapna. "French law is strict. It takes account of the spouse in inheritance matters if it's bought through a person not an SCI company. With the SCI, it is the shares in the company that are assigned to the partners so each partner can choose what they do with the shares."

Thomas said, "Bring the notepad. Let's put down any questions we all have. I talked to my accountant in Ireland. This is the best way for us." He smiled at Sapna. "Don't worry, our wills in Ireland make sure you are taken care of if anything happens to me. And my salary there will be the valuable part of the estate."

Sapna wished she had paid more attention at home when her dad talked property and business. They had all assumed she would learn what was necessary in due time to support her husband by arranging the household budget. She did that well, but she had never been interested in money. She felt an unaccustomed urge to know more about what was going to happen to her dowry, the last of anything that was hers, originally, not now.

Sapna said, "This is an up and coming area of Paris, is it not?"

Victoria nodded. "Paris has always had higher prices than anywhere else in France. And the different arrondissements have property values that vary based on distance from the centre and other factors. My real estate friend, and Henri, both believe this area is going to shoot up in value this year or next. There's a great demand for rentals, I mean, look at this apartment, it's tiny, and still it costs a bit to rent. We'll be able to let out the three apartments in the house with no problem. And when I move, I'll pay the going rate for one of them and keep an eye on the others." She turned to Thomas. "We'll do everything through the notaire. I'll be the managing partner though, the gérant, because I'm putting in more money and I'm here, but we'll have all the rules laid out and I'll give you both regular updates."

Thomas said, "Good. Fine. I refuse to be involved with tenants or anything." He laughed. "Have the 40 percent profit sent to me, I'll be satisfied with that, no fixing broken toilets or dealing with crazy people."

Victoria smiled. "I've only four more months of crazy before I retire. I'm looking forward to dealing with rentals rather than being at the hospital." She made a sweeping gesture at the view of the tree-lined streets. "This is going to be so much easier."

Sapna watched her smile and knew it was real. Ishmael had moved over already and found the perfect house, home for them on one floor and two rentals on the upper floors. Sapna found herself wishing, as she did every time she'd read Victoria's letters in the last year since Victoria had met Ishmael, that she could find that smile in herself.

Sapna

Paris, France

Sapna wondered what Ishmael looked like now. Her memories of him were of a shy boy paled into quiet by the charisma of his brother, Reza. Everyone remembered Reza. And now their memories of Reza included the delicious wisp of scandal. Now they were not allowed to remember Reza or speak his name. And Lalitha's. But Sapna remembered Lalitha every day at first, and then every other day, and then only when Thomas reminded her in a look of contempt veiled behind admonishment.

The image most closely associated with Lalitha now was the disgust on her mother's face. And Sapna knew only one or two other things would create that level of disgust.

First cousins. On their father's side seemed more distant somehow than if it had been on their mother's side which felt like they came from almost the same womb. But on their father's side, there was a psychological distance. Sapna wondered if Reza and Lalitha thought that, comforted themselves with that. Or with each other. They had each other, but their actions, the consequences were hers.

And maybe Ishmael's too.

The man entering the café was familiar to her in what must be the original sense of the word. His brown skin did not stand out in the room, but his features, his likeness to her family, was an imprint in her mind.

He scanned the room and his face lit up in a smile the moment he saw her. The smile her father said he passed on to Sapna. Her uncle had passed it on to his son.

She stood.

Ishmael glided through the chairs and people, his eyes fixed on her. His voice was smooth, husky, his accent tinted with Indian and English and French, "Sapna? My word. It's so good to see you again." He held out his hands. He looked unsure for a moment, whether she hugged in greeting.

Sapna hugged him. She leant back and smiled. "Little Ishy."

He laughed. "It's been a long time since I heard the name. Hey! I'm not much smaller than you or younger."

Sapna nodded. "I know, I know, but I always feel like an auntie to anyone I meet from those days."

He pulled out a chair, waited for her to sit, and dropped into his seat. "It's always packed here. Wow, how long has it been? I think I last saw you when we were visiting India in '91. You haven't changed a jot."

Sapna laughed. "I was what, fourteen, fifteen, then? I'm an old married woman now, I've changed."

Ishmael picked up the menu and shook the plastic at her. "Less of the old, please, we're in the prime of our lives. What would you like to eat? You got a drink?" Ishmael gestured at the lemonade in front of her and waved at the waitress. "I hope this place is okay for you? It's not fancy, but the food is delicious. I wasn't sure if you'd want to experience French food in a posh restaurant, but I come here all the time and it's the best Vietnamese food in Paris." He smiled. "I didn't know what you would be like now, if you'd be the same as I remembered or if you were now a new European. You never know how people will be when they move to a new culture."

The waitress put an espresso on the Formica table top. "Ishmael, ca va? Ready?"

"Bien, merci, et toi?" Ishmael turned to Sapna. "I'm sorry, I talk too much when I'm nervous. Have you had a chance to decide what you want to eat?'

Sapna said. "I thought I might let you pick, I haven't had Vietnamese food before." She smiled. "So, I'm not the only one who's nervous. I'm more relaxed already."

Ishmael smiled. "Me too." He handed the menu to the waitress. "We'll have the petites nems, and the crevettes farcies to start, and then the riz avec porc emincés and the soupe saté ou bouef." The waitress took the menu and nodded. Ishmael turned to Sapna. "Blast, I didn't check, you're not vegetarian, are you?"

Sapna shook her head.

Ishmael said, "Why am I nervous? We're cousins."

Sapna smiled. "And you don't know who I am now and whether I'll be cool with the fact you were gay, but now you're my female friend's boyfriend. And I'm the one who introduced you."

Ishmael smiled in surprise. "Yes. Exactly. You probably never meant to be a matchmaker when you were growing up, did you? Or even meet gay people."

Sapna laughed. "No. It's not exactly what I visualised as my role. Especially in India as I wasn't aware what gay was then. And when I did, it was only as almost the worst thing in the world to be."

"I did." His eyes were sad though his face smiled. "I may not have

known the term, but I knew I was different."

Sapna nodded. "Yes, I do have a memory of you not really hanging out with the others."

Ishmael kept his gaze on her as he sipped from the espresso. "Do you remember the time when we visited you guys? In '91?"

"Not clearly. Well, I remember playing rounders, and Reza decided he was going to be captain."

"That's our Reza." Ishmael nudged the saucer with his finger. "Are you in contact with Lalitha?"

Sapna knew the question had been coming but the loss still stabbed at her. "No." She sighed. "We're not allowed. It's not said, but Appa…" The words trailed across the table between them.

"I know." He shook his head. "It was always that way. Reza doing whatever he wanted and everyone else picking up the pieces."

Sapna smiled. "Same as what I thought with Lalitha." She chuckled. "This isn't in the slightest bit funny, but the two of them did that all their lives and then ended up running away together."

Ishmael grinned. "Not funny at all. Pity about the blasted consequences for everyone else. If you think about it, it's a pity they're first cousins, they're perfectly suited for each other."

The waitress brought their appetisers, and Ishmael gestured at the plates. "Do you want to share? It's the best way to eat Vietnamese food."

Sapna nodded and he split the dishes, giving them a roll and a square of fried pastry each. "The nem is a spring roll and the crevettes farcies is stuffed shrimp, here, have salad too. I love coming here, it's nice sometimes to just sit in the noise of the place. It's always packed and sometimes you end up sitting at a table with strangers, but most people are friendly. Victoria doesn't appreciate Vietnamese food as much." He laughed. *"Only Indian for her. I swear, she's more Indian than me."* He took a bite of the roll. *"Mmm. It's good."*

Sapna smiled. *"She ate my cooking, she must love Indian food."*

"Hey, she said you were a great cook. And she's English and speaks her mind, so I'd say you must be." Ishmael wiped the grease off his mouth. *"And Thomas? Does he like your cooking? Does he cook, or is that too much to expect?"*

"He was brought up in Saudi. His mum decided he'd better be able to cook at least a couple of dishes before he went to England." She smiled. *"He taught me those dishes. I make them for us when he doesn't eat at work."*

"He eats at work usually?"

"Yes. Or at one of the restaurants near the hospital after work."

Ishmael said, *"So you eat alone mostly?"*

She nodded slowly. *"I guess so."* It had become a routine, she didn't dwell on it much.

Ishmael said, *"Victoria would have a fit if she knew. She should have a restaurant. She loves having company, cooking for everyone."* He smiled. *"She should own a restaurant and employ a chef."*

Sapna said, *"This is yummy. I've had Chinese food, this is as good."* She cleaned off the last drips of sauce on her plate with the spring roll.

Ishmael leant back. *"May I ask you a question?"*

Sapna looked up. *"Sure...?"*

"Are you happy? I mean, with Thomas?" Ishmael reddened. *"I heard what happened after, of course, but the wedding was a crazy thing happening in the background. We were busy with the other stuff, with all the relatives who wanted to find out what was going on, but were pretending to give a damn."* He smiled. *"I was the England outpost. They*

thought I'd have news for them, but I never hung out with them before, damn if I was going to just because they wanted to pump me for info."

The sadness was back in his eyes, in his hand as it cradled the espresso cup. "Appa and Amma, on the other hand, they were right there in India. I never went back. I wasn't there for them then or later."

Sapna put her hand over his. "It was Reza's doing, not yours. He should have warned them. He should have come back and faced the music himself."

"Lalitha should have as well. Instead, you ended up having to marry a stranger."

Sapna said, "There was no other way. Who knows? I might have had a marriage arranged for me which was worse." She squeezed his hand. "Do you not go back because you were gay?"

He nodded. "Can you imagine what it would do to them? Only two children, and one son runs off with his first cousin and the other...something worse. Perverted. Dirty. Unspeakable."

Guilt crept through her. She didn't think of Ishmael or Garry or John or any of the others in that way, but she was a part of such thinking every time she imagined two women together.

Ishmael closed his eyes. Opened them again and sighed. "I admire you. I couldn't have made such a sacrifice for Reza."

Sapna frowned. She didn't deserve the admiration, she'd never once stood up for people like him.

She said. "Do you remember Sholay?"

"The movie?"

"Yes." Sapna smiled. "I used to watch it over and over again. When we had our first VCR. Which, by the way, was a present from your uncle and aunty, they sent it over from London with you guys. I used to watch

that movie every afternoon after school."

Ishmael smiled. "I watched it too, in London."

"The scene where Hema Malini dances in front of Gabbar Singh and all his villains."

"And Dharmendra tied up from the gallows thing? Wearing a light blue shirt and a navy t-shirt under it which she rips off him as she's falling, when she can't dance anymore."

Sapna chuckled. "Of course you'd remember that part."

He grinned.

She continued. "I loved that song. I always remember the scene. It embodies sacrifice. It's what we're trained to do, isn't it?" She quoted the words from the song, translating what she remembered. "As long as there's life, I'll dance, love never dies, it doesn't even fear death."

He sighed. "I remember. I thought she was so beautiful." He smiled. "I wanted to be her."

Sapna smiled. "Me too. You mean, to love the hero? Did you have a crush on Dharmendra?" She wondered for a moment why she couldn't feel the same, she didn't remember having a crush on the hero.

He shook his head. "Yes, I did. But I guess I wanted to look like her. You do, to a certain extent."

Sapna frowned. "I do? No. You mean Lalitha. I'm more the quiet widow, Jaya Baduri's character. Always covering herself away in white."

Ishmael smiled. "Funny how we see ourselves. I always thought of you as the beautiful heroine, the lively laughing one."

Sapna shook her head. "You're definitely thinking of Lalitha. I was the quiet, reserved one."

The waitress arrived with their main courses. They laughed as they split the dishes, the liquids more awkward than the appetisers.

Ishmael wiped his hands with the napkin. "I always wanted to tell you what you did for me."

"Me?" She gulped at the lemonade, the sauce was unexpectedly spicy.

He nodded. "You probably don't remember. It was that last time we visited. There was a party at the house."

Sapna thought back to that summer. She remembered the two boys being there, along with the nine cousins from her mother's side and the kids she played with who lived in the neighbourhood. It was noisy and there'd been a number of parties with sodas and sweets.

She said, "I think so."

Ishmael said, "I was eleven, so you were fifteen?"

She nodded. "Going on fifteen."

"I was sitting on the porch, in one of the wicker chairs your folks used for their card games."

She smiled. Her parents' porch was an outside room. The bougainvillaea tumbled down the sides, the warm air moved slowly through the gaps but left the cards in their place on the glass tables. She remembered all the sandals lined up at the entrance as the players laughed and joked over the game which could go on till the early hours of the morning, occasionally interrupted by yells and good-natured ribbing. Her parents' house had been the hub of the neighbourhood, now quietened by the scandal.

She said, "They used to have so much fun. When everyone came around. Was the party on Reza's birthday?"

Ishmael smiled. "No, it was mine. I was hiding outside, it was loud inside, Reza was doing one of his magic shows. You came out and you were wearing this salwar kameez that was only stunning. Red and gold."

Sapna smiled. "I remember it. One of Kamala's hand-me-downs that didn't fit Lalitha."

"You came and sat down in the next chair and you said, 'Hey Ishy, what are you doing out here alone at your own party?' and I didn't say anything." Ishmael cleared his throat. "I couldn't talk and you didn't mind. You chatted away, the jasmine you were determined to grow, the bird you were training to eat out of your hand whenever you saw it, and I still couldn't speak, but you didn't make me feel bad. I couldn't say what was on my mind, I couldn't say it to myself at the time, even now, but you seemed to have a sense. And then aunty called you in for something and you got up and you were going into the house, but you stopped and came back to me. And you said, 'Ishy, it doesn't feel that way to you now, but you're the beautiful one. And you'll always be.'"

Sapna remembered now. It had been important to let the kid know the truth.

Ishmael said. "Only a few words, but it had a huge impact on me. More than you will ever know. Or I can ever thank you for." He shook his head as she opened her mouth. "I felt awful when I heard because of Reza you ended up having to," he quirked his fingers in an air quote, "save the family honour." He held her hand. "It wasn't my fault, well, not really, though Chandy only knew of your family through me, and I've meditated on it and it's Reza's deal, not mine, but I've had to deal with consequences that weren't what I would have hoped for my life, I'll always have to hide being gay from my family, and more. I hope at least you're happy. That's what I wish for you."

Sapna tried to find the words to reassure him. But she found no words coming to her rescue.

They sat in silence, their own pocket of quiet within the dense noise of the restaurant around them.

Sapna said, "I never expected this life. I dreamed of love that would make me never fear death, would make me dance until I fell, because dancing would keep my love alive. A love I would give my last breath to protect. Thomas can be very," she searched for the word, "charismatic. Convincing. He was furious Lalitha jilted him and ran off with her cousin. What man wouldn't be? I overheard the aunties gossiping before the wedding and they said what a good man he was for accepting me as a substitute? They said how lucky I was, that I had passed the age when I could get a proper marriage and Thomas was a doctor and only 36 and nothing wrong with him except his brother had gone and married an English girl and that affected the parents and delayed his proposals." Sapna looked up at Ishmael, said the words without thinking. "I didn't want to be the heroine in the movie, I wanted to love her." She stopped. Frowned. Shook her head. "I'm in a marriage with a man who makes me fear love. For no reason. He has done nothing wrong, but I can't put my finger on why I feel that way. I know life is never going to be a movie, but I never expected the grimness of this reality either. And there is no other option. Reza took away your chance to be you around your family, Lalitha took my chance. I guess the sacrifice I was meant to make was for my family, not for my love.

She knew from his eyes Ishmael had heard the words she'd never spoken aloud. And she'd heard the words he hadn't said. There had been more he'd hidden from his parents than just being gay. He wanted to look like the heroine.

Somehow it felt right to sit in a Vietnamese restaurant in Paris and talk for hours on every subject except those words and what they held. And the knowledge she could never say those words aloud again, or silently.

CHAPTER TWELVE

The courtyard basks in the sun, sand-dust ground hurling yellow at the sandstone walls, dripping brown into the shadows.

I glance around once more before slipping into Frank and Ishmael's cottage. The heat is enough to keep everyone indoors, either at the bar or by the lake. I'd heard the yells of children playing in the water, as I left the restaurant where the two men are helping in the service prep. I want to find Lana's belongings, get in and out fast.

My mind is buzzing with the confusion of being in another world, a world of make-believe. Or is it truer than the façades of the people here? I'm hoping that the letters provide more clarity.

The cottage is quiet, and the sense of homeliness is still present. It is neat with few obvious storage areas.

I race through the cupboards in the kitchen and the shelves in the living room. No boxes, just knick-knacks from countries they visited, a Galway Crystal bowl, a leaning tower, a tulip-shaped keychain.

I climb the stairs, careful not to make noise though the neighbouring cottage sounds empty.

Two bedrooms are separated by a landing and a bathroom. Both have personal items on top of the dressers, clothes in the closets. One bedroom does have a more shared quality to it and I pause when I see the cerise shirt hanging on the closet door.

I stroke the material and the scent of cologne touches me, a light musk I associate with Ishmael. A tingle goes through my fingers. He looks like his sister. And she is stunning in a take my breath kind of way. That's why I get this tingling.

I feel safe around Ishmael, he's a guy and gay, and he's so easy to talk to, I understand how Chloe became close to him so fast. I'm tongue-tied near Isabella, and while the flirty interactions with Ishmael do confuse me, I like him and we hang out more than I do with her. New old friends. Which is nice, but also useful as I search for Lana. And I shouldn't beat myself up for befriending him to get information on Lana, or possibly even locate her. If the character in the novel is Ishmael, then he is keeping things from me too. If he is Lana's cousin and Reza is his brother, then who is Isabella?

There is nothing upstairs that might hold Lana's things. Maybe Frank moved the stuff to the house, where Isabella lives.

I stare out of the bedroom window. At the sandstone of the main house, the yard, the flower beds, the fruit trees. And a small barn I hadn't noticed when I was standing downstairs.

§

The barn is unlocked. There are gardening implements and empty flower pots stacked against the walls, resting on loose hay. The rectangle of light from the entrance falls short of the back wall, but it lightens the shadows enough to show four boxes, branded, with pictures of the equipment they once held. The dust and shreds of grass settled on them appear undisturbed.

I check my watch. I judge I have time to hunt through them if I hurry, Isabella was busy in the restaurant, but Henri or any of the vacationers could return soon.

The first three boxes have the Styrofoam cut-outs of power tools. The fourth, on the bottom, has another box in it. Plain brown cardboard, with clear tape sealing it closed.

The air is musty and I strain to suppress an oncoming sneeze, but it emerges as a muffled squeak. I wait, pulse thudding, but there is no sound from outside.

I'm taken aback for the moment by the tape. There are garden shears hanging on a nail, and I use them to slice through the layers of plastic. I'll have to return later with more tape and seal it up again. The box seems untouched, but Frank might check it and I don't want him to suspect anyone has been at it.

The sparse contents are barely an inch in height.

I lift the papers out, pages curled together. My heart beats faster, they are the letters. Photos lie loose and in a thin pile at the corner. I pick them up, scraping at the last with my nails to ease its edge off the cardboard.

My fingers bump against an object and voices intrude at the same time.

My heart clatters against my ribcage.

I freeze, listen.

The voices are coming from the cottages behind the yard.

I let out my breath, move everything to my left hand, and scrabble at the bottom of the box with my right. A ring, gold, topped with a small diamond. I hesitate and then slide it into my hip pocket.

I fold the photos into the papers. Stack them in the waistband of my jeans, lower my top over them. They might be visible, but it will have to do.

I return the boxes to the state in which I found them. Smooth out my clothes.

I wait until I hear the voices again and they're more distant, towards the front of the cottage. Slipping out the rustic Z-frame door, I swear under my breath when the papers catch in the closing gap, pulling at my shirt.

I adjust my clothes, pass the large windows at the side of the house, unhurried, a forced casual stride. My pulse has slowed, but races again when I arrive to find Zara unlocking our gîte, Chloe standing beside her.

§

Chloe accepts the beer with a smile. "I need this." She picks up a letter. "Lana worked at the lesbian bar in Galway, do you know it?"

I say, "Depends on which year. There were different versions over the years and at times they were mixed gay as well as lesbian."

She flips to the first page. "There's no date." Lana's letters are water-damaged, ink smeared into the paper, faded navy blotted on cream.

Zara leans forward on the couch and rifles through the papers on the coffee table. "Could you contact the Gemma who was her boss at the bar?"

"I should be able to find her and the girlfriend. There wouldn't be other Gemma and Tracy partners where one is the owner of the only lesbian bar there at a time." I taste the wine. I've discovered I like *rosé*. "Could track down Gerry and John, Frank's friends."

Chloe says, "Garry." She frowns. "They might say something to

Frank though. We can't risk that."

Zara nods. "I agree. Don't get in contact with them. Just the ex-boss."

"Lana was pregnant!" Chloe breaks in, she's waving the paper,

Zara and I glance at each other. The expression in her eyes changes from curiosity to a more serious note.

Chloe repeats herself, each word distinct. "Lana was pregnant." She lowers the letter. "There wasn't mention of a baby."

I say, "So she might have been pregnant when she left."

She shakes her head. "She doesn't sound happy. David was working again after a long period of sitting at home without a job. Her last day at the bar was to be that week, she couldn't afford for him to find out she had worked in a lesbian and gay bar, or she had gay male friends."

"Here, let me see." I take the papers from Chloe's hands.

Zara gets up and opens the sliding door, letting in a warm breeze from the yard. "He sounds incredibly homophobic."

Chloe says, "The culture is almost fanatically anti-gay. He can't help it if he comes across as homophobic. He can't deal with these things in the Western way. And what with his wife maybe being lesbian, it must have made it worse."

I put the letter on the pile. Lana doesn't come right out and say it but her words hold an undertone of fear.

I shuffle through the photos again. Some are stuck together. They are of Frank at tourist sites in Galway. He was wearing the same jumper and trousers and I assume the photos were taken on the same day. I recognise the Galway Cathedral, Eason's bookshop on Shop Street, the outside of Tigh Neactain's pub, the Quays, the Claddagh. We'd passed them on the Pride march.

One of the stuck photos is of different quality. It's blurred and darker and is inside a room. I pry it off the other photo, taking care but narrow strips of colour remain on the white backing. A thrill goes through me. An Indian couple is posing by a fireplace. It is a copy of the one I'd found in the shed, now in my bedroom at Zara's house.

I say, "Hey, look, this has got to be them."

Chloe and Zara lean in on each side of me.

The room was dark and dwarfed the marginally lighter faces but, despite its damaged surface, the photo captured the perfection of Lana's features, their coffee coloured symmetry soothing, nothing to jar the eye off its smooth path over her face, no specific feature on which to focus. A smoothness which gripped your mind for an instant, before melting away again, slippery, impossible to hold. Lana appeared to be a woman who, if you saw walking down the street, would cause you to steal a second glance, mainly to check if you had seen right the first time, but also because you wanted to experience that instant again.

"She was beautiful." Chloe's tone is hushed.

In a recess of my mind, I wonder why I automatically thought about Lana in the past tense, as Chloe just has.

I stare closer at Lana's face wishing it were clearer. There's something unsettling me.

Zara says, "David looks grouchy."

I realise I haven't paid attention to the man yet. Part of his cheek and nose is missing, peeled off, now. From what remains, he's good-looking, in a dark, unshaven way. Not my type. The thought steals in and I wonder where it came from.

Chloe says, "I'm not sure that's him. It's only a minor resemblance to my David. A friend, or his brother? And he looks tired, more than grouchy."

Zara shakes her head.

I say, "I don't know, Mam, I've to agree with Chloe. He's smiling."

My mother snorts. "His mouth might be smiling." She pokes at the face. "Look at those eyes."

We stare. Into his eyes. It might be an effect of the damaged photo, but I have the urge to reach into that time and room and scoop out the woman beside him. A shiver sweeps through me.

I switch my gaze to Lana, say slowly, "Doesn't she look familiar?"

Chloe holds the photo closer to the light. I stand beside her.

I say, "A little like Isabella." They are similar, but Lana's face is thinner, or it could be the flatness of the two-dimensional image. Same impression of beauty, of skin colour, of thick dark hair. The poor quality and the damage are frustrating.

Chloe says, "You're thinking of Isabella so much, maybe that's why. They're both beautiful women." She puts her hand on my shoulder. I take in her warmth and softness for a moment and then she moves to grab her beer and takes a swig.

She coughs. "I should be going."

Zara smiles. "Will we meet you for dinner later? I want another chat with Isabella now."

Chloe nods. Says to me. "By the way, how was your trip with

Ishmael? He took you on a tour?"

I hope the heat creeping up my neck is not visible. "It was very nice."

She slings her bag on her shoulder.

I ask, "How long has Ishmael been with Frank?"

Chloe arranges the letters and photos into a neat pile. "Can we leave these here for now? Then replace them when possible."

"Remember we need clear tape."

She nods. The bag spins green as she turns to go. "Ishmael has been with him for a few years. They were going out when Frank was in Paris. Frank was friends with Isabella, then she met Henri who was based in Paris and they moved here after she married Henri. From what I gathered that's how Frank got involved in the property. Ishmael wanted to be near his sister and I'd say it made sense for Frank to be here too and work directly in his investment."

I say, "Lana mentions property in Paris. Have to get my head around the details, I'll look through the letters again."

And the novel. Lana seems to have changed the names of three people in it, hers, and David's and Frank's. It's looking less fictional the more I hear of Lana, but Thomas does not match with Chloe's description of David.

I haven't shown them Lana's notebook. I said there were pages of class exercises. Her writing feels private, even more so than her letters to Frank. And if it is fictional, then it would not be fair to fill Chloe's mind with that too.

No.

Not yet.

Zara collects the material together and sits at the dining table, "I'll help."

Chloe smiles. "Thanks you two."

I say, "I understand why you're so fixated on finding out about Lana."

Chloe nods. Her movements are slower, smaller. "I'm glad you're both here. I'll see you later."

I get the feeling Chloe is regretting her curiosity.

I'm annoyed at her twisted defence of David. But then he may not be anything like the supposedly fictional Thomas. Other characters have been changed, what's to say his wasn't as well.

I can't let Chloe, or Zara, read the novel yet. It has worked its words into my mind and I'm not thinking clearly. For all my need to protect

Chloe, I want only the truth in my armoury. Even though I'm worried, I dread their rational dissection of Lana's novel or any railing against her to defend David.

I realise I'm feeling protective, holding her words close, keeping them from my mother and my ex.

And I'm the one who is fixated on Lana now.

The click of Chloe leaving is quiet.

I stay on the couch studying photos and letters as Zara hands them to me. The novel is waiting, but holing up in my room poring over what is only supposed to be a few writing exercises will raise suspicion.

The sun is at its peak outside, blazing onto the table where she sits, and the gîte is filled with lazy warmth when my mother finally decides to take her afternoon nap. I slip away to my bedroom and retrieve the notebook.

Sapna

Galway, Ireland

Sapna smiled at the young dyke. "Thanks, but I can't drink on duty." She could have accepted the drink, but she certainly didn't want to give the wrong impression. And she never flirted with the customers, though her boss laughed and said Sapna didn't have to, her smile and exotic appearance brought in enough extra custom.

She pulled the handle of the Guinness and watched the dark clouded liquid churn into the pint glass. She waited until it was the right level and then set it aside.

A woman was waving a twenty euro note. Sapna had to concentrate, working with the register and the change to euro. They were all still thinking in Irish punts. Everything has gone up in price, not only the actual increase with conversion, but the prices being charged everywhere. At least Gemma hadn't hiked up the drink prices, not yet anyway. Once the drink suppliers put the pressure on, even her stubborn boss would have to comply.

Sapna topped off the Guinness and handed it to the dyke who gave her a shy smile before turning to perch nervously at the bar and survey the room.

Sapna watched with affection as her boss interacted with the customers, leaning over the bar to plant a loud kiss on a woman's lips. Gemma was a flirt with customers, a floozy for the boozy as she jokingly described herself. She ran the lesbian bar with a charm that was the only protection against closure. There wasn't enough money on the lesbian scene, and Gemma did not want to make it a mixed bar. Sapna thought that too would have to change soon.

Gemma left the raucous customers with a tray of shots and slid across the floor to stand beside Sapna. "Hey, kiddo, how's it going? Any more phone numbers?" She smirked.

Sapna smiled. "Not unless you count the ones for you."

"I'm a happily settled woman. You on the other hand."

"I'm a married straight woman."

Gemma cocked her head, "I notice you didn't say 'happily'. What's up, kiddo? Thomas giving you trouble?"

Sapna shook her head, but she could see the doubt in Gemma's eyes. She was grateful when a woman leant against the bar and ordered a drink.

Two young women got up to leave and Gemma went around from the counter to clear up the glasses. An older woman dragged down the last drops from her beer glass and all three made their way out into the night. Gemma locked the door behind them and pulled out a bucket and mop from the cupboard built into the wall behind the counter. She brushed away Sapna's offers of help and began the nightly ritual of washing the day's business from the dark stained wood floor. The chemical lemon of cleaning fluid blended with the beer smell in the bar. Outside the wind howled and spat the rain against the doors and windows.

Sapna sorted out the registers and they worked in silence, broken only by the occasional hiss of the coffee machine and the swishing of the mop. When she finished, Gemma tidied everything away and went in behind the counter and took down the open bottle of Baileys which she poured out into a glass. Sapna sat on a bar stool and sipped at the cream liquor.

Gemma poured herself a whisky and took a long gulp. "Aaah. How do you drink that sweet stuff?"

Sapna smiled. "I don't really drink. I don't like the taste of alcohol. This is more desserty."

"I know. I know. And we can't have the husband getting angry with you." Gemma twisted her mouth. "Though he is allowed to drink himself stupid whenever he wants."

Sapna stared at the water-stained floor. "He doesn't."

"Then what does he do all day now?"

Sapna sighed. Tiredness stalked her bones. "He reads, he studies, he sits."

"He drinks and he gripes at you."

"He has reason, doesn't he?"

Gemma tapped her finger on the counter. "It's not your fault he failed the exam." She tapped again. "Neither is it your fault he lost his job." Tap. "Or that he can't handle the fact that you work." Tap. "And work two jobs at that. I mean how many hours have you already done at the counselling job before you get here?" Tap. "He's a male chauvinist and I can't believe in this day and age you can't tell your husband you work in a lesbian bar. What would happen? Do you think he'll think you're lesbian, as if we infected you or something?"

Heat roared into her cheeks. She rested her elbows on the counter and placed her face in her palms, but Gemma noticed. "What is it? Sapna?"

155

Sapna laughed. "Nothing. What?"

"You've gone red. Though it is more purple in your case. Who knew Indians could blush."

Sapna said, "It's warm in here. I'm tired, long day." She looked at her watch. "Is that the time?" She scrambled off the stool, "Oh no. Thomas is going to be so angry."

Gemma frowned. "Don't let him push you around. Remember, you haven't done anything wrong. In fact, you're one hell of a woman. He's fecking blind if he can't see that."

Sapna gathered her coat and put it on, fumbling in the pocket for her keys. Gemma walked her to the door and unlocked it. The street lamps were surrounded by misty halos. They both gazed up at the night sky.

Gemma said, "Be careful driving back. At least it's stopped raining."

Sapna tightened the jacket around her waist and shivered. She didn't want to leave the warm, dry comfort of the pub. She hoped Thomas was asleep, but he hadn't been the last weeks when she got home from a night shift. He'd been in bed, but not asleep.

Her car was parked within sight of the pub door, but Gemma walked her to it and waited until she opened the door. It was a Friday night and the streets were almost empty, the pause between the pub crowd and the nightclub crowd.

Gemma pulled the lapels of Sapna's jacket closer around her neck. Her heart thudded at the touch of fingers on her skin. She wondered if Gemma could see the rising warmth of colour in her face. The streetlight above them cast shadows over Gemma's eyes.

Sapna knew Gemma was happy with her partner. Gemma never flirted with her, but Sapna caught herself wishing the woman was single, then berating herself for the thought though it was never in concrete form, more wisps of feelings that rose in her chest, danced over her face, teased her belly, and spread its silk tentacles down her thighs. Thoughts and feelings that horrified Sapna, but she could not stop them.

Gemma raised Sapna's chin, her fingers sending a tingle down Sapna's throat. Gemma's voice was soft. "You're better than this, Sapna. Don't let anyone, man or woman, convince you of anything else."

Sapna looked up at the face above her, drank in the scent of skin that wasn't scratchy, lips curved softly into a smile, eyelashes sweeping down and up in the flutter of wings. She longed to run her fingers through the thick auburn hair curled around ears, falling to shoulders that were broad and strong and gentle.

She saw an awareness creep into Gemma's eyes, and, for a moment, a long, changing, devastating moment, Sapna looked into a woman's eyes and saw a matching desire, one that finally had a name.

She closed her eyes. Felt their hearts thudding against their chests. Gemma's body had tightened, she sensed that through her jacket and Gemma's T-shirt. They stood under the lamp, under a circle of light, saying goodbye to the moments that would never happen. Lips touching her forehead burned with gentleness, and then there was only cold space pressing against her chest.

She drove home slowly through the quiet streets of Galway, manoeuvring the car around the stragglers coming out early from the nightclubs. She was not afraid of being stopped by the gardai, she was well under the limit after only sipping at the Baileys. No, she had no fear of that. She almost wished she was drunk and could get locked up if stopped by the gardai. Then she wouldn't have to go home. Wouldn't have to face his anger, the cold hatred, the red rage, the smell of alcohol on his breath as he begged for forgiveness, wouldn't have to endure his hands on her skin.

She was glad he fell asleep each night before he realised she never responded to his advances, that he hadn't gotten further than groping her breasts. She didn't think he would take no for an answer and the thought of him on her, in her, filled her with dread. She had a sick feeling in her stomach as she wondered what his reaction would be if he ever found out she now worked in a lesbian bar and not on the Samaritans helpline. He had let her work on the phone line though it was housed in the same building as the AIDS helpline because she promised him she'd never come in contact with 'the gays' all the while hating herself for referring to her friends in such a way. She thought he was fine with it because he could tell his colleagues his wife did charitable work for those people society shunned.

She couldn't bear the thought of giving up the job at the bar now. It was such a different job to anything she'd ever imagined she would do, but she'd taken to it, a duck to water, as Gemma had described it. A wee Indian duck, mind you. Sapna smiled at the memory. Tears dropped into a well inside her at what could never be. She had already tucked away the contents of her unnatural dreams, of her sick desires, and her mind was back to her reality. Her heart would follow, she would make it comply, as she'd always done.

The smile slipped off her face as she turned into the driveway of the house they still rented from her brother-in-law. The light was on in the living room, Thomas was awake.

The nausea rose again. Sapna had successfully suppressed the urge to throw up over the last client, but she was losing the fight now. Sweat broke out on her forehead as she tried in vain to listen and hear the words of her current client.

"Are you okay?" The client was perched on the chair looking at her with concern.

Sapna shook her head.

"My time is almost up anyway. You don't look so hot, no worries if you need to stop early."

Sapna nodded. The saliva poured into her mouth forcing her to swallow. "I'm so sorry. If you don't mind?"

The woman jumped up and grabbed her bag. "Sure loveen, no worries. I'll see ya next week?"

Sapna nodded.

After the client had left, Sapna sat and let the waves of nausea crash and pass.

She called Gemma. She needed to give her enough time to get a replacement for the bar tonight. Or Gemma might cover it herself, Tuesday nights were never busy.

The conversation was short. Sapna could not manage to stay on the phone for long, the sickness had lessened, but it was still there. Gemma was concerned, urged her to come in anyway and rest on the couch in the upstairs room the staff used for their belongings. Gemma didn't say the words, not to go back to the house, but Sapna could hear it in the worry threaded through Gemma's voice.

She'd never told Gemma what had happened with Thomas that night, a mixture of shame and disgust combined to keep the words down. For the last three months, she'd watched Gemma and her partner, whenever Tracy was at the bar, Sapna had stored the sight in her heart, in a secret place that believed touch could be welcome, could be pleasurable. Most of all, she imagined she could be clean again. None of it made sense to her anymore. How could the sight of two women together, affectionate, loving, touching, how could that be clean?

And now she was pregnant.

She touched her belly, wondered how a new life could make her so sick.

Sapna wished she hadn't been brought up in a family, in a society, that so hated abortion her father had stated outright a woman being raped was no excuse at all. No question, no debate. Tears prickled at her lids. She wondered if he'd be so adamant even now, when it was his own daughter. The tears fell, slid down her cheeks, carrying the knowledge it would make no difference to him, though he was an educated man, a gentle man. And to him, she would not have been raped. Not in a marriage.

And she could not face the thought of destroying her child. Not when she had always wanted a child of her own. She was not sure she could bring this child into life though.

She slipped her hand under her blouse, felt the trickle of blood on her abdomen. She lifted the cream material away from the stain and stared in a daze at the lines of red. They were not alone on her torso. They were merely the freshest.

Her fingers snatched at the buttons of the blouse. She pulled off the cotton, her movements jerky, her breathing heavy and fast. She was sitting in her office, in her trousers and bra. She cupped her breasts, watched her tears slide over them, their path obstructed, twisted momentarily, by the raised edges of the scars.

It was her birthday tomorrow. There was a new dress waiting for her. Her present.

Her future.

She knew it would be thin and gauzy. He enjoyed living dangerously now, gaining a sort of control by showing her off, excited by the risk of her bruises being visible.

CHAPTER THIRTEEN

The bamboo fence hems in a rectangle of grass and sand, its jagged tubes sawing through a sky stained crimson by the dying sun.

Zara coming in from the bathroom wakes me out of my darkening reverie.

My joints crack as I stretch, after hours sitting at the dining table hunched over my phone following one referral after the other through the Galway scene until I got to talk to Gemma.

"Any luck? Does Gemma know where she is or what happened?"

I ease out the tightness in my neck. "All we can do is wait. If she can find out anything, she will."

Gemma was shocked to hear from me, remembers Lana well, but hadn't heard from her since she stopped working at the bar.

"They'd had a going-away do for her. She'd hoped Lana would contact her once the baby came, but understood when there was no word at all." I rub my eyes. "Gemma hoped she left town and was happy somewhere."

She sits beside me. "Why did she hope that? Did she say why?"

"Sorry, yes." Worry congeals to stone in my stomach. "They only knew Lana's husband as Thomas. Lana was afraid of her husband finding out where she worked and that she'd hung out with gays and lesbians. So she stopped working there. Gemma couldn't tell me much about Thomas, just her impression of Lana's reluctance to go home and details she let slip about her life. Gemma thought he might have been drinking after he lost his job and that's how Lana could work."

Zara frowns. "Lana told them a different name?"

I select my words. "I skimmed the first pages of her writing in Galway when we found the notebooks and her main character's husband is called Thomas."

The rest of my conversation with Gemma was sketchy and, as I fill

Zara in, I'm aware it hints at a picture of fear. I'm uneasy because Lana lied to her boss and friend about her husband's real name. She used the name of a fictional character from her book. The more I discover, the less I want to share her writing with anyone here.

I wrap my palms around my coffee mug, the porcelain cold. "None of this has to mean it ended badly. Let's wait until Gemma checks it out. She'll probably find Lana and the baby are living somewhere, maybe she was the one who left Thomas or David and found a new man. Or woman."

My mother's hand warms mine as she protects my fingers and tops up my coffee from the stainless steel cafetière. "Why? Is Lana gay?"

I release my grip on the mug and catch her hand. My words are slow. "Not as far as Gemma knew. She said she wondered sometimes."

Zara says, "I did too." My palm rests in hers, and she pinches my fingertips, an unconscious habit of hers that amuses and comforts me normally.

"You did?"

"Uh-huh. The way Lana wrote about Gemma and the women. It was all matter-of-fact for Frank, but if you learn to read between the lines…"

Bitterness seeps into my voice. "Gemma hinted for someone who spent time with lesbians, Lana had this cultural thing against lesbianism. She was wonderful to the customers, but could not accept the idea of it. And she stayed with Thomas. She was having a child with him. She quit her job. She made the choice to keep whatever she felt hidden. If she even felt something."

Zara nods. "Many do. They allow the demands of their own small social setting matter more than what is in their own heart."

"Ouch." I withdraw my fingers from hers. She forgets sometimes and squeezes hard, painfully, while talking.

I rattle my phone around the mug, it rings hollow on the wood surface. "Love is love. How can you hide from it, throw it away because of your society? What's bloody society, anyway? Just another group of humans making another set of rules to control what its members do."

The room pushes in on me. I jump up, walk to the window. The courtyard shimmers as the heat recedes from the day's assault.

The pane is cool for a moment against my forehead, my breath forming a patch on the glass. "The way Gemma refers to Lana with so much affection, this happy weird wee Indian woman, doesn't gel with the Lana in the letters. She is so controlled, so proper. Telling Frank all the ordinary stuff, David this and David that, studying for his exams, then failing them, then losing his job. Where was she in there? Why didn't she leave him? And being friends with the women in the bar and gay men like Frank and his pals but continuing to judge their sexuality as wrong?"

I swivel away from the stupor and towards the table. My mother pats the seat of the chair I'd vacated and I sit, feeling the hard edge of my anger. She says, "The letters signalled more than they said. In the words that are harder to see. And she might have fallen in love with David, at least it hints at that in the earlier ones, she describes him as charismatic. He certainly had an effect on her. It's a different culture, and with the arranged marriage, we can't appreciate it here, but countless marriages are like that, with a deep bond and they last a long time. There's a need to answer to family." The blue of her eyes dims. "Sometimes people do things for their family and society, that isn't what they truly want, but the need to fit in is so strong, it's survival really. It is the same as you needing Chloe to not be bisexual. You wanting to belong to the lesbian scene so desperately that it affects your decisions, who you love, who you partner." She smiles, but her eyes stay sad. "Sometimes, my wee cub, I wonder how you are so blind in some ways and so wonderfully awake in others. You write beautifully on lesbian issues, racism. And yet I wonder if you truly understand the human heart."

I rise again, pushing back the chair, scraping the legs against the lino. "I understand enough. I understand people hurt others by trying to live to what their society decides is suitable. That you can't trust anyone to choose you over being accepted by a group." My fist clenches. "No matter who makes up the group. I mean, even if they are a crowd of judgmental creeps. Why would a woman who isn't concerned what her so-called friends think, why hide the fact she loves a woman? Why would she put those acquaintances, those strangers, the church, why ever put them before someone she *loves*, purely to remain in that group?"

"Chloe might have come around to being open about your relationship."

"Wasn't referring to Chloe." Mumble because I was. "I meant the women before her."

"And you let your feelings and your hurt from them spoil what you had with Chloe."

Glaring at her, the same exasperation rises in me. Since we met Chloe here, they've been making insinuations. As if somehow the breakup was my fault. "How on earth am I getting the blame for Chloe walking out on me? Even if it wasn't a proper state-recognised wedding, she bloody walked out on our commitment ceremony!"

Zara says, "Did you love Chloe? As in 'can't breathe without her.' I mean, really really love her?"

I sigh, raise my eyebrow. "That's a stupid question, wouldn't have asked her to marry me otherwise."

"You didn't answer my question."

"Of course I loved her. She took my breath away."

Zara shakes her head. "You still haven't answered my question."

I shove the phone in my jeans pocket. "Did so. You always took her side, anyway." I pivot, march to the front door, and swing it open. "Going to have a drink, hang around people who won't find a way to blame me for someone else's really hurtful actions."

The stubborn teenager is satisfied but the adult winces as the door slams on Zara's words. Both agree I'll be damned if I let them keep blaming me for something that's not my doing.

I'm confused by the swirling words, by the talk with Gemma, by Lana making up a false name for her husband, by Sapna lying to Thomas about her work, friends, and her feelings, though from a novel and not real, but that is what's blurred and it's making me crazy.

Zara and Chloe are confused too, and they haven't even read the rest of Lana's words. The book is waiting, but my time can't be spent reading. It's crucial to make use of my limited time here with the real characters.

Maybe I'm not showing the other writings to them because it's important to me to believe Lana, and to avoid them being drawn into the fiction. But we're probably all reading too much into it. And I'm unsettled by the novel. If it is fictional, then I have to be fair to Chloe and not permit the story to influence my view of David. Or Frank and Ishmael.

Why are all the names real, except Lana's and David's and Frank's?

Does Lana not putting her name to it suggest the novel is more likely to be made-up rather than the actual events? Or that her fear was justified.

My legs tremble, standing in the heated courtyard. I search in my pockets for the key and touch an object.

The ring.

I'd forgotten it was there. It must be Lana's wedding ring.

The sun sparks bright off the diamond, dull off the gold. One tiny circle that locks in two hearts, two lives.

I'm sure Lana did not feel the all-consuming 'can't breathe' love for David.

Will I ever feel it?

Sapna

Galway, Ireland

The sweat oozed from his pores and settled around the roots of the hairs on his forearms. The drops glittered in the candlelight. It was warm, but not that warm, she thought.

He had pulled up the sleeves of his formal blue shirt and the darker line of wet fabric cut against the muscle in the thick part of his forearm.

She pushed a piece of meat around on her plate and watched the sleeve stretch tight and loose, tight and loose, against his elbow each time he took a mouthful of wine.

"Good wine, this," Thomas said and pushed the glass towards her. "You can take a little, the baby will be fine."

She took a sip and nodded. It was awful, tasting cheap and thick despite its price, an instant corrosive in her dry mouth. She swallowed and smiled, trying to make the grimace as sweet as the liquid.

Her card leant against the bottle of wine.

They had gone to the French restaurant because he liked the thought of being a French property owner. It was what kept them in a home, he said. Not her two jobs. But she knew the income from the property in Paris was nowhere near enough, he needed to assert his manhood.

Though it was her dowry that had bought their share.

He had ordered the 'chateeyo briyandeh' and she'd seen the waiter's eyebrow twitch but his facial expression had remained chiselled on his face. Even French waiters remain polite for him she thought.

The waiter returned an eternity later placing their plates with precision and she stared at the thick red cylinders of beef sticking out of the crimson sauce, periscopes that swivelled and stared back at the two of them sitting there, dining out, as if they belonged in such a civilised place.

She heard a quiet sound every few seconds, a rasp she knew was coming from his mouth when he took the meat off the fork. His eyes had taken on the dull glaze of scratched marble as he chewed and she wondered whether he heard the whimpers every time his teeth came together. There she was, comparing herself to a dead cow, but that would be quick, being struck over the head with a mechanical hammer, no more having to control her cries till they were rumours, passed through the house, tossed and turned in the undercurrent, drowned in the music.

As she'd expected, he had wanted her to wear the gauzy dress this evening and he checked in every few minutes on what was his underneath. He had made her wear it despite the bruises with their evenly spaced indentations that lay there angry and chafed. The most recent was hours old, the oldest was 3 months old, the same age as the embryo growing in her, his baby, the news of which had sparked this fascination with her breasts as a new site.

The prize for the first bruise, though, went to her stomach, her first scream of pain and surprise rewarded with a possessive smile and then a tight-fisted grip on her wrist.

The three months of training worked well, after the years of caution, the whimpers stopped deep in her throat now. She wondered whether the expensive candlelight hid those tribal marks or whether the waiter crossed himself as he walked away grateful for his job, the worst part of which was probably being yelled at by the chef or the possible threat of dismissal.

Sapna wiped the salt water from her cheeks. The wind felt cold and bracing against her cheek after the over-heated air of the office with its cushions that smelled of despair. She was glad her work was near the ocean, close enough for her to walk to the promenade, grab a sandwich, and eat it on one of the benches facing the water.

Garry and John worked in a multimedia company right up the street from the prom. They were usually a welcome distraction from her clients and her life.

She saw their car pull into the parking area that lined the oceanfront and waved them over.

She smiled as they got their usual picnic basket out of the boot. She grimaced at her supermarket sandwich. She wasn't suffering anymore from morning sickness, but the sight of her food was still turning her stomach.

John's hug was tight. He leant back and smiled. "The bump is starting to show."

She frowned. "I put on weight, that's my stomach."

She laughed at his expression. "Just kidding. Yes, I'm starting to show."

Garry gave her a hug. "Good to see you smile, love."

Sapna said, "What else can I do?" They settled down on the bench.

"I see the ocean and count each wave as a blessing. When you hear the stories I do, you learn to be grateful."

Garry put his arm around her shoulder and squeezed.

John opened the lid of the picnic basket. "I'm grateful Garry doesn't pack our lunch every day."

Garry said, "What did I forget this time?"

"Only the thermos with the tea."

"Oh bugger." Garry got to his feet "Okay, be right back."

John took out the wraps, set aside Garry's and peeled off the cling film. "Have you heard from Victoria recently?"

Sapna said, "I got a letter last week. I didn't get a chance to write back yet."

"Did you tell her about the baby?"

Sapna nodded. She had mentioned being pregnant in the last letter, but she'd phoned Victoria after and talked to her. Victoria had sensed something was wrong. Sapna wasn't sure if her reassurances were convincing, they sounded hollow even to her.

John said, "You need to tell someone else about this too. She could help. Or you need to let me help."

"If Thomas found out Victoria knew anything or she is with Ismael, he'd find a way to destroy her. Especially now Thomas holds the majority share in the business. And nobody would believe me anyway. He's the one who has colleagues and friends who respect him. I'm the one who sat at home, who never went to any of his work parties. They don't know I wanted to, but he preferred to go on his own."

John glanced over his shoulder in the direction Garry had left to go to the supermarket. "I've been in your position before, I can understand. Garry wouldn't, why you don't leave, he'd jump in there with all guns blazing." He put the wrap down, unbitten. "But I'm not sure how much longer I can sit back and not do something, Sapna. That bastard deserves to be in jail. Or at least beaten up and left in an alley somewhere." He turned. "Hey, I know people who would oblige?"

Sapna shook her head, worried at the seconds delay in her response.

"What about your family? Surely your parents would help."

"My father is sick. I can't worry him. They were so happy about the baby."

"You told them?"

"No, Thomas got to them first."

John frowned. "He's still the golden boy to them?"

Sapna nodded. "He's expert at that. My aunt thinks Thomas is the sweetest guy for taking on the older sister of a woman who disgraced her family. They all think he's been so understanding, so heroic. And he feeds off that, fills them up with it. He told my mother I had become withdrawn from his friends, I wasn't able to make friends. And she believed him. I think they laughed at my quiet ways."

"How is the savings fund going?"

Sapna clutched at her belly. "Slow, really slow. It's a bit better since Thomas went back to work. He's stopped drinking. He says he's going to pass the exam this time, for his kid."

"Don't tell me you believe him?"

"I believe he believes what he's saying. He doesn't remember what he's done. He has this whole new vision of us, of himself, doesn't see what he did. I'm afraid to set him off again. It's as if the past year never happened."

John reached across the picnic basket and held her hand. "I ran away. I couldn't tell anyone, not after my fight to be accepted as gay, and then I end up with a guy who abuses me. I get that, I get you can't tell your folks. I'm so lucky to have Garry. You'd have us. Granted that's scary, but you wouldn't be totally alone."

Lana said, *"I couldn't stay in Galway."* She glanced back at the hotels looming over the pavement, aware Garry would be back soon. As sweet as he was, as caring as he was, she didn't want anyone to know. The shame slithered under her skin, *"I should have left before, but he was never physical with me, not like this. Now there's the baby to think of. He'll never let me leave now. This baby is proof to the world he's still a man. That he's as good as his brother, he didn't deserve to get the leftovers."*

"He said that? About you?"

"Not in so many words, though it was pretty close. And now he's cleaning up and being sweet and it makes me sick. I'm some kind of vessel for his glory." She sighed. *"I'm going to have to give up working."* Her eyes filled. *"It's my last night at the bar on Friday. Will you two come to it?"*

John squeezed her hand. *"Of course we will. I'll make sure Garry gets off his arse and comes out. He was so happy when the bar became mixed, but then we never go out."* He looked past her. *"I'd better let him back, he's been standing at the car with the tea."*

Sapna said, *"Oh no! And lunchtime is almost over."*

John waved at Garry. *"He can eat fast. This was important."* He smiled as he reached into the picnic basket and moved a thermos flask aside. *"He'll make a great father someday."*

Sapna smiled. *"I wonder what Thomas would do if I asked you both to be the baby's godfathers."*

John gave a short laugh. *"Whatever you do, don't tell him that."*

Garry sat on the bench, on the other side of John. He handed John the carryout tea. "Don't tell him what?"

Sapna said, "We're not going to tell Thomas his baby is going to have two gay guys as godfathers." She chuckled.

Garry's eyes lit up. "I'm going to be a godfather?"

John patted his knee. "Only if you keep it quiet. Otherwise we'll all be swimming with the fishes."

Cold spattered pinpricks against her skin. She wasn't sure if they were from the ocean spray or the thought of Thomas finding out she had gay friends, had been working in a lesbian bar. That she was exactly what he made her out to be, crazy. Because she had experienced desire for a woman, more than she had ever for him.

She had to stop working at the bar. Not for his sake, for hers.

Sapna watched from the other side of the bar as her replacement chatted with Denise and felt a stab of envy. The woman was a boi dyke as Gemma had described her, short blonde hair slicked back, handsome with a face that looked like she was in her twenties though really in her thirties. She had piercings in her lip and in her eyebrow and the simple silver rings added a touch of rakishness. Sapna had a flash of what her mother's reaction would be to this woman, not that her mother would call her a woman, more a mentally ill deviant. Sapna shivered, trying to get the injected venom out of her system.

"What can I get you, and your friends? It's on the house, of course." Gemma leant over the bar to give Sapna a kiss on her cheek.

A deeper pain settled in her chest, not one of envy, but of regret. Not only for losing the company of Gemma and the friends she'd made working at the bar. For the times she could have had, the loves she might have experienced. But she knew it wouldn't be real love, it couldn't be, not between two women.

She smiled, "They're having real drinks. Or beers at least. Two Heineken, please. I'll have to have a glass of non-alcoholic beer since we don't sell non-alcoholic cream liquor." She was aware she'd said 'we' and she'd have to stop thinking that way.

Gemma chuckled. "Coming right up." She took the pint glasses down and pulled down at the handle. "I'm going to miss your weird Indian ways."

Sapna laughed. "Weird Indian ways? I think the weirdness might just be me."

Gemma set the pint glasses on the counter in front of Sapna. She was grinning. "No clue of any other Indian woman so I'll have to take your word for it." She laughed and shook her head. "Though I haven't met anyone who could work at a lesbian bar and get on with all women while thinking it is wrong." She got a bottle of Beck's out of the bar fridge, scooped ice into a glass, and filled it with the non-alcoholic beer.

An unexpected craving for alcohol surged in Sapna. The thread of fear tightened in her stomach. She was not going to harm the baby growing in her, but the need to lose control, leave her body behind, the need screamed at her as she stood there in control at the bar and let her life become a prison.

And she was aware losing control of herself might open up a floodgate of emotions.

"Sapna?" Gemma waved her hand in front of Sapna's face.

Sapna pulled herself back into the room, saw Gemma's concern in the knot of her eyebrows. Sapna smiled. "In case I don't get a chance to say goodbye, I want to thank you, you have no idea what you and the bar have done for me."

Gemma walked around the counter and took her into a hug. She whispered into Sapna's ear, and Sapna could hear the shake in her voice through the chatter and music, "I wish we could have done more. Please take care. Leave him if you can, not for anyone, for you."

The tears prickled behind her eyelids. She nodded, the movement brushing Gemma's shoulder. "Soon. Maybe soon."

Gemma leant back and smiled. "You know I'm going to make a wee speech now, don't you? We all kind of love you, didn't think we'd let you go without embarrassing you, did you?"

Sapna's throat was tight, her voice thick. "Of course not, why would tonight be any different? As long as you don't mention my first attempt at pulling a pint of Guinness."

Gemma grinned. "But that's my favourite memory! You hold the record for the fastest pint of Guinness pulled here. Maybe in Galway. Maybe even in all of Ireland."

Sapna laughed. "Okay, okay." She kissed Gemma's cheek. "Why on earth did you give me a job in the bar when I'd never had a real drink before and I thought lesbians and gays were mentally ill?"

"That's why I'll make it someday as a businesswoman, I see potential in people. You can't help what you were taught. You turned out to be one of my best employees." Her eyes were sad. "And a good friend." She frowned. "No getting sad. Time to give you a proper send-off, Galway style."

Gemma turned and rapped the empty Beck's bottle on the counter. The sound did not make a dent in the noisy bar. Gemma climbed up on a stool and yelled, "Hey! Shut up!"

Sapna smiled as the crowd quietened down after a couple more requests. She was used to Gemma's going-away speeches for her bar staff or women from the scene and had always been touched by the response from the people at the bar, most of whom she had become friends with in a way that had warmed her heart on many nights over the years.

She knew they considered her a bit of an oddity, a straight Indian woman working at a lesbian bar. Sapna sensed that for the first months. She knew they found it hard to understand her culture didn't allow her to accept their actions, but she thought they understood she accepted them, liked them, and even loved some of them. She realised now as she felt the matching tears in her eyes and the laughter at another of Gemma's teasing remarks, that for most of the time she'd felt more at home here, in their shared refuge from the day, than anywhere else.

CHAPTER FOURTEEN

The noise level is at early evening chatter, not yet the shouted orders stage. I recognise faces and exchange greetings with a few. There are various flavours of tourists, the majority English or French from another part of France, and locals who divide into those who are friendly and welcoming, and those who nurse their double whiskies and Coke and dispense sullen scowls to the foreigners, as they refer to anyone not born in the village.

Ishmael and two young French women are working the bar. He greets me with a smile and gets a demi-glass, adds the grenadine syrup and taps in beer over it. I've taken to their weird custom of wrecking the beer by adding different syrups and using half-glasses.

I sit on a stool and gulp at the red-stained liquid. It doesn't wash out the creepy taste in my mind. Or the determination that burns in me to find Lana.

I ask, "Is Isabella working tonight?"

Ishmael nods at the dining room. I swivel. Isabella and a man are sitting at a table, she's facing away from us, dark locks glossy under the low chandeliers.

He says, "Her husband, Henri."

The man is pleasant-looking. I'd put him at mid-fifties. His hairline is a few centimetres further up his forehead than it probably was in his youth, brown hair, brown eyes. He could have been described as handsome if his ears cosied up more to his head.

I say, "He looks kind."

The frown on Ishmael's face dissolves when I turn. "A decent guy."

"Then why the look?"

He smiles. "You caught me. Well, he is kind, but also chairman of the hunting club."

"Ah." I point at notices on the wall. "So, the petition to protect our little deer could not have pleased him?"

Ishmael grimaces. "No. And he's upset his wife and her brother are the ones who put the notices up here. And we're on the side of the group that wants to let the deer stay in the herd of cows."

"How did Isabella meet him?"

A man leans against the counter and orders a pint of Heineken. He's wearing shorts and his shirt is open, exposing red hairs lost on a plump sunburnt chest. The smell of sweat and alcohol assails me, memories of a street in Dublin, but the futility of slathered suntan lotion and his cheeky grin are innocent. He addresses me, "Pardon-moi Mademoiselle, I voulez beer."

Ishmael bends to grab a pint glass off a shelf under the bar. He pours the draft beer and places it on the counter, gestures and moves to the register at the other end. The man grins again at me before grabbing the pint and following.

I watch Isabella's table between the ebb and flow of people.

Only her back is visible, but I catch an occasional glimpse of Henri through the crowd. He is focused on her face and the couple appear to be in an animated discussion but his mouth isn't moving much.

Ishmael has returned. "They met in Paris. Henri was working for a large insurance company. He always wanted to set up a branch here, in his home village, but they sent him to the city for a long time. Isabella was heartbroken over a breakup and I suspected it was a rebound thing. She insisted it wasn't, she was tired of confused people and Henri was a gentle and decent man who loved her and made her happy."

I say, "Who did she break up with? Someone in Paris?"

The space is filling up and customers wave to get his attention. Ishmael offers me an apologetic smile and hurries to serve them.

I drink my beer and study Isabella and Henri, trying to put my finger on their mismatch as a couple. She is full of pent-up energy, colourful, and soaring, he, a balloon in her slipstream, bearing an infinitesimal unhurried leak.

An image of Lana fills my mind. Isabella is the same height and the same slim build, similar skin colour, a shade darker in life, but the photo light was bad and I picture Lana as fairer in life. Her tresses falls thick and dark over her shoulders, same as in the photo.

"Are you admiring Isabella?" Chloe's voice almost topples me off the stool.

She and Zara are standing beside me, drinks in hand.

I right myself. "In fact, I was thinking of Lana."

Chloe is wearing a green dress which matches her eyes and shows off her blondeness and tan. I think she notices my appreciation because she blushes. "I love shopping with Zara. She picked this out for me."

My breath whistles out. "Good choice. My mother has excellent taste, especially for other people's clothes."

Zara laughs. "Do you not like what I'm wearing?" Her jacket is a silky patterned mix of greens and browns, worn over a purple silk chemise and cream trousers and a turquoise bandanna clutches onto her silver hair.

I say, "Actually I do. Nice, mam."

"I got the jacket today at the store in Rochechouart, isn't it lovely? They have wonderful old churches, but don't have the fashion style here of Paris, though there are hidden treasures if you know how to put it all together."

Chloe says. "I'm eager to see what you put together for the wedding."

Zara examines the piece of lint she's picked off my jeans. "I bought a dress for you for the party on Wednesday evening. Tonight, I'm going for the Dame Judi Dench look, but I'm glad I brought the Jane Fonda outfit, I'll wear it for the dance."

I brush at my cotton top. "Thought it was just a local band on the terrace, I didn't realise we were going formal on it."

Chloe grins. "We weren't, but Zara got excited shopping and hey, it's a party after all." She touches my cheek, how she used to when teasing me about my stubbornness over something or the other. "You look great as usual, but I confess I'm looking forward to seeing that dress on you."

My heart is pounding, at the memories, at her nearness, though she is out of reach.

She stops, holds my gaze for a few seconds, then moves her hand to her bag, peers at her phone. "Are you hungry?" She swallows, gestures between Zara and me to the kitchen doors. "There's a stand-in chef covering until the main guy gets back on Monday and he's first-rate too."

Zara nods. "I'll eat any food you put out for me. Doesn't even have to be French."

I mumble. "Could eat too."

Chloe says. "Let's grab a table then. Frank is off tonight, so he'll be coming."

I was hungrier before Chloe mentioned next week when we return to Ireland. Before she looked at me, for those familiar seconds.

§

"You created a wonderful place here." I recline in my chair and sigh, content.

The restaurant has turned over twice at least, except ours, Isabella's, and a table of eight, a family having dinner together, their French loud and cheerful.

Frank says. "I'm proud of it."

Chloe says, "Henri said it used to be rundown."

Frank tugs at his beard. "Yes. He was overjoyed when we bought the buildings. So was the commune. The town council were pleased too, and the Mayor did what he could to sweeten the deal. This building had been sitting unused for two years though it was a successful enough business before. The whole complex had so much potential and I'm proud we developed it in a manner that works for everyone."

I say, "How did you discover it?"

Frank swallows a mouthful of lemonade. The red liquid glints in the wavering flame of a candle resting in a tin holder. "I owned a house in Paris. A holiday rental. Henri was the broker who handled our insurance needs there. He's from the village, born and bred here. His family used to own the place many years ago, the restaurant and bar. He was upset it was sitting empty. Told me I'd be better off to sell the property there and buy here."

Zara says, "Ah, so you got your partner, this David guy to invest?"

He nods. "We were already partners in the rental property. It made sense."

I say, "So did you guys get to use the rental? For holidays and stuff?"

Frank is nudging an asparagus spear on a tour of his plate. "I moved over to stay in one floor of the building and they came over every once in a while for the weekend."

"They? David and Lana?" Chloe reaches across me for the salt. I get the scent of her perfume, light and floral. She's using the same fragrance and it spurs a flash of memory, of her spraying it on my wrists, laughing when I crinkled my nose. I'd been wearing a dress, a lace black one, and we were preparing for a Christmas party at her workplace. We attended as friends.

Frank says, "Yes. David and Lana."

Zara says, "That must be so nice. Doctors don't get paid as well in Ireland as they do in other countries, but they certainly get more than most other professions. What did you do before you retired? Do I remember Chloe mentioning you were a surgeon in England?"

Frank nods. "Worked in general surgery for decades. I retired early and moved to Paris immediately before the boom, lucky me."

I say, "It was lucky too to have David as your partner. In college in Galway many Indian medical and science students were unpleasantly surprised when they discovered I was doing an Arts degree."

Frank's fingers desert the asparagus and lightly tap on the red and white checked tablecloth. "I found that too. There were a heap of Indian doctors in London. That's how I met David. He and his brother, Cherian, both were at college there. They grew up in Saudi Arabia."

Chloe asks, "Was Lana from Saudi Arabia too? I hear women are treated horribly there."

"No, they had an arranged marriage. David went to India to meet her. Her dowry is how he could afford to buy into the Paris property."

I say, "They still do the whole dowry thing? That's crazy."

Frank waves his hand. "Isn't it?" A sheen of red creeps up his neck, into his beard and cheeks. "I couldn't get over the way David assumed it was his total right to make the decisions for them."

Chloe is gripping her fork and knife, her knuckles pale.

Zara says, "Indian men can be misogynistic. They're raised with a sense of privilege. Taught in subtle ways women are there to serve them. Their mothers don't help the problem, they treat their sons as gods and aim to find a wife for them who will treat them the same."

My mother has voiced her opinion on this before. She's also told me my father was a college student in New York when they met. Her family, Irish Catholics, wouldn't have approved of the brown man. And his family, Indian Hindus, wouldn't have approved of the white girl. She was willing to tell me the little information she had on him, but I had no wish to know. What he'd given me was all I needed from him. I wanted no more from someone who could leave his love, and his unborn child, for the sake of his family or society.

Isabella approaches our table, Henri trailing behind.

Zara waves at her. "Join us, please. We can move a table over." She pokes me and I jump up as does Frank.

Isabella smiles. "Thank you. I want you to meet my husband." She moves aside to let him near the table. "Zara, this is Henri."

On closer scrutiny, Henri is vaguely handsome, his beige suede jacket smooth except for a patch on each arm rubbed in the wrong direction. He gives Zara a warm smile. He leans forward and presses a kiss on each cheek. "Madame Zara, a great pleasure to meet you." His voice is melodic, the French accent present, but tamed, more city than that of the locals.

Isabella kisses me twice, lips soft on my cheeks. This time her scent is wild and musky. "Jaya, my husband, Henri."

Henri and I do the embarrassed shuffle, but we manage the two-kiss greeting. His jowls are smooth, with an edge of stubble.

"*Enchanté*. I do hope you are enjoying your visit to Saint-Sebastien-du-Lac?"

I nod. "It is beautiful."

"I hear our Ishmael has been showing you the touristic sites. You are welcome to come to my office and I can give you brochures." He includes Chloe and Zara. "All of you. Or the town hall. They provide good material. Will you be attending the, how do you say *vide-greniers*, on Thursday evening?"

Frank fetches a chair for Isabella and she sits beside me. He explains, "Vide greniers are a mixture of a car boot sale and a village fete here."

Henri winces. "A vide-graw-niere." He drags a chair to the other side of Isabella, sags into it, the corner of the table pointing at his stomach. "Yes, I believe that is similar to your village boot sales. I am organising it this year. It is excellent. If you want to attend, it is free."

Isabella says, "It's charming. Our one has mostly private sellers so the prices are good. You should both come."

Chloe smiles at me. "Let's go to it on Thursday." She asks Isabella, "Doesn't Ishmael have a stall there?"

Isabella nods. "He has." She twists to include me. "He makes these amazing wood, what to call them, pieces, sculptures?" Her manicured hands flutter in a graceful arc. "He started a few years ago, after he did a course, and now his work is in Limoges galleries."

Henri says, "They are becoming collector's items someday, I tell you." He smirks. "And then I can proclaim I am the brother-in-law of the famous wood artist."

Isabella pokes him in his ribs. "You need that fame stuff. His art is as good today whether some nose-stuck-in-the-air Parisian art critic decides so or not."

Henri laughs. "I am in insurance. It is what we do. We must decide the value of everything."

She gives a deep sigh.

Frank strokes his beard in an exaggerated motion. "Proud to be the partner of the great wood artist." He chuckles. "Though I wouldn't mind if a Paris critic picks his work and praises it. We could sell it for a great deal more."

Isabella opens her mouth to speak, then pats her cheeks and tuts. She waves at Ishmael who is working the register, out of earshot. "An artiste is never celebrated in his own time."

Ismael quirks an eyebrow, but returns the wave.

Henri murmurs to me. "Isn't he so sweet? And handsome, no?"

I frown inside, but my face remains relaxed and I smile. I guess Henri doesn't realise I'm lesbian, if he is trying to match us up, and why with Ishmael who's with Frank. "He's been so nice. Taking me places. We're going to visit the friendly deer early tomorrow."

I catch the change of expression in Henri's eyes. The smile drops off his face.

Isabella exclaims. "Isn't that amazing? This wonderful little creature trusting us so much?" Her voice turns irritated. "I don't understand this place sometimes. Why are we discussing, why must we do petitions?" She angles away from Henri. "And my own husband is one of them."

Henri shows his wrist, a gold watch, inlaid circles of blue. "It is late." He stands. "We need to leave though I am sure we have the pleasure again very soon. I must organise more vendors and I need to pass the final list to the mayor. The Thursday comes rapidly." He touches the top of Isabella's chair. "*Cherie?*"

Isabella purses her lips. She doesn't take Henri's proffered hand but rises. "I'll see everyone tomorrow? *Bisou?*"

Chloe goes around the table and they kiss cheeks twice. Zara and Frank and I do the same.

We watch as the couple leave.

Frank drops into his seat. "Someone's in trouble." He takes a swig of the lemonade as though he wishes it were stronger.

I sit. "I hope I didn't say something wrong?"

He grimaces. "No. Ignore me." He frowns at his brushed silver watch. "Why do I only become aware how old I am at this time of the night? You'd think my body knows by now I should take it easier during the day."

Zara laughs. "Young man, don't even go there."

Frank chuckles. "I'm only a trifle younger than you, but you come across as thirty years younger." He gets up, stretching. "Okay. I'll bid you adieu, folks."

He pauses at the bar to give Ishmael a peck on the lips.

Zara says. "I like him."

I smile. "All anyone has to do is call you young-looking and you're theirs for life."

She laughs. "And? What's wrong with that? Shows they have a discerning eye."

Chloe holds up her glass. "I'll drink to that."

We touch our glasses together and our eyes meet. The candlelight shines in hers and my heart skips a beat, my breath catching in my chest.

She blushes. Sips wine. Laughs at something Zara has said.

My pulse drums out the thought. I have less than a week to figure out whether the spark is real.

§

The dining area is empty except for Chloe and me, and quiet apart from the occasional scrape of pans and gush of water in the commercial dishwasher rumbling behind the kitchen door where Pierre is finishing the post-service routine.

In the dimmed bar, the flame of the candle chases shadows with our breath.

We've talked for the past hour, aware of the unsaid, of the reasons we were together and the mystery, to me, of why we aren't. It's mostly easy, this, sitting here, near her, and it's also moments of piercing pain, the memories sifting through my skin with every familiar smile, every tug of teeth on her lower lip, every light touch on my hand when she makes a point, or the moment when she strokes a loose strand off my forehead, *that* hurt like the devil had poked his head over my shoulder, stuck a pitchfork in my side and murmured that he thought I was done.

The moon joins in, broken and twisted in glimmering pools on the polished terracotta floor.

I say, "I couldn't help my views on bi people." Because we've landed on the usual topic.

"And I couldn't help being bi." Chloe stretches to pick up the bottle of red wine. She fills my glass and empties the bottle into hers.

"But surely that shouldn't have been enough to separate us. Surely we could have worked it out."

She nods. "Possibly. But everything came full circle to you not being able to let it go."

This is not what I want to hear, she was at fault, the one who left. Me, I was the one left behind, in the right. I had the right to an opinion.

My elbows grind against the table, my face pushing against my palms. "I don't understand it. I mean, I found my place when I came out, falling for a woman, the most natural space where I belong. Can't imagine being with a man."

"So what is this thing with Ishmael?"

I lift my head out of my hands and stare at her. "What thing?"

"Jay, I know you. And it's obvious Ishmael reacts to you too, I mean, I figured something was up when he held on to your photo, but it didn't enter my mind it was because he was interested in you like that."

The heat races up my neck. "He kept my photo?"

She leans forward. "He's so handsome, pretty almost. And you two seem to have hit it off, you spend more time on him than you do checking Isabella out."

The blush burns my cheeks. "I think Isabella is extremely attractive, and Ishmael is a copy of her. He's gay, and he's a man, and I am not bisexual."

She sighs. "And there's no way the lesbian activist you are will ever admit it to anyone, especially not to yourself."

"That's not why!" The blood is rushing carrying wine to my brain, confusing me more. "How can you say you love women and sleep with men? That's a betrayal! Like you weren't really a lesbian, you were just waiting for a man and you were experimenting on women."

Her sigh is a deep breath. "You won't forget the bad experiences you've had with women who weren't even bisexual. Your reasoning is so twisted by that."

Ishmael's face flashes into my mind. His eyes, his smile, looking into me.

I don't want this. I can't.

Chloe stretches. I watch the smooth skin of her arms, her slender neck, blonde nestling on her shoulders. I want to escape to the world I know, for everything to settle, into the right shape, hers.

She sighs, her hands folding into a tent on the table. "It's frustrating having to explain how I am, I shouldn't have to, but you need to hear it, for your own sake."

I frown.

She says, "Say you love blondes, does that mean you haven't fallen in love or been attracted to a brunette or redhead?"

"Well, I guess not. But that's not the same. Big difference between someone's hair colour or whether they're a man or woman."

"Just hear me out." She takes a gulp of wine, swallows hard, and waggles the glass at me. "So, you're attracted to blondes, brunettes, black, etcetera, what would you feel if a woman who has decided they can only love your particular colour..." She pauses, stares at me, not directly, more a brush of her eyes through my hair, "Not exactly brunette and I didn't really have words to describe your hair colour except that I loved how your highlights sparkled like the sun on a slow-moving river."

Her gaze returns to the wine glass in her hand. "Anyway, what if this Jaya-colour-loving partner of yours tells you you're wrong for having the potential to love redheads and brunettes and black-haired women and grey-haired and purple-tinted and on and on, but not only that," Her lips tighten, "What if they are afraid to love you in case you leave them for a purple-tinted-hair woman because you simply cannot be trusted near other women, not that you're flighty or anything considering you've never looked at another one since you met them, but you clearly might be more likely to fall for someone else because you get to choose from a wider range."

Her glass ticks against the wood, the wine rippling waves, barely contained. "As if because you are open to an additional set of options, you're suddenly and *automatically* less trustworthy than the woman who can only love blondes. I mean, it's not like there aren't a fucking variety of shades of blonde and they might cheat with the strawberry variety as any other type, because they're an untrustworthy person in the first place cos they're an asshole."

She stands, her breathing faster, searching for a sign that I have understood. I have seen it and heard it knocking at the door, but the thought must stay locked outside.

Instead, I say, "I'm not untrustworthy. Never looked at, never even noticed anyone else after I first saw you."

She looks bone-weary from her trembling lips to her narrowed eyes to the whispered breath of her hand grazing my cheek, falling away as she turns and is gone, leaving her words pulsing in the air that had lived between us.

"Neither did I."

CHAPTER FIFTEEN

Framed by the window, the moon shines bright, a perfect circle save for one rough edge. Gentle snores sift down the hall from Zara's room.

Sleep is evading me. The wine and the conversation with Chloe, followed by Lana's novel and the desperate hope that it was imagined.

I sit up and flick through the notebook again, wishing the story didn't end so abruptly.

Ever since I encountered Lana's writing, worry has been simmering under my skin, bubbling over occasionally.

As it is doing now.

The novel just stopped. No more chapters. I searched through the pages, desperate to find more words. But the lined pages were blank, curled at the corners.

The other notebook lies on the antique locker beside the bed. The loose pages of writing exercises peek out and I remember I didn't read all of them before starting the novel. I pull out all the sheets and flip through to the missed ones.

Lana M.

Intermediate creative writing class

Week 6 assignment

The Meal

The sweat oozed from his pores and settled around the roots of the hairs on his forearms. The drops glittered in the candlelight. He had pulled up the sleeves of his formal blue shirt and the darker line of wet fabric cut against the muscle in the thick part of his forearm. She watched the sleeve stretch tight and loose against his elbow each time he took a mouthful of wine.

"Good wine, this," he said. She took a sip and nodded. It was awful, tasting cheap and thick despite its price, an instant corrosive in her dry mouth. She swallowed the sip down, her smile as sweet as the liquid. Her birthday card leant against the bottle of wine; he'd draped the necklace over it, casual even as he held jewellery worth 55,000 Euro. She knew the price because she'd seen the receipt for the identical one he'd bought last year and given the maid. He'd left the receipt and necklace on his dressing table.

He ordered the 'chateeyo briyandeh' and she saw the waiter's eyebrow twitch but his facial expression had remained chiselled on his face. Even French waiters remain polite for him she thought. The waiter returned an eternity later and the thick red cylinders of beef, sticking out of the crimson sauce, periscopes, swivelled and stared at the two of them sitting there as if they belonged in such a civilised place.

She heard a quiet sound, a rasp coming from his mouth when he took the meat off the fork. His eyes had taken on the dull glaze of scratched marble as he chewed and she wondered whether he heard the whimpers every time his teeth came together. There she was, comparing herself to a dead cow, but that would be quick, being struck over the head with a mechanical hammer, no more having to control her screams till they were rumours, passed through the house, tossed and turned in the undercurrent, drowned in the loud music.

He had wanted her to wear the gauzy dress and he checked in every few minutes on what was his underneath. He had made her wear it despite the crescent scars with their evenly spaced indentations that lay there angry and chafed. The most recent was hours old; the oldest was three months old, the same age as her baby, his baby, whose birth had sparked this fascination with her breasts as a new site. The prize for the first scar, though, went to her stomach, her first scream of pain and surprise rewarded with a red-tinged smile and then a fist. The two years of training worked well, the whimpers stopped deep in her throat now. She wondered whether the expensive candlelight hid those tribal marks or whether the waiter crossed himself as he walked away grateful for his job, the worst part of which was probably being yelled at by the chef or the possible threat of dismissal. She now had a job for life, she had been signed and paid for; she'd seen the briefcase. He'd used a calfskin briefcase, soft and supple, funny how her life was measured in dead livestock, mothers and babies.

That passage is familiar. I wonder for a minute if I'd already read the exercise, then remember it with the names Thomas and Sapna.

From the novel.

Were the class exercises a way for Lana to write parts of the novel?

Or were they parts of the novel she changed for class?

Was any of it based on reality or merely written from the imagination needed to produce a piece of writing before the next class.

Usually, classes had writing prompts too.

Lana M.

Intermediate creative writing class

Week 7 assignment - poetry

Love Letters in Smoke

This is my love letter

and my goodbye letter

to all those who have loved and said goodbye because they could not love

This is my love letter to the wraiths, the ghosts, the enamoured visions of lovers, spewed from the obsessive spurt, the compulsive grab, the narcissistic break from the movie of itself to get supplies.

And this is my love letter to me.
Because I refuse to travel further down that trail.
For what lies in wait in that landscape is not home.
It is a cavern from which any light, any spirit, any colour, appears heavenly,
but even heaven can search for meaning,
and even heaven can wander lost and fade if trapped in the darkness.

I am no heaven,
but now I sit on the edge of the abyss and drop love letters into your depths,
not for you,
but for me,
to see the smoke rise, to show myself that there is no smoke without fire.

Don't Pay It Forward

What do you do when you arrive at the last page in the book,
your heroes lying exposed as antagonists
dead on the basement floor,
and your true love story turns out to be a cold case special,
when the visions came true,
but the reality you'd escaped was truer.

When you wish there was an epilogue that tied it all into a story that made sense,

when you realise there are no cliffhangers for the sequel

just loose strings that hang meekly from the exalted rafters of your hopes,

ceilings shattered with naive exuberance,

and now no more limits worth reaching,

no more chapters worth reading,

no more words worth trusting.

What happens when you believe the travelogue of the world as you know it

that turns out to be propaganda for the charismatic, the charming, the insane, the unreal, the hyped-up dreams of a society that needs to feel truth, but cannot deal truth.

There are too many damaged who pay it forward.

Not enough who say

No.

Enough.

Pay it back.

From the Journal of my Narcissist

The Imprint of Me

I have terrified someone until I saw her eyes hide.

I have watched her flow back into her pain and not come out the other side.

I see the woman lift her face from the water

and smile for me, eyes dead,

I see the child in her stay face down, eyes under,

watching pictures that show

she drowned herself.

Because I made her believe that.

I held her head under the raging

and screamed into her ear

that she was killing me.

I left her there,

dried my hands, my face, my body as it shook.

Then I walked away,

full of power in the pain that I felt.

Because I could have loved her

and now I can't.

My fingers smooth over the typed words. I skim again through the first set of exercises when Lana was in Week 1 and 2. They were more innocent, still dark, but the later pieces had more of a tone of knowledge, as though Lana was writing from a place of studying dark minds. What was her writing like when she started, in the Beginner's level?

I pick up the last sheet, the exercise for what was probably her final class.

Lana M.

Intermediate creative writing class

Week 8 assignment–prose

1. All Voice

The dormitory is large, cavernous, stretches for twenty beds on either side. Beds holding young children in rows facing each other across an aisle the width of a tall adult lying down. The only adult in the building at night is down the hall. Down the hall, on the right, in what looks like a warm room, when the door is open warm yellow light spills from that room into the hallway. The hallway is cold, the bathrooms are far away in another land, a land of white porcelain and relief. Far away past the corridors the height of two adults standing, past the piano room the size of a small church choir, past the dining room that stretches for fifteen tables by five each surrounded by its clutch of eight huddled chairs each the size of an adult sitting that in the day bears the weight of a child, past the grey kitchen with grey pots and grey pans that could fit six children, seven at a push, hanging in grey darkness, cold air accompanying you as you slip down the black and white squared floor trying to be silent, trying not to awaken the ghosts that are whispered about by the herds of children shepherded by masters and mistresses who sleep through the nightly visits of the predators gathered at the edge of the circle of light, cold light, not the light of a fire, fluorescent lights, blue-tinged lights of corridors, flickering bulbs, buzzing overhead, the chill crawling into your bones as you creep past the sound of a piano playing in the empty music room.

But there is no refuge for the refugee in the land of the Dormitory. Fear and cold are constant, companions in hell, comrades, in arms that hold you down, to the sound of lust held behind clenched teeth. It doesn't matter to you that there's a taste of fear underneath the noise, it doesn't matter to you that the arms are only a little older than yours. It doesn't matter to you that it happened to the boy in the previous bed the previous night. It matters to you that you're quiet, that you know it will be over soon. And it will happen to the boy in the next bed the next night. And it doesn't matter to you that you can't save them, any of them. It doesn't matter to you that you can't save you.

It mattered to you for the moments before you landed in the land of no return. It mattered to you before you were thrown onto the path less travelled, more on it than you'd think, no help to each other though, eyes averted, faking reality until it became your reality. For seeing, saying words to a fellow traveller meant you both saw the path. Meant you saw your bare bleeding child feet instead of your expensive adult shoes. Meant you knew you were not on the other road, the blacktop gleaming highway where all the shiny adults sat in their shiny cars with their shiny children.

And it doesn't matter to you that you can't save them, any of them. It doesn't matter to you that you can't save you. Not anymore.

2. Less Voice

The dormitory is cavernous, with beds in rows facing each other across an aisle. The only adult in the building at night is down the hall in what looks like a warm room. When the door is open, cosy yellow light spills from that room into the hallway which is cold. The bathrooms are far away, past the corridors, past the piano room, past the vast dining room, past the kitchen with grey pots and pans hanging in darkness. Cold air accompanying you as you slip down the tiled floor trying to be silent, trying not to awaken the ghosts that are whispered about.

Fear and cold are constant companions as arms hold you down to the sound of laughter. It doesn't matter to you there's a taste of fear underneath the laughter, it doesn't matter to you that the arms are only a little older than yours, it doesn't matter to you that it happened to the boy in the previous bed the previous night. It matters to you that you're quiet, that you know it will be over soon. And it will happen to the boy in the next bed the next night. And it doesn't matter to you that you can't save them, any of them. It doesn't matter to you that you can't save you. Not anymore.

3. No Voice?

The dormitory is large, with beds in rows facing each other across an aisle. The only adult in the building at night is down the hall. The bathrooms are past the corridors, the piano room, the dining room, and the kitchen with pots and pans hanging in darkness. Cold air accompanying you as you slip down the tiled floor trying to be silent, trying not to awaken the ghosts that are whispered about.

Fear and cold are constant companions as arms hold you down to the sound of laughter. It doesn't matter to you there's a taste of fear underneath the laughter, it doesn't matter to you the arms are only a little older than yours, it doesn't matter to you it happened to the boy in the previous bed the previous night. It matters to you that you're quiet, that you know it will be over soon. And it will happen to the boy in the next bed the next night. And it doesn't matter to you that you can't save them, any of them. It doesn't matter to you that you can't save you. Not anymore.

My gut says this exercise relates to Thomas, Lana searching for a reason, something to explain him, and I mourn with her at the loss of innocence that created the character of the man in her book, while it doesn't excuse him.

I had taken writing classes in Dublin and loved being part of the group, all of us earnest and in awe of the possibilities. The homework submissions were often thinly veiled slices of real-life massaged into the shape of the assignment. I learnt a lot about my fellow students, their relationships, families, attitudes. And all from them reading short passages of prose and poetry, fiction more real than the 'tell the class about yourself' introductions or the chats in the bar afterwards.

If Lana had been in class, I would have been captivated, and probably thoroughly infatuated. By her, her own particular style, and her ability to write from the point of view of the perpetrator in the last pieces. The content hurts, that she experienced such darkness. She worked as a counsellor though, she might have learned from her clients too.

Are her words from personal experience or from deep empathy?

I don't have the answer so I still can't tell if David is Thomas.

CHAPTER SIXTEEN

Ishmael is almost skipping as we walk through the forest. The road, downgraded into a grass-clumped track, wanders with purpose through the trees, silver-barked and slim with leaves bunched on their lofty heights, others brown and solid, leafy branches elbowing into our faces.

He halts and points.

"Beautiful Demoiselle."

I scan the wild grass verge.

"See, there." He stoops. "Isn't she interesting?"

The object of his attention looks like a cross between a butterfly and a dragonfly. A long green tube with a bronze tip, and bronze translucent wings slanting up and away.

"What did you call it?"

"Beautiful Demoiselle. This is a female, the males have blue wings." He smiles, groans as he straightens. "I made a sculpture of the Demoiselle, in wood." He spreads his arms in a wide embrace. "This place is full of wildflowers and butterflies and birds. It's wonderful, a free studio, provides great subjects."

"Yes, Isabella mentioned you are an artist?"

He says in a soft voice, his cheeks reddening, "I don't know if I can call myself an artist. I produce wood sculptures, yes. Some folks appreciate them." He walks on. "I'll show you my studio later if you'd like? It sounds grand, doesn't it? But it's really a shed in the woods."

I catch up with him. "I'd love to see it."

He seems content to meander, pointing out other creatures, plants, trees. I watch him as he speaks, enjoy the brownness of him, in the play of light on his skin, the swirling depths of his eyes. I wonder at myself, I'm not used to admiring brown.

Houses at the village outskirts come into view. There are figures near the pasture.

Ishmael says, "I've been coming here every day since the little deer arrived. I've met more humans because of a wild animal. It's become a morning ritual for a few of us. Later the parents bring the kids, but our early outings are a meditation with nature. A celebration of the beauty and innocence that can exist. And a testament to trust." His smile for me is gentle. "We stand around and dream we could be good parents, those of us who are not. When we meet for our baby deer fix."

I'm riveted by the glow in his eyes. We remain suspended, facing, seeing into each other, and he is silent, a delicate butterfly hovering with dragonfly force.

He must feel it too, this connection, this irresistible pull.

He shakes his head as if to break a spell and the moment stirs and fades, the trail of a candle flame smothered by a whispered breath.

"Ishmael."

We look up, jarred by the voice though it is quiet, reluctant to intrude.

Henri is motionless on the road, his hand raised, palm exposed. His face is that of a man trying to stay calm, to pass on that calm, but resigned to the fact there will be none.

Ishmael says, "Henri? What are you doing here?"

Henri says, "You should return to the restaurant."

His pitch rises, "Is there something wrong with Isabella?"

"Non, no. *S'il te plait*, do as I say."

I glance beyond Henri. Notice men between us and the fencing wire. Cows through the barbed lines. The uniforms. My heart beats faster. This doesn't look right, not the same as the other day, with the parents holding their child over to be kissed by the deer.

Ishmael advances, the same doubt slamming onto his face but Henri blocks his way.

"*C'est vrai*, Ishmael, you should to go home."

Ishmael chokes out. "What have you done? What have they done?"

"I try to stop them." Henri stares at me. "When you say you are coming this morning, I arrive before them and try halt them." His voice weeps of fear and regret.

Ishmael nudges Henri aside and strides towards the field. I follow. His pace quickens and then he stops. Dead.

I can't decipher any words, but he's running and a howl of pain hangs in his wake.

Henri says, behind me, "I try to stop them."

The men are in navy military-style uniforms. One stands out in a tan and white camouflage suit and a bright orange pinny. I notice with a dull thud in my chest that he is carrying a rifle.

Ishmael is six feet from the wire. A uniform steps into his path, but Ishmael swerves by him.

The cows are standing. They are standing. They are not chewing or grazing.

One is lying down.

Ishmael reaches the fencing. He holds on to the barbed wire, stares over it.

Henri slips by me. He puts a hand on the arm of the camouflage man.

I run past them.

Ishmael's voice is low. "Why? What have we done?"

I arrive at his side. It is not a cow lying down but the deer. The brown body, that had blended into the safety of the herd, is not moving.

Ishmael swivels to the men. "Why? What did you do? Why?" His voice is getting louder.

Camouflage-man brushes off Henri's hand. The blue-uniformed men are silent, appear to defer to him.

Henri says, "It had to be for the security of the people. Deers carry disease."

Ishmael ignores Henri, yells at camouflage-man. "This deer did not. This deer came here trusting us. The farmer was fine with it staying with his cows. You only wanted to show your power. How much power does it take to shoot a defenceless trusting innocent creature? Did it come up to you, you bastard, did it walk up to the fence for you? Did you even have to move your fat backside to chase it any distance?"

The man understands enough. He spits, missing Henri's shoes by an inch. He lifts the rifle and places it on his forearm so it lies pointing at Ishmael.

Ishmael lurches forward. Stands in front of him. "Shoot me then, you snivelling piece of shit coward. You think you are a big man, a strong man because you act tough but what can you do except kill innocent creatures. But you are too cowardly to go into the forest to hunt, you have to wait for the poor deer to offer itself to you and only then can you shoot it. You are not a man, you are a boy with no balls."

A giggle escapes from the group of blue-uniformed men. A red mist of rage seeps into camouflage-man's eyes. He raises his weapon.

I move forward and hold Ishmael's arm. He is rigid.

Henri edges between them. "Ishmael, leave now. You cannot talk to the National Guard in such a way. *S'il te plait.*"

Ishmael stands firm. The muscles in his forearm tremble under my fingers.

Henri moves closer. Grips Ishmael's upper arms. "This man is not local. They are not too friendly to brown men either. Please, I have to answer to Isabella for the deer, she will not forgive me for you."

Voices behind me. I glance back and see villagers walking to the field, their pace quickening as they notice the commotion.

They halt, hushed, then a woman's sobs pierce the air.

Henri says, "I make sure she is buried with dignity. *Desolé*. I did not understand." He looks at the group staring through the wire at their baby, then at Ishmael. "Please not to advise Isabella it was me. Please advise her I tried to stop them."

Ishmael turns away from Henri, to the people, most in tears. His eyes stay up as though they're held up by ropes and he will fall if he sees the slight brown body.

Ishmael's words struggle to emerge from his mouth. "Jaya, can you get a lift back?"

Henri says, "I take Jaya. I need to talk to Isabella."

I nod. Rub Ishmael's shoulder.

Ishmael walks away, towards the forest. He stumbles and then picks up speed. He is running when he disappears into the trees.

Henri whispers. "*Qu'est-ce que j'ai fait?*"

I cannot find words. I hate these men with a passion, but the words won't form.

I wheel around, walk to the cars parked on the verge.

CHAPTER SEVENTEEN

Isabella and Frank are having morning coffee in their corner of the terrace. Isabella is laughing, but the laughter fades when we jerk to a halt across two restaurant parking spaces.

I stumble out, the fresher air welcome though warm. Henri stays in his seat.

Isabella hurries to the steps. Her hands fly to her mouth when she sees my face streaked with tears. "What's wrong? Where is Ishmael? Is everything okay?"

The shock thuds through my body. "They killed the deer. Ishmael ran into the woods."

Frank appears beside Isabella.

Isabella frowns. "What? They did what? *Who?*"

"Henri said he was the National Guard. The man with the rifle. Men with blue uniforms, the police?"

Isabella shakes her head. "*Gendarmerie?* Why would the *gendarmerie* kill the deer?" She glowers past me at her husband's shape huddled in his car.

Henri climbs out, trudges towards her. "The National Guard did it. They said it was a security risk."

Frank's face is flushed. "You called the National Guard for a baby deer?"

Isabella's face darkens. Her voice rises in tone and volume. "*You* did this. *Why?*"

Henri's words rush out, a pleading stream. "I had to inform them. That is all I did. They made the decision. I tried to stop them this morning."

Her volume stays high. "So you knew last night it was going to happen, and you didn't tell us. You didn't give us a chance to protect it, to get it somewhere safe?"

"Where would you have taken it?" Henri flaps his hands. "There was not anywhere safe. *Cherie*, these are the laws here. It is a rural place."

Isabella says, "Rural should not mean inhuman. What is this place? That a poor sweet deer who trusts us cannot be left in peace. Even the cows are more human than you are."

"Isabella, *cherie. S'il te plait.*"

"Please get out of here. I cannot look at you." She pivots and walks into the restaurant.

The muscles in Frank's throat are moving under his bristling beard, but he stares down at Henri, then follows Isabella.

Henri's shoulders slump. "I cannot do anything right anyway."

I say. "This was so wrong. There is no right here at all."

He nods. Takes a deep breath, shrinks as he expels it, his shirt sinking onto his frame, sweat circles bunched under his arms.

I rub at my eyes, my cheeks. "I need to find Ishmael."

He is quiet beside me. "Please tell him again I'm sorry. Tell Isabella I will meet her later after her work. I must finish preparations for the *vide-greniers*. These are my duties. We are not in the city anymore."

The car creaks as he crawls in. The engine rumbles and dies away behind me. I climb the steps, the bricks hot beneath my feet, onto the cool tile of the terrace.

The interior is gloomy after the sunshine, the only brightness from the sun dripping off the suspended wine glasses onto the polished wood of the bar. Frank is holding Isabella, her sobs muted against his shoulder.

He asks me over her bent head. "How was Ishmael?"

"Shocked, distressed. Where would he go?"

Isabella's words are muffled. "His studio." She straightens up and takes the napkin Frank offers her. "I'm going to look for him there. Frank, can you handle finishing the prep?"

His voice is thick. "I'll get Pierre to come in early. Go on, I'll find you when he gets here." He blinks rapidly and I sense he does not want us to see him cry.

Isabella grips Frank's hand. "Why did we come here?" She releases his hand. "Nowhere escapes cruelty."

She inclines her head to me, "Come with me?"

I step closer. "Yes."

Her fingers are cool on mine. "Come. Let's find Ishmael."

§

The wooden shed sits in the middle of a clearing, surrounded by trees, their leafy branches hiding the studio from the sky. Strands of green, red, yellow, blue tumble over the scalloped edges of the flower boxes on the window sills.

Isabella opens the door and peers in. "He's not here."

I follow her into Ishmael's studio and gasp. The Beautiful Demoiselle. The tube body is an arrow pointing down to earth, the wings soar towards the sky, tender, delicate, laced wood.

"It is stunning, is it not?" Isabella traces her fingers over the interstitial fibre of the wings.

I whisper, "We saw a live one today. This is more beautiful. And more fragile, but it is wood."

"He is amazing. Me, I cannot create anything. Not painting, or drawing, nothing." She smiles. "Though perhaps now I could make creations with food." She wanders from piece to piece, touching each.

I scan the studio. There are other pieces in various stages of forming. "You said Ishmael only started sculpting a few years ago?"

"Yes. Only after we got to the Limousin. He attended a class in Limoges."

"And he didn't show this talent earlier? When he was younger?"

Isabella hesitates, her body shielding a sculpture. She beckons me over.

It is the unfinished bust of a deer, features chiselled, emerging smooth from the rough block.

Her eyes fill as she places her palm on the cheek of the fawn. "He was always artistic, but no, he didn't do anything like this." She faces me. "He is a gentle soul. We are all we have. Me and him and Frank."

"And Henri?"

She looks back at the sculpted wood. "And Henri."

"Where are your parents?"

Her voice is halting. "They passed away when Ishmael was a teenager. He travelled as much as he could. Me, I stayed in Paris."

My finger follows the coil of a wood knot behind the ear of the deer. "You are devoted to him now. As he is to you"

She sighs. "Yes. I love seeing him happy. I didn't expect it to be with

Frank, but I am happy for him."

"You are close to Frank too. Were you friends with him before he went out with your brother?"

"Yes, you could say that. They met through me."

"And how did you meet Frank? Through Henri?"

She hesitates. "No. I lived in the neighbourhood where Frank had his rental property. We used to meet on the street, in the *boulangerie*, sometimes at the market. I met Henri through Frank. Henri insured the property in Paris. And got them to invest in the restaurant here."

"So, did you ever meet Lana and David?"

Her face lies in the cone of sunlight from the window so I notice she has a visceral reaction to the names, that her pupils dilate despite the brightness.

She says, "Once or twice. Yes, when they came to stay for a weekend. Frank would bring Lana to the boulangerie. David didn't come along."

I examine the wall, the tools on the shelves, measure my words. "I am so fascinated with them. Maybe it is because there aren't so many Indians in Ireland and it sounds like Lana was a beautiful woman."

Isabella says, "I guess she was. Frank thought so."

"You didn't?" I spin back to her.

A pink tinge creeps up her neck. "Sorry. Yes. Of course I did."

My eyes are drawn to her cheeks, the changing shades of brown to russet. "From how she has been described, I get the impression you look like her."

Now the russet spreads into a definite blush. She smiles. "Is that the Irish charm or the Indian charm?"

I return her smile. "Both."

The curves of her face are similar to Ishmael's, her eyebrows smoother than his, but with a matching elegance. Their eyes are the same almond shape, colour a shade of pure cocoa. I'm looking into hers as I stared into Ishmael's earlier and her beauty is formidable, but not in the riptide surge of my blood with him that threatens to submerge me, to drown me, in the drumbeat of my heart.

My cells tingle with panic. If I have unwanted reactions with anyone, surely it should be with Isabella, not Ishmael.

And if, as I suspect, she is Lana, then I am already enraptured, tangled in the web of her words.

She drops her gaze from my lips and brushes by me to stand at the entrance. She stares out at the cloudless sky.

I say, "Where do you think Ishmael went?" I've been avoiding the reason we are there. We both have been.

She rests against the jamb, her shadow falling onto the porch and tripping down the wooden stairs. The worry creeps into her voice. "I don't know where he is if he isn't here."

She swivels to the inside. "Chloe trusts you."

I'm surprised by the subject change, but nod.

She continues, "You observe so much. I cannot figure out, though, who you are observing the most. Chloe said you are lesbian."

I nod again, my brow furrowing.

"But I see you with Ishmael and there is a chemistry there."

I shake my head.

"He's into you."

"He is with Frank. And I'm with Fiona." As the words emerge, I wonder at myself. Who our partners are is *not* the reason I should be denying my strange feelings around Ishmael.

"Yes, he is." A hint of sadness creeps into her eyes. "We cannot control our attractions." She takes a step towards me. "I love my brother. He has had doubts about himself." She stops.

"Doubts?"

"This is so private to Ishmael." She grips the door frame. "He would have to tell you himself. If he wants." Her brow and cheek muscles tense. "If he does, please be gentle. It is a difficult place to be."

I hold up my palms. "No plans to be cruel to anyone, but I have no clue what you're warning me about."

"I watch people too. You hide behind yourself."

"Now I have no idea what you mean there either?"

She moves close. "This image of yourself you allow others to see. We all do."

I frown, with a smile. "What you see is what you get with me."

"Is that really true?" Isabella smiles. "I don't judge anyone. I can't. We all hide, especially when we are afraid. You are a lesbian. From what Ishmael told me, you couldn't accept Chloe is bisexual, no?"

"And wasn't I right? She left me for a man. Not directly, but she's marrying one."

"Though you feel something for a man yourself. But the difference is you won't even consider the possibility. Do you know how painful that is to someone who cares for you?"

She's not talking about only me. Or Ishmael. There is a pain in Isabella's eyes from a time outside this shed, this forest, this time. "The poor deer, I'm desperate not to imagine it, but I can't stop." She shakes her head. "Going to return to the kitchen. After checking his gîte. Are you coming with me?"

"Would it be okay if I stay here? Ishmael did say he wanted to show me his studio, I don't think he would mind."

She quirks an eyebrow. "It's easy to get back from here." She swivels and points the way we came, "Simply follow the path that's been used." Her lips curl in a lopsided smile. "I guess you could call it, how do they say? The road well-travelled."

CHAPTER EIGHTEEN

I sit on the floor of the shed, beside the deer. The wood wall is rough against my back, the light streams in and slants over me into an oblong at my feet.

The forest nestles around the studio, whispering through the open door, the rustle of wind in the leaves, the singing of birds, interrupted occasionally by squawking, the movement of animals through the undergrowth.

My hand rests on the smoothened surface of the fawn's head.

Chloe had wanted a child. I hadn't. Not at the time. Not until she was gone.

I wonder whether my biological clock has suddenly decided to swing into action. Whether that's why I'm experiencing this pull towards a man. I warm towards my theory.

I had teased Chloe about men. Pointed out attractive men and asked her if she was interested. I cringe at the memory now. Chloe never mentioned men in that way in the two years we were together. I was the one who brought up the subject. I wasn't interested in them, I was testing Chloe. Over and over again.

The studio is cool despite the sunshine outside. Particles of wood dust float in front of my eyes, but the air is heavy on my skin.

I can hear Gemma's voice describing Lana. The affection for the wee Indian woman as Gemma referred to her. They'd enjoyed ribbing Lana at work, she took it all in her stride.

I strain to picture the woman in the photo, but I keep seeing Isabella behind the bar, laughing with the customers.

I wish I'd visited Galway in those days. That I'd had a chance to meet Lana, when she was weird and happy, not as I see her now, with fear in her eyes. Her letters to Frank had a thread of anxiety through them. They did spend time describing her life with David. But they showed a woman who was interesting and thoughtful, even funny at times. And the novel, the exercises for her writing class. I wish I'd known her.

What happened to the baby?

I have babies on my mind.

I stroke the nose of the deer and tears roll down my face.

There is a noise outside and through the shimmer in my eyes, I make out a shape at the fringe of the clearing.

I haul myself up and limp to the door, working out the cramp in my calf. I've been sitting here for almost an hour.

Ishmael is sprawled on a bench, facing a patch of wildflowers around the exposed roots of a tree.

I cross the clearing. I hadn't noticed the bench when Isabella and I came into the clearing. It's partially hidden behind the shrubs at the forest edge.

Ishmael is staring at the base of the tree trunk.

I say, "Would you prefer company or to be alone?"

He straightens up and shifts along the bench and I take that as an invitation to stay.

I see a niche in the trunk, a foot off the ground. There's an object in it. A wooden box.

We sit in forest silence.

He says, "We came here for a quiet life."

A bird squawks loudly above us and he smiles. "Not quiet in that way. I adore the sounds of the woods. There's a stream nearby and I can sit by it for hours and listen to the chatter of the water, to the conversations it carries from all the towns and villages, from the forests, taking them to the sea. To join the conversations from all the others."

I imagine him sitting alone by the stream, listening. The picture should feel lonely, but he doesn't.

His voice is soft. "When we hide, we lose the chances we're given. To love and be loved in return. But when we trust, as that poor deer did, seeking the safety of the herd, we lose so much more." He nods his head at the tree. "Like Isabella did. Did she bring you here?"

I say, "Yes. She was worried about you." I consider the wooden box. "What did Isabella lose?"

"Too much." I sense his gaze. "Chloe will be back with Matt soon. How is it going, your study of whether Chloe really prefers men?"

I turn. He is smiling.

I say, "Not very well. But that's not exactly what I meant. I mean, I don't think she prefers men over women." I stop. I don't know what I mean.

I love how his eyes crinkle up at the corners when he's trying not to laugh at me.

I make a snap decision to take the subject by the horns. The conversation between the fictional Ishmael and Sapna in the Vietnamese restaurant is playing on my mind, his wanting to look like the heroine of the movie. My breath catches, I clear my throat. "I keep getting the feeling you want to tell me something. And it's not related to Chloe or Isabella."

The smile fades from his face. He turns his head away.

I say, "I don't mean to pry. I'm confused. Isabella mentioned you had doubts, but it was private to you and I got the impression it had something to do with me. Is it to do with being gay? About being with Frank? You said your sexuality was different from bisexual or gay?"

There is a silence that spans a minute. I wait in the ripples of his breathing, in the tranquillity of the clearing.

He says, "They've watched me struggle for a while now and they're concerned." He takes in a deep breath. Glances at me. It is there linking us, in the quickening of my heart, what's always been there, but made no sense.

He says, "There is too much to say and too much to hide. Not for my sake, but for others." His hands grip each other. "You saw what happened. What cruelty is here. Everyone must fit into their own field or forest or village or town or city. Or else they are destroyed or killed or lose their place in where they were or where they want to be, where they feel they belong." He sighs. "Frank is a good man. I love him and he loves me. As a man loves a man. But inside me, deep inside me, there is someone else, someone who has been pushed aside." He stops, stares at the ground.

A part of me surfaces, one that has comforted my friends through their troubles. It takes over from the part of me that has been reacting to a man in a manner that bewildered me. "You feel you are really a woman inside, like born in the wrong body?"

He tenses, his shoulders straightening.

I say, "It's okay if you need to talk, I'm not very experienced, but I'll try and understand."

He lets out his breath. "It's hard to talk to anyone here."

"It must be. You've said something to Isabella?"

He nods. "Frank and Isabella." He glances at me. "I talked to Chloe about many things, but not this. She showed me a photo of you."

"I'm confused." I smile. "My predominant emotion now."

The blush starts at his collarbones. "I was confused too. I felt like a woman inside." He inclines his face away. "I hadn't been with Frank as a man for a long time, we settled into a new way of living together, friends. Friends who loved each other deeply and took care of each other. I could not dream of living as a woman, it would affect Frank, in mostly bad ways. Especially here, in this village and we wanted to stay here. Frank has to. So I settled for life as it was. Gave up on being myself. Gave up on feeling what I was and that heart-blowing-open love for anyone."

I know exactly what he is describing. I had given up on that too. I realise the thought has crystallised in my mind for the first time. Along with other thoughts, churning, taking shape, tinged with shock.

He continues, "But I kept your photo. I explained away my fascination with you as being a good friend to Chloe, if she wanted to share memories, painful or pleasant, from her past. We discussed various things, including her love for Matt. I saw it in her. I was happy for her. I tried not to be envious of them, for finding what I could not find or believe could exist for me. Especially not while I was this." He makes a sweeping motion, his hand travelling from his neck downwards, to rest on his knee.

I sit back. My mind is reeling, balancing on a precipice, on one side the darkness of uncertainty, on the ground side the certainty of me, of who I love, what I am.

He says, "And then you arrived here. In flesh and blood. I came out of the kitchen and you were there. And all I could do was smile and stare and get you a drink."

I say, and it sounds so calm, these words dropping from the swirl of my thoughts, "I thought you were smiling and staring because it was good to see someone else with brown skin."

"No." He smiles, looks at me. "No. That wasn't why. Though it is always good to see more brown here."

I am staring now. Into his eyes. Into his smile. I'm sinking, I will drown. The air presses down on me. The wind whispers through the leaves hanging over my head, *this is not how anything is meant to be*.

I tear my gaze away. I jump up, flash my watch. "Zara will be worried." My voice has come out a croak. I clear my throat, keep my eyes on the shrubs behind him. "Are you coming back now?"

There is a smile in his voice, and sadness too. "I'm going to stay and do a bit of sculpting. I need to finish a piece for the *vide-greniers* tomorrow."

I turn to go. I say, "Your sculptures are amazing. I love the Beautiful Demoiselle, thank you for showing her to me this morning. Your version is even more beautiful."

I walk out of the clearing without waiting for his answer. Wondering why the tears want to fall.

§

The restaurant is empty, but there is a clatter of pans from the kitchen. I sit at the bar, on my usual seat by the register where I chat with Ishmael or Isabella when he's between customers or she's taking a break from prep.

Why am I not at my cottage with Zara?

I can't be around her.

She can see through me most of the time, and right now I don't want to be see-through.

I need a coffee.

Pierre frowns up from his prep when I peer into the kitchen. He recognises me and smiles.

I hold an imaginary cup to my mouth. Try new French words. "Je fait café. Vous voulez?" I hope that means I'm making coffee. And offered him some. He smiles again and shakes his head.

I struggle to remember Ishmael's instructions as I work the heavy-handled coffee filter, filling it with a dose of granules, moving it back and forth in the dispenser, the dark liquid dripping into the white porcelain cup. Ishmael had been patient with my lack of focus, my fascination with the noisettes, a mix of espresso and Nutella, which was more an infatuation with the hazel chocolate spread I'd never tried. Isabella had watched us from across the counter and laughed as I played with the machine and teased Ishmael with the Nutella.

I'm not paying attention and the blast of steam sears over my left forearm. I yelp and drop the heavy filter which lands with a clatter on the metal drainer, knocking the cup over.

The crash of steel in ice cuts the air.

His fingertips are cool, the ice-filled towel over my arm makes me shiver.

Ishmael holds the makeshift ice pack in place and leads me out of the bar and into a small room. He places me in an office chair, hunkers down so he's facing me with his kitten-caring eyes. "Are you okay?"

I nod. There are tears in my eyes from the steam burn and I push them away with the back of my right arm.

Ishmael lifts the corner of the towel and examines my arm. "This might blister, but it's not as bad as it could have been." He adjusts the ice so none of the cubes are in contact with my skin and wraps the towel as a bandage holding everything in place.

He looks up. Tears have escaped from the corners of my eyes. His expression changes and he lifts himself off his knees until his face is level with mine. His fingers are gentle as he touches the tears. His eyes are filled with care and I get that feeling again, like I've known him forever, his eyes in front of me, looking at me this way, like he can see into my heart.

I let my gaze wander over his face, over the slope of nose, the blush of cheeks, the smooth curve of eyebrows. My heart beats loud in my chest, in my neck, in my head. I'm worried he can hear it too, in this quiet space.

I return my gaze to his eyes. Which are focused on mine. I close my eyes, but my breath is coming out slightly faster between my lips, matching my heart, giving me away.

The touch of lips on my cheek, the resting of weight against my temple, the tensing of his jaw.

He whispers in my ear. "We both feel this." He pulls back. "But I'm still Ishmael now. And you are not able to deal with that. Or with the fact I might always be."

I stare at him, my fingers aching to run through his hair, to pull his face close, to touch my lips against his. But my mind is gathering itself together and registering where we are and who we are.

He senses the withdrawal and closes his eyes. When he opens them seconds later, there's a shield separating us, and a spear drives into my chest, so sharp I wonder how a stranger can cause more pain than I've experienced before with any person, even Chloe.

He's gone and I slump into the chair, my arm now throbbing, scalded, but only skin-deep. The fear, the panic rising in me now, is that the fire crackling in the distance will burn so much deeper.

CHAPTER NINETEEN

"Is it easy for Algerian citizens to live in France?" I ask Isabella. "Or are you both French citizens?"

We are sitting in the yard behind the house where she and Henri live. The wrought-iron chairs are placed inside a circle of flowerbeds. The barn where I found the letters is at the far corner. The front of the restaurant is visible from here, as are the backs of the cottages.

We're waiting for Pierre and the servers to finish the afternoon post-service cleaning and Isabella wanted to show me around, to take our minds off the horror of the morning. Zara is having lunch with Chloe at a restaurant in the next town. I was invited, but it feels wrong being around them. Everything feels wrong, out of place. The shock of the morning tunnels in my veins, crawls over my skin.

Ishmael is sitting with his body at an angle to us, viewing the lake. He answers for them. "We were both born in France, so we are French citizens. No problems with staying." He smiles. "Except, of course, for the brown skin not being French."

Isabella nods. "Yes, but that is changing. With so many more brown-skinned people now being French citizens, they have had to change their way of thinking." She gestures around us, at the *gîtes*, the lake, the empty parking space. "Not as much here, in rural France. But then, they are suspicious of anyone who comes here from outside. Even though Henri's family are from the next village, when they owned the restaurant they were considered foreigners."

I say, "That's crazy! So how do they deal with real foreigners coming and buying up the place?"

Ishmael leans back and picks up his coffee mug. He says, "It was a shock to their system, but they were desperate to revive the area. And the French do respect people, no matter where they come from, who attempt to learn the local customs. And the language." He smiles. "Frank made the effort to learn French and they respect him for that." His smile widens. "Even when he is using it badly to curse their bureaucracy."

Isabella laughs. "Can you blame him? The bureaucracy here is insane. They have a desperate need to complicate everything. There is an official for everything." She sighs. "The *vide-greniers* tomorrow. My God, if I hear one more time another piece of paper Henri has to submit to the *maire*, I will hit him over the head with one of your sculptures. Speaking of which, did you finish what you needed for the stall tomorrow?"

Ishmael shakes his head. He returns to studying the lake. "I couldn't."

He'd come to the restaurant shortly after I had. He hadn't worked on the deer sculpture. None of us can bring up what happened this morning. Their eyes are red-rimmed and I know mine are too.

I say, "If you were planning to put the one you were working on up for sale tomorrow, the deer bust, do you mind if I buy it instead? When it is done. Or as it is."

Isabella's eyebrow rises and I say quickly, "I love it. It doesn't seem right for it to go on sale at the village *fête* after what happened."

Ishmael stands. "It wasn't your fault I didn't finish it. You don't have to feel guilty." His smile is sad. "And it would be difficult for you to get it on the plane back."

I say, "It's not guilt, though I did get in the way of your work on it this morning. I really do love it. I'll find a way to get it back."

My mind floods with images. Chloe and David getting married, me leaving this place, leaving Ishmael, Isabella. And then the two images that haunt me, both intertwined, until I see Lana's body, lying in the field, unmoving, holding the baby deer.

I rub my eyes, trying to dislodge the image, and the worry.

And I see instead Ishmael's smile on the first day when I walked into the restaurant, the thudding of my heart reminds me how I've known for every moment where in the room he's been when he's present.

Ishmael says, "If you insist." I realise I'm staring at him again. The same awareness is in his eyes and it suddenly becomes important that I need to stop him thinking I can fall for a man.

Because I can't.

Not if my life until now has meant anything. Not if my love for Chloe meant anything or means anything now. I pushed her away for as much as allowing the potential of being bisexual.

"I'll work something out with Zara. We should be able to get it home." I swivel to Isabella. I force a smile onto my lips, into my eyes. "Have you ever been to Ireland?"

I see Ishmael's face out of the corner of my eye. I see it fall, and fade. And I am guilty, but I can't afford to feel anything.

Isabella says, "No. Not yet. I want to visit." She chuckles. "Though, I'm a sun-worshipper. Is there ever any sun there? From what Frank says, I think not."

I search her face. There are lines of strain through the cheer. She watches Ishmael gather the mugs and spoons, the milk jug and the sugar bowl. Load it all onto a tray. It rings in me, the clinking of porcelain off iron, small and tight. His movements, small and tight.

Isabella says, "We might all come and visit you in Dublin."

I smile at her, my eyes following the figure carrying the tray into the house until he is swallowed up by the tall doorway and the high-ceilinged kitchen. "You would all be welcome."

Isabella sighs. "I wouldn't mind leaving here right now, the way I'm thinking about this place." She leans forward and whispers, "You are perhaps the same way now, that it is all too much. You look more worried now than when I first met you." She smiles. "Though I have seen you laugh a lot too. When you came here, you were angry, not worried. Now you are more alive, but anxious."

"You watch everything as well, don't you?"

Her eyes are sad. She sweeps her hair off her neck. "I've seen too much. Sometimes I wish I could forget everything, wipe out the slate, and just live life. Have the innocence of a child."

Lana in the field.

Her baby beside her.

I flinch.

She asks, "Are you okay?"

I nod. Rub away the images. "Seeing things through a child can be so freeing. Did you ever want kids?"

She has her hair in her hand and lets it fall over her face. "I did, but I can't have children."

"I'm so sorry."

Her hand moves again to gather her hair in a ponytail. "I haven't been lucky in some ways." She lets go and gestures around her. "And in so many other ways, I'm blessed."

I cannot hold it in anymore. I blurt out, "Isabella, do you know what happened to Lana? I can't stop thinking about her."

Isabella's face betrays an instant of fear and surprise. She recovers quickly and smiles. "Why would you be thinking of Lana? Because you think she is beautiful?"

I nod. "She intrigues me. As I said, there aren't many Indian women in Ireland. I'm training to be a journalist." I smile, try to sound relaxed. "Well, I'm writing articles for magazines, and I hope to do more of that. It's the way I am. Something catches my attention and I can't let it go until I know as much as possible. Lana and David, they make me wonder. I'm thinking of going to find him when I get back."

Isabella gasps. "You are?" She reaches casually for her coffee, but the movement of the mug to her lips is shaky.

"I thought, why not? I'm writing on those issues, brown skin, growing up in Ireland, living there as an outsider in my skin, and here is this Indian woman who fascinates me, so why not write about her. There is so much more I want to know." The panic is building in Isabella's eyes though her lips stay fixed in polite interest. "I've already found out she worked in a lesbian bar, I mean, how different is that? I talked to her ex-boss and I want to get an idea of how the women, the lesbian community, how they interacted with her, not only as a brown Indian woman but as a straight woman."

Isabella is paler, under her brown skin. She says, "You talked to her boss?"

"Yes, Gemma. There was a group photo of the staff from when Lana worked in the bar. Gemma is going to scan it and email it. She sent a photo of the photo, but it's not clear at all."

She turns her head and I can't see her eyes anymore, but her voice is shaky. "That's interesting. I certainly did not get the impression when I met Lana that she was lesbian."

"No. No, I don't know if she had any leanings that way. I mean, she was married, and straight people can work in gay bars. But there was something in the way she was in the photo, like she was at home, one of the women. If I had only seen the photo without knowing she was straight, I might have wondered. I usually have a good sense of these things."

Do I anymore? I'm beginning to wonder if I have a good sense of anything to do with people being lesbian or gay or bisexual or transsexual or queer or any other fecking letter in the cloudy soup.

A surge of anger knocks me aside. I'm chasing Lana for Chloe's sake. To figure out if she can trust the man she's marrying instead of me.

In my annoyance, I ignore Lana's effect on me, as I got to know her, to care, to worry about her. The anger makes me push harder.

I say, "Gemma said Lana had gone away. I'm thinking I'll go and find David and ask him. He'll probably tell me she left him to run away with a woman." I give a short laugh. "That's what my instinct tells me anyway. Or she finally realised she was gay and left him. And then I'll go and discover her on the scene somewhere."

Isabella is looking behind me, to the back door to the house. For a moment, it's as if she's asking for help.

"Isa? Everything okay?" Ishmael's voice is full of concern. I turn with a fright. He threads his way through the flower pots and chairs on the deck.

Isabella smiles. "Yes. Of course." She jumps up, knocking the table with her thighs, rattling cutlery and plates. "How late it is! I promised to help Henri with the preparations for tomorrow." She picks up her empty coffee mug and turns to me. "It was very interesting talking with you, I'm sorry I have to run."

She hugs Ishmael, leaning on him. "Tell Frank I'll see him this evening. I have to do this for Henri otherwise he will sulk for days."

Ishmael nods. "I'll see you later."

Isabella hurries off the patio and disappears into the house. Moments later she appears, striding away on the road to the village. Ishmael's face as he watches her makes me feel like an awkward clueless cat that has landed amongst the French pigeons.

CHAPTER TWENTY

Gemma's voice on the phone had been worried. She'd given me the number I'd asked for, David's neighbour's number. Lana's book had mentioned a Mrs Flynn, the neighbour on their right. I remember the house with its lace-curtained windows from when the lads and I had gone to the estate.

The woman has a landline.

I hand the paper with my scrawls on it to Zara.

Zara hands me her phone to dial and I pull back the paper and punch the numbers in, give her back the phone after I hear the ringing at the other end.

I hear the voice answer.

Zara says, "Mrs Flynn? Is that you?"

She gives me a thumbs up. I gesture at her to put the phone on speaker. She pokes at it and I take it back and touch the speaker icon.

The voice at the other end is shaky. "Yes. Hello? Hello? Mrs Flynn here."

Zara says, "My name is Zara Dillon. I wonder if you have a minute to talk?"

"Who? Dillon?"

Zara says, "You can call me Zara, Mrs Flynn. Would you mind a quick chat? I am a friend of your neighbour and I've been trying to get in touch with her."

"Bridget's friend. You say you're a friend of Bridget's. I don't remember her being friends with the Dillons. Where did you say you were from, is it the Ballinasloe Dillons?"

Zara laughs. "No. The Brooklyn Dillons. I think we were from Sligo originally though. Or Roscommon, I can never remember."

"Brooklyn in New York? America?"

"Yes, that one."

"Now I know Bridget definitely did not have friends in the Brooklyn Dillons."

I sigh. This might take a while.

Zara says, "Bridget might not have had friends there, but Lana did. Your neighbour on the other side, Mrs Flynn."

There is silence on the line.

"Mrs Flynn?"

"You mean the Pakistanian one?"

I frown.

Zara says, "Yes. The Indian woman. Lana."

"Was that her name?"

"Yes, ma'am."

My gut curls. How long had they been neighbours, living side by side?

The voice is slower, thoughtful. "Lovely young woman, that one. Such a sweet smile."

Zara says, "That's the one, Lana."

"You know, they were the only coloured people here."

My frown gets deeper.

Zara says, "That must have been difficult for them."

Mrs Flynn's voice is sad. "Maybe it was, my dear. I wanted to talk to her, several times, I did. I don't know why I didn't. I think it was him. The husband. Were you friends with him? I didn't think he had many friends, though he always smiled at everyone here, very charming."

"No. I didn't know him. Only Lana."

"Yes. Lana. That's a nice name. Such an exotic name. It suits the lass. She was beautiful. In a dark way, you know. She was the first coloured woman I saw and I thought they would all be like her. But they are not. I see more now, in the supermarket on a Thursday when my son takes me to Aldi. Some of them are as ordinary as us. In a dark way, though."

"Yes, she was beautiful. It's nice you have a son who takes you shopping in the week."

"He's a good one, my Barry. He used to live in America. Thank the Lord he came back after the Celtic Tiger thing."

Zara says, "Is Lana still living there? I can't get through on her phone anymore. I'm calling from abroad."

"Sure, loveen, why didn't you say? And here's me, gabbing on about my boy. The telephone charges will kill you."

"No. No. It's okay. I'm on one of those plan things. I can talk forever on one of those. I think."

I sigh again. I should grab a beer and take a ringside seat.

Mrs Flynn says, "They don't live there anymore." Her voice lowers to a whisper. "That did not end well."

Zara whispers, "What happened?"

I can sense Mrs Flynn glancing around herself before talking. "No one can make out what happened. But they talk, you know."

"And what do they say?"

"They say she pushed your man down the stairs. Well, Mr Boyle says that. He said he has a cousin who works in Casualty and the cousin said an Indian man came in with broken bones from a fall down the stairs. But Mrs Given, down in number 34, she said he fell off a ladder because there was one out the back and it was on the ground. All I know is there was an ambulance next door, I remember the lights being so bright, but I only saw it going away, I think I didn't wake up when it came because of my sleeping tablet."

I'm frowning. This is unexpected. Zara's eyebrows are raised as well.

"Was Lana there? Why did they think she pushed him?"

"Oh, you know how all these people talk. They have nothing in their lives so they make up stories. As if she was crazy or something. Me, I don't participate in gossip. No. That's something I do not do."

"I'm sure you don't, Mrs Flynn. Was Lana there that night? When did she leave?"

Mrs Flynn's voice descends into a dramatic whisper. "You see, that's why everyone says these things. We never saw Lana after that." She coughs. "Not that we saw much of her before, but I can say for sure we never saw her after that night. Mrs Given does not remember seeing her after that. So of course, Eddie Boyle makes up all these stories. He was always one for the stories. That man, you could not get him to shut up. Poor man, rest his soul, what a way to go."

"Who? David?"

"David?"

"Lana's husband, David."

Mrs Flynn says, "Is he dead?"

Both Zara and I sigh.

Zara says, "You said, 'poor man, rest his soul'. Did you mean David?"

"No. No. I meant Mr Boyle. He passed away last year. What do you call them, hit and runs? In the cold. They found him too late, frozen stiff on the road. He was a cold stiff, that's what the cousin said."

Zara shakes her head. "Poor man, rest his soul. Now David. Did he say anything about Lana after that night?"

Mrs Flynn gives a nervous laugh. "Sure, loveen, I never talked to him when they were there. I think he was in hospital a long time, he wasn't here. But he got a new job I think the next year. Or he came into money. Or possibly that was his brother, the one who owns the house. Nice new Mercedes-Benz. With all the shifts those doctors have to work. I think he is a doctor. I don't know why he was staying here, you'd think a big-shot doctor would move to where the others are. They cleaned up the house after. Made it nicer than most in the estate. Not mine, of course. My Barry would not have that. He put in the new garden which was better than next door's. When I said to him the house was manky next to theirs. Straight away, the next week, everything was new here. The house was empty for a while, you know how it is, when stories get out. But the young ones are there now, college students, like used to be there before."

I mouth the word 'Lana' at Zara. She nods.

Zara says, "It was a while since I saw Lana. How was she looking when you saw her last? Still pregnant?"

Mrs Flynn is quiet for a moment. She sighed. "So she was pregnant. I thought so. That last month. She looked, I don't know, fuller. And she looked like she was going to vomit sometimes. You know, she was working a lot, and then one day she stops. I think she stopped. And the husband used to go out again, you know, he was always home before, except some evenings when she was working. I would see him going out, all dressed up. And sometimes I would hear him taking out the rubbish before she got back. A bit noisy, the rubbish, as though there was glass in there."

She is silent, then says slowly, "I thought of going over there a few times. You know, when she was on her own. To tell her to come on over for a cup of tea. She looked like she needed it, the poor mite." She sighed again. "But you know how proud people can be. You never know what their religion might tell them too. I didn't know if she was allowed to talk to us Christians."

I want to speak, to say Lana and David were probably Christian too. The name 'David' should have given them a clue. The surname 'Matthews' should have confirmed it.

Mrs Flynn is quiet.

We are all quiet.

The image of Lana sitting at her kitchen table, alone, pregnant, afraid, keeps pushing into my mind and reflects in Zara's face as well, and in the silence over the phone.

Zara says, "She smiled at you whenever she saw you, didn't she?"

Mrs Flynn says, "Yes."

"And you smiled back?"

"Yes. I did. You could not help but smile back even if you were like Mrs Given and not inclined to be friendly to anyone else, you would smile for her."

"That must have been good for her. Must have made her feel less lonely."

Mrs Flynn's voice sounds lighter. "Yes, thank the Lord, yes, that must have helped a little."

"You're a good neighbour, Mrs Flynn."

"I'm sorry I could not be of more help."

"When was it, the night when David had the accident?"

"Let me think. My Barry was not home yet from America. He visited when the husband came back months later. I remember because I told Barry I was not happy living next door to a man whose wife had left him, the husband never went out for days on end. Then he cleaned up and started to work. Let me see, my Barry has been moved back only a couple of years, but he visited in 2013. I think the accident was in 2013. Yes, it was. I remember because I said to my Barry it took years for him to decide to move home to help his poor old mother. And of course, there was that whole thing with the brown woman who died in the hospital here because they would not let her have an abortion. Sad, so sad. You can't have an abortion. It's not right. It was on the news every night, not only RTE you know, the foreign channels also, BBC and that American one."

My heart skips a beat, but then I realise it wasn't Lana. I'd followed the Savita thing with a broken heart, those photos on TV, a smiling Indian woman mauled in our Catholic hell.

Zara says, "Is there anything else you can remember about Lana at that time? Did David ever say to any of the neighbours where she had gone?"

Moments pass and then Mrs Flynn says, "He told Eddie Boyle once that she had gone back home, to her parents. I think he said he was going himself to visit them."

Zara raises her eyebrows at me and I raise my shoulders. No more questions come to mind and I don't think Mrs Flynn has any more answers.

Zara says, "Mrs Flynn, thank you so much, it has been so nice chatting with you. I live in Galway myself, and I'll be sure to come and visit if you'd like."

"I would, loveen, you're welcome. The house is looking lovely, it's a shame not to have visitors."

They say their goodbyes and I reach over and put off the phone.

My mother and I stare at each other across the table.

She doesn't seem to want to talk and I'm not in the mood either.

We sit quietly and I know Lana weighs on both our minds.

CHAPTER TWENTY-ONE

Zara waves me over to the table and I walk towards them on the transformed terrace, conscious my dress is clinging to my hips, aware of Chloe, Ishmael, Isabella, watching me. As are Frank and Henri, but they're in the corners of my vision.

A vision blurred now by confusion.

Lights have been strung up and a space cleared for the stage and dancing.

Frank is closest to me and stands up to pull out a chair. "Jaya, you look lovely."

I thank him, and my eyes meet Ishmael's and I blush.

Chloe says, "The band is excellent. Three English lads and they play covers we know."

I try not to stare at her, but she's radiant, in a deep purple dress, her skin aglow in the warm light of the terrace. Her hair lies gold on her bare shoulders.

Taking a deep breath, taking in the ache of the known contours of her beauty. She can see into me, she always has.

I tear my gaze away, catch Ishmael's eyes before his lashes lower and tremble against his cheek.

Isabella places her hand on Chloe's. "It's a pity your fiancé had to miss this night. But you're getting this band for your wedding, aren't you?"

Henri says, "Yes. It was my recommendation for the lovely couple."

Chloe smiles at him. "Thank you, so sweet of you." She turns to Zara, "Matt and I were dancing to this song when he proposed."

Zara clapped her hands together. "I love a romantic gesture."

I had proposed by our fireplace, coal burning red, shadows dancing with us when she said Yes.

There is a hint of pain in Chloe's eyes. I know we are both seeing into the same room.

Chloe swallows a gulp of wine. She says, "Any requests? These guys say they can sing pretty much anything."

Frank says, "If you get them to play anything by Van Morrison, I'll even get up to dance."

Chloe jumps out of her chair. "I'm sure I can get them to play something. Only if you dance with me." She smiles. "If you can bear my two left feet."

Frank laughs. "You're sweet, pretending it won't be my fault if we stagger across the floor."

Frank gets up and waits beside the table as Chloe goes to talk to the musicians. His hand rests lightly on my shoulder and gives a gentle squeeze before he joins Chloe and they walk onto the dance floor.

Isabella smiles. "The two of them can dance. Frank says he's clumsy. Gets him out of going to parties."

Henri gets up and gives her an elaborate bow. "Would my beautiful wife dance with me?"

She waves him away, but gets up and lets him lead her to the dance area.

Zara says, "That leaves the three of us, and my legs are hurting from all the walking today." She turns to Ishmael. "Jaya is not in the slightest bit averse to dancing as far as I know."

My heart pounds faster. I frown at my mother as Ishmael stands.

He smiles, "I'm not the dancer Frank is, but I usually don't bruise anyone's feet too badly."

He's wearing black trousers and a blue silk shirt that moves loosely against his skin. He stands near my chair and I shoot Zara with a look before standing.

His hand is outstretched and I place mine in his. His palm is cool and dry, his grip gentle as he leads me through the growing crowd of couples. Chloe is smiling at Frank, talking to him. She sees us walk onto the floor and her brow crinkles for a moment, and then the crease is gone and she resumes her conversation. Isabella looks at Chloe and Frank and then at me. She is facing them and she smiles at Ishmael before turning her head back to them.

We have reached an empty space. Ishmael waits until I turn around to face him. He puts his hands on my waist. He is only an inch taller than me, his breath whispers on my cheekbone. He holds me like precious china, reverent in the polite distance between our hips. The straps of my dress are thin, leaving bare skin that tingles against blue silk.

The first notes of the song are familiar. The guitar wails and the drums beat a slow pulse into the warm air. The singer is English, but he takes on an American accent as he croons the song. 'Wicked Game.'

Ishmael murmurs in my ear. "He sings this almost as well as Chris Isaak, doesn't he? I love this song."

I do too.

My nipples rub raw against the cotton shield between my breasts and the silk.

I lay my head in the crook of his shoulder, his fingers tighten against my sides, his chest moving with more effort. I want to be pulled close, to be held as if I could be crushed but won't break. My hands move from around his neck, down to his waist, the way I'm accustomed to dancing. I turn my head, remaining cradled, but now my breath flows over the smooth line of his throat, into the dip between his collarbones. Our breathing has quickened and I know I'm stoking a flame in me, in him, that will burn, but I can't stop. The words of the song wrap around us, holding us in a web of music.

Ishmael sways with me, but he is holding me up and must sense the tension stiffening my spine as the music fades into the last lines.

I remember where I am. *And who I am.*

I whisper, "I can't do this. I'm lesbian. And I'm with someone, a woman...And I'm so confused. Chloe..."

Ishmael pulls away, leans across, kisses me on the left cheek and then the right cheek. I can't see his face before he turns away.

Frank and Chloe are leaving the floor and Ishmael bows to them.

He takes Frank's hand and they return to the middle of the dance floor.

I look at Chloe, my familiar heart, the woman I pushed away for having the potential to be with a man.

I hold out my hand.

She hesitates. Her bare shoulders and neck betray a darkening of pink under the tan.

I say, "I won't bite."

She smiles. "They *are* playing our song."

I pay attention to the music and smile. "Okay, one of our three songs, your one."

The singer is strumming his guitar, singing low into the mic. An Adele song, 'Someone Like You,' and he's singing it pretty well.

She takes my hand. I follow her to a bare space and she turns and we stand awkwardly for a moment before folding into the contour of a familiar embrace.

I can feel her heart in my chest and I know she can feel mine.

The music comforts us into a gentle swaying and this is where I want to stay, without thinking, without confusion, me and this woman in whose arms we are perfect.

§

The bar is emptying out. The young servers who were employed as extra hands for the music night have helped clear up and are giggling and messing with each other as they wait for their parents to give them a ride home.

Zara left an hour earlier, horrified when she checked the time, pleading to make friends with her bed.

Isabella and Frank and Ishmael are finishing the closing down of the kitchen and bar.

Chloe wanders the terrace wiping already clean tables.

I sit on the terrace steps and watch the stars. The sky is thick with them. They weigh down on the air around my shoulders.

Someone sits beside me and I know from our dance and from the scent of her perfume it is Chloe.

The night is pleasant, but her shoulders are bare. I ask, "Do you need a jacket?"

She shakes her head, her hair reflecting the single lamp from the terrace. She gestures towards the lake. "Want to go for a walk? It's beautiful at night."

I nod and she gets up and offers her hand.

I take it and we walk, hands loosely entwined.

The tarmac parking lot ends in a crescent of low-cut grass. I stop and take off my shoes with my left hand and she does the same with her right hand.

The grass is cool under my feet.

The lake is surrounded by a sand beach that falls away from the grass. We are silent as we walk under the trees, the moon winking between the leaves, twinkling on the surface of the silver lake. My hand hangs forlorn when she lets go of it to sit on the sand.

I sit beside her. She leans on me and her bare shoulder is soft and warm against mine.

Her voice wanders between us. "What are we doing?

"I don't know." I turn my head. Her hair caresses my cheek. "All I know is this feels right, to be sitting here with you. More right than anything that has happened since I got here, and the last three years should never have happened. This is right, the years of hell were wrong."

"Until last year. For me, it was hell for a long time after I left you, but the last year has been different."

"You feel this. It isn't solely me."

"Jay, I feel what I've always felt for you." She pulls away. "Except for the commitment to spend the rest of my life with you. I can't get that back. Something broke inside of me and I can have all those emotions when I'm with you, the effect you have on me is the same. But a new part of me can't trust us anymore."

The sand shines pale beside my legs. The tears seep into my eyes.

Her fingers lift my chin. I keep my eyes closed so the tears don't show. Her body moves towards me and her lips are on mine and her tongue is pushing into mine and I'm holding her face and kissing her. My hands sink into her hair, drawing her closer, her breasts against mine.

I have an image of Ishmael's face, for a moment. I push it aside, into the shades of my mind.

Chloe pulls her mouth away. She rests her forehead against my neck. Her breathing is fast, matching mine.

Her voice is soft, slightly breathless. "We were always good together physically. And I love you. As a person, a woman, a feisty little nut as well as a brave big-hearted warrior. We had a chance, but we missed it."

Through the confusion of rushing blood, her declaration warms me. Even as I ache with loss.

My heart continues to race. I breath in, to slow it. I smile. "Who are you calling a nut?"

Her laugh is a release. She sounds relieved. "I do love you."

"Not enough to marry me."

She leans back into me and I hold her.

She says, "I did. Love you enough to marry you. But you weren't ready. While I don't need the type of love that blows me away, I realised

I would like it if it comes with the steady love too. I love David deeply. I wouldn't have agreed to marry him if I didn't. For me, I need to be attracted physically and to love the small quirks of a person as well as their true character. I need us to fit and I choose whether to work at the relationship. I couldn't get by your distrust of me. And I sensed deep in me you needed more. Don't you have that with what's her name, Fiona?"

"I don't know what I have with Fiona. I care for her of course. And I'm grateful."

"You don't stay with someone because you're grateful. And you don't get yourself on the cover of a lesbian magazine with someone as the face of the gay marriage fight if you're merely grateful."

"We'll be one of the faces, well, two of them. There will be other couples on it too. They're doing the story on a few of us. I might be the token brown woman."

Chloe sighs. "Jaya Dillon, what are you doing?"

"It's your fault." There, I said it.

"*My* fault?"

"Well, you never seemed truly there. You know, committed. I get it more now, but at the time it felt like at any moment you could have gone off with a guy. And I left everything behind for you. I left the place where I believed I belong, on the scene, with other lesbian women. That didn't go down too well with anyone. And then the Pride march happened and the stabbing and Fiona was with me at the hospital and my friends came and set up camp there and the media was all interested. It kind of went from there."

Chloe leans forward and swivels to stare at me. "So how is it my fault?"

"I was angry at you. When I went to the march. You'd left me and now I wasn't welcome in my own group, the one place where I felt I belonged. You always got to choose where you went. You never have to feel like an outsider, even being English in Ireland, you could fit in, being white and all."

Understanding creeps into her eyes.

I say, "I'll never fit in there, not as Irish. But with Fiona, with the women, I'm one of them, one of the women, a lesbian fighting alongside, not outside." I don't want her understanding or her pity, I want her to see me. "When you hide the lesbian side of you, when you make me hide, it is like we're nothing. And I know straight women who fall for a woman and then run from the difficulty of being lesbian, not from the feelings."

Chloe touches my lip with her fingertip. "I'm not straight, I'm bi. Which means to me I was, still am, attracted to you. And I loved you as a lover, a woman. My fears of being out weren't to do with you, they concerned my father and his religion. I was confused then. I've been scared to tell David because I can't deal with another partner who can't trust me. That took such a toll on us, Jay. You could never trust I loved you, always sniping at me going back to men. I don't want David to do the same to me, always wondering whether I would return to women." She moves her finger away, gazes at the water. "I want him to be convinced I love him for him, so when I tell him he won't fear me leaving him for a woman." She smiles. "Or at least, we'll simply have the same concerns as any other couple, not double the worry."

"And yet you are here, with me. Seems as though he would be right to worry."

She sighs. "Yes. I guess so."

Her shoulder tenses against my chest. "Anyway, you can't argue with me anymore about being bi. Not when you're so into a man."

"A man?"

Her voice holds a smile. "I know you too well, Jaya Dillon."

The years of battle press down on me, but she's right, I have no weapon anymore. It is damaged, rusty and useless, in the confusion that is Ishmael.

She leans back and snuggles in closer. "I understand the trust thing now. I can't stop worrying about Lana, whether David is hiding something from me. It's affecting me and I know how that kind of worry and lack of trust can ruin a relationship." She laughs, a soft rumble against my chest. "Here I am. Talking about trust. After kissing my ex-girlfriend. And I haven't told David about you yet, that I'm bi. I'm going to tell him as soon as he gets back. Going to ask him straight out about Lana. We need to clear these things from our way and start with no skeletons in the closet." I hear the smile in her voice. "That sounds so inappropriate on both levels, doesn't it? Didn't mean to. I don't know why I'm relieved, but I am."

Her body relaxes into the spoon of mine.

I cannot let it go like that. I want to get to Lana without going through David. I'm not ready to trust him.

We sit, me holding her, both of us facing the lake, watching the moon dance on its surface.

She shivers and I realise we've been there almost an hour. The moon has gone to sleep behind a cloud and the light in the sky is from the early rays of the sun, deep pink streaks hinting at its presence waiting behind the horizon.

I tighten my hug. I whisper. "We should get you into bed." I smile. "I mean, you need to get to bed."

She sighs. Stretches. "There I was thinking I'm a young kid who can pull an all-nighter." She gets to her feet, slowly, leaning on my shoulder, giggling.

She helps me up and smacks the sand off my backside.

We walk to the restaurant, our shoes low-heeled, but wobbly on the tarmac.

She grins. "What's this called, a dirty stop-out?"

I say, "What's going to happen? With us."

She stops, turns to me. "I have no regrets." She leans into me and places her lips against mine and I know this is our last kiss and my mind is filled with a mixture of loss and gratitude. Losing her is a painful rooting out of my centre, of what's kept my heart going since I met her. And I'm grateful I recognise the last kiss, I didn't know the day I walked into the room and she was gone. My heart is trying to catch up with my mind. It doesn't want to let her go.

We move apart and I open my eyes. The baker's van is parked beside the restaurant. Ishmael is holding a bundle of bread rolls and turning to go into the kitchen. His field of view includes us, but his face shows no emotion as he turns away. Isabella is standing at the kitchen door. Her hand touches his shoulder, her eyes show an emotion that looks like hurt.

CHAPTER TWENTY-TWO

Lana walked into the restaurant through the kitchen door. She was surprised to see Jaya sitting at the bar counter, head resting on both hands, eyes closed. Lana stopped and stared for a moment, while she had a chance.

She looked without any chance of being seen.

And no chance of being loved.

Even if Jaya had not been kissing Chloe hours ago. Lana in hiding would never be able to reach Jaya. And the fear of Jaya finding her. Lana knew she was playing with fire, Jaya had already gotten dangerously close too often. She had to withdraw, distance herself, stay safe.

But that pull grasped at her again, and she moved to stand beside Jaya, helpless, a moth drawn.

Lana said, softly, in Jaya's ear. "You must be tired."

Jaya spun around on the stool. She cleared her throat. "What? Why?"

There was a cup of coffee in front of Jaya. Lana needed one. She walked around the counter and behind the bar. She started the ritual of making coffee, conscious Jaya was watching her.

The smell of roasted beans floated in the air, mixed with the sunlight.

Jaya sighed. Her eyes were bloodshot, from the lack of sleep, probably from the turmoil of emotions.

Lana smiled. "Late nights can be tough at our age."

"Hey!"

"We don't have to worry as much though, with our brown skin."

Jaya said, "You don't have anything to worry about." Her voice was envious though she didn't need to be. Her skin was smooth, the colour of the coffee as Lana poured in the cream.

Lana turned to Jaya. Her right eyebrow arched as she saw Jaya was staring again.

Lana watched the shade of pink rising, an infinitesimal reddening of the sandstone colour. That was how she thought of Jaya's skin, red clay mixed with white sand. Jaya's eyes were stained with tiredness, but the autumn green irises lined by forest green were startling in the earthy setting. Startling at first glance, then riveting, inviting into their depths.

Lana turned away. She had to stop staring at Jaya.

She cleared her throat, and her voice came out husky. "Will you keep drinking it with Nutella when you go back to Ireland?" She put the cup on a saucer and placed her coffee on the bar, taking care to keep her hand steady. "You *are* going back, aren't you?" She hadn't meant to say that, hadn't meant it to sound judgmental, inhospitable. She saw the hurt flash into Jaya's eyes, for a second, and then it was blinked away.

Jaya said, "You can't wait to get rid of me? You all think Chloe is so much better off with Matt?"

"I didn't mean that." She couldn't say what she had meant. That she couldn't face the thought of Jaya not being here. Or the thought of Jaya loving Chloe. But Jaya was out of bounds. So she shouldn't be having any of these feelings, too many consequences, all bad, came from allowing them any air.

"What did you mean then?" Jaya glanced behind her, at the parking spot where Lana had seen her and Chloe kissing.

Jaya turned back. "You saw us this morning?"

Lana shook her head. "I saw nothing. It isn't my business."

"You've both been making it your business since I arrived. Why stop now?"

Lana felt herself starting to blush. She'd been trying to get close to Jaya, first trying to protect their secrets, and Chloe, to stop her making a mistake, to keep Matt and Chloe together, but then to stop Jaya from finding Lana. At least that's how it had started. Not because Jaya took her breath away, from the moment she'd first seen her, from the first smile. For every moment since, even as she watched Jaya watch Chloe.

Jaya and Chloe kissing this morning. It brought it all back. Gemma with Tracy, the women at the bar. The churning confusion, the sickening fear.

Lana lowered her gaze. "I don't want anyone to get hurt."

"But you think it's more right somehow? Matt and Chloe together?"

Lana grabbed a cup from the stack and put it on the grill. She scooped the dark powder into it. Then realised she'd already made a cup of coffee. It was sitting there, beside Jaya's cup.

Jaya's voice was bitter. "Because straight people deserve to be happy. The world makes sense then, doesn't it?"

Lana leant her head against the silver coolness of the coffee machine. Nothing made sense. "Yet you are a lesbian woman attracted to a gay man and *that* makes sense?"

She heard the cup clatter into the saucer. She turned. Jaya was wiping at the drops on the counter with her fingers. Lana picked up a napkin and placed it over the spill.

Jaya mumbled. "A gay man who wants to be a lesbian woman. Tell me again how this isn't all fecked up."

They stared at each other and for a moment it was like they would drown, and then they laughed, suddenly, spontaneously, and it poured out of Lana, this need to let go, to live, really live free for the first time in her life.

"What's so funny?" Chloe's voice broke into the moment.

Lana saw Jaya's startled movement, the change in expression. Jaya swivelled around on the barstool.

Chloe and Zara were standing at the entrance, both smiling.

Lana watched Jaya straighten her shoulders, sensed the painful image being gathered up and added to all the other images.

Jaya sighed. "Just life."

CHAPTER TWENTY-THREE

I watch Chloe enter the restaurant and I'm seeing her with new eyes. My heart lets go, tearing fibres as the old love wrenches away. There is a soothing that comes from the new love I have for her, one without conditions, purely the wish for her to be happy.

Ishmael confuses me, especially with my attraction to Isabella, but I recognise the same love for him intertwined in those same fibres, along with an attraction matching what I felt for Chloe and the other women I had desired.

It is strange and fills me with wonder, this new unconditional love, the tugging at my soul for Ishmael so soon. That I trust it now I realise I did not trust the version of it I had with anyone else before, the men or women I let into my heart before this.

Chloe smiles at me. She is different too, something has happened.

I smile back at her, shy with knowledge.

Zara sweeps in, wearing a purple velvet hat.

I look back at the coffee machine but no one is there.

I hear voices in the office. Isabella mentions the *vide-greniers* and I realise we are all going to be late if we don't get a move on.

Chloe says, "Did you get any sleep?"

I turn to her and Zara. Shake my head. "Not really."

Zara puts her bag on the counter. "I don't know whether to get coffee here or wait until we're at the market." She sips at my coffee. "I'll wait," she says.

I smile. "You might as well finish mine then."

Isabella comes out of the office. "Ishmael has gone ahead to set up his stall, he left it so late." She sounds exasperated.

My heart jumps at his name, but at Isabella's presence too, her beauty has that effect. I wonder for a moment whether I am just susceptible to beautiful women, in an indiscriminate fashion. My head shakes, no, I've been around many and I don't react this way.

Isabella says, "Yes, he can be disorganised sometimes." I assume she has mistaken the reason for my head-shaking.

"When does it start?" Zara gulps down more of my coffee.

Isabella says, "In approximately 30 minutes, but I'm always pressured to be there early because of Henri. Do you want to come with me or follow later?"

Zara sounds sheepish. "We have decided to fly to Galway tonight so we should probably go with you now."

I swivel on the barstool. "What?"

Chloe steps forward. "It's my fault. Matt got back to Galway late last night and called me this morning. He is all shook up, his mother died and he's been trying to reach me."

I frown. "I'm sorry."

Chloe bites her lower lip. Lets out a deep breath. "He was trying to reach me last night and I'd left my phone in the gîte for the party and then I didn't get back until this morning. He said he's sorted everything out and got an annulment and wants to get married as soon as possible. I thought we could all travel together. I'll have to arrange everything there, he wants the wedding in Galway. I could really use Zara's help."

The distress in my eyes must be evident because Zara puts her hand on mine.

I say, "That's fast. I thought you wanted to get married here?"

Chloe nods. Glances at Isabella hovering behind me. Chloe's voice is quiet. "I did. But Matt sounds so excited and wants us to start our life together properly. I only have a month or so to plan the wedding there."

Zara says, "Let's head down to the market and talk on the way." She gathers her bag to her. Takes my hand again and helps me off the barstool.

Isabella says, "You are paid up until after the weekend, aren't you? A few more days."

Chloe nods. "I know. I'm sorry, Jaya."

Isabella says, "Jaya could stay if she wanted."

She's right. And I hate to leave here this way.

I look back at Chloe. She smiles. Her voice is gentle. "You should stay."

Zara pats my arm. "Yes. You should. Chloe can drive me back in the rental car and we have to get her ticket anyway. You should stay as long as you need to. But get back before the referendum next week. If they are doing a what do you call hashtag to get emigrants home to vote Yes for same-sex marriage, then we can for sure get back to vote."

Chloe nods. "I can change your plane ticket or get a new one. Or you could go back by ferry if you want?"

I inhale and nod, breathe out the fear that has suddenly invaded my chest.

§

Stalls are being set up in the tarmac rectangle in front of the town hall, arranged under the shade of the trees lining the square and the central lawn is filled with simple folding tables draped in cloth and crowded with items, and spindly-legged tables covered with cream, green, yellow, multicoloured fabric as a shelter from the coming sun. People are unloading their cars and I recognise faces from the bar. We get waves and greetings as we pick our way through the newly-installed day market.

There are makeshift aisles emerging as order is slowly imposed on the chaos. Each vendor space is marked off with a pegged flag.

Isabella leads the way. She says, "Ishmael is at his usual spot. I always get him that slot as he is shy and does not push his sculptures forward."

Zara says, "It's a pity we are flying, there are several things here I'd love to get."

I say, "I already know what I'm buying." I think I'll take the ferry, that way I can carry the deer sculpture easily.

Isabella smiles back at me. "Ishmael has finished the deer. For you, I think."

Fear and shyness emerge again, and I push them down as I follow Isabella.

My mind and heart are so confused right now.

The other stalls fade away as I see Ishmael standing at the front of a stall with a cream fabric acting as the backdrop to an array of wood sculptures. The other people fade away as he turns and spots us coming and that smile emerges.

Isabella says, "Can I leave you with Ishmael? I need to help Henri."

Zara says, "We'll be fine, so much to explore. Let us say hello to

Ishmael and then we can get a coffee and a croissant? How about it, Chloe, last indulgence before we leave?"

I can hear Chloe's voice agreeing. I don't want coffee or a croissant. I want to stay and be.

Ishmael kisses the three of them on both cheeks. He is wearing white again, a loose shirt, gathered below his wrists, the soft cloth glowing against his skin. His face is drawn, but his smile blazes through me.

Isabella says, "Your stall looks wonderful as always." She scans the sculptures. "You didn't bring the deer?"

Ishmael blushes. "No." He moves to include me in the greetings.

Isabella smiles. Looks at me. "I think it might be your most beautiful piece so far."

I move closer to Ishmael, kiss his cheeks, his lips soft as he returns the greeting.

Zara exclaims from within the stall. "These are so beautiful, Ishmael. I wish I could get some of them, but we can't take them on the plane tonight."

Ishmael's face tightens, the smile slipping away. He turns to Zara. "Tonight?"

She nods. "Sadly, yes." She waves at me. "I'm going to get these amazing sculptures, you can deal with moving them." She turns to Ishmael. "You'll probably be busy all day with this. Chloe and I are going to get coffee and croissants, would you like something?"

Ishmael shakes his head. "Thank you, no, I had better finish setting up here." He turns away from me and I shiver at the chill in the resulting space. He picks up a smaller version of the demoiselle and puts the carved figurine on the other end of the table from its bigger sibling.

Isabella says, "Henri is already angry at me. I'll go now." She hurries away towards the church building on the far border of the square.

Zara and Chloe wander away in the opposite direction, towards the café, perusing the stalls.

I say, "Can I help you with anything?"

Ishmael doesn't look at me. He nods. "If you don't mind helping me put out all of these. I was late today."

We work silently, taking the wood pieces out of their boxes. He has transported them in the empty cardboard boxes they use for the produce in the restaurant. The brown tones gleam and dance in the shade and sun.

"Do you work all year on these for the market?"

He nods. "Most are for here. I take a few of the bigger ones to Limoges to a gallery there. Occasionally they sell."

"Do they sell for much?" I'm blushing. "I mean, as Zara said, the deer sculpture is the most beautiful and I want to buy it."

His warm presence is beside me, but I can't meet his eyes.

He says, "I kept it aside, but I haven't completely finished it. And how are you going to carry it on the plane? I think the weight restrictions will cause the airline to charge you for another seat."

"I'm staying until next week. And then taking the ferry."

The wooden bird in his hands pauses in its flight. He smiles. "You must really like the deer."

I say, "I do."

§

"A good day, you sold most of them." Isabella surveys the stall, her eyes wide. "And the day is not yet over."

Ishmael laughs. "I had a good salesperson."

Isabella turns to me. "I see that. You must have smiled at everyone who came near the stall. We could use you at Henri's mother's stall." She grins. "Even Madame LaForge would soften up."

Ishmael snorts. "Your mother-in-law is sweet with me, it must be you who makes her grouchy."

Isabella smacks him gently on his arm. "You cannot talk. If Jaya was not here, you would not have sold as many. Remember last year?"

Ishmael holds up his hands. "I do, I do."

Isabella says, "Jaya, your mother and Chloe are going to take the car to the *gîtes* and load it. They will either come back to say goodbye or I can take you later."

The fear screams again and I glance at Ishmael before shaking my head. "I'll go with them now."

I have been distracted, but I need to speak with Chloe, one last attempt to persuade her to slow down, at least until I find something to show Lana is alive and well, and get her to expose David as Thomas, or to determine for myself that Lana's novel is nothing more than her imagination.

§

"You didn't think to show me this before now?" Chloe's face is red, her voice angry. The notebook is trembling in her hands.

I say, "I didn't know whether it is fiction or the truth. I didn't want it to affect you. Not until I found out for sure."

Zara sighs. "Now is definitely not the best time for this."

I say, "I know. I was a bit distracted. Last night, this morning, today. And I knew Chloe would think I'm just doing it to get her back."

Chloe says, "And are you not? Doing this to get me back? You don't want to admit you are attracted to a man and it's so convenient to use me as an excuse."

"No!" I take the notebook out of her hands. "I've accepted we are over, that I love you as a friend. And because I do, I can't just let you walk back into the arms of someone who might have done something so wrong. Who might be a monster."

Chloe's voice rises. "A monster? Where do you get off calling my fiancé a monster? He's been nothing, but sweet." She turns towards Zara. "Zara saw how I've been since I met him. He's so wonderful. I'm the one who has kept things from him."

Zara holds my hand and squeezes, does the same to Chloe's then picks up her bag. "I can't be involved in this conversation." She walks to the door. "I love you both and I'm here for both of you, whatever you decide. I'll wait in the car." She goes outside and her footsteps sound slower as she makes her way through the courtyard. Chloe must have told her about our kiss, our early morning together. She seems to have set herself up for things being one way, Chloe going back to David, and she doesn't want to deal with any more change.

Chloe swings to face me. "See! Every time you come back into my life, there's chaos, drama, always. I want a quiet life, to be loved, to be married, have kids. A simple life. I'm not an activist. I never was. My dad, same thing. Everywhere we ended up, he'd get into a battle with a person or some group, he was always trying to do the right thing. And my mum had to live in chaos until she left. And then she dies, when she gets away. I got away from him, from all of that. No. I've had enough! Is it too much to ask for, to be able to settle down somewhere with someone who loves me for me, who takes care of me, who doesn't question everything."

The blood rushes to my head. I drop the notebook. "That's not fair! I was prepared to settle down with you. Did I not ask you to marry me? Aren't you the one who walked out on our wedding day? Did I not separate from all my friends to be with you? I want a quiet life too, but not at the expense of the truth. I can do the white picket fence too, but don't ask me not to speak up when I see something going on that's not right."

Chloe is holding her hand to her face, pressing her thumb and finger against her closed eyes.

I continue, my words jumping over each other to get out. "I don't want us to get back together. That's not why I'm asking you to wait a bit longer. I am terrified David is not what he is showing to you. Or he is, but there's another side to him. I'm scared for Lana. I've grown to care for her. I think Lana is hiding out as Isabella. I think Lana didn't kill herself, she ran away to Paris, to Frank and Ishmael and they all moved here and changed her identity." I move closer to Chloe. I put my hands on her arms, lower her hands from her face. Her eyes are tired, strained. "Lana describes a husband who is terrifying, who had everyone convinced she was crazy. What do you want me to do? Walk away from her? Be like all the others who didn't listen to her when she couldn't talk?" I drop my hands from her arms. "Sometimes the cries for help are not heard through your ears."

Chloe is silent and the words lie there, weighted down by the past, by the helplessness of years of conversations. There is too much between us, behind us, to let us see anything except through the lens of distrust, of change, of growth. I realise her vision is no clearer than mine.

Chloe's voice is low. "I need him to be who he has shown me. I love him. He fits me so much. He sees me. From what we know of Lana, she was confused. On the very issue that is David's weak spot. He cannot be around gay people, not because he is a bad person, but because his culture has taught him what to think of them, and his only experience with them is a woman who turned away from him, left him, took his baby, to be something taboo to her as well." She draws in a deep breath, her voice shakes. "Jaya, I need to be loved the way he loves me. I need everything to be normal. I can't put him through the same uncertainty as he went through with Lana and I don't want that distrust in my life again. Even if it means hiding a part of my past and myself from him. I cannot go questioning him, especially not when I have you hidden in my past."

Her words make cuts in me. "You are not even going to say you were with me, that you once loved me? Just because I am a woman?"

Tears slip down her cheeks. "No. I can't. And I didn't only once love you, I still love you, but it's not enough. It is enough with David. It's not about man or woman. I was as attracted to you. It's how he makes me feel completely loved. You and I weren't in the right place and time." She takes my hand. Her fingers are warm. "And you love me, but not in the way you love Ishmael. I can sense that from here, from the short time you've known him. And it doesn't matter if he's a man. Don't let that hold you back. Don't spend your energy trying to convince yourself to fight for us, solely because you can't admit to yourself or to your society you love a man."

"I might be unsure what I feel for Ishmael. And Lana or Isabella. But that's nothing to do with why I'm saying you should slow down with David."

She frowns. "What you feel for Lana or Isabella?"

I exhale. "Screwed up, isn't it?"

She can't seem to help her smile. She blows out a shaking breath. "Totally."

I find myself laughing.

She holds out her arms and I move into them.

We stand together, in each other's arms, holding on as the minutes slip away.

I hear a sound behind me, at the door. Chloe looks up and lets go of me quickly, almost guiltily. I glance around, but there is no one there.

Chloe says, "I'm going to Galway with Zara to prepare for my wedding in a few weeks. You should stay here and sort out who you love, Ishmael, a man who could be your soulmate, or Lana, a woman who you might not have met, or Isabella, who you have, or Fiona who you're supposed to be marrying soon." She smiles. "I think my love life is a bit simpler compared to yours."

I sigh. "You might be right." I give her a last hug and let go.

She picks up the notebook from the floor. "I don't need to know anymore what you find out about Lana."

I take the book and hold it against my chest. I nod.

She smiles and picks up the car keys. "But I do want to know how you are and who you end up with. And believe me, I want you to be happy."

'Only if you believe me, that I also want that for you."

She offers her hand. "Deal."

I shake her hand, pull her towards me and kiss her gently on the lips.

"I love you, Chloe Evans."

She smiles. "I love you too, Jaya Dillon."

She turns to go, stops, turns back to me "Are you not going to follow him? Ishmael was at the door and he looked pretty upset."

I say, "I've messed things up with him so often. And I still don't know what I'm doing."

She grins. "When has that ever stopped you before?"

CHAPTER TWENTY-FOUR

The rain came and went so quickly and ferociously that the birds sound as surprised by the change in the day.

I don't know where I am. I thought I'd be able to find my way to the studio.

My hair is wet, my shirt is hanging, gripping my hips, but parts of me are dry, the soles of my feet and my chest where I'd enclosed myself in the shelter of my arms.

The path looks familiar. I was certain when she'd brought me here, that Isabella had turned off the road at the farmhouse with the woodchip machinery. Then we'd walked through the trees and up a hill.

But I can't find the trail leading down from the top of the hill to the clearing. I should have come to it by now. We hadn't walked this far. But the sun had been shining then.

I sink to my knees on the path.

The air is thick around my head, heavy with the scent of green. Drops of rain are sliding down the blades of grass, abandoned there after the sudden deluge.

I want to cry, but nothing comes out.

§

I hear shoes on the stones behind me. I smell the musk of his cologne in the air beside me. I see drops on his eyelashes as he kneels in front of me.

His fingers tremble against my skin as he smooths the wet strands of hair off my forehead, away from my eyes.

His gaze focuses on my mouth and I'm aware of the pulse beating in my lips.

His fingers move down my damp cheek until they are resting beside my mouth. His thumb outlines the top of my upper lip, tracing then touching, gentle then tense.

He looks into my eyes and I see he's struggling. His body keeps swaying towards me, but he stops and pulls back.

I tilt, forward.

He waits, motionless, all of him except for his eyes.

His skin radiates warmth, an inch away. The world has gone silent around us and all I can hear is his breath.

I move that last inch knowing the distance is much more. But I don't want to know, I don't want to think anymore. I simply want to feel.

He moans as our lips meet, like he's releasing a breath held for a lifetime. Or it might be me, making the sound. I have no thoughts, no images, just the rush of tongue against lips, the roar of my blood racing.

I cup his neck, my fingers dipping into his hair. I pull us closer, bruising my lips against his.

He growls gently. His fingers leave my face and he grips my waist with both hands. He's holding our hips apart, and trembling.

I whisper, into his lips, "I won't break."

He leans his forehead against mine. His voice is husky, strained. "I 'm not sure how to do this. I mean, I know what I want to do, but I don't know if it will be right. To do this as a man."

I realise he's never been with a woman. Or he hasn't been as a woman.

The thought is so alien. I hadn't recognised it in all my confusion and avoidance. It's not only me this changes.

And I remember No more thinking. Not anymore. Not for now.

I say, "Where's your studio?"

His lips move in a smile. "It was the track you passed right after the rain came. I called after you, but the rain was too loud."

"So, it's not far."

He shakes his head. "Five hundred feet or so."

"Take me there. Please."

"I'll give you the sculpture if it means that much to you."

I jerk my head back, but he's smiling.

I say, "If you don't want to, that's fine too. I'll be heading back then."

He grins, but he's on his feet in seconds and reaches for my hand.

§

We are quiet as we walk. Every sound hums louder in my ears, the whisper of leaves, the random drops of rain, the gossip of the birds.

The sun is busy drying off the forest and the clearing is bright between the branches.

Ishmael moves from my side to open the door. He says, "I was working last night, it might be dusty in here."

I step inside. Warm air hugs me.

The deer sculpture is more defined now, smoother.

I turn to him. "It's beautiful."

He takes a step inside and closes the door.

His eyes are dark and liquid and the warmth becomes heat spreading through my veins.

I say, "You're not allowed to look at me like that."

"Like what?" He stays by the door.

"Are you coming in?"

He clears his throat. "Only if you want me to."

I nod. Say the word out loud, we both need to hear it. "Yes."

He moves towards me, takes my hand, puts his lips to my palm. The touch shoots through me and I groan in surprise.

He gasps and his lips move to mine.

He whispers, "I want to touch you, to look at you." His brown skin is smudged with red. "But it doesn't seem right being seen or touched while I'm this."

I say, "You are beautiful as you are." A smile jumps to my lips. "This is obviously weird for me. I don't know what to do either."

"Show me what you want." His eyes are troubled. "I only want to do what you like."

"If I think this through, I'll lose my mind."

He smiles too. "I see. So we're not going to think."

I watch the light in his eyes when he smiles, the sun rises in my chest. I whisper, "Maybe if you tell me how you feel, if we just sit here together and feel who we truly are."

His eyes fill. I get the sense it's the first time he's been asked.

He nods, trying to hide the tears.

I take his hand and lead him out of the studio, across the clearing, to the bench. Drops of rain puddle on the wood. He guides me instead to the tree and sits with his back against the trunk, cradling me in his arms. His heart beats against my back. Rain drops from the leaves.

His voice whispers against my cheek. "I don't know where to start."

"At the beginning. Wherever that was for you."

I can hear the smile. "How much time do you have?"

"As much as you need."

His voice is choked and thick, but gradually clears. "There are things I can't tell you, believe me I would love to, but I have to respect the safety and privacy of others. What I need to tell you is I've always been a woman inside and from my earliest memories, I've always been attracted to women. From watching the heroes and heroines in the movies and wanting to be like them, proud, open, able to sing their love for each other without fear, without being considered sick or dirty or a taboo that would cause my own parents to regard me with disgust."

It's an effort to imagine experiencing disgust at my sexuality in Zara's eyes. I don't have an image of my father, but I can see, theoretically, he would hold the same views as Ishmael's parents. But I can't relate to that, the only way I can is with the disgust I saw in the eyes of some of my teachers at school, or strangers on the street, at my skin colour, at being lesbian. I'm trying to wrap my head around seeing repulsion in a parent's eyes.

I say, "But you could have been with women without any taboo? As a man."

His chin bumps against the top of my head. His words are slow and thoughtful "But not as a woman as I wanted, that's what I was. I could never be a woman with a woman. I lived the lie, of being with men as a man, of trying to be with women as a man. Because the truth is I should be with a woman as a woman. And if even I cannot see the path clearly, *I* cannot accept this truth about myself, *I* consider it as abnormal and taboo. So how can I ask another to take that on, how can I ask my society here to accept that, how can I ask any society to accept what I myself cannot."

I lean my head back, against his shoulder. "I grew up with a mother who accepted me for who I was and yet I find myself trying not to be brown, trying not to be different. I'm able to accept the fact I was born lesbian easier than that I was born brown. I can't imagine being straight now, or being bisexual because that's what is frowned upon by people around me, the people that make up my home, and I really need to belong there, to belong somewhere."

He leans forward, his lips curve against my chin, his words breathe down my neck. "So, we find a part of us we've been told or shown is wrong and we hate that in ourselves and try to find a safe place outside of ourselves, when the enemy is inside us."

"Yes." I smile. "What do you do when you carry the enemy around with you. I've been arguing for so long against choice, against a woman being able to choose or feel love for a man as well as a woman, as if it's a choice. Because being brown, being different is not a choice and I can't hide my colour, but a person can hide who they love and can gain in society by hiding that, and can hurt others so much. I never thought I was hurting anyone by trying to expose that or by distrusting their actions."

Ishmael's voice is sad. "I guess I've gained so much by being a man. It's possible I didn't have the courage to show myself in case I lost the privilege I have. By being a member of the majority, by being respectable, I don't have to lose anything. Except myself." Tension suddenly enters his arms around me. "If you feel something for me, if you want to be with me, as I am, you will lose too."

I frown. "What do you mean?"

"The identities we have created to protect ourselves. One of us will lose that protection if we are to be our true selves. If this is something true and real."

The air in the clearing presses down on me again. I can hear the voice in me, the one that lies deep in me, I can hear her say she knows, she knows without question, without doubt, this is real and true. She is saying she knew the moment she looked into Ishmael's eyes, truly saw, without the demands of all the other voices inhabiting her, all the voices that grew from the seeds of other people's thoughts, other people's beliefs, all the voices that said she could only love in a way that was acceptable to whatever group she wanted to belong to.

She is not confused because she sees Ishmael, beyond a man or a woman. She is not confused, not one bit.

But I am.

All of these voices are now a part of me, as hateful as they are.

I thought I was courageous. I have faced thugs with knives that ripped into me. I would do the same again for anyone else.

Except for me.

I don't know if I have the courage to do it for me.

And I need to find Lana. To protect Chloe, but also to meet the woman in whose words I have immersed myself. The woman who has pulled me into herself, into her world, her words.

I say the truth. That is all I can do right now. "I feel it is real and true between us. But I am terrified and I don't think I have the strength right now especially when I am so confused."

He sinks into the tree that is holding us up. "Are you still in love with Chloe?"

I let myself imagine being with Chloe again, her face, her smile, her presence. "No. I am not in love with her."

What I see is Ishmael.

And Isabella. Not Isabella as she is, as much as Lana in the photo, Lana in her writing.

I pull away, out of Ishmael's arms. I turn and face him. Look into his eyes. The person I am drawn to, without reason, without rules. I will always be truthful with this person, as much as I know what is true.

I say, "It is like I have known you forever. I might have let you in as a person because there was no possibility I would complicate our connection by falling in love with you, as a man, or you falling in love with me as a gay man. I am attracted to you and that confuses me in the way I've experienced straight women, or women who thought they were straight, get so confused and fight against their attraction to a woman."

His breath has slowed, held back, waiting with a tiny furrow in his brow, but his kindness shines through his eyes as I fight with the familiar words.

I swallow. The fear, the confusion, the hiding, they will all be over for me when I confess, but my next words will pass to him, infect him. I am compelled to say them anyway. "I have to tell you I've been confused as well by my reaction to Lana, a woman I've never met, by her words, by the character she is in her novel. I've been searching for her, and I'll admit it, so I could use her to win Chloe back, but on the way that became less important than finding her for herself, and to know she is safe and happy somewhere. That has become crucial to me."

I continue though Ishmael's eyes are fixed, with fear in the widened depths of his pupils. I am all the way in, I won't hide the rest. "I believe Isabella is Lana. I need to convince her to tell me whether Thomas is David, to warn Chloe if he is."

Ishmael's body has stiffened, his arms tensed against the tree, hands twitching in the soil beside him.

His voice is high, through the tightened muscles of his throat. "What character Lana is? What has Lana got to do with winning Chloe back?" There is a dawning in his eyes now. "Chloe's fiancé...Matt? You want Isabella to warn Chloe about David? Matt is *David*? *That's* why you've been fascinated with Lana and watching Isabella?"

My head is shaking, but that was what I was doing. At the start. When I didn't know, and love, Ishmael and Lana.

His voice trembles, deepens. "Do you realise what you would be doing? What will happen to us?"

"Why would anything happen to Isabella if she is who you say she is? I know from Lana's book, if it isn't completely fiction, she had a cousin named Ishmael, Ishmael was with her friend. And I suspect Victoria was Lana's way of hiding and protecting Frank. The part seems real where Ishmael did not know what he was, that he felt like a woman inside. I would never put anyone else in danger, but if there is a reason to fear, then I can't let Chloe walk into marrying David."

His body is shaking, tight, held together. His eyes close. He whispers, "All this was merely a way for you to expose David, and Lana? To get Chloe back?"

"No! I promise I didn't..." I put my hands on his shoulders. "And I won't do anything that might harm Isabella."

He gets to his knees and my hands fall off his shoulders.

He turns to the base of the tree, to where his body has been covering the hole in the ground. I see the wooden box again.

His hands are slow as he reaches for it, brings it out into the fading light. He is kneeling in front of the simple hand-carved case.

He says, "Isabella has already been harmed. She can recover, however slowly, however long it will take. But a baby cannot."

The pain hits me in my gut. Lana's baby did not survive.

"What happened? Please tell me. Did Lana get away or did she jump into the river? Did she go to you and Frank in Paris? Did you all run here? Why did no one confront David?"

He places the box back in its resting place and rises to his feet, his movements heavy and without his usual grace. He looks at me with fear in his eyes and turns. I watch him walk away, out of the clearing, and I know I have to find out, for Chloe, for me.

CHAPTER TWENTY-FIVE

It is almost dark now and the rain that had hesitated before begins to fall with confidence. We have been moving in the general direction of the village. His pace quickens suddenly as though he has heard me in pursuit. He turns into a side track and I lose sight of him. I hear his shoes clicking off metal for a few seconds before silence, and then a muffled curse. I run around the corner. The heel of his shoe is stuck in the metal slats of a bridge. In the darkness and the rain, I cannot see the rush of water that burrows under the structure. Its metal claws cling on to the two banks and its ribbed floor arches as high as it can to clear the water. Lamps on its railings form puddles of light in the pool of darkness. He is sitting in one of these, swearing at the offending heel trapped in the gridded surface.

I walk by him and stop at the height of the arch. I rest my hands on the aged wooden rails and stare through the rain at the flowing glints of dark and light. The solid roundness of the wood is strong and reassuring. Who had stood there holding on, how many had let go and let themselves fall? The cursing stops behind me and I turn to face him. He is crying softly into knees drawn up to his face. I push myself away from the rails and sit down beside him on the cold wet metal. We sit in silence on the bridge while the rain falls through us into the river below.

"Do you know what Ishmael means?" His voice, husky with tears, is barely audible.

I shake my head and then realise he can't see the movement, his face buried in the comfort of the cave of arms wrapped around his knees.

"I don't think I've heard it before," I offer hesitantly.

He raises his head and stares at the empty street, the lamp lights broken and dissolved in his eyes. "It means secret," his mouth smiles, "I don't think my parents knew that when they named me."

The rain falls heavier and he raises his face, eyes closed, and lets the drops wash away his tears. "For all of us, a renaming, a rebirth, but we remain tied..." He shakes his head, sprinkling drops on my face, "Why did you come here?" The tone abrupt, demanding now. "Lana has stayed safe for long enough no one will need to find her."

"I didn't know any of this, Chloe came to check out the place. Did you read Lana's book? Is what she wrote the truth or fiction?"

"What do you think?"

I say, "I'm all jumbled up. Chloe told me the little information David shared. That Lana got confused about her sexuality, she went into a depression, she went to writing classes and hung out with lesbians and gay men. That she might have had a lesbian affair. She became paranoid and it got worse when she became pregnant. That she was convinced her family were turning against her and David was out to harm her baby."

"And you read the book and what do you think?"

"Both accounts of what happened are second-hand." I press my fingers into my brow. "I don't know. Chloe loves David. She describes him as kind and generous, loving and sweet. He helps so many people. He set up a group for people who'd lost their partners through mental illness, through suicide. Lana's book could be fiction, though all the characters are based on all of you, but was she writing it as an account of what happened or simply using the people she knew and the exercises she was doing in class to write a novel? The writing I saw is from an Intermediate level class, it is quite dark. Would she have taken a Beginner's class, was it lighter and then got dark as she got more disturbed or things happened as David says."

"Why do you need to know, why do you need to push this, to find her?"

We are balanced on a knife edge. I ask, "What if it was your sister, Isabella, who was going to marry a man whose wife might have killed herself, who might have been living in fear?"

"But you've heard Chloe describe David. Does he sound like a man who would inspire that kind of fear? You desperately want to hear something bad about him, you've possibly built this up in your mind so if you can't pull Chloe away from him, at least you might push him away from her."

"No. No. Not anymore." I'm shaking my head vigorously but the disbelief remains in his eyes. "I admitted to you I might have seen an opportunity to do that when I didn't know Lana except as a stranger, but I would *never* consider doing that now. And I care for Chloe, but I'm not in love with her anymore, and not in the way I can now experience love.

This has been such an intense time, and I've been so involved with Lana and searching for her." Shyness sweeps over me when I look at him. "And meeting you."

He has his mouth open to say something, something sharp, combative, but he closes it when I say the last three words. The struggle in his eyes, the gentleness of his nature, his feelings for me, he can't completely hide them from me.

We stare at each other in the shattered light of the rain-soaked night.

I say, "Chloe and Zara will be back in Galway tonight and Chloe will go to David tomorrow. She thinks I've been trying to warn her off David because I want her back, that I'm using Lana's ramblings as she calls them, Lana's overactive writer's imagination, to twist the situation to suit myself. She's furious I kept the novel from her and I believed it over David. She wants her picket fence even if it wraps itself around the two of them and chokes them."

Ishmael pulls his knees in tighter. "Some people want so much to believe their dream and will see it as real though it is fake. They believe their own mind's eye and nothing can show them the monster behind the curtain who knows what they want to see and projects it, because the monster believes it too, for a while. It is the truth for both of them, for a while."

"So, David really is Thomas? The book is not fiction?" Acid drips in my stomach, the fear for Chloe battering away inside my chest.

"It is a true account from Lana's point of view."

I push myself upright. "You have to help me. Isabella has to help. We can't let this happen when we could stop it."

Ishmael looks up at me, his eyes sad. "What makes you think Chloe will believe anyone over the perfect partner that is David. That she would believe the crazy ex-wife who tried to kill herself because she was gay and killed their baby instead and ran away."

I slump to my knees. "Lana killed the baby?"

Ishmael stands. His fingers clench and unclench against the metal rails of the bridge. "Go back to your safe world, Jaya, to your cocoon of lesbians. If you break the rules and love a man, no one from your world will believe you are valid anymore, not in any other area. Lana broke the rules and now she doesn't exist anymore."

"She exists to me." I get to my feet. "And I know she would not let Chloe or any other innocent person be harmed when she could help. No one else might have believed her, but I do."

I turn to the road to the restaurant. "I'm going to ask her to come back with me. To show Chloe what David truly is. If she won't, I'll go myself."

Ishmael's voice is quiet. "She can't. Don't judge her too harshly because she can't. She already gave her life up once. And there are other lives that would be destroyed."

I walk away from him and this time the tears fall freely. I would have left the safety of my cocoon, for him.

CHAPTER TWENTY-SIX

There are no more chapters to read. Not in the notebooks I left behind in my room in Galway. Lana's book stopped abruptly, with a razor to her throat, to Sapna's throat.

My search for her ended as suddenly, with less of an obvious threat. Walking through the restaurant, through the gîte complex, by the lake. Knowing Isabella was gone, and Ishmael too. Frank regarding me with contained anger, blaming me, for all of it. He didn't ask me to leave, but there was no reason to stay. Frank wouldn't elaborate on the people in Lana's book. Henri and Isabella had gone on holiday according to him, the restaurant was closing for a two-week break as they prepared for the busy summer season. Ishmael had gone ahead with his sister, Frank was to join them when the last of the booked guests had left. I was the second-last. I didn't wait for the weekend to pass, I left the next day. I didn't make it to Galway, instead I stayed in Dublin. The ferry was packed to the brim with people coming back to Ireland to vote in the same-sex marriage referendum.

Fiona dragged me to the polls a week later. I voted. I laughed. I smiled as if I was not a shell. Living through the best thing that had happened in Ireland for a long time, forever for some of us.

And I was a traitor.

Fear, rational and irrational, ate at me. If they knew my secret, I would be exposed, thrown out, abandoned.

It's been three weeks since I returned to Ireland. I didn't want to come back to Galway, but I'm sitting on the floor of my bedroom, beside the A4 legal pads and flicking through the pages, wishing again they were not blank, wishing I had a plan. I did not get closure with Lana, in any of her forms.

I did not get to say goodbye to Ishmael.

I miss his face, his eyes, his smile. I miss his spoken words as much as I miss Lana's written ones.

I can hear Zara and Fiona downstairs, clattering around the kitchen. I smell the baking and my stomach lurches, knowing it is for the wedding.

David has hired what he calls the best catering company in Galway for their wedding party tonight, but he's charmed Zara into baking a special cake for the happy couple. Fiona isn't coming to the wedding. I don't want her there.

My own mother does not believe me, that David is covering his true nature. I don't blame her. They think I have nothing to lose except Chloe. Fiona is upset at me for being upset. She thinks what they all do.

I'm too upset to make the effort to persuade them otherwise.

Three weeks of going through the motions. Fiona does not mind we haven't had sex since I got back to Dublin. She assumes we're being appropriate since we're going to be partaking in a traditional wedding, one of the faces of the New Ireland. An Ireland that regards us now as equal citizens, including me, the brown one who never belonged here.

I'm walking through someone else's perfect life, everything falling into place in a way that was always a dream, but does not fit anymore.

I check my email again. There is still no reply from Ishmael to the daily messages I've sent for the last two weeks. I've told him my heart, sent it out into the silent digital space, hoped for an echo, a sign of life, of love. I've explained to him what I'm doing, marrying a woman I do not love, but I doubt he understands. I don't.

"Jaya." My head jerks up as Fiona knocks on the open door. Her gaze falls on the open notebooks.

I close the pages and stack the notebooks in the cardboard box in which I'd found them.

"Hi, I'm just clearing away all this stuff." I get up and stretch.

She comes into the room. I can sense her examining the evidence.

Her voice is bright. "We're going to be part of history soon. I can't believe my folks are going to come all the way from Sligo for their daughter's gay wedding."

My panic must show in my face.

Her smile falters. "Jaya?"

I smile. "I'll be ready in time, I promise."

She grins. "At least you don't have to wear a dress. The guys at work threatened to wear dresses and the women were going to come in uniform, but I told them your family were coming up from the country and they'd be too scared to come to the ceremony." She nudges me. "Where's my Jay?"

I make the effort. "Hey, it's your crowd who need to be scared of the cops. My side are the respectable ones. You do know I'll be arriving at the hall in Padraic's white van, don't you? Fits with my Traveller looks."

"Well, you'll be the most beautiful Traveller bride ever." She kisses the tip of my nose. "Now, no more talk of white vans. My nerves can't take it. Your mam is cool, but I'm not sure how to explain her to my folks, you know how they can be."

I realise I don't. I'll be meeting them for only the second time tomorrow. The first time was when they came up to Dublin to meet me and ended up going shopping in Brown Thomas with Fiona while I sat in a café and read the paper. I got the impression they found me exotic and didn't think I could hold a conversation with them. Fiona explained later they'd been intimidated by me being a foreign city girl while they were simple country folk. I sighed when I heard that. My Irish accent mustn't have come out that day.

Fiona scans the room. "You are going to get ready soon, aren't you?"

I nod. She turns to go.

I say, "Fiona."

She stops.

"Fiona, are you sure?"

She says, "Yes." She turns. "Aren't you?" She frowns. "You're not happy going to your ex's wedding." She doesn't wait. "You've been different since you came back here and went to France. With her."

"I didn't go with her. I didn't know she was going to be there."

"But she was. Did you two get up to something? Over there? You're not talking to each other now, but it's not the same as before. And watching that Indian movie, making me sit through hours of it. Since when do you watch Bollywood movies?"

I'd been able to download *Sholay*, watched the seventies movie several times, the heroes and heroines, the dance, dwelling in Lana and Ishmael's presence, Lana wanting to love the heroine, Ishmael wanting to be the heroine."

"Jay, what happened in France?"

"Do you really want to know? Why now? You didn't want to know anything when I got back."

"The referendum was coming up. It was crazy for everyone."

I frown. "You've been so involved with the whole gay marriage thing. Is that why you want to marry me? So we can show the world we're as normal as everyone else?" I know I'm not being fair, but I want to break through this wall, this invisible glass screen separating her from me.

"Is that what you think? Is it the reason *you* want to marry me?"

My head is starting to pound. "No."

But what am I doing? I care for her, but I don't love Fiona. Not in the way I love Ishmael. Or I loved Chloe.

I press my hands to my temples.

"Do you have a headache?"

"Uhuh."

She walks over to me and puts her arms around me. "You'll feel better after you get today over with."

I nod.

"You don't talk about Chloe in an angry ex way anymore. Did you make friends with her in France? Think of it that way. You're going to the wedding of a good friend. Who is marrying a dreamboat doctor from the way your mother describes him."

I rest against her. Going with the flow is so much easier than fighting against this river. And there's no one waiting upstream for me.

I whisper into her shoulder. "I've been a bit of a wet rag for a while, haven't I?"

Her chest moves as she laughs. "Just a wee bit." The remnants of worry in her voice are mixed with relief.

I lean back and look into her eyes and hate myself for not being able to hurt her.

She kisses me lightly on my lips. She whispers against my cheek, "Are we okay?"

I nod. I can't trust my voice. At least one of us can be happy, I argue with myself, better than none.

She turns to go again and this time my voice is stronger, "Fiona?"

I need to be a better person than I've been. My confusion is no excuse. Fiona deserves better.

She doesn't face me.

I say, "I'm sorry."

Her back is rigid. Then her shoulders slump.

I walk up behind her and put my hands on her hips. She stiffens. I hold on, turn her around gently.

Her eyes are closed and a tear is trapped under her eyelashes.

"Fiona, I don't know how to say it without hurting you." Breathe in. Breathe out. "I can't marry you. And if we stay together it will be because I'm confused and I want to keep you as a friend. And you deserve a whole lot better."

Her eyes open and the tear is joined by another. The blue of her irises is blurred.

I say, "It isn't Chloe. And if I'm truly honest, it isn't anyone else though I do love someone else. I don't want to continue in something out of fear of not belonging somewhere. You've sensed that, haven't you?"

She nods.

I squeeze her. "You have every right to be mad at me. I'm going to be here for you to yell at me if you want. And I'll listen to every angry word. Because I want us to be friends, as soon as you are able." I smile. "And not just because I don't want a guard as an enemy."

A hint of a smile surfaces on her lips. She rubs at her eyes and says, with an effort, "Not with the way you drive."

CHAPTER TWENTY-SEVEN

"It's good to finally meet you." David's smile doesn't quite reach his eyes, which have more of an air of sadness than I expected. Then I remember he recently lost his mother.

His handshake is firm.

I return a smile. "So Chloe has mentioned her friends in Dublin?"

David nods. "It's nice to know she has a few friends, since she doesn't have a big family. I'm so glad she had your mother to be a second mother to her." He looks around the church foyer. "Speaking of your mother, do you know where she is? I'm a little lost and she is to show me what they've planned."

His suit is impeccable, the grey classy, the cream waistcoat braided with gold lifts the occasion. The colours in the flower arrangements at every turn are all coordinated. I haven't seen Chloe yet, but I know she will be stunning, and they will look like a dream together. He is handsome and he knows it. His features are straight and smooth, a shade of milk chocolate.

I say, "She is fretting over something floral. Don't worry, she'll be right in."

He turns, smiles. "Thank you." His eyes sweep over me. "I have started to pay attention to those who are a mixture of Indian and white. I haven't met any in person in Ireland, but there were a couple in England who were a mix, different heritages though." This time the smile reaches his eyes. "I'm encouraged by the Indian Irish combination."

"I'll take that as a compliment. I haven't met any Irish Indian mixes either."

"Definitely a compliment. Zara mentioned you grew up in rural Ireland in the seventies. I must say I was curious as to how that was. I find it interesting, the reaction of Irish people to my skin colour." He laughs. "I say interesting, but the word doesn't cover the half of it."

I smile. "I guess interesting as good a word as any to describe the experience."

He says, "I would love to talk with you about our experiences, I'd say there might be similar ones. When you are visiting Galway and your mother again, we could all go out for dinner. I hear you are getting married as well soon." I realise he doesn't want to describe the wedding of his fiancée's gay friend as a wedding, but he's trying. I watch him and I can't see the slightest hint of the monster in Lana's novel.

I nod. "That would be nice."

His gaze flicks to the church door. "Here's Zara. Who I am adopting as mine, by the way. My mother can't be here now and Zara is so wonderful."

I turn to Zara. She is dressed in grey and cream too with gold and blue and green accessories, and her hat is purple. She reaches us and I smile and say, "You look great."

She pats my arm, holds it in her grip for a moment.

She says to David, "Chloe is now in the sanctuary room. The guests are going to start arriving soon, did you want me to walk through the church with you?"

He nods and turns away.

Zara releases my arm. She says to me, "Why don't you go in and say hi to Chloe and make sure she's okay."

I watch David walking through the big wooden doors into the main area of the church.

I whisper, "I don't trust him, mum."

"It's only been a short time since you met up with her again, my wee cub. Not much chance to prepare and let go. This will be tough for you no matter who Chloe marries."

The familiar helplessness rises in me. This is not about me. But no one wants to hear. No one wants to believe. They would rather believe him, an upstanding member of the community, a doctor, a man who spends his spare time helping those who are suffering. He is handsome, charming, kind, and obviously in love with Chloe. And he dotes on Zara. And if I didn't know more, I would have been saddened by the wedding, but I would have deemed him as a positive for Chloe.

Zara gives me a nudge. "Go on. Set your feelings aside and go and help Chloe." She points out the way she came. "You have to go out and around to the side."

I walk towards the entrance to the church.

She says, "You look beautiful."

I turn back.

She says, "You really do." She smiles. "I'm glad I chose that dress for you, the turquoise is perfect with your eyes and hair. And you are beautiful inside too. It's not any lack in you. Simply love and chemistry and the right time and place."

I don't say anything, merely smile my thanks and leave.

I'm wearing shoes with only one-inch heels, but I stumble in the grass bordering the church. I find my footing on the steps leading up to the sanctuary and knock on the wooden door.

Chloe's voice is muffled as she calls out, "Come in."

I poke my head through the gap. She is sitting in front of a mirror propped on a dresser. Her reflection smiles at me.

I go into the room. "Are you not warm? I look around and spot a heater attached awkwardly to the stone wall. "Will I put that off?"

"Yes, please."

I leave the door open and switch off the heater.

I face her. "Okay, let's see you."

She stands. She is wearing an ivory wedding dress and the beads sparkle gently as she moves.

"Wow. Just wow."

She smiles. "I'm glad you're here."

I grin. "Wouldn't miss it for the world." That's true, but the grin is not. I am worried sick for her, about the life she will face if Lana's book is not fiction. And I fear she will not tell me or let me help if things go bad, the way Lana did not let anyone help. I begged Ishmael to get Isabella to contact Chloe before the wedding. I got Isabella's email address and begged her too. No response from either of them.

The best I can do is believe her if she does find herself in difficulty.

She exhales loudly. "I shouldn't be nervous. Why am I nervous?" She sits down on her hands. "You look amazing, by the way." She smiles, all teeth. "What will you wear for your famous wedding?"

My grin remains mostly in place. I don't want to get into my breakup with Fiona now. I say, "Dungarees."

"What?!" She sighs. "Okay, you got me."

I want to say something, anything, that could change her mind, but instead I say, "I will be there for you no matter what."

She says, "You sound like I'm walking into the gas chamber." She smiles. "Marrying a guy isn't that bad, remember Ishmael?"

I wince and her smile falters. She says, "I'm sorry, low blow." She turns to the mirror. "Have you heard from him?"

"No. Nothing since." It happens again, the tearing in my heart at the thought of Ishmael. I put a hand on my chest and push the feelings down.

"Why are you marrying Fiona?" She is staring in the mirror, at herself, then her eyes search for my reflection and meet mine.

"What? Why are we talking about my wedding at yours?" I brush the air away, trying to keep my movements casual.

"Lana is gone, there wasn't a time and place for you to be with her. No one should judge you for who you love. It shouldn't matter that he is a man. You love Ishmael."

I say, "It doesn't matter. Ishmael and Isabella wouldn't help. And they believe that I only got close to them to get you back. Ishmael will not reply to my emails."

"It is not as simple as that."

It is not Chloe's voice. And it came from the door. I spin around.

Ishmael steps into the room. His face is haggard, with dark shadows under his eyes. He has lost weight.

My mouth hangs open.

Chloe jumps up and exclaims, "Ishmael! How wonderful! I didn't realise you were taking us up on the invitation."

Ishmael's eyes are tortured. "I'm sorry. I didn't come for the wedding. I came to speak to David. On Lana's behalf. She is too afraid to come herself."

My hope grows.

Chloe says, "No. You can't do this now. It's not fair to David on his wedding day."

Ishmael says, "It is not fair to you. But nothing he does is fair to anyone else. Nothing will change, he will marry you, but Lana cannot rest unless she at least makes one effort to stop you making the biggest mistake of your life. You won't believe her, but she hopes to at least warn David she will be watching." He closes his eyes. "To let him know no one will believe him if the same thing happens, not if it happens to you."

I take a breath. He is right. It is the only way, the only small way to do anything.

I say, "Chloe, if you trust David, at least let Ishmael talk with him, give him Lana's message. If Lana was as crazy as David says, then he will be able to take the message for what it is and he can have closure too. If none of it is true, he will also know you stood by him and waited for him to sort it out with you."

Chloe frowns. She says. "That makes sense in a weird fecked up way."

Ishmael lets out a sigh. He doesn't seem relieved, more resigned.

He turns to me. "Can you get him to come here? Don't mention Lana. Say an old friend wants to pass on their greetings for his wedding but needs to leave soon."

I nod.

Chloe says, "I'll go into the church from here when I hear him knock. I know this is all screwed up, but even then, I don't want bad luck if he sees me." She struggles to produce a smile.

Ishmael smiles sadly. "I need to talk to him alone anyway."

I open the inside door to the church and step into the relative darkness of the next room. I say, "You could wait in here."

I cross the room with its coats and robes and open the door at the other end. I hurry along the aisle, a trickle of guests have already made their way into the nave and I hear chatter at the main door. Zara and David are standing at the entry, talking to an older man. I join them.

Zara says, "This is my daughter. Jaya. Jaya, Chloe's father, Philip Evans."

For a moment, it flashes through my mind I'm meeting the man who would have been my father-in-law. He bows slightly, his back as ramrod straight as the grey hair bristling on his head. His smile is wide and charming like Chloe's, his palms rough against mine. "Jaya, I'm so pleased to meet you. Chloe spoke highly of you. You've been a great friend to her here in Ireland."

I keep my voice from shaking. "She'll be so happy to hear you've arrived. She wants to meet up with you before it starts." I turn to David. "There's guy who says he's an old friend of yours and wants to pass on his greetings, but can't stay. Would you mind coming back around with me?" I say to Zara, "Chloe will be in the room over there," I point back the way I came. "Could you take Mr Evans to meet her?"

Philip Evans says, "Call me Phil. I can't wait to see my Chloe. She must be nervous." He smiles at Zara. "Thank you for being her mother for today."

Zara says, "Ha, not only for today. Ye are stuck with me now. Come, let's find her."

I watch them walk into the eaves. I say to David, "Your friend is waiting in the sanctuary room, but you're not supposed to see the dress, so if you could go outside and by the side?" I smile apologetically.

David's brow is furrowed, but he is polite. "Do you mind standing here then? Until I get back? I don't want the guests to come in and wander around."

I nod. I'd rather be outside the sanctuary door, just in case. But Chloe and Phil and Zara will be in the next room to him and Ishmael. He won't do anything to Ishmael. Nothing openly anyway.

David has disappeared outside before I remember Ishmael is Lana's cousin. Not only is there the family resemblance, he is the brother of the man who ran off with David's betrothed and Thomas had hated them as much as anyone else.

CHAPTER TWENTY-EIGHT

Lana – 2013
Galway, Ireland

Lana woke up with a fright. She lay without moving, the adrenaline seeping out of her chest.

She didn't know if David was in the bed beside her.

She lifted her head an inch and moved her eyes to her left. She breathed out. He was not there. She saw through a twisted slat of the blinds that it was dark outside, the foggy darkness of a Galway morning. The streetlamp at the junction of their road and the crossing road was a faint orange reflection in the droplets on the window pane.

She dropped her head back onto the pillow and put her hands over her stomach. Hugged the life inside her through the fading bruises.

She breathed out again. Relief washed in with her next inhale. He had gone to work early, maybe there had been an accident and they needed him.

She stretched and turned to the right, needing to use the bathroom.

He was sitting by the bed, in a chair. Staring at her.

Her heart stopped and then raced into action.

David frowned.

She could smell the alcohol on his breath from here.

He held out a bottle of Vodka. It was half empty. "Did you have this for a reason?" His voice was slurred. He threw the bottle and it landed with a dull thud on the covers above her stomach.

She searched her mind for an answer. She couldn't remember why the bottle was there, and then it came back to her. She'd transferred the plastic bag from the tyre well to her closet. A woman from the bar had given her the bottle as a joke for after the baby was born.

She said, "I wouldn't drink while I'm pregnant. That was a present."

He leant forward, his frown deepening. "Who would give you a present? You have no friends. You can't make any friends the way you are."

Lana said, "I have to get up. I need the bathroom."

He thought for a moment, then lifted the covers off her. "Get up then."

She edged past him and went into the ensuite. She turned to close the door, but he shook his head.

She peed, willing herself to be quick, but the pressure on her bladder made her take longer. All the while, he sat and stared. She got a sense though he wasn't looking into the room.

She wondered whether she should call for help. He was drunk and the beast was near, she could sense it in the bristling of his skin, the distance in his eyes. But he hadn't done anything except look at her.

She decided to get outside instead.

She cleaned herself and flushed the toilet. She peered into the bowl and said, "Oh no." She looked at David with an expression of worry, which she didn't have to fake.

He got up, held on to the back of the chair. "What? What is it?"

She said, "I've had pain, only a tiny bit. I think there was a hint of blood in my pee. The doctor said to go to her if that happened, they need to keep an eye on my bladder."

David blinked at her. His words were slurred. "You didn't tell me that. Why? Do you have a UTI? Are you screwing around with your doctor? If I knew then you screwed women, I wouldn't have arranged a woman."

Lana let out her breath. "No. Of course not." He'd arranged her doctor to keep her away from his clinic. She knew that, but she didn't know what exactly he said about her at work. She assumed he did what he could to gain their pity, for him having to deal with a crazy wife. He didn't remember now she hadn't been able to visit her doctor yet, not for a few more months he said. The bruises were fading, but there.

He waved a hand at her, steadying himself with the other. "You're lying. I know you. You're a liar. You've damaged my son."

Anger rose in her, threatening to choke her. "I am *not* a liar and I have *not* done anything to hurt my baby."

He frowned. "*Your* baby?"

He took a step towards her.

Then another.

His hand was wrapped around the neck of the bottle. "*Your* baby? That's *my* son. Once you deliver him, you're nothing again."

Her voice was shaking. "You are not going to take my baby from me. Never."

He smiled and she saw the beast in his eyes. "He will have a good mother. Something you can never be. My family already know you are crazy. Your family." He stopped smiling. "Your family know you are not normal."

Lana saw she would not be able escape the bathroom without passing within his reach. He took another lurch forward and the gap narrowed further.

She tried to gather her thoughts as they flowed away in the river of adrenaline. The baby was all he wanted. He wouldn't harm her while the baby was there, in her belly. She needed to get herself and her baby out of there and as far away from him as possible. Not here. Not in Galway where anyone who knew him thought he was perfect and kind, the long-suffering husband, healer of everyone, sad because of his wife. She knew that now when she remembered the limited interactions she'd had with his colleagues.

She said, her voice soothing, "Let me go back to bed. We can call your doctor to come and check on your son. But, right now, me standing in a cold bathroom is not helping him. Don't you want your son to be healthy?"

Tears sprang into his eyes. He swayed, holding the bottle in both hands to his chest. "Of course I do. He will be the only boy in the family. The first grandson. He is going to be a prince."

Lana nodded. "Yes, he is." She stepped forward. "So, can I go to bed, please. I need to rest with no excitement."

He closed his eyes. Stumbled back and waved her towards the bed.

Her muscles trembled as she moved, but she walked to the bed and climbed on. Covered herself.

She waited, heart thudding in her chest. She heard him fall onto the chair.

She did not have her Irish passport yet. She had no right to stay in the country if she wasn't with him. She couldn't escape to her family in India. There was one week to go before she had to present herself at the cluttered immigration office to renew her permission to remain. She needed to go through the procedure one more time, get it renewed for a year, and then get out and away.

She lay, tears dripping into the sheets, until she heard his breathing turn heavy.

§

She stared at the stamp on her Indian passport. It allowed her to come in and out of Ireland freely, for another year. She hated the process to get it, the stale odour of sweat, the officers, the others frightened, wondering.

But it was her way out.

She slipped her passport in her jeans pocket. She didn't want to deal with a handbag. She had enough euro in cash in her pocket to get to Paris, with a couple of hundred more in case of emergency. The rest of her savings were in a credit union account in her sole name Gemma had helped set up months ago.

Lana hadn't talked to anyone. She didn't want a trail, didn't want any of her friends dragged into this mess. David would be angry enough with her, she couldn't risk what he might do to them. She couldn't leave until he was asleep, then the drive to Dublin and the ferry to England. Then Paris.

She hid the soft travel bag on the upper shelf of the closet. There was nowhere in the house where he couldn't find anything if he chose to search, but he'd been quiet over the last week, considerate even. He seemed busy at work, tired, falling asleep almost immediately after he got home.

He didn't remember. In the in-betweens, he didn't remember anything. His conscious was as innocent as a newborn baby's heart.

She wished she had that luxury. In all the charm of his outside self, and he was a man she had loved, she could now not see him without the mask of the beast that was printed on her eyes.

She put her hand on her belly.

Lana shook her head. She would not let him mask her baby for her too. The thought was always there. Would the baby be like him?

Lana shook the feeling out.

No. Not if she could do anything about it.

§

She waited for his breathing to slow to heavy.

Waited five more minutes.

The bathroom light was on as usual, a thin line showing under the door, enough for her to work her way there without knocking into anything.

She closed the bathroom door behind her. She had her jeans and top on underneath her pyjamas. Her shoes were by the hallway table as usual. She had left the car unlocked, the keys hidden in the middle console. She'd decided to wear the pyjamas as far as the car. She could always tell him she'd forgotten something in her car.

What could she have forgotten? She searched her mind.

Her antacid pills. Yes. That would work. He'd gotten them for her after establishing there would be no effects on the baby.

She needed to pee. Quietly.

She pulled down her pyjamas, unzipped the jeans and worked her underwear down with the two layers.

She was sitting on the toilet when she saw them.

Between her feet.

Red spots on cream tiles.

Her eyes moved slowly to her underwear hidden in all the material. She spread her knees. Saw darkness on the navy of her panties. Saw more on the jeans, vague outline against the dark fabric, but red stain clear on the beige of her pyjamas.

Fluid dripped from her into the toilet. The cramp of adrenaline shot through her gut. That's where she prayed it was. In her gut.

But she knew it was in her womb.

The first stab of pain took her by surprise and she moaned out loud. Held her hand over her mouth.

The second stab was followed by a rush of fluid.

She screamed. Looked up.

David stood at the bathroom door, blinking. He was reacting as he always did for work, almost on auto-pilot. There was confusion in his eyes though.

He reached her in seconds. Knelt in front of her, held her shoulders. The concern in his eyes was genuine and for a moment she thought it was for her.

"When did this start?" His voice was edging on panic.

She forced the words out, between gasps. "A few minutes."

"Why didn't you call me right away? You might have killed him." He moved his hands to her knees. Stared at her legs, at the pile of clothes gathered around her ankles. Frowned.

Her eyes followed the path of his scrutiny. Her heart slowed, then began to beat painfully.

Her jeans were cradled in her pyjamas, the top of her passport flopping blue against the floor.

His face was immobile, his gaze moved from her ankles, up her legs, to her stomach. She followed. Saw the same as he did, the brown shirt peeking out from the beige.

The mask covered his eyes, the beast for the first time visible without the cover of alcohol and it terrified her more than on any of its other visits.

She said, "We need to get to the hospital. Quickly."

She lifted herself up an inch, two inches, her hands pushing off the rim, but his hands held her in place. Pushed her down.

His hands moved up her thighs, gripped and separated them further.

The toilet water was pink and red, clotted, denser fronds of tangled tissue.

She said, "She's still in there, I can feel her. I know." She appealed to the man, but the man faded and the beast was all that was left.

"She? The baby is a *she*? You lied to me about *that* too?"

Lana said, "I had to. You wanted a boy so much. I was afraid."

"Afraid of what? What have I ever done to you to make you so afraid of me? You're the one who is so crazy. You lie, you change everything."

"No. That's not true. You keep saying that, but it's not true. I'm not crazy, I'm afraid and I'm confused, and I'm losing my baby."

He said, his voice tortured and tight. "You were leaving. You were leaving and taking it with you."

She shook her head, but the evidence was damning.

A thought tapped at her mind. This was the first time he'd called the baby 'it'.

"I was going for a drive." She knew the effort was pointless, but she couldn't think of anything to say that would help.

She tried again. "She needs us to get to a hospital. David, this is your daughter, she needs you."

She cringed at the pain in his eyes. He appeared to be in another world.

Lana couldn't wait for him to come back. She put her hands on his arms and tried to move them, but his grip tightened.

He raised himself to his feet and put all his weight on her. His hands moved up her body until he was pinning her against the cistern.

Another cramp gripped and she gasped. She screwed up her eyes. "Please, David, please. I need to get her to a hospital, they can save her."

He grunted. Grabbed her arms and lifted her up and fluid trickled down the inside of her thigh. Tears slid down her face. Her muscles tensed with anger at him and fear for her child.

She moved without thinking, screaming. Her hands gripped his throat and she pushed hard, as hard as she could.

His eyes were filled with surprise as he fell back against the counter.

She turned and ran, but her feet flailed inside the three pairs of holes, the three loops of fabric enclosing them. She fell heavily, her head hitting the carpet of the bedroom, her bare belly jolting off the tiles in the doorway.

She lay stunned for a moment.

She grabbed her jeans and dragged them up, and crawled towards the hallway door, her hands trying to shed the pyjamas from her feet.

She felt him approaching. Heard his breathing.

Lana reached the door frame and pulled herself upright. Felt his hand grip her arm. Shook it off and ran, holding her jeans around her thighs. The hallway was short, a few more steps to the staircase.

The pain in her scalp registered seconds after her body kept running but she wasn't getting closer to the stairs.

She screamed as his grip on her hair stopped her forward motion, then slowly dragged her backwards. He used his other hand to grab her shirt and pyjama top.

She saw the ceiling pass in a white blur above her, the scrape of her skin on the carpet relieved by the cool bathroom tiles.

Her head lay cradled by the base of the toilet. Her body pulsed with pain. The darkness approached, stole into her mind and she struggled to stay in her body, to keep her baby alive.

He stepped over her and closed the bathroom door. She heard the lock click.

His feet padded on the tiles. She could see the strands of hair on his toes as he stood beside her. She heard the cabinet door open and close.

Lana saw his hand drop into view, the scalpel shine dull against his thigh.

CHAPTER TWENTY-NINE

Lana – 2013
Galway, Ireland

The darkness lightened in shades. She was floating in a womb, warm and wet, weightless. The sound around her, or rather the lack of sound, was a blanket, wrapping her up in a cocoon.

The thoughts came rushing back, a train roaring through her mind. Her hand flew to her belly. She tried desperately to remember what had happened. Then wished she hadn't. The pain didn't comply though. It screamed through her, from between her legs, from the clotted blood gluing her thighs together, refusing to let them part. Her sobs were soundless, just gasps for air, for mercy from the memory waiting at the corner of her awareness, a grinning clown.

She moved her head. She felt drunk. The smell and the dizziness were sober and real, but she moved as if she had been drinking. Her mouth tasted like the dregs of a glass of alcohol, she didn't know what type.

Her fingers moved across the slippery sticky tiles beside her legs. She couldn't figure out where the blood was coming from, why bits of it were still wet. She couldn't feel it trickling out of her, not between her legs. She explored further down, touched soft tissue. Not paper. Her insides. Her mind skirted around the meaning of that thought, the clown's grin got wider, showing blood-stained teeth. She rolled onto her back, the noose of underwear and jeans wrapped around her ankles.

Liquid tickled down her arms. The searing pain announced its presence. Her wrists. She retched. Grabbed each wrist with her other hand, stopped the leak of blood. The room spun around and she closed her eyes. Tears ran down the sides of her face, trickling through her hair. She squeezed her eyes tighter, stopped that flow too.

A part of her held on to the belief her baby was alive, depending on her.

She opened her eyes. Saw the blurred shape of towels hanging from the rail above her. She grabbed one with her right hand and wrapped it tightly around her left wrist, using her teeth to help. Lifted herself up until her upper body was pushing against the wall. She pulled down another hand towel and used it on her right wrist. The makeshift bandages were enough to stop the trickle. She wasn't sure how long she had been lying there bleeding. She held on to the rail and pulled herself all the way until she was standing. Her head swam and she rested it against the cool tile, her hands holding her up.

The lamp from the street behind their row shone through the frosted glass. It cast a dim orange glow into the room. Lana felt her way along the wall, to the door to the bedroom. She leant against the door, her ear pressed to the painted wood. She couldn't hear anything.

Her heart thudded in her chest as she eased the handle down and pulled the door open, the whisper of air between wood and tile like a scream in the silence. The street lamp on this side of the house shone directly into the room. The bed was empty. If David was still there, she thought he would probably be sitting in the living room. She realised her cloth noose was hanging off her right foot. Her eyes moved along the carpet to where the pyjama bottoms lay crumpled in panic. She pulled her underwear and the jeans up, forcing the thick denim over the stickiness of her thighs. The towels wrapped around her wrists made her movements awkward. Her bare feet left smudges on the cream carpet as she edged her way along the bedroom to the hallway. She opened the door quietly. Exhaled as she realised she had been holding her breath. The hallway was empty and dark.

Lana moved slowly, as carefully as she could. She got to the end of the hallway and sighed as she'd avoided any creaky floorboards. She turned to the stairs and a jolt of adrenaline flooded her body.

He was sitting halfway down the stairs, facing the front door, his body slumped against the railings. She tried to catch her breath, struggled in the silence of the house to remain unnoticed. Light reflected off an object beside him and she realised it was an empty bottle of Vodka. She hoped he had drunk it all and was not merely asleep, but passed out.

The second stair creaked, the lightest of sounds, but was a hammer beating against her eardrums. She waited, but he did not move. The seconds treacled by like long minutes as she took each step at the slowest pace possible when what she wanted to do was run as fast as she could. All she needed was to get to her car without waking him. She focused on the movement of her feet.

She could hear him breathing now, steady, almost a snore.

Lana kept her eyes on her feet, placing her left foot on the step beside him, her body leaning towards the wall on her right, away from him. She got her right leg to obey, to slide past her left leg, her right foot taking her weight, her left foot following. She was past him now. She wouldn't look back, she wouldn't look at him, she wouldn't do anything to him, though her mind blurred with fear and hatred. She needed to get her baby to safety, to someone who could help her. Her baby girl. He'd wanted a son so badly, he'd have destroyed her and the baby sooner if he had known.

His hand on her shoulder made her let out a scream.

She stayed frozen, her foot dangling over the next step. Three more steps.

His grip tightened and he pulled her back until his chin weighed on her collarbone, his stubble against her hair and cheek. The smell of alcohol was present, but not strong.

His voice was quiet. "You're not going anywhere."

Lana turned to face him. Saw in his eyes. He was all beast, no man in sight. The last hope faded from her, that he would have come to his senses, would be begging for her forgiveness.

She said, "I am going to get my daughter to a doctor."

He smiled. "I was right. You lied to me about everything. You are a liar, a charming, cheating, barefaced liar." He put his hand up to her face, ran his finger along her cheek. "You were so beautiful. You still are, but I see you now. Truly see you. The monster you are. The beautiful crazy monster that is my wife."

As she said the words, she recognised their futility. "*You* are the monster, how can you even look at me after what you've done?"

He frowned. "What *I've* done? No, no, my beautiful crazy wife, *I've* done nothing. I am a broken man. I am a decent man, a good husband, whose wife cannot live with herself because she is a crazy lying gay, who killed her own baby before it got a chance to take a breath. Who hid the fact she was pregnant with a baby girl because she had a crazy cultural bias against bearing a girl child, and instead lied to her devoted husband who has been joyfully sharing the good news with his friends and colleagues."

The horror dawned on her. She knew she had not done those things in the way he said them, but she had lied about the baby, and her feelings for women. If, for the briefest of moments, *she* doubted herself, what chance did she have of anyone outside believing her over him.

His fingers tightened on her shoulder. "Go back upstairs to the bathroom. I am going to call for an ambulance soon."

She stared at him. *Soon.* Not now, but soon. When he was sure there could be no hope for her baby. Or for her.

His expression changed as he saw the understanding creep onto her face. His grip moved from her shoulder to her upper arm and he pulled her up two steps. She didn't struggle, the darkness was approaching again and she needed to hold on to whatever strength she could.

She was now on the step above him, his hand pushing into her back. Her body shivered, her skin clammy with sweat sliding through drying blood.

It was now or never.

CHAPTER THIRTY

I can't stand here on the steps inanely greeting strangers as they arrive for my ex's wedding. Not when Ishmael is going to face down David on his own. I know Thomas and Sapna are fictional, that my thoughts of David have been tainted by the character in Lana's novel. Ishmael has not told me what really happened with Lana and David, but I can't stop the fear.

I smile at the couple walking up the stairs. They're hurrying, but they have time. There's a half hour to go before the wedding. I turn and follow them back into the church. There are a handful of people sitting. I walk down the side to the door and knock.

Zara opens the door. "We were just coming out. I think Phil is making Chloe more nervous."

I walk into the room. Chloe is sitting on a chair, her father standing beside her awkwardly.

I say, "Why don't ye go and greet the guests as they arrive. I'll stay with Chloe."

Phil nods. He places his hand on Chloe's shoulder. "Your mother would be in tears at how beautiful you are. And how happy. I'll be outside, ready to give you away." He smiles. "Only in name though."

Chloe looks like she's going to burst into tears. He pats her shoulder and marches out past Zara and me. Zara shakes her head. "No crying yet. You'll make a mess of your makeup." She straightens Chloe's dress and gives her a careful hug.

"It's okay, mum, I'll wait with her. You go and deal with the guests. Promise me no one will rush Chloe, she'll be out when she's ready." I want to stand by the door to the sanctuary, to make sure Ishmael is safe.

Zara frowns but gives Chloe's hair a last tweak and leaves. I close the door behind her and rush to the other door.

"You're going to listen?" Chloe whispers.

I nod. Hold my finger to my lips as I ease the heavy door open an inch, enough to hear, but I cannot see into the room.

Chloe moves away, stands at the opposite corner of the room, beside the rack of coats.

The murmur of voices doesn't change, I assume they haven't heard the door. I push it another inch and lean my head closer. I can now hear their words a little more clearly.

David's voice is low-pitched, from the centre of the room. "- think you are? Coming here like this. You and your family wrecked my first wedding and now you are trying to do the same to my wedding today. But it won't work this time."

Ishmael's voice is further away. Muffled as if he is facing away. "I had nothing to do with your first wedding. That was Reza, not me. And you married Lana. You didn't know either of them before. You didn't lose out."

"Do you not think being humiliated is losing out? Having your fiancée run off is bad enough, but to do so with her first cousin? Did you not feel the shame? Or are you as brazen as your brother. Unashamed as you commit the worst sins, the biggest taboos."

Ishmael's voice is shaky. "How are the sins you committed not the worst sins? How do you get to call other people's actions a sin when they were based on love? How can you live with your actions? With your hatred?"

David sounds like he is smiling. "Your family is so dramatic. Same as Lana's. But then you are all happily related, aren't you? Probably been intermarrying for generations and paying the matchmakers not to say anything. And I heard the talk about you. In London. It was at least good I never had to meet you."

"Nothing you heard about me can match what I know of you."

"Is that a threat? Whatever you heard comes from the mouth of a woman who lost her mind. You shouldn't believe what crazy people tell you. Probably how you ended up that way, listening to the crazy London people."

"Lana was not crazy."

David snorts. "How would you know? You didn't have to live with her."

"She told me what happened that night."

David's voice is tenser. "What night? You mean the night she killed my baby and tried to kill herself?"

Ishmael says, "Yes. That night. Unless you want to talk about the night you held a scalpel to her throat. Or the night you raped her?"

"Are you serious? I was her husband. I never raped her. Is that what she told you? And you believed her? Cheh, I can't even hear the word without feeling sick." He moves a few steps, further away from me. "See what happens when a sheltered woman associates with perverts. Working in a lesbian bar. Do you know she took a job as a counsellor? Probably had her mind twisted further by her clients. And then those writing classes. I stopped her after the first set of classes. I found her so-called writing."

So that's why the intermediate class exercises and the notebooks were hidden in the attic. I glance back at Chloe. She is watching me, but she can't hear the words. But David has not admitted he did anything wrong.

I can hear the desperation entering Ishmael's voice. "Lana was not crazy. She might have been confused, but she was not crazy."

David says. "If that's what you need to believe, go ahead. I don't want to have to deal with any of your crazy family anymore. And I don't have to. Lana is gone. She's dead. I've annulled our marriage in India. She didn't manage to kill herself in the house so they are declaring she jumped into the Corrib river and was taken out to the ocean. Do you know the number of people who do that every year from the same spot where her car was found? What that does to the people left behind? What it did to me?"

Ishmael sounds closer now. "Lana is not dead though. She cannot risk coming anywhere near you again. She wants you to know she will be watching you, watching out for your new wife, making sure nothing happens to her."

I hold my breath. I need to hear in David's voice that he is rattled. It's the only way I can live with walking away from this wedding.

David laughs. A quiet, confident sound that reaches out and grabs my throat.

"Nice try. The last whine of a crazy family who simply can't let it go." His voice is moving away. "This isn't the rushed arranged marriage to the sister of the woman who ran away with her first cousin. I love Chloe."

Ishmael says, "But you said that to Lana too." He sounds defeated. His voice is closer, he has moved further into the room,

"I guess I must have." There is a creaking sound of the door opening. "Give it up Ishmael. Go back to wherever you came from."

"No." Ishmael's voice is firm.

David sounds surprised. "No? No what?"

"No, Lana won't crawl back into hiding. Not anymore. Not from you, not from anyone."

The door closes and David moves back into the room.

I frown. Something feels wrong.

"What are you talking about? Is she going to show her face here?" I can imagine David standing over Ishmael, trying to intimidate him.

Ishmael's voice, still quiet, now has a tone of steel running through it. "I'm talking about you, your façade, the good guy image you show everyone, the one you showed your wife at first. I'm talking about how you believe it yourself which makes you so convincing. I'm talking about the years of training, the subtle and not so subtle ways you controlled your wife until she didn't know what to believe, and no one outside believed there was anything wrong. I'm talking about the night you got her to slit her wrists with a scalpel and left her to bleed out on the bathroom floor. But most of all, I am talking about what you did before that, when you forced her to use a coat hanger to try to abort her baby."

There is silence in the room. The fear Lana must have experienced is echoing through me. The terror, the pain. Tears are running down my face and I barely notice as I wait for David to answer.

CHAPTER THIRTY-ONE

Lana – 2013
Galway, Ireland

Lana turned to face the upstairs.

His breath rustled in her hair, his hand in the small of her back.

She raised her foot to the next step, waited for a second until his body moved back slightly as he lifted his foot to follow her.

She swivelled and pushed him hard, saw the surprise on his face as he started to fall backwards. She stepped forward and ducked under his flailing arms and shoved him in the chest.

The adrenaline filled the gap left by her blood loss and she felt no pain, just the urge to fall as well, to keep moving, to get away.

He tried to grab onto the handrail.

She rushed past him knowing he would have to find his grip before he could chase her. She slipped on the last step, landing with a heavy thud on the hallway floor. She didn't look back until she reached the front door and opened it.

He had broken the force of his fall by grabbing onto the handrail. He was starting to pull himself out of the twisted position.

She ran out onto the driveway, her feet bare, every step a pin in the pain that was her body. She cursed and sobbed as her hand slipped on the handle of the car door, but she got it open and shut and locked it.

The key took more precious moments to find.

Her last sight of David was through the side window of the car as she raced away.

He was standing at the open front door holding the hallway phone to his ear.

§

Her hands gripped the wheel, pushing the now familiar darkness away. She consciously moved her foot off the accelerator. An ambulance screamed by her, its lights making the inside of her car a dance hall from the depths of hell, like there was a disco ball rotating red.

She pulled the car to the side of the road, tried to get her bearings, tried to think of a plan through the pain and the shock and the blood. Her baby needed a hospital. The nearest hospital was where David now worked. She couldn't risk that. Her thought processes felt slow, sluggish. The smell of the alcohol he had forced into her would get her arrested for driving if anyone found her. In the fog, she thought of the other women who had been lost because of an attempted abortion.

The next hospital was the clinic where David used to work when they first moved to Galway. She couldn't go there.

She heard the ambulance in the distance. Saw the red lights dance in her rear-view mirror. Watched in fascination as the red grew closer, filled the car, dimmed again.

She pulled out onto the road. Followed the ambulance. She should have been a lawyer, here she was chasing ambulances. She smiled, wondered what was happening to her. The sogginess in her jeans, the slipping of the steering wheel through her hands, reminded her with a wrenching scream. She focused on the red flashing lights, saw them turn into the hospital gates. She steered the car through the lanes after the ambulance, came to a stop a hundred feet behind it, where they wouldn't notice her.

Her brain was clogged. She watched as the ambulance doors swung open and two EMTs dragged a stretcher out with someone on it. Follow. Follow. Follow. She managed to crawl out of the car without falling. The towels had fallen off her wrist during the journey, but the bleeding was under control. She pulled down the sleeves of her pyjama top and then remembered she was wearing a shirt underneath it.

She stumbled on the kerb, stopped her fall by grabbing a concrete post. She heard voices and instinctively slid to the floor, hiding behind the post and the dark night.

The two ambulance men stopped on their way back and took out cigarettes and lit them.

"Fucking hell, I don't want to get married if that's what happens." The man drew in a loud breath and exhaled smoke.

"Crazy foreigners." The other man sounded older. "That's what they do in their country and then they bring it fucking here. Jesus H. Christ, and the woman demanding an abortion a few months ago. Foreigner too. Hey, you got a light?"

"Yah, I guess they do." There was a pause and she heard the snap of the lighter. "You'd think yer wan would just off herself. Why try take Dr Matthews out as well?"

"You know they keep these Pakistanian women covered up and hidden away for a reason, right? Fucking whackos. I asked one of them out years ago, she wasn't all covered up like some of them, only the head thing. You're not supposed to talk to them."

The younger man snorted. "Maybe she just didn't fucking want to go out with ya, you thought of that?"

"Ya sure. She'd be so lucky. I'm fecking lucky I didn't shag her. I'd be in Casualty in the next bed to yer man."

The younger man sighed. "Wouldn't mind a fecking shag. The wife is pregnant, no way José, she's decided. An executive decision she says. Fucking hell, these fecking magazines."

"New Age shite." He blew out. "My cousin lives in that estate. I don't think he knows them though."

"Who?"

"The Pakistanians. Do you think your wan has killed herself? If I was the guards, I'd check the river first. That's how I'd do it, drink a bottle of gin and go down by the Corrib, jump off the Salmon Weir."

"You know gin makes you suicidal? The wife, she read that in another one of those fecking magazines."

The older man laughed. "Good one." He coughed. "Ya, that's how I'd fecking do it. None of this razor shite. Man, I'm tired of blood. If she's alive, she's in fucking trouble. To do what she did to an innocent wee baby. If she doesn't get years for pushing your man down the stairs, she's gonna get what she deserves for trying to do a fecking abortion. With a coat hanger, for fuck's sake. We're not a shite Third World country."

A pager sounded. The younger man said, "Ah for fuck's sake. Can't even finish a fecking fag in peace."

Lana heard their footsteps walking fast towards the ambulance, the squawking of the radio snapped off by a closing door. The red flashing lights swept over her, but there was no siren as the ambulance sped away.

She let out a long shaky breath. David was in there. They would be looking for her, not to help her, but to arrest her. What had he done?

Thrown himself down the stairs after she ran?

Her mind was swirling. It fixed on a thought, Frank was a doctor. But he was in Paris. Frank and Ishmael would help her. She needed to get there. Without the guards catching her. Garry and John would help her. And Gemma, but David knew the bar now. And David could never know. If he knew she was alive, none of them would be left untouched. He would find a way to destroy them all.

She would have to convince him she died tonight. And if she was blessed, her baby might live.

She needed to get to Oranmore, to Garry and John's house. Before she passed out. One goal at a time, one step at a time.

She realised with a jolt her mind had wandered and she was lying on the ground. Her car was fifty feet away. She was thankful for the night, the darkness, as she crept towards it.

CHAPTER THIRTY-TWO

Lana held her breath and waited for David's answer, but she knew nothing Ishmael said would get through David's barriers. She knew those barriers well, knew how painful and damaging it was to try and bargain with him. He had no concern for others. She knew that now, after years of bewilderment, years of manipulation. Until she studied his behaviour, his condition. Until she understood she was not crazy or depressed, as she counselled victims of other narcissists. Until she learned there was nowhere to go and nothing she could do to heal him. Running away, no contact, that had been the only path to stay alive, to heal.

And now she was back here.

Her legs shook. No more hiding. She willed herself to have the courage to face him, but the memories slammed into her body. As she watched David stand before Ishmael, her mind and her body cowered underneath the lashes of every whip he had used against her.

But she was stronger now. She had experienced love in its true form. For herself, her lost baby, her friends. And Jaya. Her heart was with Jaya, no matter her society's repulsion, and its final erasure of her for loving a woman.

David said, "No one is going to believe the rantings of a man like you, from a family of crazy people. Shall I list your sins? You are the worst, a gay, your brother is another abomination, marrying his first cousin, your mother killed herself at the shame. What's left of your proud family? Your hermit of a father? Locked away in demented isolation?"

The anger pulsed through Lana. Ishmael stepped forward. "My family suffered so much because of people like you, judging everyone on who they loved rather than who they hate."

David frowned. "What?"

Ishmael continued, taking another step forward. "I paid a price I didn't need to, to atone for what great sin? My sister married a man she loved. It happened to be my first cousin. But there was no justification for my punishment, my family's suffering."

David shook his head. "What punishment? Your sister? You don't have a sister, Ishmael"

Ishmael frowned. "Do you not realise what you did, every day of your marriage?" He took in a deep breath and let it out. "Or does it not matter what you do or who you do it to? If you believe someone did you wrong, humiliated you, that's all the justification you need?"

David said, "What are you rambling on about? You are crazier than Lana. Does crazy run so deep in your families?"

Lana steadied herself. Stepped out of the shadows.

Ishmael turned to face David fully. Slowly lowered the hood.

"Look at me, David. Really look at me and tell me what you see."

David frowned. Took a step closer. Ishmael watched David's face, tried not to let the fear show on his. David remained handsome, more so now with the sheen of good health, the streaks of grey more pronounced, his hair worked into a distinguished style.

"What do you see, David?"

A smirk played on his lips. "I see a wimp of a man, a fag as they say."

"Look closer, David."

The smirk disappeared. His lip curled. "Don't tell me you hold a torch for me. I'm not that way inclined. I'm as much of a man as you can get."

"You're less than a man than Ishmael ever was."

David sighed. "I have a wedding to get to. Mine. To a beautiful woman. If you have quite finished with your stupid games." He turned towards the door. "Tell Lana to do a better job of killing herself next time. Save us all the pain of dealing with her craziness. That's if she's alive. I wouldn't put it past your crazy family to pretend she is."

"David." Lana raised the volume of her voice only slightly, but the quality changed.

David stopped. His body went rigid. "Lana?"

He turned, slowly.

CHAPTER THIRTY-THREE

Lana – 2013
Paris, France

Lana opened her eyes. The light beside her was yellow, soft, casting a tint onto the room. She was in a bed, covered by a duvet which smelled of apricots. Her wrists felt tied, her insides torn apart.

There was a woman sitting in a chair beside the bed. Long dark hair fell forward over her bent head. She appeared to be asleep.

Lana tried to remember where she was.

Paris.

Frank and Ishmael.

No. Not Ishmael.

Frank.

And Isabella.

Isabella and Henri.

The woman stirred. Jerked awake. Pushed the curtain of hair away from her face.

"You're awake. Thank goodness." The woman got up. The mattress dipped as she sat. Held out her hand and smoothed the strands of hair off Lana's forehead.

Lana smiled. It was a small smile, but the best she could manage.

Tears ran down the woman's face. "It's wonderful to see that smile again."

Lana searched for her voice. It came out as a croak. "Did they save her? My baby?"

The woman's hand stilled. Then soothed again. The tears dropped onto the beige duvet.

Tiredness drenched Lana from inside her. Along with guilt. She should have gone into Casualty, not saved herself.

"Frank said there was too much damage to your uterus, nothing could have survived."

Lana's throat tightened. "He did that with a scalpel?"

The woman shook her head. "No. Probably a coat hanger. The scalpel was for your wrists."

Lana turned in the bed. Faced the wall. There were no tears left in her. She had lost her baby.

And deep inside her, she knew she had also lost the chance of any other babies. But that was a horror for later.

The covers rose and the bed sank beside her and then an arm slipped around her. Gentle pressure pulled her into the warm hold of the woman's body. She closed her eyes and let herself return to a merciful sleep.

§

"Henri is coming to visit Frank today." The panic was obvious in Isabella's voice. She dropped her coat on the floor. "We can't keep hiding you from him." She looked around. "Where's Frank?"

Lana put down her coffee. "In bed." She stared out at the trees. "What does Henri know? Has he been talking to David?"

Isabella gathered up the coat and hung it on the peg by the door. She said, "Henri talked to him again about the property in San-Sebastian. And then David told him you vanished and the police were saying it was suicide. Henri is so curious, but he knows not to ask David anything."

"I'm sorry. Me coming here has put you in trouble. And screwed up the deal for Frank." Lana put her feet on the ground. "The best thing is for me to go."

Isabella strode into the living room of the apartment. "We are not quitters." Lana saw her examine the coffee table, the glasses left out from the night before. Her voice was low. "Has Frank started drinking again?"

Lana sighed. "Can you blame him if he has? I would if I could hold down anything stronger than a little Baileys."

Isabella sank onto the couch. "No. I can't blame him. But I'm not sure I can handle getting him sober again."

Lana picked up her coffee again. "Just as well then. Neither of us has started drinking. As far as I remember, it was some icky soda mix we drank too much of pretending it was whisky. The rest of the bottles are in the fridge if you want to check."

Isabella let out a breath. "Good. We have enough to deal with right now."

"I'm sorry."

"Oh, don't be. We'd already created enough of a mess before you arrived."

Lana smiled. "You certainly had."

Isabella giggled. She sounded surprised. "I'm not laughing. I can't believe I'm laughing."

Lana took a sip of coffee. "Laughing is better than crying right now. What does Henri know?"

"He knows Frank used to date a guy called Ishmael. I can't remember if he was aware that Ishmael was Lana's cousin. He might not, Frank didn't want him to let that slip to David in case he figured out Ishmael was Reza's brother."

Lana bit her lip as she thought. "Henri is eager to move back to San-Sebastian, isn't he?'

"Yes, he wants to be home. And the restaurant means a great deal to him. I think he figures if he can't buy the complex, then if Frank is there running it, I might be persuaded the innards of rural France are not as dreadful as I imagine." She sighed. "I call him a sweet optimist, but he's probably just focused on getting what he wants."

"Do you love him?"

Lana watched the blush move up Isabella's smooth neck. Lana wondered if that surgery had been minor compared to all the others.

Isabella said, "He's a nice man who adores me."

"If he loves you that much, he might accept who you were."

Isabella shook her head. Her eyes were sad. "No. I don't believe he will. He is an old-fashioned man. And at heart, he is a rural country man, as much as he gives the impression of being a Parisian."

"So how long can you live the lie?'

"What is a lie? This is the truest to myself I have ever been. Why should it matter who I was in the past? We all change, sometimes for the better, sometimes for the worse. He loves the woman I am, and that is all that matters."

Lana nodded. "But you love Frank. That is not being true to Henri."

Isabella's eyes filled. "I loved Frank. But he cannot be with me as a woman. So we are now trapped in the dance of a love that cannot be. What should I do? Wait around and hope Frank can love the true me as much as he loved the other me? I'm still the same person, but he is not allowed to love a woman."

Lana got up and walked over to the couch. She sank into it and put her arm around Isabella's shoulders. "I understand you both and it is so confusing. I know what it is to care for a woman and refuse to allow such feelings even if it kills you or kills any hope of a real love. And I know what it is like to hide my true self and to desperately wish to change, to openly be who I truly am."

They sat in silence.

Isabella frowned. "Did you ever meet Henri? I mean, in person?"

"No. David and Frank dealt with all of the property stuff. I went to meet you that day. Remember? In the Vietnamese restaurant. Why?"

"I'm thinking."

"Always a bad sign."

Isabella smiled. "Not always." She pulled back and examined Lana's face. "Stand up."

Lana quirked an eyebrow but stood. She opened her arms out in a gesture.

Isabella's stare made her aware of the floppy grey sweater, the loose sweatpants. Lana swept her hair back, fluffed it out.

Isabella stood. Put her hand on Lana's arm, stopped the motion. Her eyes calculated as she gathered Lana's hair in a bunch. Her face was thoughtful. "I modelled my look as a woman on you. Did you know that?"

Lana shook her head. Winced as her hair pulled in Isabella's grasp.

"I always loved the way you looked. As I said, Hema Malini was my idol and you were so like her to me."

Lana smiled. "I thought we established I was Jaya Badhuri's character, not Hema Malini's."

"And I thought we established I have a better eye for style than either of them or you?"

Lana laughed. "That we did."

Isabella said, "I wouldn't normally say this because you had the perfect body before you started getting so anxious and thinner, but you would have to lose a smidge more weight for this to work. And we'd have to cut off most of your beautiful hair."

Lana said, "For what to work?"

"Think about it. If David finds out you are here, that Frank helped you, that Ishmael is now Isabella, what do you think he will do to all of us?"

Lana's heart contracted, pain sliding through her blood.

Isabella said, "If Henri finds out who I was, I will be lost as well." She winced. "I have lost so much already, I cannot face him finding out. You have suffered so dreadfully. Frank has lost, but he made the choice, even then I don't wish for him to lose more. He wants to be in the country, wants to make the restaurant work. He is so happy there, maybe he will forget he loved a man who became a woman. He might enjoy playing the part again, being with a different Ishmael while he and I live as friends. I would have to introduce you to Henri as my brother, that would be less trouble. I'd have to give you all my old paperwork as Ishmael and my new identity would have the same name. I'll make it work. But we must be French-Algerian. That's who I am with Henri." She sighed. "Is there not a line somewhere, the crazy web we weave."

Lana let out a breath. The idea was crazy, but it was so bold, it might work. No one knew her here in France, especially not in a tiny rural village hours from Paris.

And now she didn't feel herself a woman anymore, however wrong that was. Not after they had cut her infected uterus out and taken her ovaries too. All the words she had ever heard from David, all her fears, all the hopes and dreams of a true and real love, all would vanish.

A new Ishmael would be born and a broken Lana would die.

CHAPTER THIRTY-FOUR

I hear the word, the name being spoken by David, but I can't see who has come into the room. Did Isabella come as well? Has she been hiding nearby?

I hear a whisper and I jump. I didn't realise Chloe had been standing beside me. "Did David say 'Lana'?"

I nod.

"What happening?"

"I don't know." I push the door another couple of inches. I figure it is out of David's line of vision.

I say, "I can't see anyone else in the room."

David is facing Ishmael, eyes narrowed. Ishmael's back is to me, the hood gathered on his shoulders.

David says, again, "Lana?"

I frown. My mind is swirling.

Chloe says, "That's it. I'm going to find out what's going on." She pushes past me and walks through into the room. "David?" Her voice is low and David doesn't look away from Ishmael.

She walks further into the room. I follow.

Ishmael turns to us. There is an expression on his face I cannot read. He holds my gaze, and then he smiles.

He turns to David. "I will not be quiet any longer, David. Yes, it is me, Lana."

David staggers, the slightest of movements, and he corrects himself quickly. He has noticed Chloe standing behind Ishmael. His voice is steady. "Chloe, meet my ex-wife, Lana. I'll let you judge for yourself if she is mentally capable."

Chloe says, "Ishmael?"

Ishmael turns again. This time there is doubt and fear in his eyes. "I'm sorry, Chloe. I could not tell you the truth at the time."

Chloe says, "The truth? What truth? I don't know who is lying anymore. I trusted you though I didn't know you. And you all lied to me. You, Frank, Isabella." She pauses. Turns to me. "Even *you?*"

My eyes feel stretched, the room spinning and distorted. I find my voice, it comes out thready, but forceful. "I didn't know."

Chloe says the words as though they're hitting her one after the other. "So that's why you wouldn't admit you had fallen for a man. Because he wasn't a man. You knew and you couldn't tell me."

I put my hand out. "No. No. I promise. I didn't know. And I was so caught up in how it appeared to others, to me, to feel that way for a man."

I realise David is frowning as he watches us talk. I realise if he knows Chloe was with me, he will take it out on her, but he might let her go.

I open my mouth, but the words don't come out.

My hand falls. I say, instead, "Lana came back here to help you. To warn you. The man she was married to is a monster. They are still married." I turn to David. "You are married to Lana, you cannot marry Chloe."

David frowns. "I got it annulled in India. She's crazy. And here in Ireland, she has been declared dead, by suicide. Are you sure you want to open that can of worms? If she comes back now, in the guise of a man and has to answer for her suicide attempt and her abortion, who do you think is going to jail? Chloe can now see what I had to deal with. Lana cannot even decide if she is a man or a woman, if she is a gay. She wrecked my life for years with her mental illness. At one point, I thought if she just admitted she was ill, that she needed help, we could have gotten her the therapy she needed. If she was telling the truth, why did she not tell anyone?"

He turns to Lana. "Have you not done enough to me? You killed my baby, in front of me, and then tried to kill yourself. You pushed me down the stairs and left me to die. I tried to protect your memory when they told me your car had been found near the river, but they could see what had really happened. The countless people I have had to comfort after I opened the group for those who lived with someone like you, that is how I survived. Knowing I was not alone, that those people would be there, would understand, would support me. They all heard my story, they all know what I went through."

He swivels to Chloe. "I gave up hope. But then, finding you. Someone who was so settled in herself, so willing to love and be loved, just me and you. You promised to be mine, and I promised to be yours. To trust each other with our hearts. I believed in you. That's why we are here. To get married, to say to the world what we have been saying to each other." He put his hand over his eyes, the tears rolled under his palm and down his face. "If you cannot say it in this room to us here, how will you say it in front of all our family and friends?"

I see Chloe's stricken face and I know he has won. That is how he will see it. Though there are no winners and losers, that is how he will see it. I see Chloe's guilty glance at me and know she has lost. That is how I see it. We have all lost.

Lana sees it too. She steps forward. "Chloe, he can be convincing. I may be a lot of things, but I've spent time thinking and learning. That's what being with him does. It forces you to look deeply at yourself and to pull yourself out of the darkness by yourself, by knowing who you truly are and believing it always." Her back straightens. "He tried to own me. I learnt that self-respect can be lost, damaged, and destroyed, can be borrowed and stolen, but it can never be owned by another." Her voice is sad, but strong. "True self-respect will recover and heal, and it will always find its way home."

Chloe holds her face in her hands. She says, "I don't know who anyone is anymore. But David is the only one who hasn't lied to me. And I know myself. I want to live a normal life, to be married to a man I love, to have children with him. I know myself enough to be sure of that."

She turns towards the room we had been in, towards the main church. "There's a crowd of people out there. They are waiting for us." She takes in a deep breath, holds it in for a long moment.

She holds out her hand. "David?"

He exhales. He wipes at his eyes and takes her hand.

Chloe turns to me, "I'll explain to Zara you had to leave, you couldn't handle being here. But that you wish me well."

I try a deep breath, can't find enough air. I say, "I will always wish you well."

David has a frown on his face, flicking from me to Ishmael, me to Chloe. I see what it looks like, I am a lesbian who loved Chloe and couldn't deal with her being straight. I now have a thing for his crazy ex-wife who has been living as a man. We are as crazy in his mind as he always thought.

Chloe smiles. "I wish you all the happiness you deserve, Jaya. Thank you for being here. Ishmael, Lana, it was nice meeting you, I hope you find what you are looking for as well."

She walks away, holding David's hand. I hear her voice. It sounds shaky but determined. "I know you wanted a traditional wedding, but none of this was part of the plan so seeing the dress before we get to the altar is relatively minor."

I don't hear David's reply, but Lana and I watch in silence as the couple through the door into the church, holding hands.

CHAPTER THIRTY-FIVE

I look at Ishmael, at Lana. Her thin face, short dark hair tucked behind her ears, the loose jeans and shirts. The impression is of a young man, pretty, rather than handsome. I can see how it had worked, this refuge from her past, this gender disguise.

Lana had been beautiful, that I had seen from the photograph, as bad as it was, but when I attempt to conjure up her face in my memory I realise I can't. In my search for her, I had stared long and hard at that photo. Now I can only see her in Ishmael's eyes, the rest of her lost in the process of mentally invoked transformation.

But, it occurs to me, I can close my eyes and continue to see Ishmael clearly, as though the transition had etched her features more clearly, sharpened and defined them until they now held their own, until they now demanded a place in your memory.

We are in the sanctuary of the room. We've been standing here for two or three minutes, unsure of what to do. Me staring at Lana, still Ishmael in my eyes.

Lana shivers and I walk across the room and turn up the heater. The coils glow and crackle as the electricity flows through them.

Her voice is soft. "Thank you."

I say, "Come and stand beside the heat."

She moves up to stand by me.

We hold our hands out to the red coils. Her jacket sleeves fall away from her wrists.

I reach out and gently turn her hand over. The scars are healed, but deep. I remember the long sleeves.

She is still shivering. "Know what was a surprisingly hard part of keeping this going?"

I say, "There must have been a lot of things."

She nods. "I was never overweight, but I was, how do you say, I filled out my clothes nicely." I sense a smile in her voice. I glance at her body. As usual, it is mostly hidden by the shape of her clothes.

She says, "I lost weight before I ran away. But I had to lose even more weight when I became Ishmael. That was easy, I'd just lost so much in my life, I was not bothered with eating, or sleeping, or doing much to stay healthy. But after a year of living in the village, of lowering my guard somewhat, it was more difficult." She smiled. "It became harder to bind the curvier parts of me."

I smile too. "I hadn't thought of that. To be honest, I'm not thinking properly now. What happened to the real Ishmael?

She places her hand on my arm. "Isabella."

My mind is starting to cloud again. I'm rewinding a film and trying to see everyone as different actors. And my reaction to them.

"From what you wrote in the novel, Ishmael wanted to transition." I frown. "You told me you wanted to transition." My heart sinks. "All the things we discussed. So much truth twisted."

She is silent.

"Did you mean any of it?" I turn back to the heater. "Of course you didn't. You were not Ishmael. You were playing him, being him." The loss seeps into me. "You were not Lana either. So who did I fall in love with? No one?"

Her hand grips my arm. "You fell in love with me, Lana. I did not say anything as Ishmael that Lana does not believe even if it was based on Ishmael's experience. You accepted loving Ishmael despite his physical presentation, not because of it. You fell in love with who I am in this strange limbo, with the woman you said you were drawn to from my photo, from the likeness of the me Isabella modelled herself on. You were attracted to Isabella, but you didn't spend much time with her, did you? You told me, me Ishmael, you were torn between him and Lana. And you fought it because in your eyes that was loving a man, but you couldn't help falling in love with the person you met and spent time with."

I say, "I'm glad you can figure it out, me, I'm so confused."

She says, "Do you know how long I fought the love I knew I could feel for a woman? It took meeting you to understand I cannot ever experience true love until I accept who I am. I fell in love with you the moment I saw you. You were grumpy and tired and I think angry or hurt. But you gave me the most beautiful smile and you were so natural with me, you let your guard down and simply related to me as a person. I couldn't give my identity away, but it was so difficult not to tell you all that time we spent together, talking, feeling the attraction, the love."

I know she is right and yet the uncertainty tugs, the fear of the unknown woman beside me.

I say, "I opened my heart to you. I told you so much. And after I got back here. I wrote you my love for you though you were a man, or at least I thought you were, and loving you was breaking every rule."

She says, "I know. I couldn't reply, but I listened to every word. That's why I came back to face my worst fear. For Chloe, yes. But mostly for me. And for you."

"I was getting married this year. I didn't know why, but now I do. I felt so wrong, so marked out by my betrayal, hurt by your silence. I couldn't cast myself out of my group, the only place I belonged."

She says, "That's understandable. You've fought for so long to belong somewhere."

"No idea what is what. Everything is surreal." I'm fixed in place, my hands held out to the heater, my palms hot, my back cold.

"Look at me, Jaya."

I can't move. I want to stay unseeing, because if I see, if I fall into Lana's eyes, there will be no way back.

"Jaya, we've both been running, desperate to find where we belong, who we are. We get comfort from being on the outside though we crave that belonging. We walk away from the parts of ourselves that get us kicked out of one society or another, but we carry those parts inside us whichever group we want to belong to. This is it. I love you. I've said those words before, but I've never understood them as much as I do now."

I know why I am terrified. All I have ever had has been a fight, either to be loved or to be accepted, but I've never allowed myself to be loved or accepted. And I know with Lana, I will.

I whisper, "This is scarier than taking on two huge Nazi bastards on the streets of Dublin. Scarier than knowing I had a knife stuck in me."

"They only had the power to damage your body. If you love me, I will have the power to damage your heart and mind and soul. As you have to damage mine. It is strange to realise that and willingly step into it anyway."

I take a deep breath. And turn to face her.

She smiles and I fall.

CHAPTER THIRTY-SIX

The house looks great. It's always clean, in spite of all the pets and people that live or visit, but today it's the sparkle that comes from nerves, from occasion, from Zara standing around with a magnifying glass and a whip. Not literally, just her critical eyes and a tea towel.

I stand at the glass sliding doors and watch the friends and family who've volunteered to set up the garden. They're directing the installation of a large cream tent and, even from here, it's obvious from Nestor's gestures that Padraic's directions to him are driving my younger cousin crazy.

I wonder who will turn up to this wedding, of the people who have been invited. And whether they will arrive with love and understanding in their hearts or anger and judgement hidden beneath the curious smiles. I don't imagine what is in the hearts of those who refuse to attend.

Padraic looks at his watch and says something to Nestor. There isn't much time left and Nestor throwing a tent peg into the ground is not going to help. I slide back the glass door.

Fiona is walking towards me from the garden, with a grin on her face. "I thought my family was bad, you'd better sort those guys out if this thing is going to happen."

I sigh. "I've never been able to sort them out, today won't be any different." I smile. "But I know they'll get it done on time somehow."

She asks, "Feeling better? With getting married and all."

She is dashing, all decked out in her uniform.

I nod. The guilt is there, but less than when I spoke to her last.

She smiles. "You will be fine. You look beautiful."

"My mother is surprisingly good at dressing me. I refuse to wear high heels though."

"You've to do something, don't you?" Fiona says, moving past me to the open doors. "I can't wait to see if your No gay marriage work crowd show up. Especially Theresa. Can't fecking wait. If she turns up, can I say something?"

"Fiona, no," I say it to chide her, but I'm curious too. We didn't ask for RSVPs on the invitations but sent them out to everyone we knew, with a note saying we would understand if their beliefs made them too uncomfortable to be present. And to let them know there would be press there, mostly afterwards, with the documentary crew being allowed to film the whole day.

Though we were leaving straight after the reception, the crew would stick around and get interviews with the guests. They were a small crew, only a camerawoman and the producer who was the director, artist, filmmaker, activist. Her name on the invitation might draw a few of the women who knew her work.

Fiona turns. She places her hands on my shoulders. "I'm glad I was the first to get to you when you were stabbed." I open my mouth and she says, "I want to say it. I know I'm not a poetic type, but it wasn't just my job I was doing. That day was important, I don't know why it made a difference I was white. I didn't really save your life, you know, there were other officers around who would have got you to the hospital or hit the perp, and I know the press made a big deal, me saving you and then us getting together, but I'm glad I was there to hear you say your name and for you to say you are Irish though you are brown. You were the one who stood up to those guys without any weapon, just you being you. We had all the protection and the batons and if it wasn't me, it would have been someone else. But no one could have been you, standing up for you. Does that make sense? I thought you were a brave wee thing then, and I still think so. I don't understand all the race and colour stuff, but I'm trying."

I smile. "It makes perfect sense. Thank you for being there. It made a big difference to be held by a lesbian and a woman while I was lying there bleeding and it was important to me you heard what I said."

She says, "I didn't figure it out then, but it changed me, you know? I never realised before a brown or black person who was Irish wasn't Irish to me. Not when I first see them." She sighs. "It's hard. I'm not getting it right. I still have this thing when I first see someone who's not white, I don't think they're Irish. I have to stop and wait and find out."

I say, "That's progress though, isn't it? At least it's now in your mind as an option."

She frowns. "That's not good enough, is it?"

I smile. "Yes, it is. For now. For you and me."

Her brow relaxes.

My smile gets wider. "I shouldn't let you off the hook totally, but I do it too."

"Do what?"

"I've lived here all my life. It's rubbed off on me. I see a non-white person and my first instinct is to assume they're not Irish."

She frowns. "But that's racist, isn't it? How can *you* be racist?"

I laugh. "According to Zara, my father told her Indians can be the most racist people around. And he was a brown-skinned fully Indian guy."

I don't have the same sense of abandonment accompanying thoughts of my father. I know now it wasn't anything to do with me as a person.

I say, "All I can do is speak up, for me, for others who can't. I won't keep silent trying not to embarrass or anger anyone in case they kick me out. I'm Irish and I'm Indian and I'm a woman and I'm lesbian and I'm bisexual, and I'm any fecking thing I want to be, but most of all I'm real and I'm here and I'm not hiding anymore."

"That's why everyone getting married together on the first day after it became legal was so important to me."

"I know." I squeeze her upper arms. "We get to describe ourselves now, in our own words. Made it okay for me with the documentary crew being here on such a special private day."

Fiona took in a deep breath. "You know I'm proud of you, right?"

I nod. "Thank you."

She kisses me on the cheek and releases my shoulder. She turns to go into the house.

I say, "And I'm proud of you too. You've been a great friend, surprisingly great considering what I did to you."

She turns. There's sadness in her eyes, but accompanied by care. "We weren't meant for each other. You're everything I wanted in a girlfriend, but it just didn't work with us, did it?"

"No, I'm sorry."

She says, "You know when you've found the one."

"You surely do."

She smiles. "Maybe one day."

"You're a fecking gorgeous guard, I mean look at you in that uniform. And you have a sweet heart. Wait until the reception, with all the lesbians who might turn up, just wait, they'll be hitting on you so bad."

She chuckles. "Why do you think I wore the uniform." She straightens her shoulders. "I hope you invited some cute ones."

"We invited people of all persuasions. And it's like we invited every fecking lesbian in Ireland. If they come to my wedding to a man, we know they're more than just cute. I think Gemma is bringing everyone from the bar. She's cute, by the way. Single too."

Fiona smiles. "Good thinking. You know, I'm now actually looking forward to this."

"And I'm nervous now."

"You'll be fine. I'd better get that table cover before I get in trouble with your mother again. I think she said to bring in the cream one, any ideas from where?"

"Nope." I smile as I turn to the garden. "You're the cop, I'm sure you'll find it."

§

Ishmael smoothed the silk of the Nehru jacket. The lines were straight, tailored to suit a slim body outline. The mirror reflected a calm man, peaceful, on the outside at least. The hat matched the jacket, in colour and style, red and cream, mostly Indian, with the influence of the West showing in the modicum of restraint in the amount of gold woven through the red. Like Lana's mandragoti saree all those years ago. The loose cream pants were almost anonymous, visible only from the knees down, bunched at the ankles by a red and gold band. The jewelled slippers followed the theme.

Black kohl highlighted the deep brown of eyes. What had Jaya said, pretty and handsome. Ishmael smiled.

Today was for them, but additionally for something bigger. They both sensed that, but they couldn't articulate it as well as two writers should have been able to do. Having a documentary maker as talented as Rekha Surinder made them lazy. But she did draw the unsaid words out of them and Ishmael had faith the finished film would uncover their hopes and dreams, if not in words, but in images, in impressions, in them simply being themselves, telling their story.

The documentary would not cover everything. Leaving David out was part of the agreement. The film would deal with parts of the story of Jaya and Ishmael and Lana. Being brown in Ireland. The fluidity of love around gender.

Exposure was frightening, vulnerable.

But this was Ishmael's last day.

It needed to be shared.

CHAPTER THIRTY-SEVEN

"I dropped out of the womb of an Irish-American banished to Ireland by her white family, onto an Irish hospital bed so that gave me the Irish part, the shocking sight of my darker than expected skin and hair lessened slightly (and a little later) by eyes, all of me darkened by the genes of an Indian student visiting New York then gone, lightened by my mother's pale blonde blue gave the nurses and my mother's extended family pause before condemnation, gave me a chance in the depths of seventies rural Ireland, a tanned baby rather than the black babies they were instructed to be charitable to, but who'd never drop into their midst, who'd never be one of them."

"My mother's fierce protectiveness, fierce as a lioness who knows her cub is unique, damaged, different, special, beautiful, would inspire unwelcome feelings in the village, even the good feelings uncomfortable, who wants change, but the lioness banned from the wild for being too wild was not going to be tamed by the laws of rural life. She flowed through, her cub in tow, demanding the glory for having produced such an exotic seed. And the family and village, dazzled by her leonine charm, opened their hearts to the bedraggled cub who didn't officially know she was not full lion, more half-lion, half-tiger."

I stand at the bedroom door and listen. My mother is holding the framed article, her glasses perched on her nose, reading aloud, unaware I'm there.

Isabella is sitting on the corner of the bed facing the door. She glances up at me behind Zara.

Zara says, "That's my wee cub. Full lion, full tiger. Did you know the Irish Times is the main newspaper in Ireland?" She lifts her spectacles onto her forehead and polishes the glass enclosing the printed newspaper sheet.

Isabella winks at me and looks back at my mother. "I didn't know that. How fantastic."

Zara puts her spectacles back in place and peers at the print. Her voice still gets shaky when she reads the article aloud, which she does often, to anyone who will listen.

"I was occasionally reminded of my difference, not by accuracy, but by the chants that followed the Travellers when they stopped by the village. I look more like one of them, the easy-tan skin, the dark-blonde hair, and amber eyes glowing with the same wildness no matter how much I kept it hidden under the required tameness of me.

I'm ashamed I didn't stand up for the Travellers, not that they needed my help and I didn't add to the chants, but inside I found myself counting the ways I was Indian-Irish or Irish-Indian and the ways I was special rather than different, oh, your hair is so thick and lush, your eyes, holy jesus, they are something else that colour, you lucky thing, you get such a nice tan, no fecking freckles on you."

Zara nods. "I told Nona, my sister, I told her there would come a day when Jaya's voice would be heard here in Ireland. I spent a lot of time fighting for my voice to be heard, for my little brown baby to be seen as Irish, or Indian, or however she wanted to be seen." She wipes at her eyes.

"See, that's my Indian side. Though the impression most of the village had of Indians was the roaming Sikh salesmen so I guess I was an itinerant to them, anyway. I hadn't yet seen, and neither had they, the explosion of medical and scientific staff from India and Pakistan, the gentrification of the Indian image in Ireland took place in towns and cities out of view of my child eyes and happened only in my twenties when I was away from the rural, when I was in the urban of Galway, when I creaked and groaned with the growing pains of modern Ireland, growing, but yet unable to graft new shades of skin, unable to see beyond into the Irishness of birth, of soul, of thought, of presence. There were scales everywhere. I felt sorry for the blackest of the Irish born here, but never Irish to the Irish; the half-skinned, born here, but considered a curiosity, a half image of Irish; and the light-skinned right-blooded, not born here, but Irish by heritage, a full image of Irish, but still not full Irish to the Irish.

There are years and years of Irishness I don't get to claim as there are years and years of Indianness I don't get to claim either, except in my genes, but all they produce are the features that give me access, the legal right to be present. They don't give me the key to the Irish and certainly not to the Indian. They give me a door to the displaced, the window on the itinerant passing by, who at least belongs in his own world of motion."

Zara's voice trembles as she gets to the part I changed.

"I never knew my father, but his genes colour my life as did his leaving. He did not have the courage to fight his society to be with my mother. She had the courage to fight her society. For me.

For all the times she held my brown self high until I could, for all the times she stood up for someone on the outside, whether she was on the inside or not, for all the times she marched for another whether they were a part of her society or not, for her tireless fight for the right for me or anyone else to marry the person we love, for all those things and so much more - Zara Dillon is a woman I'm proud to have as a mother no matter how difficult she could make my life.

And the only person I want to give me away when I marry the person of my dreams."

She finishes reading, her voice choked. Isabella puts her hand over Zara's.

My mother rests the frame on the bedside table. "See the photo. Isn't it beautiful? That's my cub, right there. And doesn't Lana look wonderful too? They fit together."

Isabella picks up the framed article. She nods. "It's a beautiful photo. I love how no one would know Lana's gender. She could be anything."

I say from the door, "They got it, didn't they?"

Zara jerks around. "Are we late? Is the tent ready? I knew I shouldn't have left it to Padraic and Nestor, but I wanted to show Isabella your article."

I smile. "Padraic said the tent is as bent as Nestor, but I think it will get done."

Isabella giggles.

Zara sighs. "I hope so."

I say, "You're looking splendid, by the way." She is. In a mix of red and golds, blues and greens, our wedding theme.

She clears her throat, takes her glasses off and fiddles with the arm.

I know that furtiveness. I say, "What's up, mam?"

Zara says, "I invited someone."

I raise an eyebrow. "You invited loads of people."

"Yes, but this is someone different, someone you might not want here."

I frown. "Who?"

"Well, it might be someone I might be having a -," She frowns too. "I don't know what you all call it these days, but it is mostly by phone and letters." She coughs. "And email."

Isabella gives a delighted laugh. "You're having an online relationship with someone?"

Zara turns to her and nods. A smile lights up her face.

I say, "Who is he?"

Zara says, "How do you know it is a man?"

I say, "Who is she?"

"Ha!" Zara's smile has widened. "You'd now be okay with a bisexual mum."

Isabella laughs. She says to me, "Does she usually rub it in?"

I sigh. "I usually don't assume anything anymore. I slipped up cos it's mam, though come to think of it, she's the last person I can assume anything about."

Zara says, "Well, it just so happens it's a man. And you know him. A little. Well, you met him once. When I did. But you didn't stay to party with us."

"Mam, who are you sneaking around with?" I frown. "He's not married, is he? I'm more easy-going now, but that's always a no-no in my book."

"Jaya, would I?" Zara smiles, and a dreaminess enters her eyes. "It's Phil, Chloe's dad."

"Chloe's dad?" I open my eyes wide. "As in the regimental colonel stick-in-the-mud Chloe's dad?"

Zara laughs. "Yes, him. He's not that bad. Really. He's quite charming. And we share a military background."

I see Isabella choke back a laugh, but mine comes out as an involuntary snort.

Zara doesn't notice. "He's interesting. You know he was stationed in

India?" She sighs. "And very handsome."

I smile. "Okay. Enough. Not sure I can deal with my mum dating at all."

I embrace her, get the floral scent of her perfume, the familiar smell of her. I squeeze. "I'm glad, though."

Zara puts her arms around my waist. "Are you alright with Chloe? I haven't seen or heard from her since they got back from their honeymoon, though Phil has more recently. He said he'll tell me more when he gets here."

I say, "I worry of course, but there's nothing I can do. She'll call if she needs. And both Lana and I will be there for her."

Zara nods. "That's how it is for Phil and me." She squeezes before she lets me go. "Okay, let me go and rescue the poor tent from your cousins."

She leaves in a bustle of colours.

I turn to Isabella, stunning in red and gold, the saree so fitting. Now I know her, her beauty has a different effect on me. The similarities to Ishmael are not as striking, rather the differences in their physical appearance, her own individual quirks, make her the Isabella I love as a sister now. "I'm so glad you could all be here for the wedding."

Isabella's smile is wide. "Of course we made it. I would not miss this wedding for anything. Lana is not just my family of blood, she is my family of heart. I will miss Ishmael, I was able to experience him in a strange way for a few more years." Her eyes fill. "Even though it was Lana, I knew she was also mirroring the person I used to be. And I loved him. Do you know how it felt to be shown yourself through such a beautiful person. To finally see what others see? And love yourself?"

Tears are running down my cheeks, hers too.

I take a tissue from the box on the locker and touch her tears away. "I can imagine." I sit on the bed beside Isabella and she leans against my shoulder. "I'm a lesbian, and I can't see me with anyone else in the future because I love Lana and want to be with her for the rest of my life, but loving Ishmael and being free to love him opened my eyes to the possibility and to my capacity to completely and simply love."

We sit in silence for a few minutes, both grieving and celebrating Ishmael.

I ask, "You're okay with the way we did the invitations? And the documentary? It is not in any way meant to minimise the difficulties you endured, or to steal your story."

She takes my hand and rests it between hers. "I know Lana is worried I might be upset. I told her I'm honoured and relieved."

"Relieved?"

She smiles. "Yes. I want to live my life, not a cause. I was a private person before I went through my very private transition and I became the person on the outside I always was on the inside. That didn't make me a public person." She sighs. "Maybe that is not the right way and one day I might have to become more public and vocal but for now, for now, I am delighted my cousin was able to live safely as Ishmael, that she has found the love with you she has always desired."

I say, "I understand. I've always been an activist, but sometimes I want to simply be. I hope I never again judge a human being for how they love. I'm still an activist now, for various things, not only race issues, or lesbian issues, but I want to live life and connect with people through my writing. I want to share stories and experiences, to communicate and absorb, not just get on a pulpit and broadcast. Now I could be learning and writing on race, lesbian rights, biphobia in the community, or," I smile and release her, "cats and how to master them."

She laughs. "I read the cat article. I love that you called your cat 'Ishy.' And that you admitted complete failure in any attempt to master cats."

I stand, holding her hand. "I live and write my truth now. I'm glad you get to live yours too."

"And I have found happiness finally, both in me and with the person I am married to."

"Henri?" Joy wells up in me at the contentment on her face.

She nods. "He knew all along. Well, he worked it out at some point."

"He knew? That you used to be a man...I mean, Ishmael? He knew that you were finally able to live as Isabella, who you always were?" I am still awkward when it comes to the terminology and thinking around trans issues. But I'm learning, though Lana is the one who applied herself to studying, and getting training so she could counsel people going through it.

Isabella's voice is soft. "Henri loved me. He hoped I would grow to love him. He's a nice guy and I was always in charge, but now, now we're kind of equal. I don't think I love him in the intense way I loved Frank, but it's deeper, in a way I settled for him and then surprised myself by falling for him."

I smile, "I like that."

CHAPTER THIRTY-EIGHT

I'm taken aback to see Theresa, but I manage to keep my jaw from dropping.

Her voice booms out even as she tries to be discreet. "Well, well. Jaya Dillon. You're a dark horse." She reddens. "I mean, not dark as in brown. I mean you certainly surprised us all."

I smile. "You never thought I'd succumb to the institution of marriage?"

She gives a snort. "Yah sure. *That's* what surprised us."

I turn to Ginger who's grinning widely beside Theresa. I say, "Thank you for coming" Behind her, they are all there, the full contingent of the Dublin office. My voice gets a little tight. "All of you."

Ginger says, "Wouldn't have missed it for the world. I say live and let live as y'all know. You look amazing. Such a beautiful blend of East and West, isn't it, love?"

Theresa nods. She's itching to say something, but I usher them into the tent. "There are no sides, sit anywhere ye want." There seems to be an unconscious grouping though, the lesbians on one side, the others scattered. I'm pleased the only seating I did arrange has Fiona and Gemma sitting beside each other.

Margeta follows my ex-boss and Ginger, grins at me and says, "Why are you here, doing the welcoming? Should you not be hiding your dress, I mean, your outfit, from the groom?"

I laugh. "I guess this isn't a traditional wedding."

Theresa's snort is audible from a few feet away. The others file past me with sheepish grins.

I turn to the entrance of the tent. My smile fades. Chloe is standing there.

I say, "I didn't think you'd make it. Won't David be angry? Are you here on your own? I'm sorry we couldn't invite him."

Her smile is full of warmth. "You look fantastic, Jaya, I adore the way you, this whole place," she gestures around the tent, "So Indian and Irish at the same time."

"We all worked on it. There are similarities with the Celtic and Indian designs and music and all." I take a step towards her. "Chloe, are you okay?"

She takes in a shaky breath, lets it out slowly. "I know you won't take any comfort in this, any 'I told you so,' but no, I'm not okay. Being in Galway brings it back."

I take her hands. "What happened?"

Her eyes fill. "I'm not going to cry, not today, and not for myself. I cannot promise not to cry during the ceremony though. I completely reserve the right to sob through that, tears of happiness for both of you. Especially now, for Lana. She deserves every single bit of joy she gets. You do too."

"What happened? Did he hurt you? We'll do something, Chloe, I swear we will. You're not in this alone."

Her smile is sad. "He didn't do anything. Nothing physical, apart from lose his temper. But that was when he reached the end of his patience with me, when I refused to accept we weren't right for each other. After four months."

"He said that? So soon?"

Chloe says, "Yes. But he withdrew, he changed before that. All the crazy love he swore for me, the obsession, it seemed to tire him out. He got irritable, wanted space, almost immediately after our honeymoon. And when I was hurt and surprised, he lost it. Said I was a crazy woman too. That Lana and her craziness, and the chaos was too much. He'd thought I was different, but I was just the same, another beautiful, but intense and crazy woman."

"I'm so sorry. That's why we haven't heard from you?"

She nods. "I left Galway. Couldn't face anyone. He made me believe I was the crazy one. I travelled for a bit and then went to stay with my dad last week." She smiles. "My dad came with me today." She gestures in the direction of the house. "He wanted to see Zara too." She examines me and I get she's trying to figure out if I know.

I smile. "I found out today. That was an unexpected union."

"Yes. It's funny how things turn out, isn't it? I'm shattered by David, but a part of me is grateful to be alone and to reconnect with my dad." She smiles. "And we're both dating. He's dating Zara and I'm now taking it easy and being happily single, dating nice people, women, men." She quirks an eyebrow at me.

I laugh. "I'm not the jerk I used to be when it comes to bisexuals."

She smiles. "Good." She scans the crowded tent. "Did Frank, and Isabella and Henri make it?"

"Yes. And Maurice."

"Who the hell is Maurice?"

"Frank's boy toy. Almost as pretty as Ishmael."

Her eyes widen. "Ah, I see. And Isabella is okay with that?"

I nod. "She's fine."

She spots Isabella leaning over in her chair towards Henri. "There they are, I'll go sit with them, there's a chair beside her. Now, you should go and get in place. Yikes, there are many more people here than I thought would be."

"I'm surprised. And touched. The ones who know I am lesbian think I'm marrying a man, and the others who assumed I am straight think I'm marrying a woman."

She looks back at me. "They are your friends and family. They're here because they love you no matter who you're marrying." She smiles. "What a great way to test their acceptance." She turns to me. "I don't think I've ever seen you look so beautiful. And it's not just the usual way. You're different. Glowing. Happy. At peace?"

I smile. "All of that, and more."

§

Red paint. Red painted hands. From the tips of fingers to the intricate bands circling delicate wrists. Lines of love that ran over the scars, not hiding them, healing them. A single tear dropping on its downward journey left no trail on an unpowdered cheek and landed with a clear splash. On hands so lovingly and patiently decorated by Zara. Ishmael smiled, this was no well-bred well-seasoned Indian bride marrying a stranger.

The red *mandragoti* sari was draped in waiting over Jaya's Aunt Nona's arms. The gold flecks on it glinted and winked at them. The sari would be laid at their feet to signify their new state. It would not be worn later in the ceremony, its soft folds would not enclose anyone in marital servitude. The blue and gold of the Nehru jacket Lana was wearing for the second half of the hour-long ceremony was as beautiful. No matching hat though, her long black hair would lie loose and free.

Ishmael focused. The moments were flying past now. After all the waiting, the preparation, all the moments would be treasured, were being treasured.

A moment of panic. The first half of the ceremony, the 'red half' as opposed to the second half pictured as the "blue half", was almost over. Both were as meaningful to them, but after the first half, Ishmael would be gone forever. What took his place was yet to be defined in terms of formal identity. Lana could not safely be the woman she had been when she was in Ireland years ago.

The documentary would help to define her as a woman. Lana would keep her first name and the share of the gîte complex in France. She would become Lana Dillon and they would throw themselves into the pile of uncertainty that was the Irish immigration system.

She knew they could live happily in rural France, helping to run the complex. And they would, on occasion, but the house they had bought and renovated here in Galway with Jaya's share of the apartment in Dublin, was already becoming the home neither of them had ever imagined they could find, but always dreamed was possible, with family and dogs and cats wandering through, her clients accommodated in a warm and cosy therapy room, Jaya's writing flowing freely for her new magazine.

She had been lost in thought. Jaya was turning to her with one of the two identical rings, a simple circle of gold.

Her mind relaxed slightly as she remembered the filming taking place. She would get to re-live every moment, their faces smiling from the screen.

She lost focus again, this time willingly, her mind and her body were as present anywhere as they had ever been. And now her soul was too. Joined with the soul of the beautiful woman beside her, in the eyes of the law, the family, the church.

Most of all, joined in their own eyes.

There is so much we have to learn about each other and sometimes I am swimming in a sea of confusion. I wonder if Lana feels it too, that wish to begin again, to meet when the other is clean and new, already set in place with our identities and our personalities, not playing a part or hiding a side, protecting ourselves or others.

I'm shy around her sometimes, unable to look her beauty in the eye, and at other times I sing out loud in front of her, me, who never sings, except on occasion in my writing.

I watch her, worried, worried she is fragile, that what he did to her will have broken the insides of her, that she will not heal except by being in Ishmael's body and I have dragged her out into the open before she is ready. And then she looks up from her reading, from petting Ishy, from the sugar snap peas in the garden, from the shopping cart I'm pushing, from her release of a vole back into the garden out of reach of Toby, and I see her smile and I know it will be in the most ordinary of things, in the smallest of simple pleasures, in the sun rising the next day and the day after and even the day after that, she will rise too, in her cells, in her blood, in her heart. She will not need me to do that, but I will be there.

This time it is the garden, the lettuce.

She smiles up from the white green leaves. "Did you finish the article?"

"Not yet. Just taking a break." I pluck a lonely weed from the path between the raised wooden-sided beds.

She says, "Did we plant these courgettes or did they magically land here and multiply on their own. I don't even like courgettes, did you sneak in the seeds while I wasn't watching?"

"Would I?"

She nods. "Now I'm stuck with them."

I laugh. "I think it might have been Zara. She's the one who sows seeds in secret."

"You're right, sounds more her."

She puts her arm around my waist and gives a squeeze. "I love the *gîtes*, but it's getting harder to leave here each time."

We turn towards the back of the house. Ishy is mid-preen, his paw stuck up, silhouetted by the window. Toby is sprawled across the threshold, keeping a sleepy eye on us.

I say, "Frank and Isabella can handle the *gîtes* and the restaurant. You can be the silent partner. We can go there for holidays and act like lords of the manor." I let out a laugh as she jabs me in my side.

"I want to be an equal partner. With us. The house, the renovation, it's yours. Should I sell my share of the *gîtes*?"

"Not if you don't want to." I turn to face her, put my arms around her waist. "I know what the place means to you, and what it means for you to own those shares now, for yourself. The house here is ours, it's our home together, no matter what the law says or the title says. Soon we can add your name to mine, but I want you to be home."

Her eyes glisten. "I will be, wherever we are together."

I kiss her, gently.

We stand in the land behind our new home, in the untilled earth and the tamed soil, and the kiss deepens until we are breathing in as much of each other as we can. It is that way and different every time we touch, as though we are entering a foreign land we both recognise as home. As time passes, the foreignness lessens, but the newness, the wonder, the open-mouthed exclamations of the tourists we are doesn't diminish and it never will. Of that we are as sure as the bodies we now inhabit fully and the hearts we now allow the truth of love into.

Lana and I are finishing the novel together. She hopes our pen name on it will help mask the identities of the people she's always wished to protect, Garry and John, Gemma, Isabella, Henri, and Frank. All their names will change, she had been using placeholders for the others in her draft, but couldn't bear to write her name or David's into the novel. She hopes the novel will reach others who are not believed, who are struggling to understand what they are living, confused by the charismatic mask and the benign façade that is the defence and the attack of those on the scale of personality disorders, the borderline, the narcissist, the sociopath.

She counsels others now. We set up her therapy office at the back of the house with a separate entrance, and her clients can arrive and leave in privacy. It is a light-filled, brightly-coloured, and warm room. As are all the rooms in our new home. My family wander in and out of the main house, and not only for occasions, and Zara has a room she has commandeered as hers when she's fed up with her neighbours. The house is near Galway but surrounded by nature, deer, hares, sheep. And cows who stick their heads over the stone wall and chew at the blackberry bushes. They moo in disbelief when I wag a finger at them, and then they return to their rumination, confident in their security. I see Lana watch the deer and they watch her. She moves closer each day, some days a few inches and others, a few feet. She holds her hand over the stone wall when the baby deer arrive and her hand shakes as much as their legs tremble. She does not want to get close to them even when they trust her, but I know her and I know she will let them in because she is love and she is stronger than fear.

I help Lana write the novel, but it is all hers. It hurts to experience her tear open the wounds, pour her blood onto the page, her fingers holding the pen, but the visible scars on her wrist and the hidden scars inside are what drive her. She can manage three or four hours of writing in the mornings and then she gets up and holds on to me in a long silent hug. We watch the grass grow outside, the leaves waving as they grasp onto to the branches in a final attempt to stay aloft. The leaves will fall, but Lana knows I will always be there for her to hold on, as I know she will be my root, my trunk, my branch, my leaves, for as long as we breathe.

THE END

ABOUT THE AUTHOR

R J Samuel was born in Nigeria, to Indian parents. She spent many years qualifying to be a medical doctor first in Nigeria, then Ireland, but ran away from home to do a Masters in IT. She settled on IT as a career rather than Medicine as she thought computers might be more logical than people, but that hasn't always proven to be the case. She remained Ireland for many years, apart from a few years in the southwest of France where she ran a restaurant-bar despite having absolutely no interest in restaurants, except for eating in them. She considers herself almost Irish, almost Indian, and almost American. She now lives in Atlanta in America where, in her latest creative outburst, she wants to establish an artist retreat in a mostly unusable property.

Her story 'Helmets' was shortlisted for the 2011 Over the Edge 'New Writer of the Year Competition' and she was the only entrant to have both her fiction and her poetry long-listed for the Doire Press '1st Annual International Fiction and Poetry Chapbook Competition' in January 2012. Her fiction entry, 'The Vision Painter,' went on to be shortlisted for this competition and was the basis for her second novel, 'Falling Colours – The Misadventures of a Vision Painter.' Her short stories 'Parallel Lives' (2012) and 'The Alleyway' (2013) were shortlisted and her poetry entry was longlisted (2016) for the Over the Edge 'New Writer of the Year Competition'.

Her published novels – 'Heart Stopper', The Vision Painter series ('Falling Colours', 'Casting Shadows') which received an Honorable Mention in the 2013 Rainbow Awards, and 'A Place Somewhere', which was a finalist for the Ann Bannon Popular Choice and the Tee Corinne Cover Design Awards, are set in Ireland, India, and America. 'An Outsider Inside' is her fifth novel.

SOCIAL MEDIA

Website : www.rjsamuel.com
Blog: www.rjsamuel.com/blog
Twitter: www.twitter.com/r_j_samuel
Facebook Author Page: http://www.facebook.com/RJSamuelAuthor

Check out the extract of A Place Somewhere that follows.

A PLACE SOMEWHERE

PROLOGUE

There are so many steps I took along the way that felt wrong. My feet landed, but there was no earth beneath them. It is too late to say I wish I had picked my way more carefully, that I had not listened to the wrong voices, that I had been able to hear my own voice, the little voice that spoke to me in the moments between the closing and opening of my eyes.

Will my life have meant anything to anyone except for me? Or even to me? I did the wrong things for the right reasons. Now, I am about to do the right thing for the wrong reason.

I should be able to live for myself, but I can't. So this is the right thing to do. I have lost the one I would have lived for. This is the wrong reason to die.

But what is one more wrong to add to the wrongs I have done.

The loss of hope, of belief, of innocence. That to me is the death of a soul. This is just making it real for the body.

I wish I had never gone to that place.

The woman lay on her back in the lifeless room. A breeze trickled through the window and along the walls, caressing the lock of hair that fell across her forehead and battling to wrest the piece of paper from under her hand, but the paper rested, weighted down, agitated only at the corners.

Outside, the wind raged at its loss.

CHAPTER ONE

Alex pushed the hangers of red T-shirts apart and stared at the woman she had pursued for weeks through an online maze. The woman was a cheap imitation of the blonde in the photographs. Her clothes matched some of those on the racks that sheltered Alex; a leopard-print blouse hugged tight black leggings. An employee name badge that proclaimed her true name hung lopsided in black and white against the jungle print.

Alex knew she was avoiding the inevitable, taking refuge in the solace of the assembled clothes and in their colour changes over the full spectrum from reds to blues to greens, every shade provided in a department store in one of the busiest malls in the U.S. The air-conditioning chilled the sweat on her forehead that was due in part to the sweltering heat outside on Queens Boulevard and in part to her nearing the end of the chase, to the discovery of the quarry, and the imminent confrontation. She wondered if she would ever get blasé about this part, no matter how much she tried.

The woman had finished folding the T-shirts back onto the display shelves. Her skin was pale against the vivid colours, her hands mottled with sun stains. She looked like she was going to leave Oversize and Alex straightened herself out of the clothes rack and walked in a diagonal line towards Petites. She had watched the woman for an hour. She knew this was the right one.

The woman reached the aisle before her and Alex picked up her pace as she followed the scrape of sandals on shiny floors. She was not sure how she was going to play out the end of this search. Judith just wanted the truth, good or bad. Alex wanted more. She wanted answers. And something else. She wanted some release from the anger and pain, and this woman did not deserve gentleness.

It was almost lunchtime. The woman grabbed a blue leather handbag from behind a counter and waved at another employee before walking out of the exit to the store and into the stream of shoppers. Alex followed dodging the knapsacks and shopping bags, keeping out of sight behind the teenagers glued to their smartphones. The two women were separated by an escalator of people as they descended into the food court and Alex used the slow ride down to pick what food she would get to hide behind. She wasn't hungry though she hadn't eaten since she had booked the flight from Orlando. That had been yesterday and she'd flown in to New York this morning. She probably wouldn't be able to eat until tomorrow morning, when she had slept a night in Boston. After this job was over.

The Food Court was busy and Alex tracked the woman's movements with tired eyes. The journey had been hot and awkward. Everything here seemed hot and awkward to her. The crowds of people, the noise, the humidity. She felt the longing for her old home of Ireland the most at these times. For the uncrowded quiet, the cool dampness of air.

She aimed for an outlet that offered salads and watched the leopard-print join the queue at the Chinese counter. Alex bought a salad and waited until the woman was seated at a table. A bamboo plant fanned out of a pot right beside the table and shaded it from the ring of lights suspended from the ceiling. Alex sat at the next table, edging her chair closer, angling it so that she could see and now, could be seen.

The woman was on her phone. Her voice was loud but it barely made a dent in the hall of echoed conversations. She teased at her yellow hair, straightening reluctant strands between pincers of blue fingernails.

"I told you not to pull your sister's hair. Brittany, how many times I told you? And you're supposed to be taking care of Ethan, not bullying your sister." The words were muffled by the noodles she was pulling into her mouth with the plastic fork in her other hand. "I don't care. I don't know why I do this. Your father can take care of it when he gets home. Don't screw with my computer. I need it tonight and if I find your dirty paw prints all over it I'm going to make sure you don't get to use Facebook again for a very long time, you hear me?"

The sound of teenage angst was still coming from the phone as she placed it down on the linoleum surface and jabbed at it to put it off.

Alex kept her voice soft. "Kids, huh. Aren't they such a pain when you need to work on your stuff?" She gave a smile as the woman looked up from her food. The smile she knew worked on straight men as well as lesbian women, and on women who'd ever thought about other women in ways they had never expected.

It worked on this woman. Alex saw the slight widening of her eyes and the wipe of fingers over her mouth.

"Yes, kids can be such a pain. You'd think I was asking for world peace." This time a stroke of her lips with a napkin. "That's such a beautiful accent. Irish, isn't it? I love that accent. My husband's ancestors are from Ireland."

Alex nodded and forced more of a brogue. "I'm just visiting, a bit lost really. Everything is so much bigger here in the States." She moved in her seat and gestured around in as helpless a manner as she could.

"I hear Ireland is wonderful. My husband always wanted to go back to visit there. Me, I was born and bred here and I don't know if I'll ever get to travel so far away."

Alex said, "You should visit. It takes less time than you think. About the time it would take to get from here to California."

"Maybe one day, maybe, who knows. Welcome to New York. I'm Pam." Pam ran a finger along her name badge which pronounced the full version.

"Hi Pam, thanks. I'm Alex."

"Not a very Irish name. I thought it would be something unpronounceable, you know like that kid actress, you know the one who has a name that is said completely different from how it is written. Or else something like Mary."

"It's short for Alyson." Alex smiled again and watched an answering smile grow on Pam's lips.

"Very nice." There was a slight huskiness to Pam's voice. "So, what brings you to New York, Alex?" She gestured with her fork at her noodles before digging in again.

"Just a visit." Alex played with her lettuce. The smell of the food all around them was making her feel sick. Or it might have been the residual effects of the sun on her black hair leaving her with a headache. "So, are you from Queens then?"

A strand of noodle drooped before being sucked in. "Yes. Grew up here and married and had my kids. Three of them, a boy and two girls."

"Have you ever lived anywhere else?" Alex asked without enthusiasm. She knew the answer. And despite the job she was doing, she hated the lies. She stuck as close to the truth as possible in everything she said.

Pam shook her head. "Never been out of the state. Well, unless you count Atlantic City. That's New Jersey."

Suddenly, Alex just wanted this to end. She wondered how jaded she could get before disappearing? After only four chases? Three of which ended like this. She could barely bring herself to be charming, to work her way into another woman's life, especially another one like this. Alex did not need these questions answered, she knew what this woman was; she just wanted to know why.

She said, "Trish?" and saw the blood drain under the tanned skin and makeup. Pam's lips struggled to decide on a position. They finally settled on open.

Alex got up from her table and moved the few feet over to Pam's. Pam's eyes darted from the abandoned salad and back to Alex.

Alex said, "Judith sent me."

"Sent you?" The words finally dropped out of Pam's mouth. "Judith? I don't know any Judith. Or any Trish." She pushed away the half-eaten Chinese food and shifted her weight to get up.

Alex didn't move. "Would you rather do this here or at your home? In front of your husband and children?"

It took a few seconds for Pam to slump back into the chair.

Alex picked up the phone that lay on the table between them. "I assume you have Judith's number on this?"

Pam mumbled something that sounded affirmative.

Alex sat down. "And I assume since you didn't tell her you were married and have three children you don't have any intention of following through on any of the promises you made to her?"

Pam crept further back in her chair and closed her eyes. The shake of her head was so slight that Alex would have missed it if not for the jangle of frizzy blonde hair against the patterned top.

"Was it even your photograph?" Alex examined the woman. "Actually, yes, it was. Photoshop?"

Pam opened her eyes, sparkling blue in the photo, a washed out grey in life. "I only sent her one photo of me. Maybe I was a little younger in it. And okay, Brittany had messed around with it a little before I gave it to them at work." Her hand was smoothing at her hair. "How did you find me?"

"That picture actually. After I checked your IP address and it wasn't in California like you said you were. I did an image search. Found that photo on your store website. Traced you through Facebook."

"But I don't use that Facebook account much."

"It was on your colleague Sandra's page. You were at her party, with your husband and kids."

Pam pursed her lips. She asked, "What does Judith want? What did she ask you to do if you found me?"

"Just to get the truth."

"You're not going to tell my husband, are you?"

Alex didn't reply, but she could feel the muscles in her jaw tense.

Pam rushed on, "Judith will be better off without me. I wish I was all that, you know, what I wrote. That I had the glamorous PA job I told her I had, but I just work in a department store. She wouldn't have wanted me anyway, would she? Not in real life. A rich widow? She has a nice life. All the Art stuff she's into, the galleries."

"She believed you, all your emails, phone calls, your protestations of love. She thinks you are someone special in her life. She just wanted me to check after you kept avoiding her invitations to the cottage in Cape Cod." A beep sounded and Alex looked down at her clenched hand. She put Pam's phone back on the table. "That's going to be the hard part. Telling her you were lying the whole time. I don't think she would care what you really work at or that you're not any of the things you said you were. You aren't, are you?"

Pam shook her head.

Alex frowned. "You went to a lot of trouble to be this other person, this perfect partner for Judith. But I guess a year is a long time and you had to fill it."

Pam said. "I found a lot of stuff online."

"Art exhibitions, galleries, a job as a PA to a famous actor."

Pam's face in person showed lines that seemed deeper, her flesh looser on her cheeks and jaws than in the posed and airbrushed photo.

Alex leaned forward. She was close enough to smell the sweat that trickled down Pam's temple.

Alex whispered. "You're a coward who hides behind her computer screen and hurts people, decent truthful women who just make the mistake of believing in you. What kind of person needs to do that to have her fun?" The words felt like acid dripping from her lips, but they brought no relief. She had a well of acid in her now.

Pam shook her head, but her eyes betrayed her guilt, and her fear. She closed them, tilting her face away.

Alex sank back. "I should let you face Judith, look her in the eyes and tell her yourself. You wouldn't have the guts to do that though, would you?"

Pam opened her eyes.

"Don't tell her anything then." There was a flicker of something like hope in Pam's eyes as they rushed to Alex's face. "Just say you couldn't find me. I'll end it with her online. I will. I'll tell her that I meant everything I said, but that we were not meant to be together. I'll find something, some kind way of letting her down easy. There's no need for her to know. Please. Alex. That is your name, isn't it?"

"Yes. I don't lie about things like that." Alex looked around at the people eating around them. How many were like her, how many like Pam? She leant back and felt the exhaustion settle around her shoulders. It would be so much easier if she didn't have to make the trip to Boston, didn't have to face another broken heart crying tears for an unknown loved one. Maybe one less cynic could actually be a good thing, pacified by the sad yet romantic words of fate. Let Pam do it her way.

Alex sighed. There were rules. She had written them for herself, guidelines on this strange path upon which she had been forced. And one of them was that she would see all cases through. She would be the truth that the women could cling to, could trust. They needed that anchor after they swam the depths of betrayal. And she needed to be real for them.

"No can do. I'm sorry," Alex said. "However, I won't tell your husband." She waited until the words registered and the look of hope was firmly installed in Pam's eyes. "But you have to answer my questions. With the truth, if you know what that is."

Pam nodded, her hair bouncing vigorously.

Alex said the words that now felt permanently etched on her lips. "Why did you do it?"

Pam frowned. She seemed to be searching for her thoughts on the matter. Like she had never considered the question before. The look was so familiar to Alex that she had named it the 'Hell if I know' look.

"I guess I wanted to have a different life for a while. You know, have someone different but not have an affair. Yes, that's it. I didn't want to cheat on my husband, but things can get a little settled after a while." Pam paused and Alex could sense her picking the words that would elicit sympathy. "See, I didn't really have an affair, did I? No one really got hurt here. Judith and I had some chats and she felt good with a girlfriend like me. Yes, you see she was lonely and she fell for me and I didn't want to hurt her by telling her I wasn't really like the person she got to know. I mean, what good would it have done? And it isn't like I took anything of hers. I just gave her a dream. What's so wrong with that? We all need something to dream about." Pam's voice had strengthened from a whisper and was now convincing.

Alex shook her head. She tried to control her voice. It came out in a low hiss. "And you really don't think what you did was wrong? Lying about loving her, lying about the interests you shared, not telling her about the family you had, building a future with someone who right now is waiting for you, waiting for what she thinks is a true love? Did you ever have any intention of going to her?"

There was a whine in Pam's voice. "What do you want me to say? Why are you so angry? It was just an online fling. It's not like this is going to break Judith's heart or anything. I mean, we never met. Just emails and phone conversations. How can she have loved someone she never met? I thought she was doing the same thing I was, you know, having a little fun."

Alex realised she was gripping the table top. She loosened her fingers and rubbed the blood back into them. Each confrontation seemed to be adding to the anger in her, rather than releasing it. The role of avenger she had taken on was taking its toll, especially when she could do nothing. No, not nothing. She could at least stop the deceit from continuing for the innocent.

Pam stood up, "I gotta get back to work. I answered your questions. You don't need to tell my husband. Besides, I didn't do nothing wrong. Not really. He would see that too. He'd probably want in on it." She grabbed her phone.

"Is there anything you want me to tell Judith?" Alex didn't know why she always asked this question. Was there another lie that could make all the other lies better?

"No. Just tell her... I mean, I don't know. I gotta go, really. Can't afford to lose this job. Tell her I said I was sorry. Yes, tell her that for me." Pam put her phone back into her handbag and wiped her palms on her leggings. "She'll find someone else."

Alex stood up. She could see the grey hairs that edged the parting of yellow at the top of Pam's scalp.

"Actually, she thought she had found her someone else. Judith is a decent woman. She is going to be devastated because she seems to love you. Or at least the 'you' that you fed her. It isn't a crime to be lonely, she doesn't deserve this." Alex felt the words were sliding off Pam's ears, dangling from her earrings. The woman was partially turned, almost fully gone.

Pam nodded. "I know, I know. No one deserves to be hurt. Tell her I'm sorry."

Alex watched as Pam clutched her handbag close and hurried into the open centre of the mall. She stood until the woman rode the escalator out of view and then sat down heavily, her legs shaking with tiredness, the familiar acid taste of anger in her mouth.

Printed in Great Britain
by Amazon